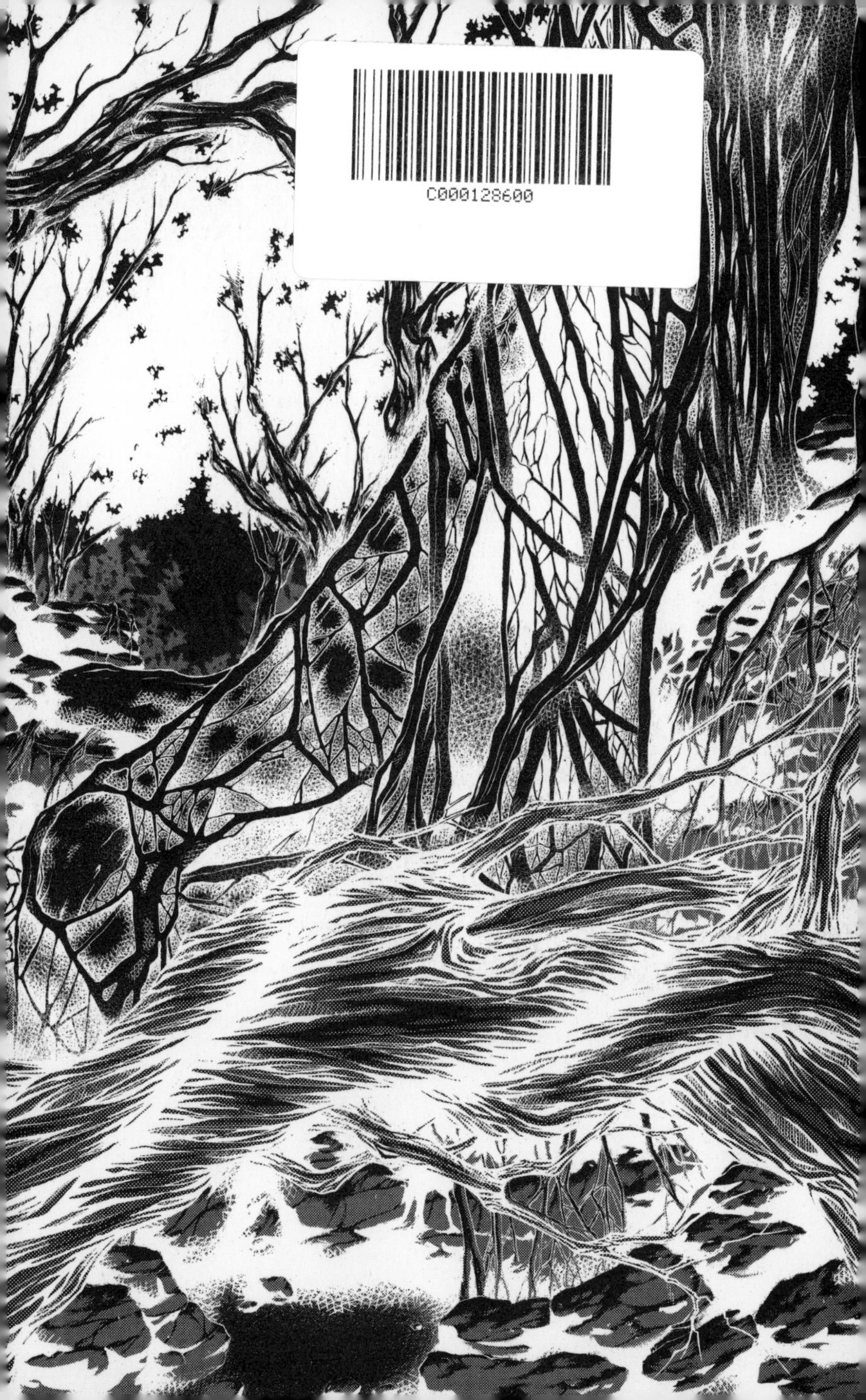

Devil's Bride Vol. 1
Created by
Se-Young Kim

Translation - Hyun Joo Kim
English Adaptation - Lorelei Laird
Copy Editor - Nikhil Burman
Retouch and Lettering - Star Print Brokers
Production Artist - Lauren O'Connell
Graphic Designer - Tina Corrales

Editor - Hyun Joo Kim
Digital Imaging Manager - Chris Buford
Pre-Production Supervisor - Erika Terriquez
Production Manager - Elisabeth Brizzi
Managing Editor - Vy Nguyen
Creative Director - Anne Marie Horne
Editor-in-Chief - Rob Tokar
Publisher - Mike Kiley
President and C.O.O. - John Parker
C.E.O. and Chief Creative Officer - Stuart Levy

A **TOKYOPOP** Manga

TOKYOPOP and are trademarks or registered trademarks of TOKYOPOP Inc.

TOKYOPOP Inc.
5900 Wilshire Blvd. Suite 2000
Los Angeles, CA 90036

E-mail: info@TOKYOPOP.com
Come visit us online at www.TOKYOPOP.com

ISBN: 978-1-4278-0496-9

First TOKYOPOP printing: March 2008
10 9 8 7 6 5 4 3 2 1
Printed in the USA

Devil's Bride

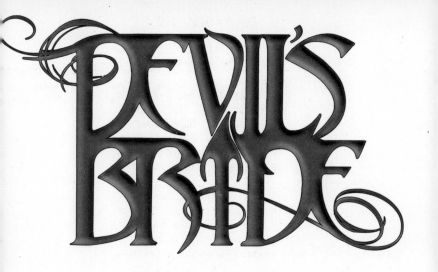

Volume 1

Se-Young Kim

Table Of Contents

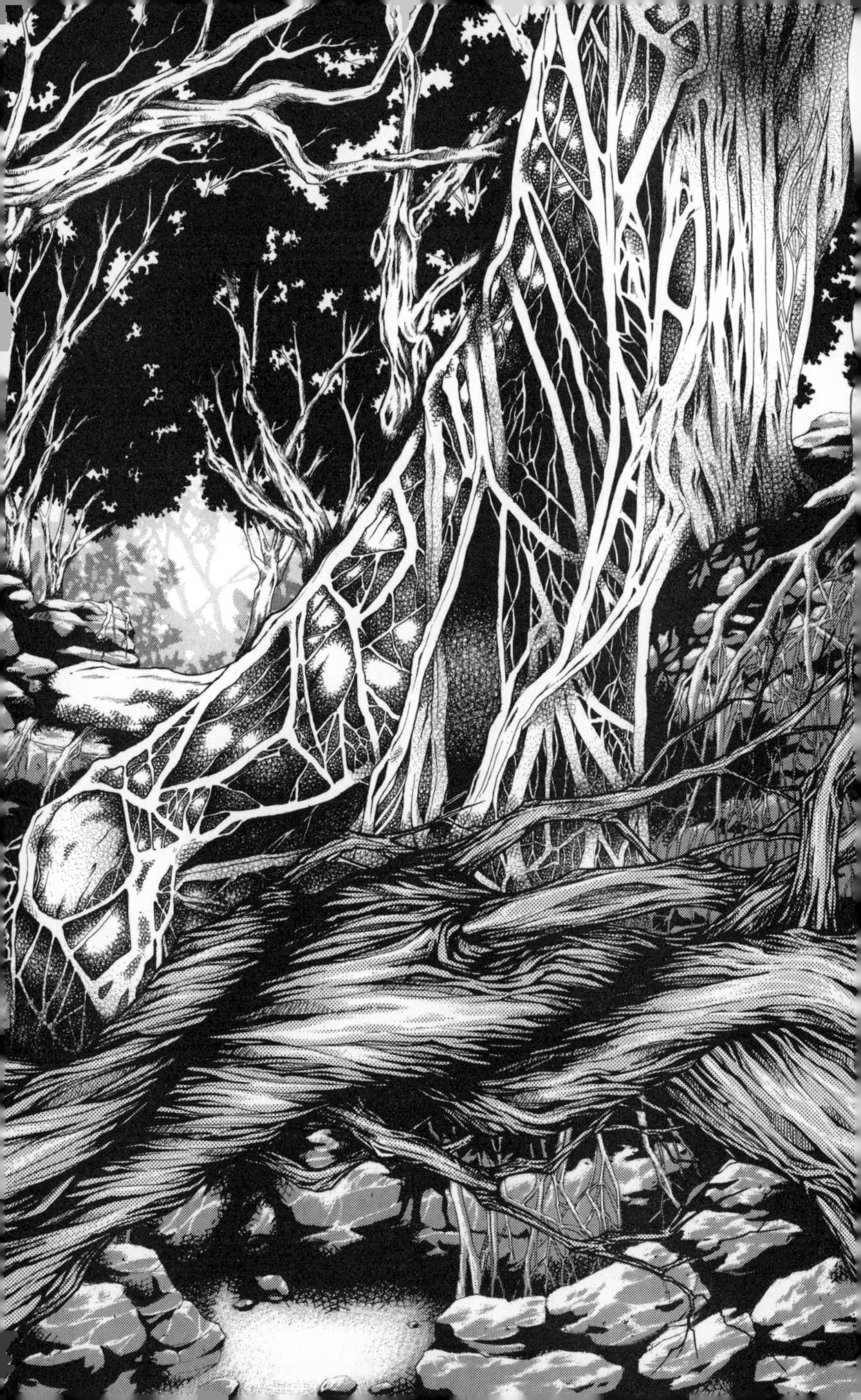

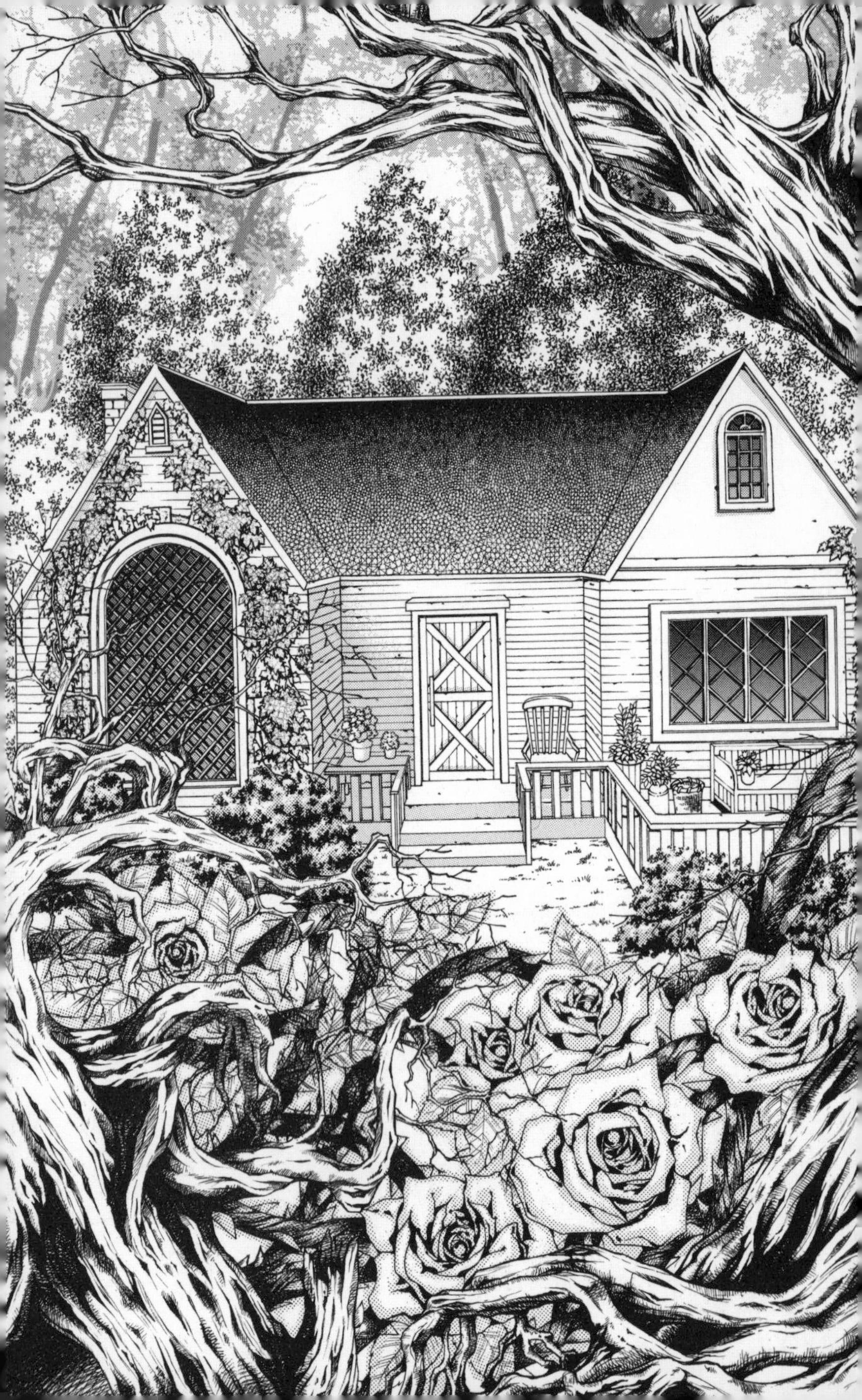

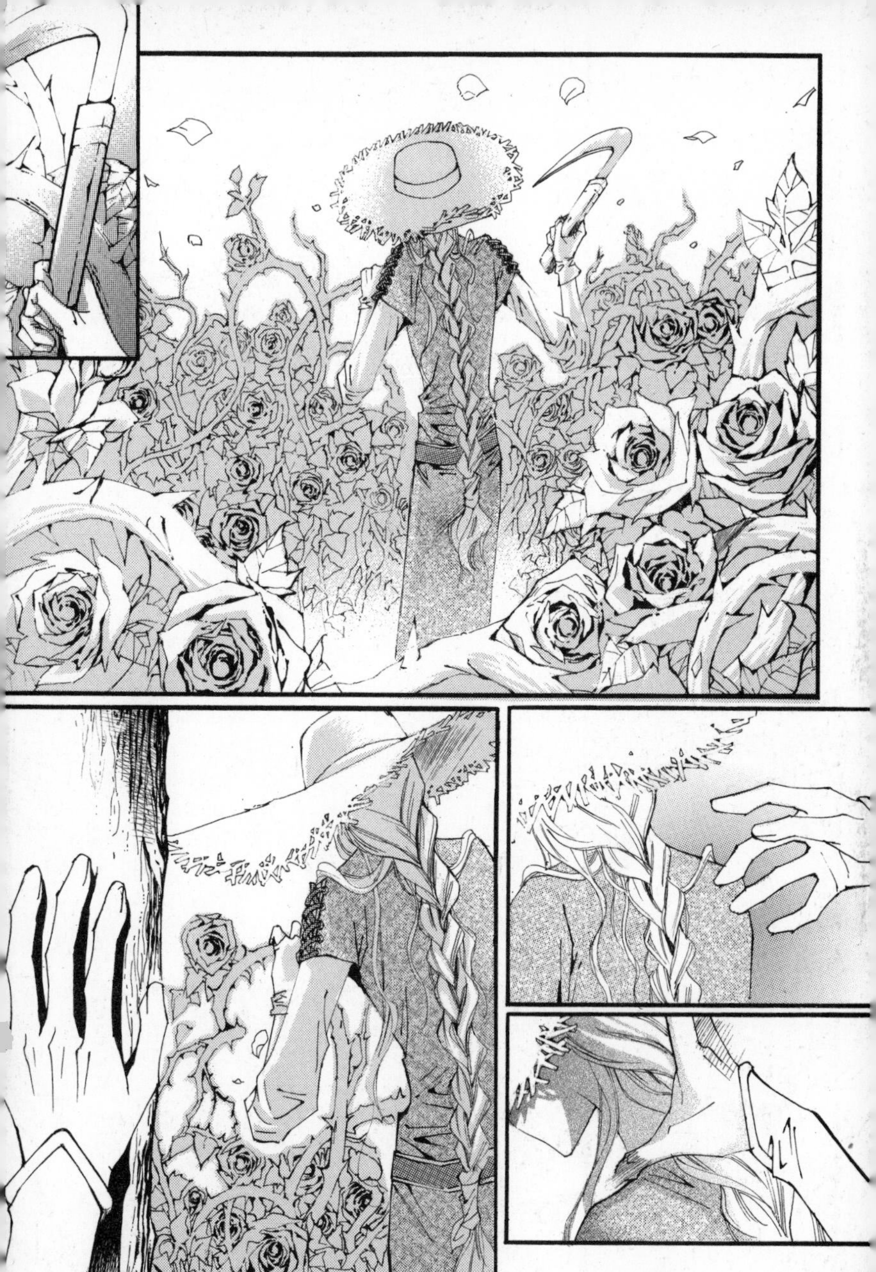

Ch. 1

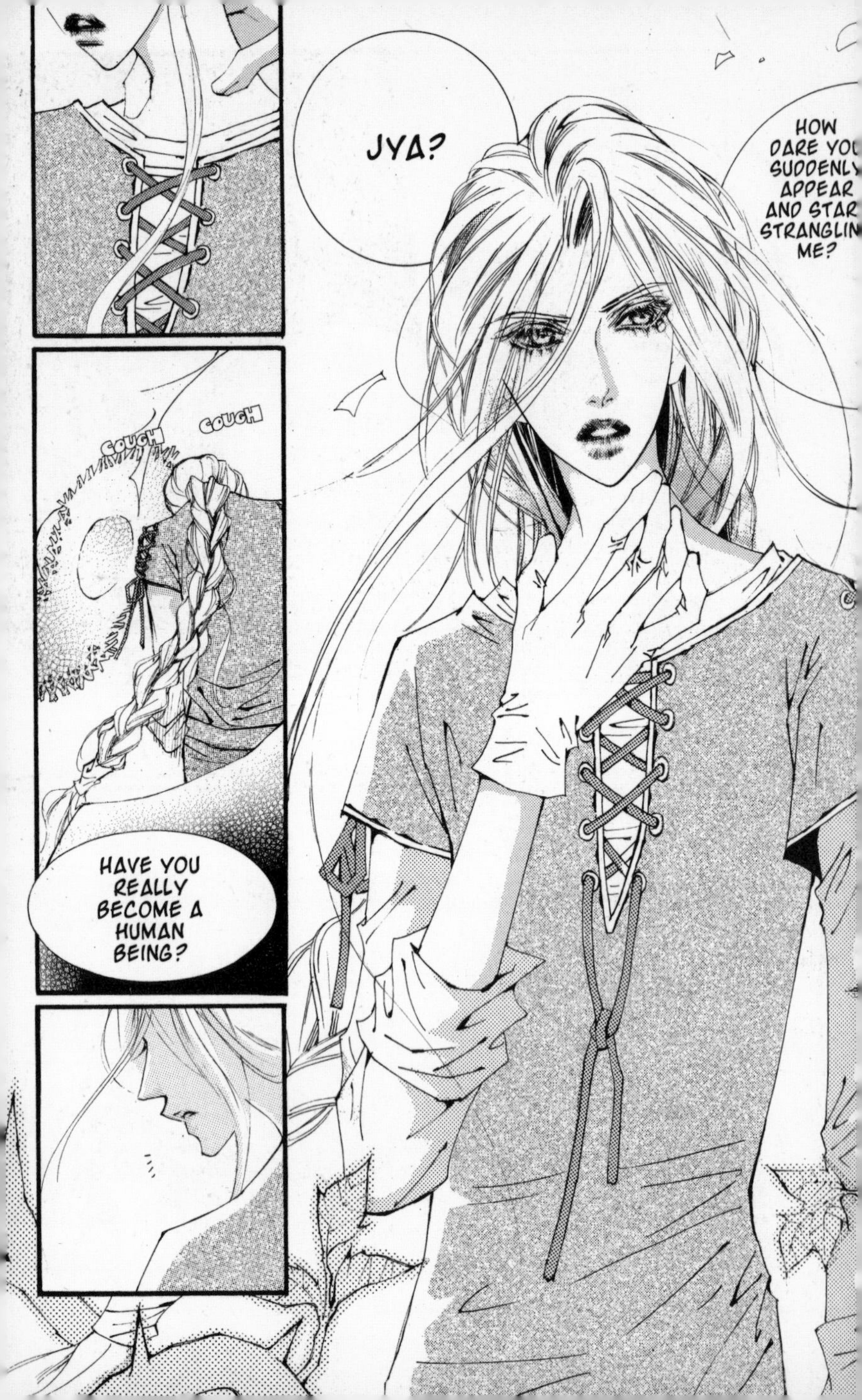
COUGH
COUGH
HAVE YOU REALLY BECOME A HUMAN BEING?
...
JYA?
HOW DARE YOU SUDDENLY APPEAR AND STAR STRANGLIN ME?

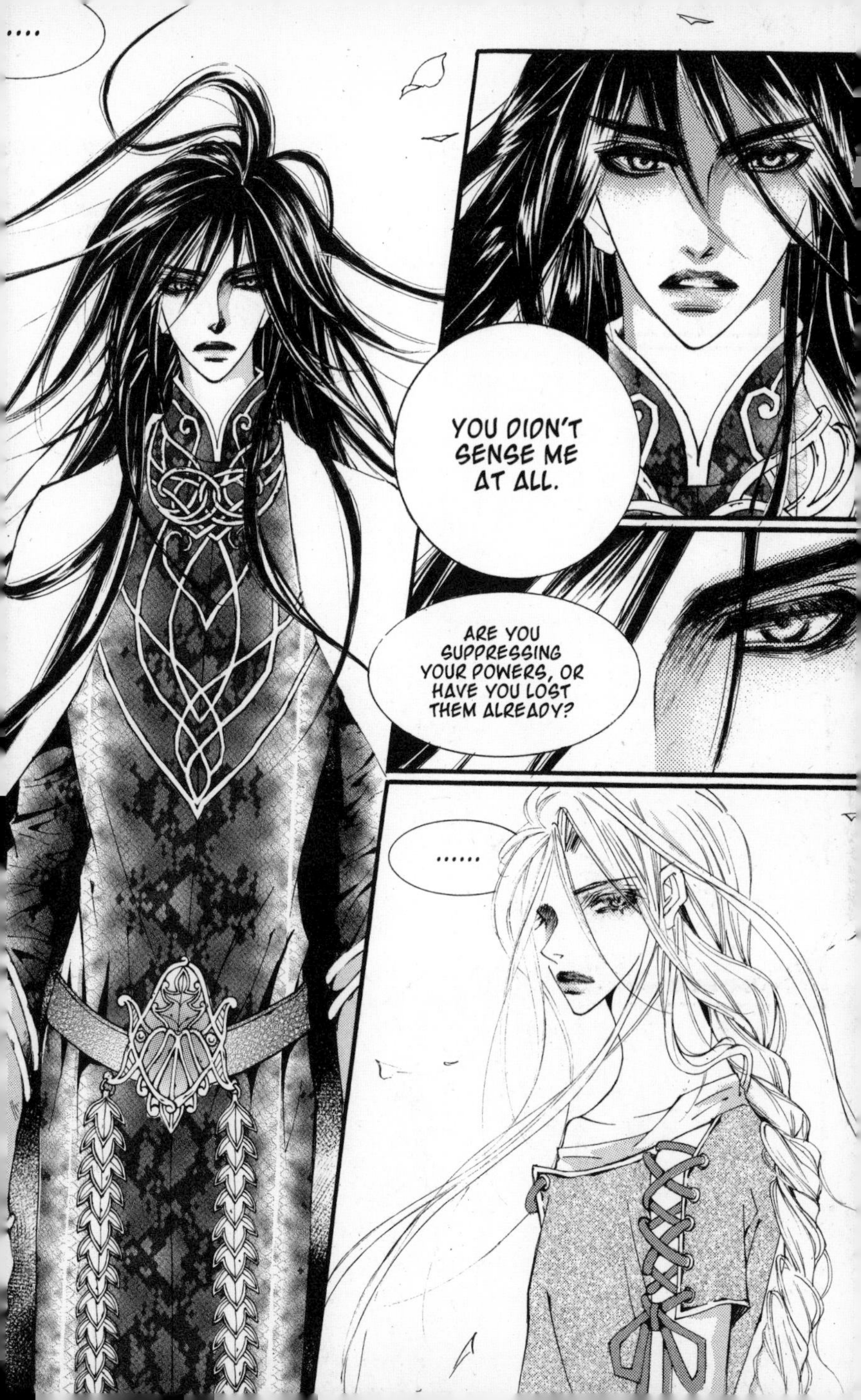
....
YOU DIDN'T SENSE ME AT ALL.
ARE YOU SUPPRESSING YOUR POWERS, OR HAVE YOU LOST THEM ALREADY?
......

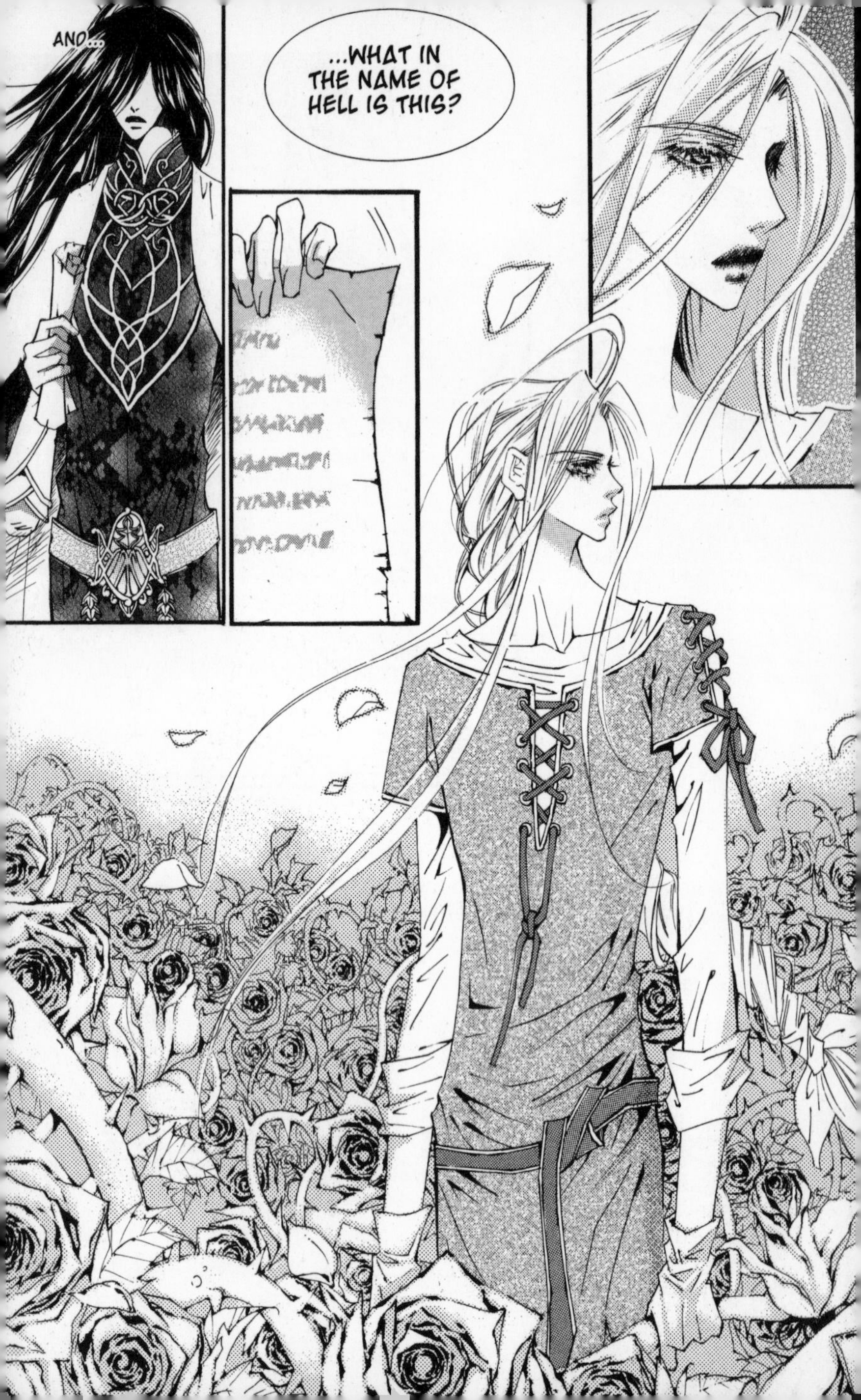
AND...
...WHAT IN THE NAME OF HELL IS THIS?

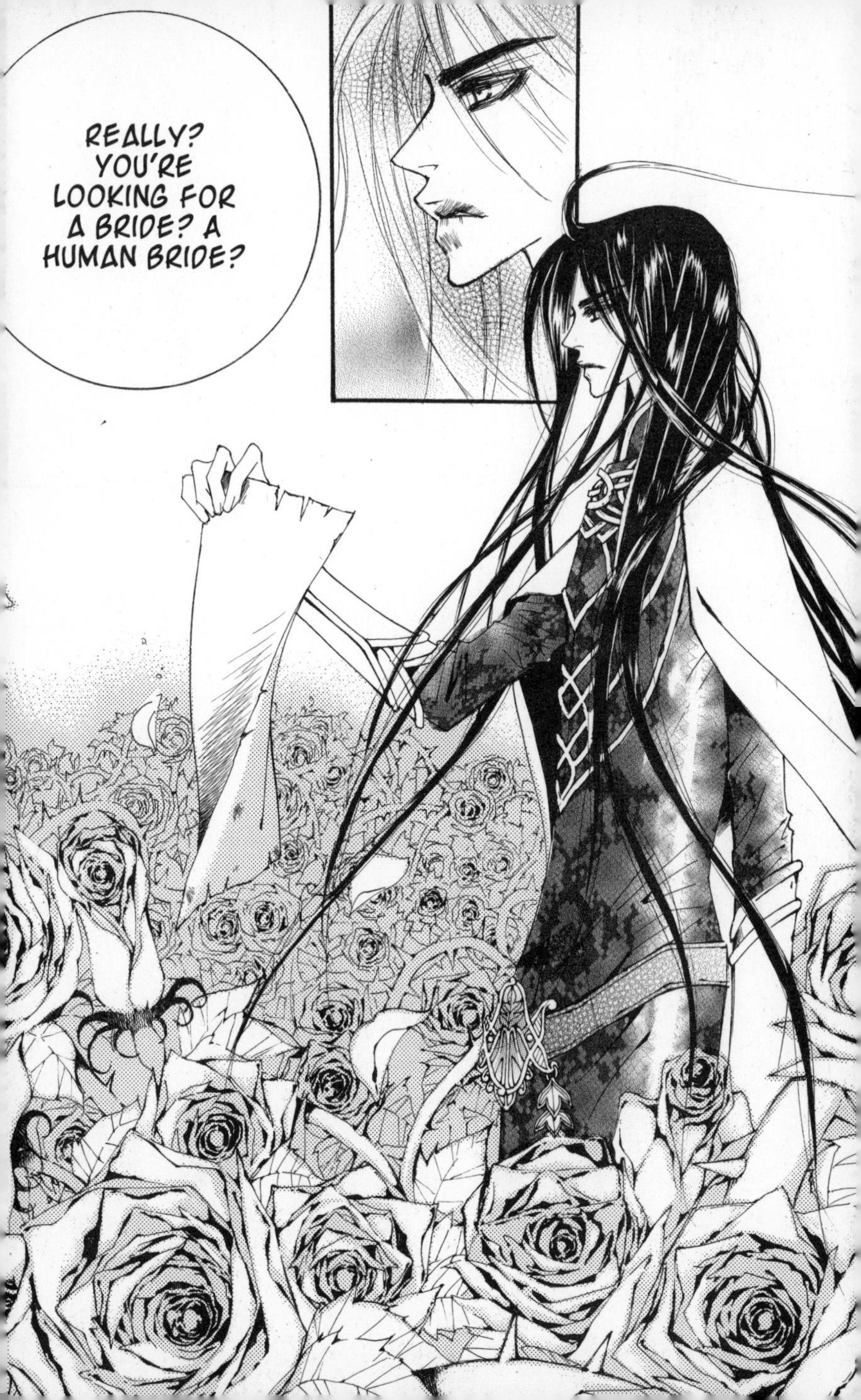
REALLY? YOU'RE LOOKING FOR A BRIDE? A HUMAN BRIDE?

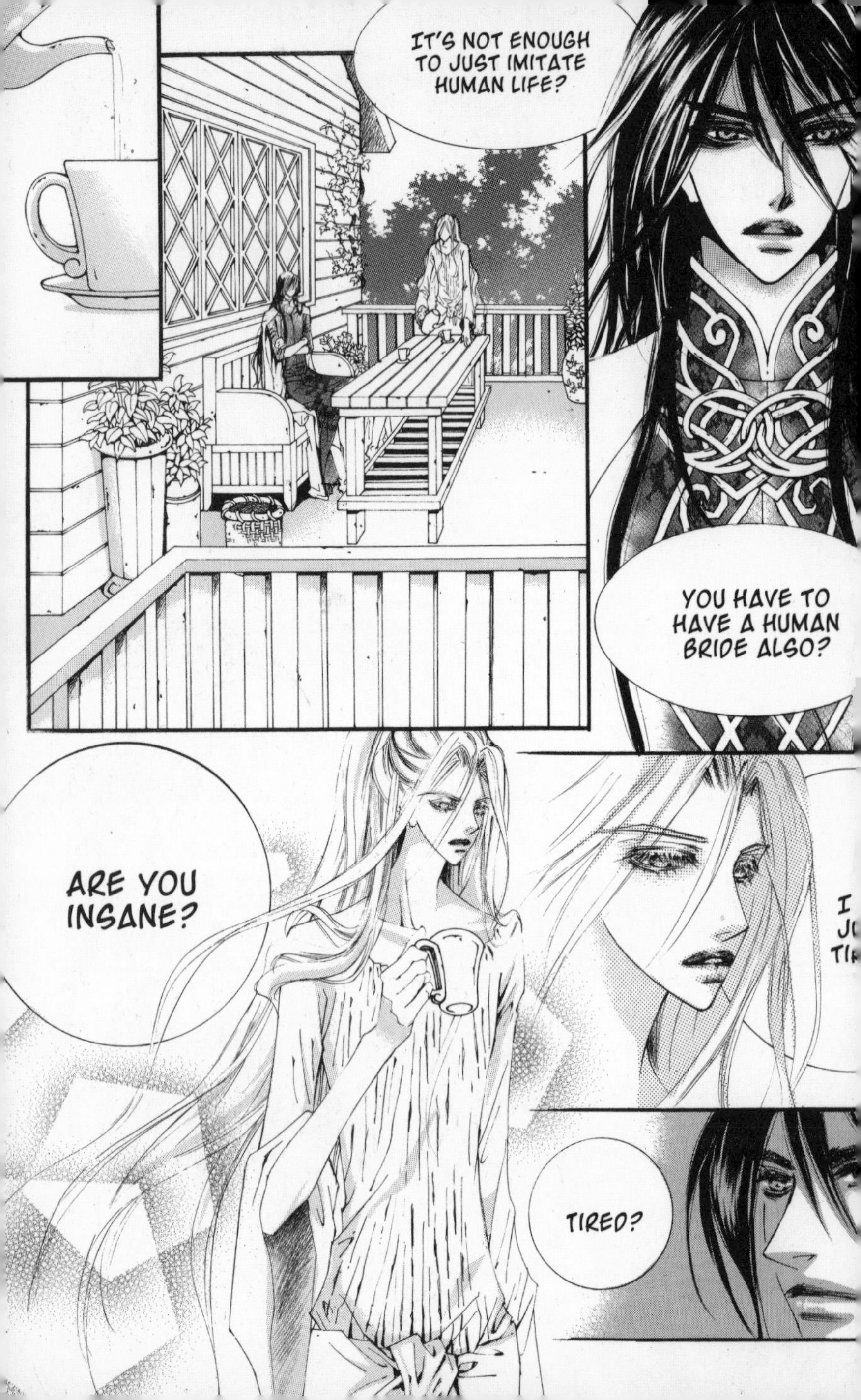
IT'S NOT ENOUGH TO JUST IMITATE HUMAN LIFE?
YOU HAVE TO HAVE A HUMAN BRIDE ALSO?
ARE YOU INSANE?
TIRED?

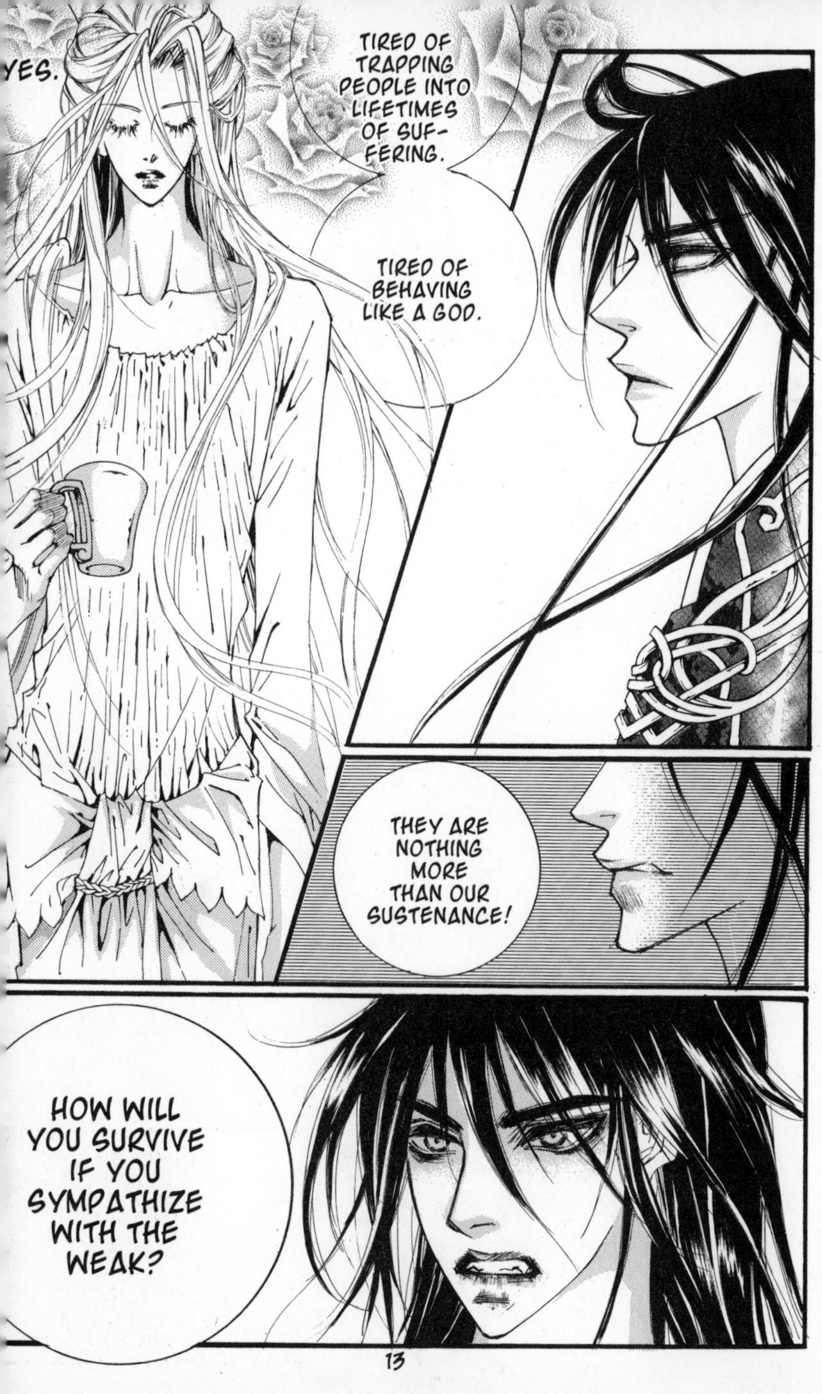
YES.
TIRED OF TRAPPING PEOPLE INTO LIFETIMES OF SUF-FERING.
TIRED OF BEHAVING LIKE A GOD.
THEY ARE NOTHING MORE THAN OUR SUSTENANCE!
HOW WILL YOU SURVIVE IF YOU SYMPATHIZE WITH THE WEAK?

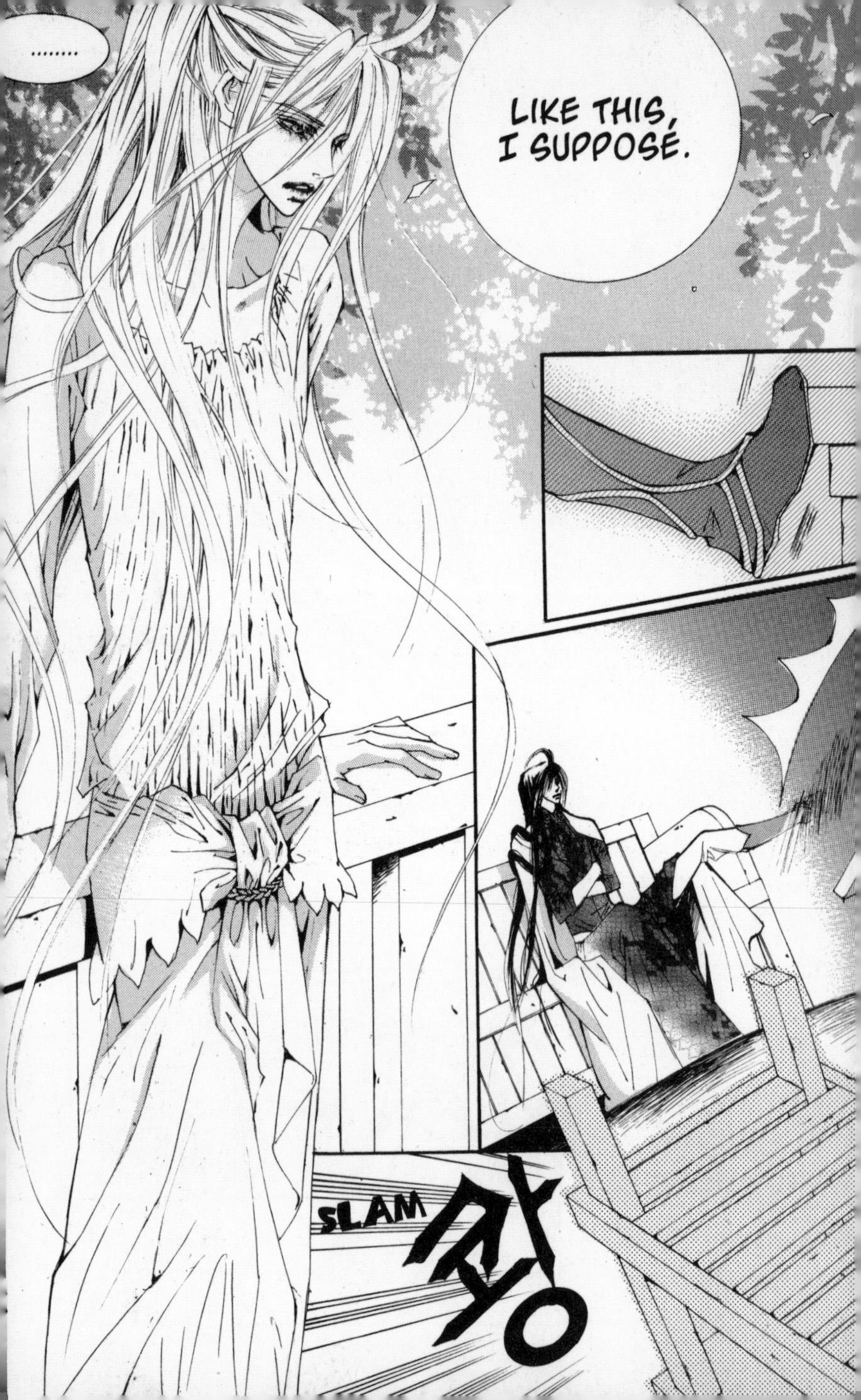
....
LIKE THIS, I SUPPOSE.
SLAM

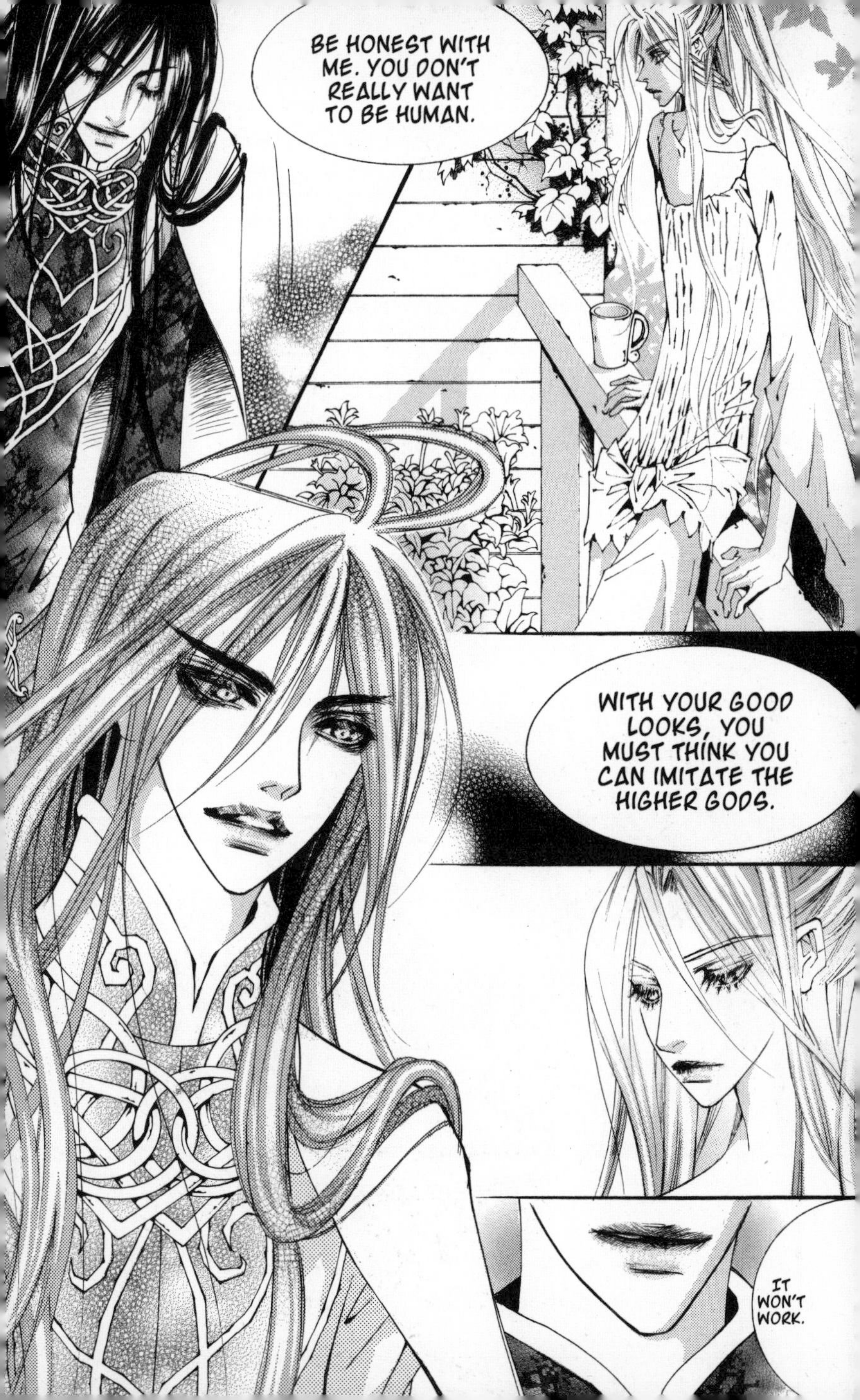
BE HONEST WITH ME. YOU DON'T REALLY WANT TO BE HUMAN.
WITH YOUR GOOD LOOKS, YOU MUST THINK YOU CAN IMITATE THE HIGHER GODS.
IT WON'T WORK.

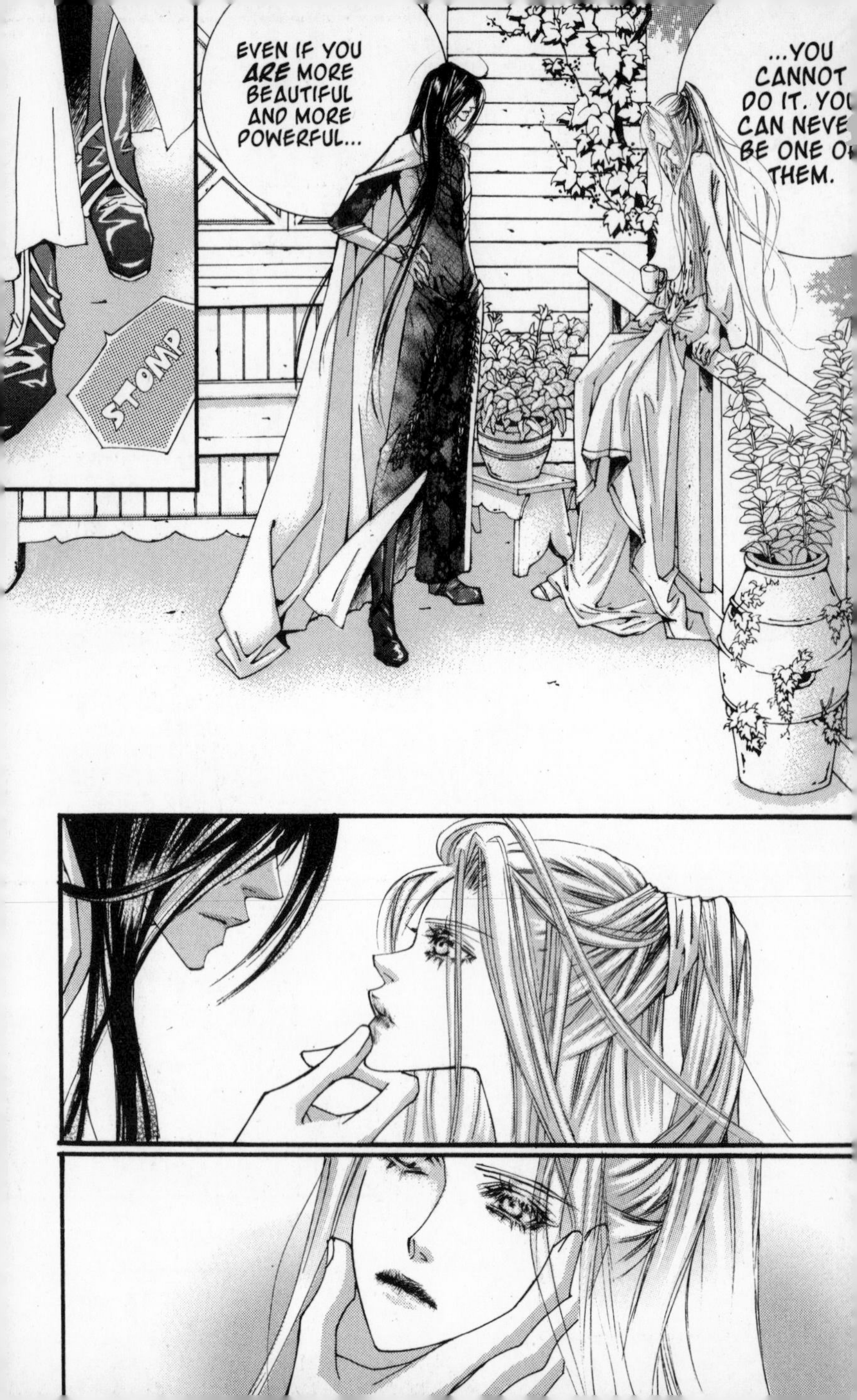
STOMP
EVEN IF YOU ARE MORE BEAUTIFUL AND MORE POWERFUL...
...YOU CANNOT DO IT. YOU CAN NEVE BE ONE OF THEM.

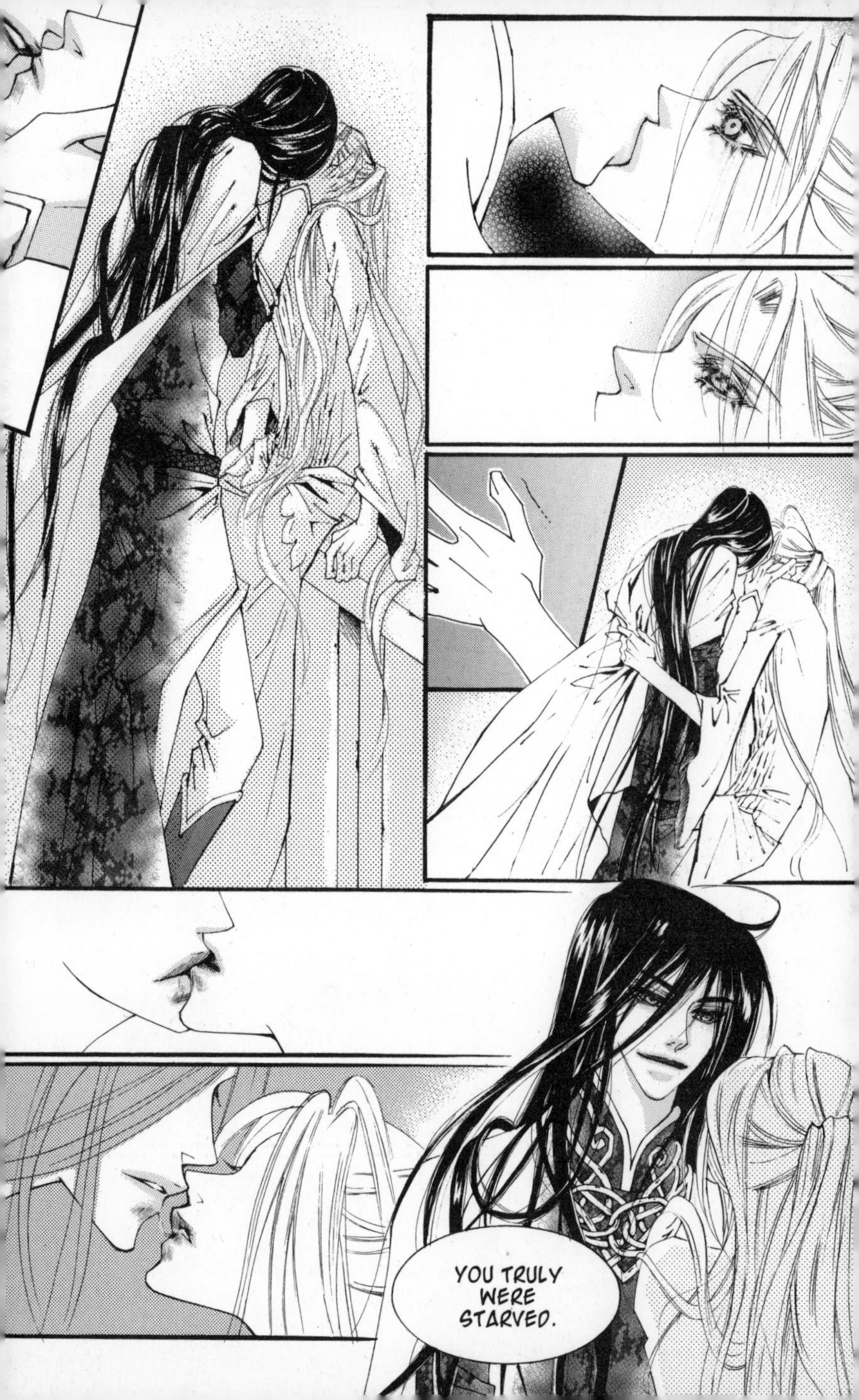
YOU TRULY WERE STARVED.

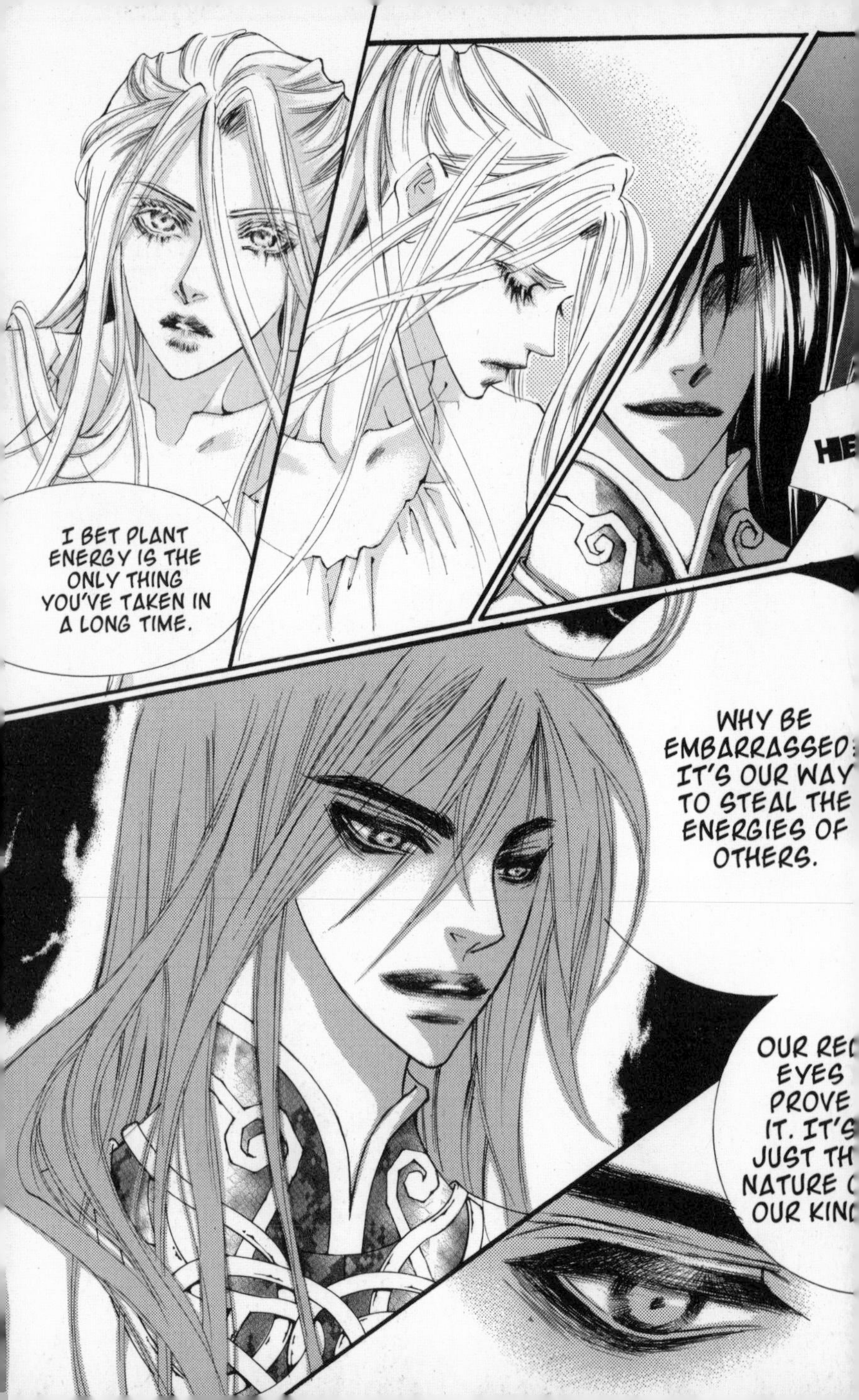
I BET PLANT ENERGY IS THE ONLY THING YOU'VE TAKEN IN A LONG TIME.
HE
WHY BE EMBARRASSED IT'S OUR WAY TO STEAL THE ENERGIES OF OTHERS.
OUR RE EYES PROVE IT. IT'S JUST TH NATURE O OUR KIN

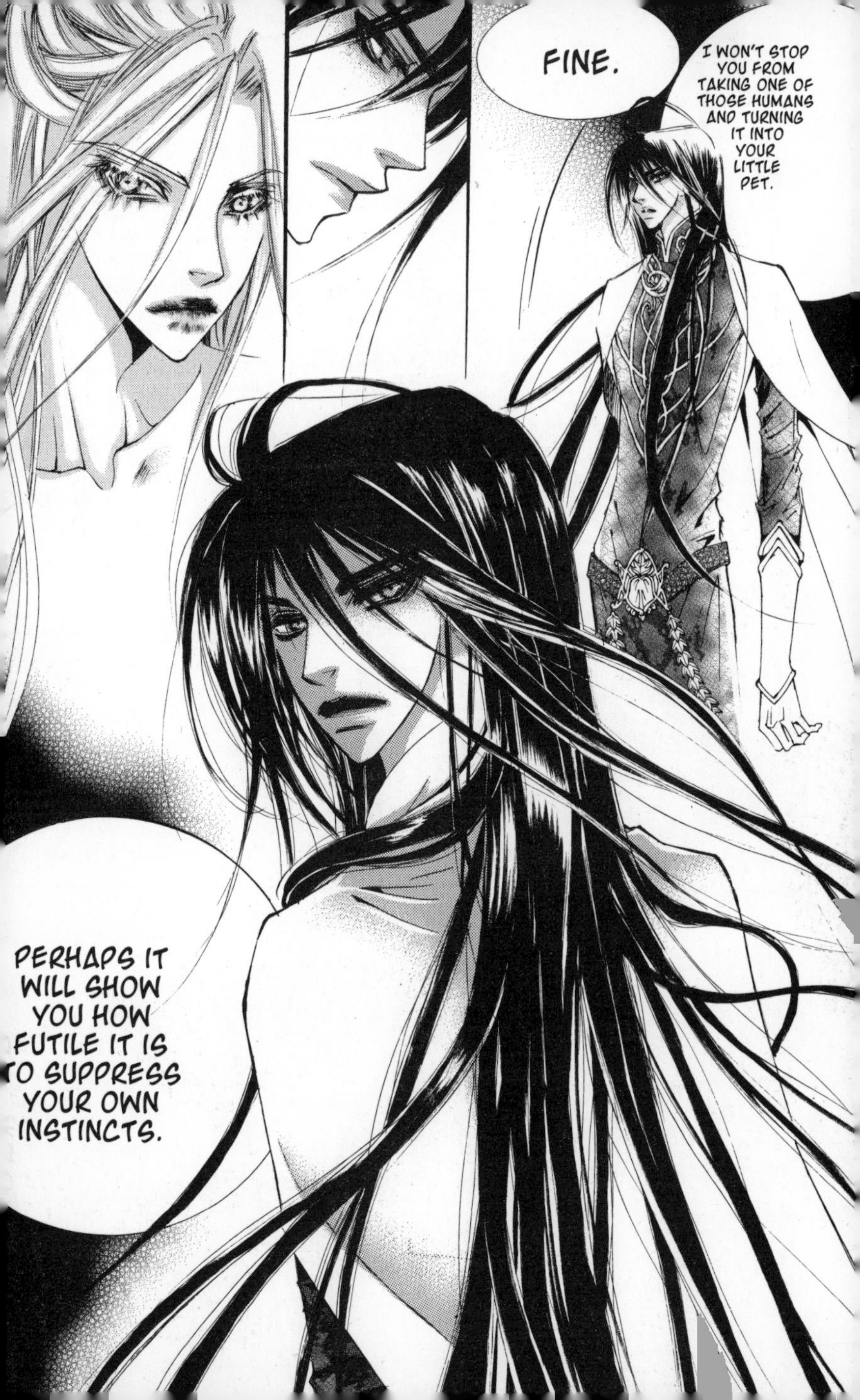
FINE.
I WON'T STOP YOU FROM TAKING ONE OF THOSE HUMANS AND TURNING IT INTO YOUR LITTLE PET.
PERHAPS IT WILL SHOW YOU HOW FUTILE IT IS TO SUPPRESS YOUR OWN INSTINCTS.

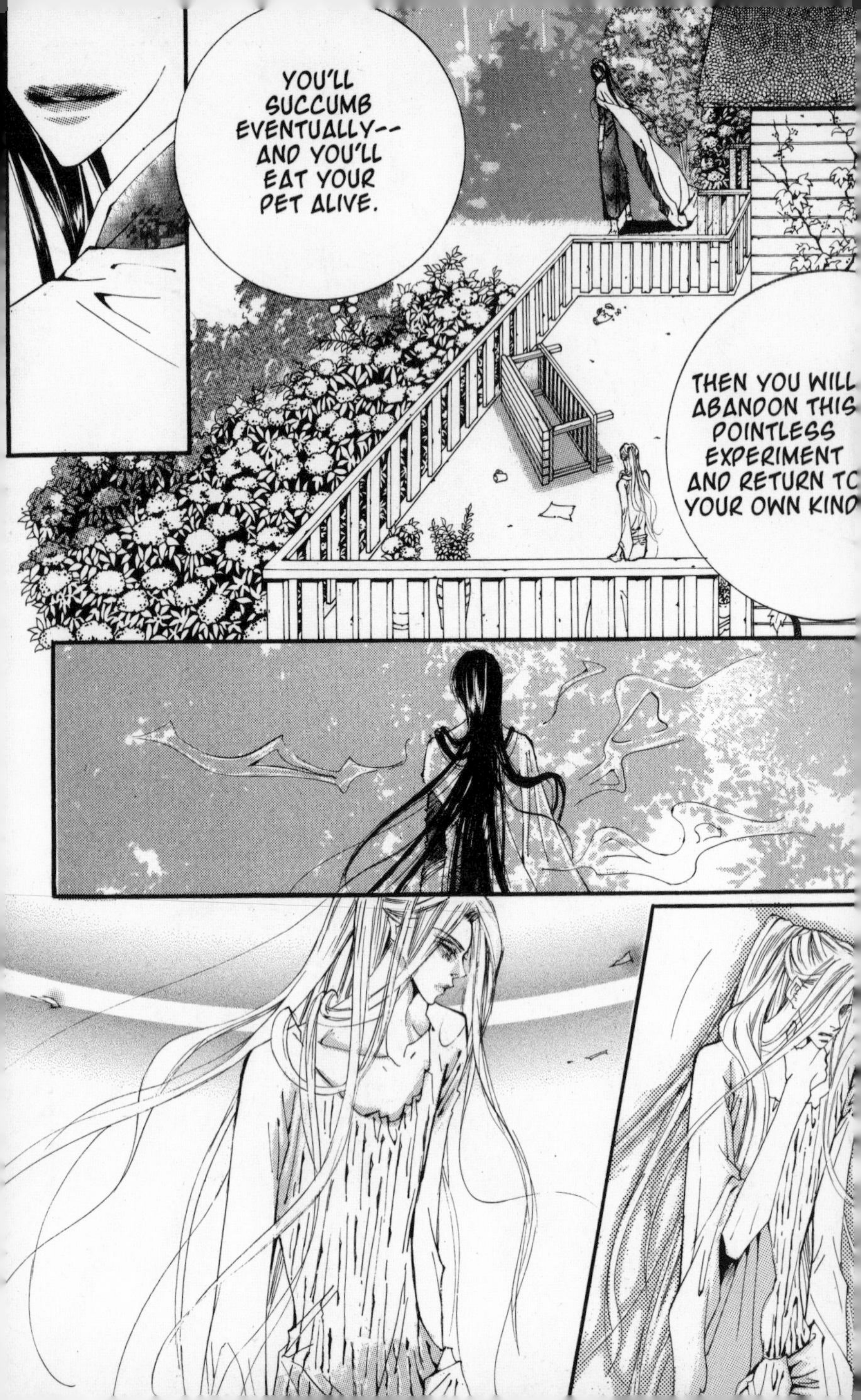
YOU'LL SUCCUMB EVENTUALLY-- AND YOU'LL EAT YOUR PET ALIVE.
THEN YOU WILL ABANDON THIS POINTLESS EXPERIMENT AND RETURN TO YOUR OWN KIND

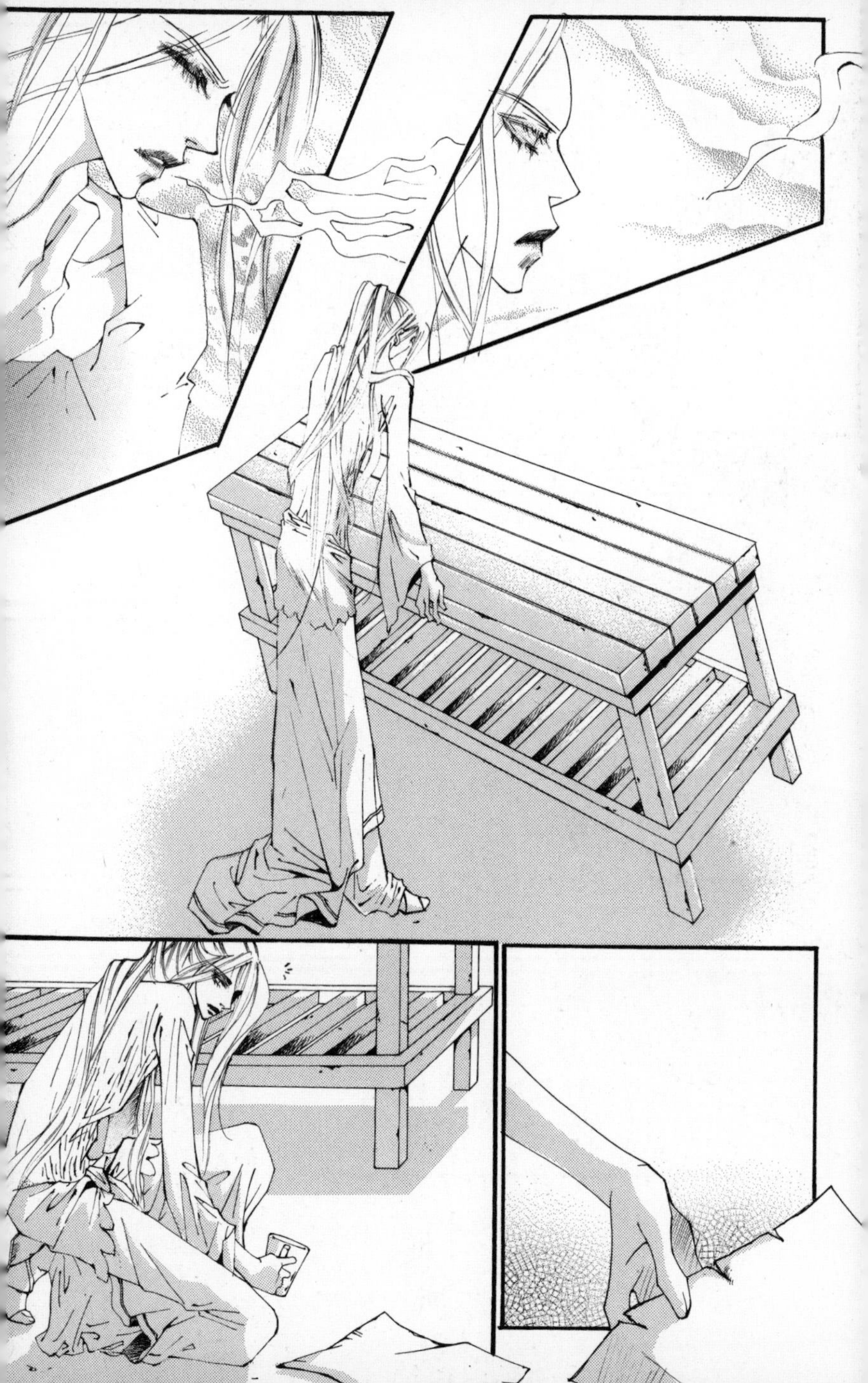

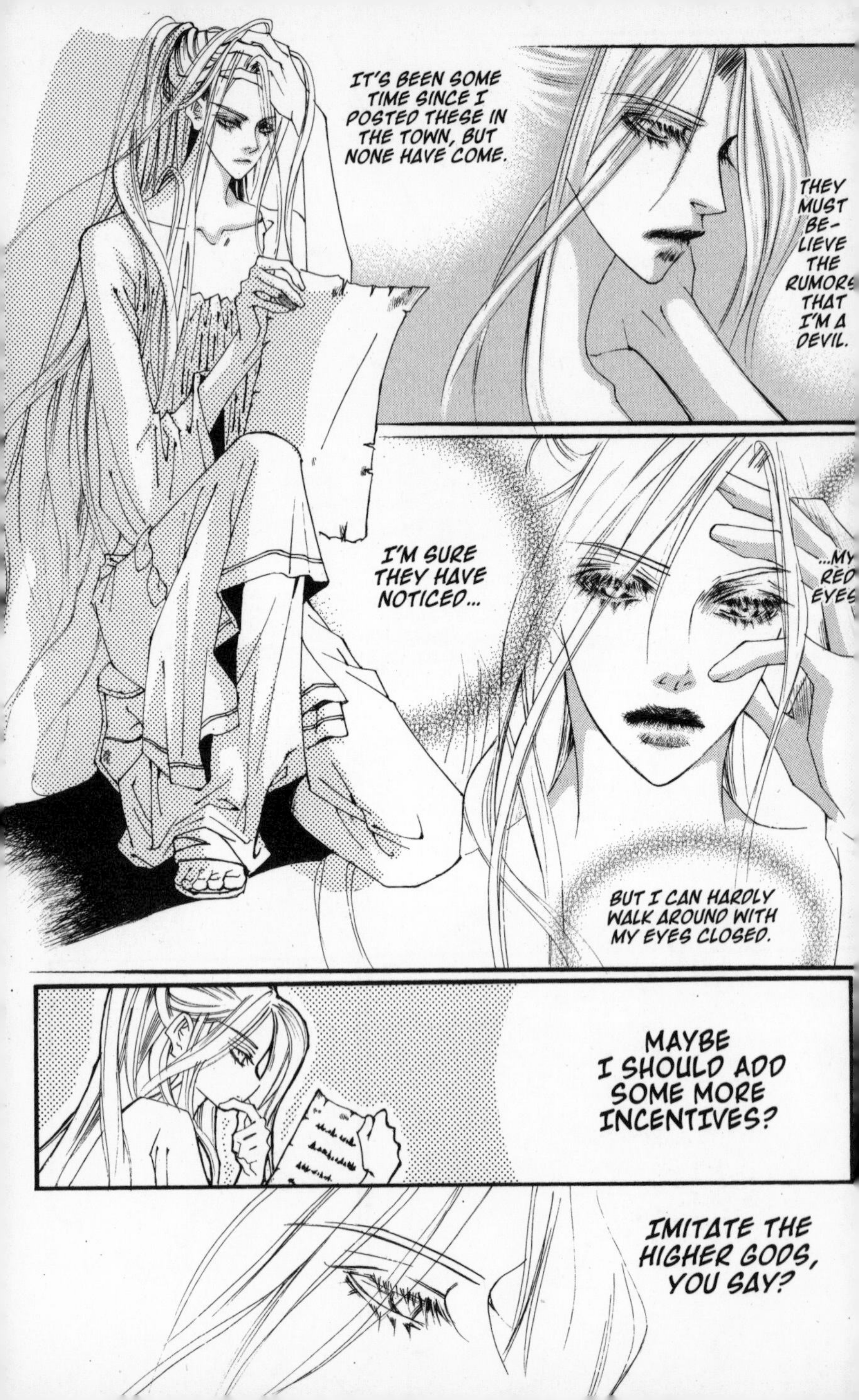
IT'S BEEN SOME TIME SINCE I POSTED THESE IN THE TOWN, BUT NONE HAVE COME.
THEY MUST BE-LIEVE THE RUMORS THAT I'M A DEVIL.
I'M SURE THEY HAVE NOTICED...
...MY RED EYES
BUT I CAN HARDLY WALK AROUND WITH MY EYES CLOSED.
MAYBE I SHOULD ADD SOME MORE INCENTIVES?
IMITATE THE HIGHER GODS, YOU SAY?

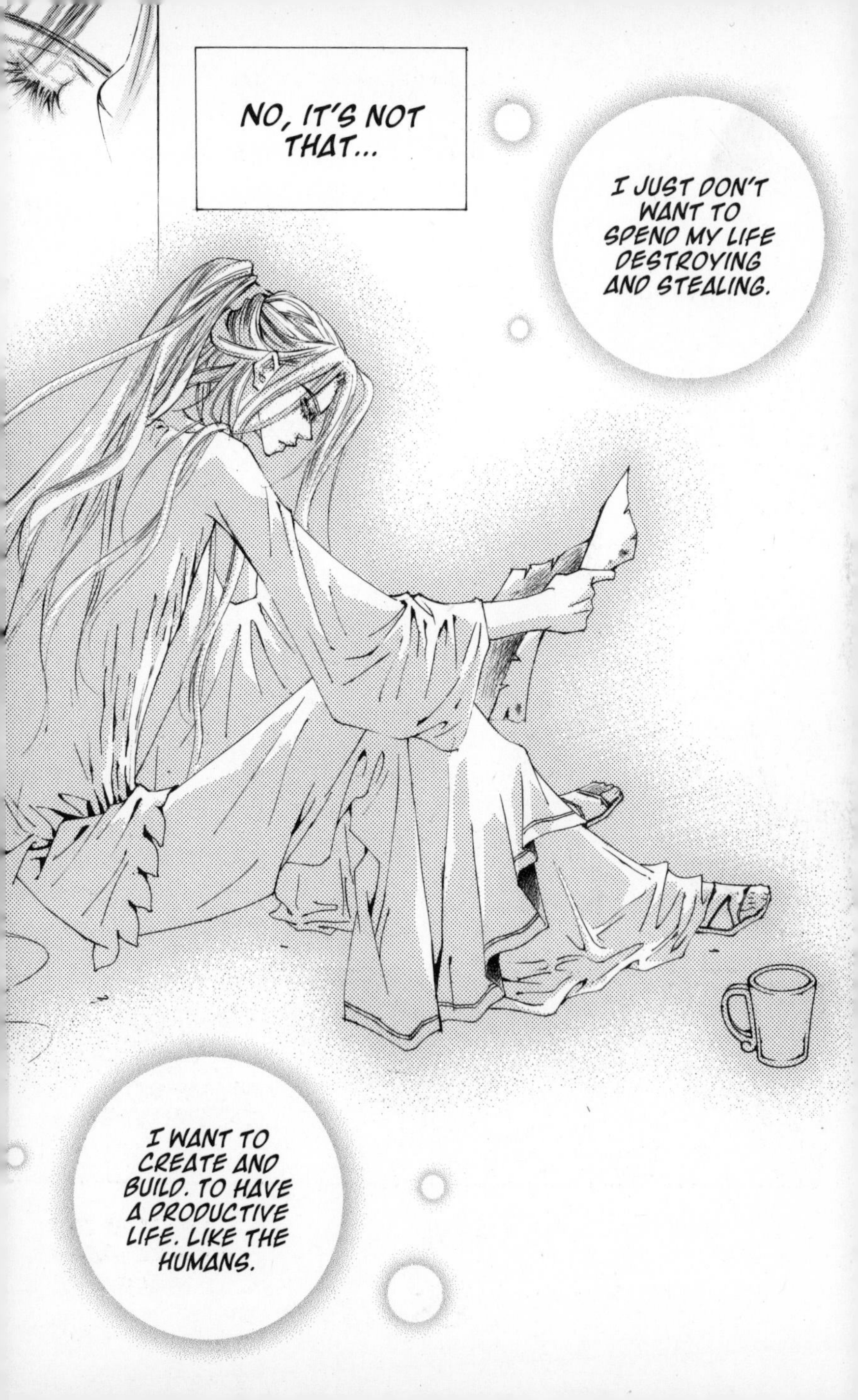
NO, IT'S NOT THAT...
I JUST DON'T WANT TO SPEND MY LIFE DESTROYING AND STEALING.
I WANT TO CREATE AND BUILD. TO HAVE A PRODUCTIVE LIFE. LIKE THE HUMANS.

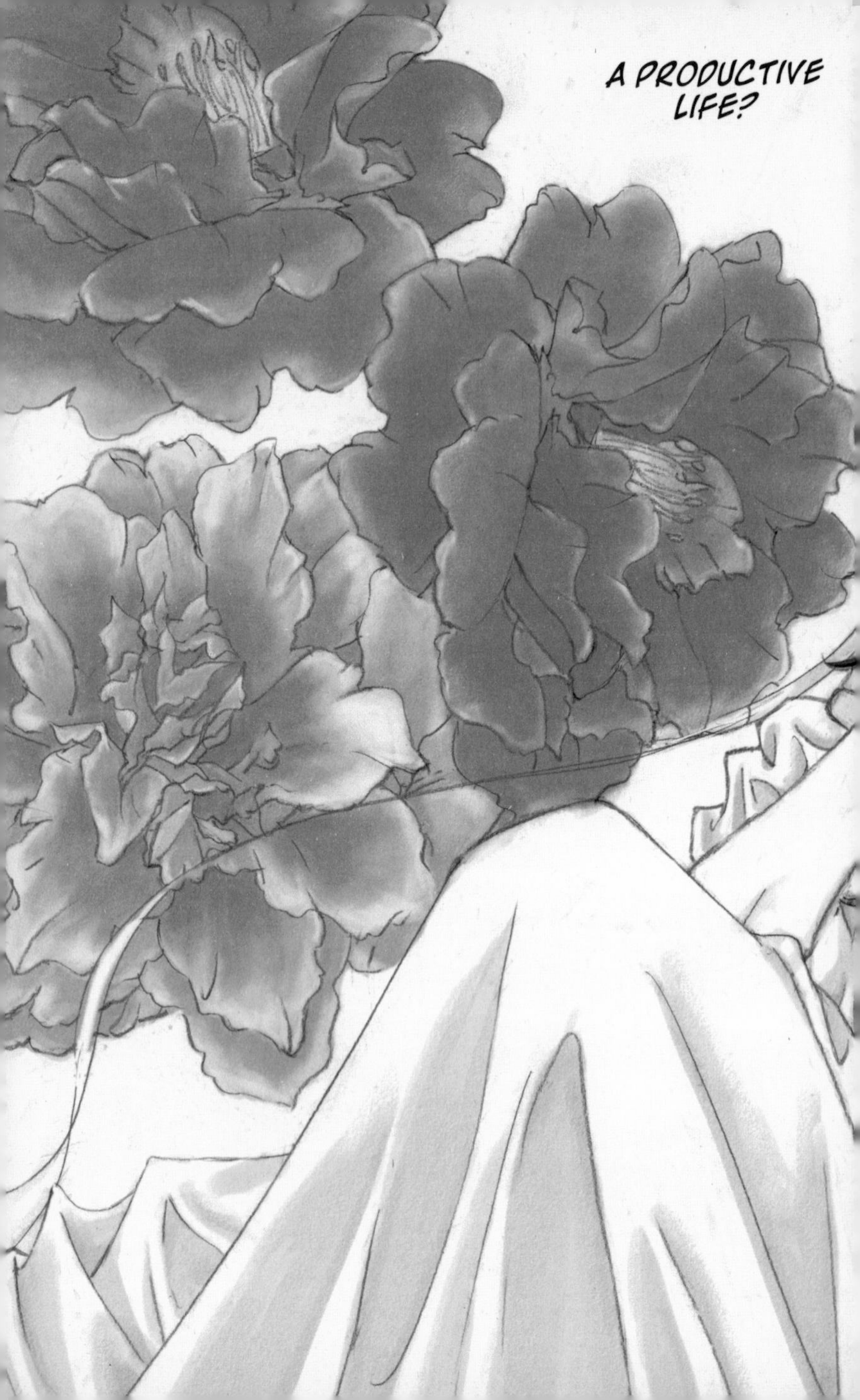
A PRODUCTIVE LIFE?

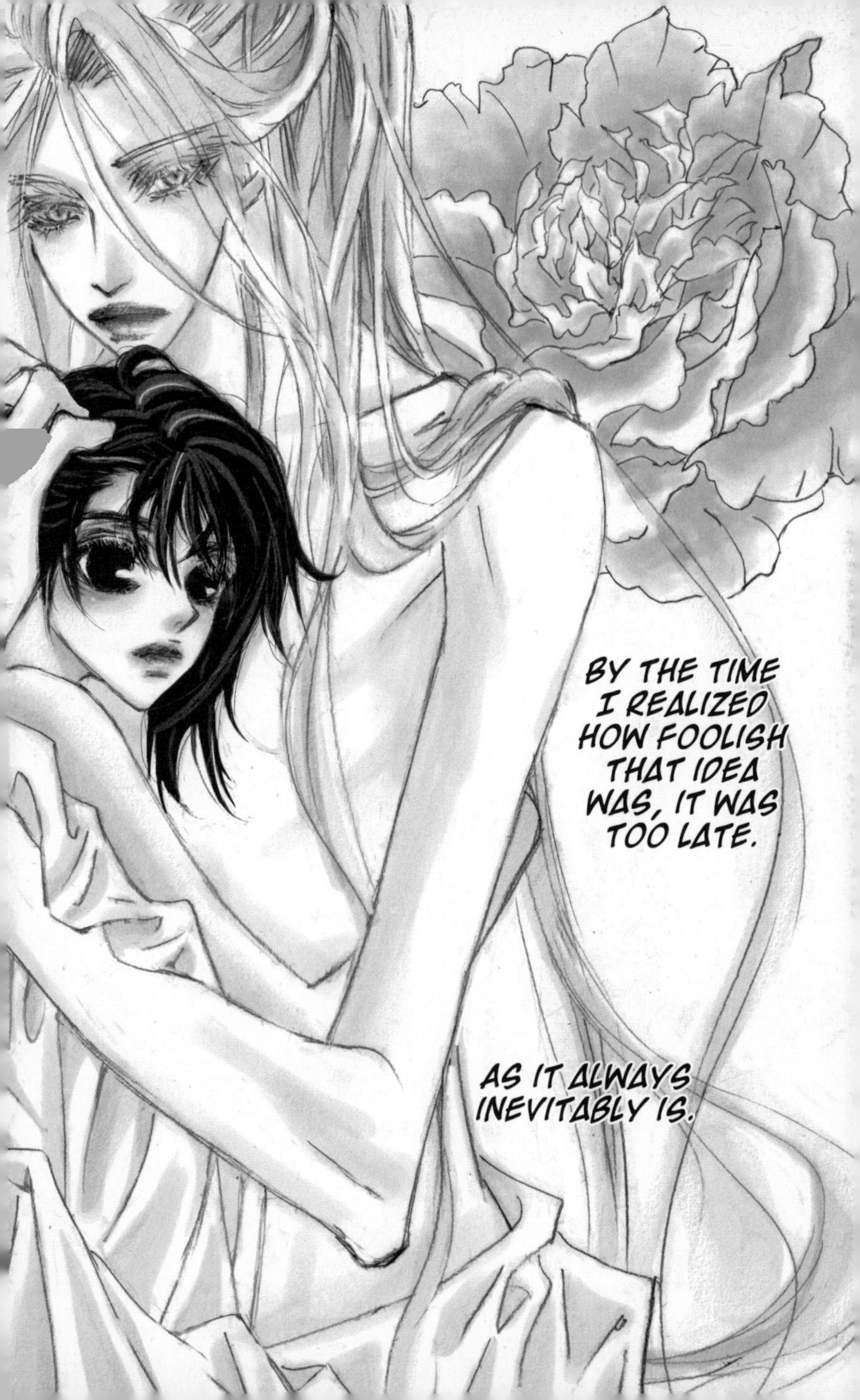
BY THE TIME I REALIZED HOW FOOLISH THAT IDEA WAS, IT WAS TOO LATE.
AS IT ALWAYS INEVITABLY IS.

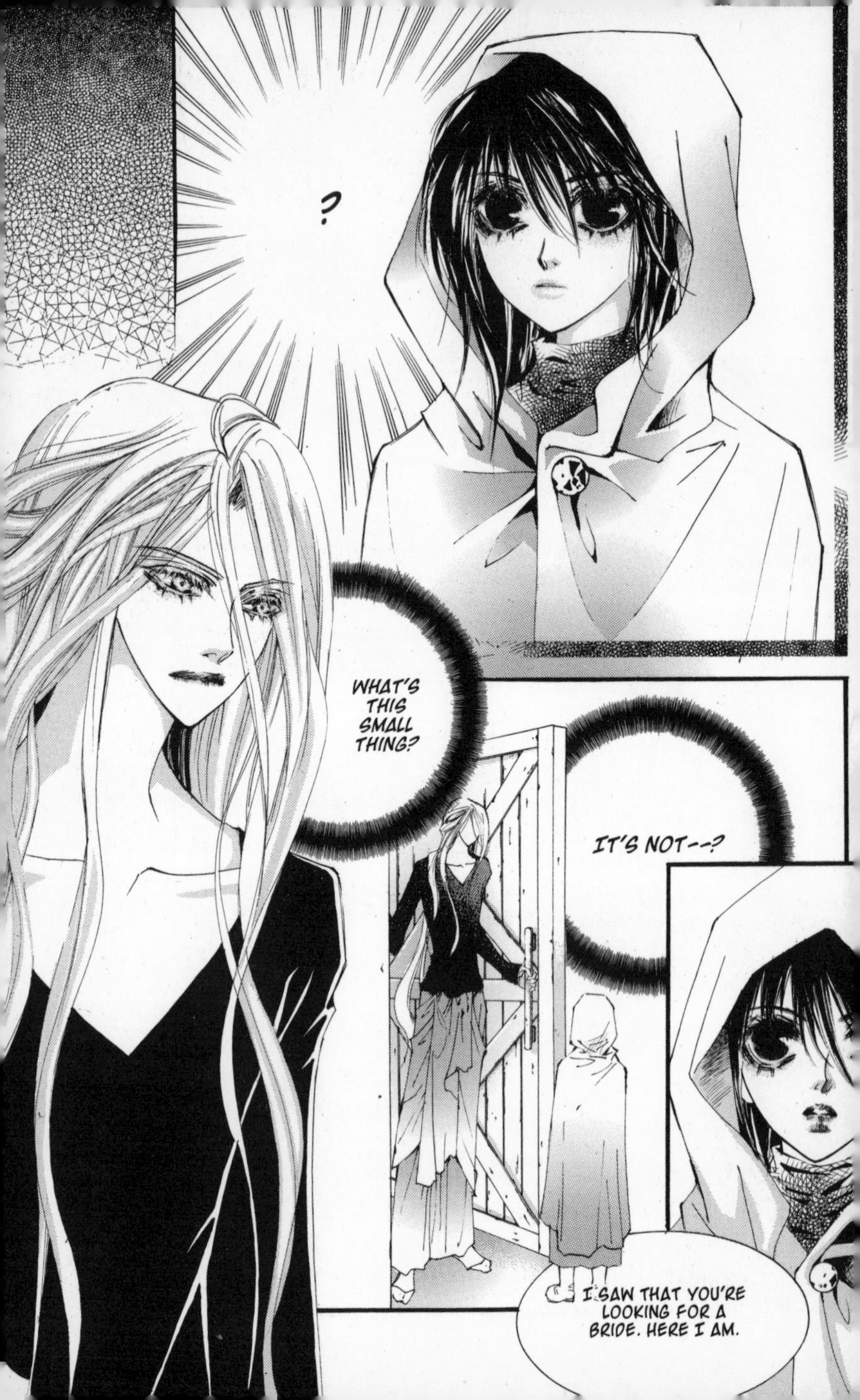
?
WHAT'S THIS SMALL THING?
IT'S NOT--?
I SAW THAT YOU'RE LOOKING FOR A BRIDE. HERE I AM.

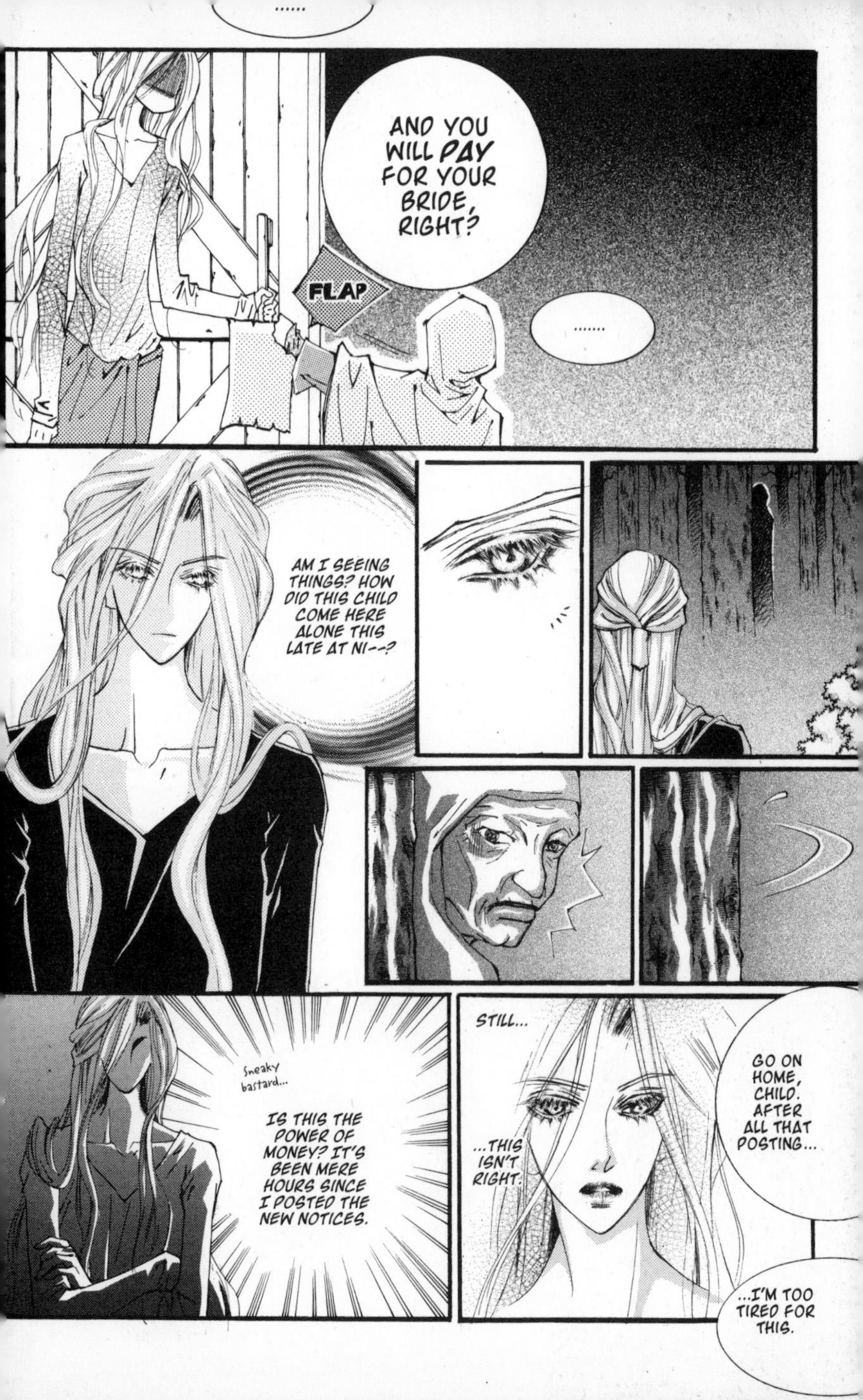
......
AND YOU WILL PAY FOR YOUR BRIDE, RIGHT?
FLAP
......
AM I SEEING THINGS? HOW DID THIS CHILD COME HERE ALONE THIS LATE AT NI--?
Sneaky bastard...
IS THIS THE POWER OF MONEY? IT'S BEEN MERE HOURS SINCE I POSTED THE NEW NOTICES.
STILL...
...THIS ISN'T RIGHT.
GO ON HOME, CHILD. AFTER ALL THAT POSTING...
...I'M TOO TIRED FOR THIS.

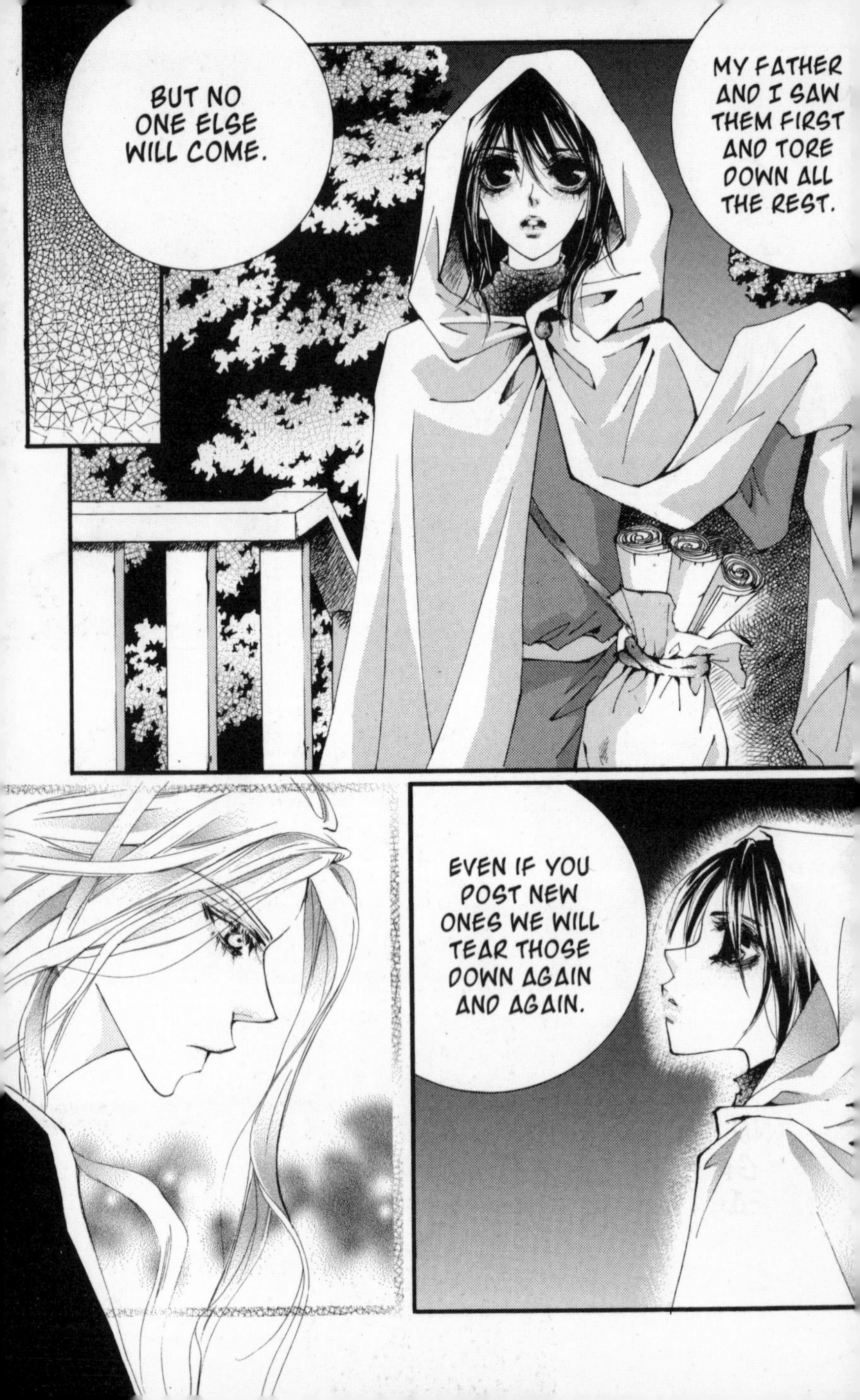
BUT NO ONE ELSE WILL COME.
MY FATHER AND I SAW THEM FIRST AND TORE DOWN ALL THE REST.
EVEN IF YOU POST NEW ONES WE WILL TEAR THOSE DOWN AGAIN AND AGAIN.

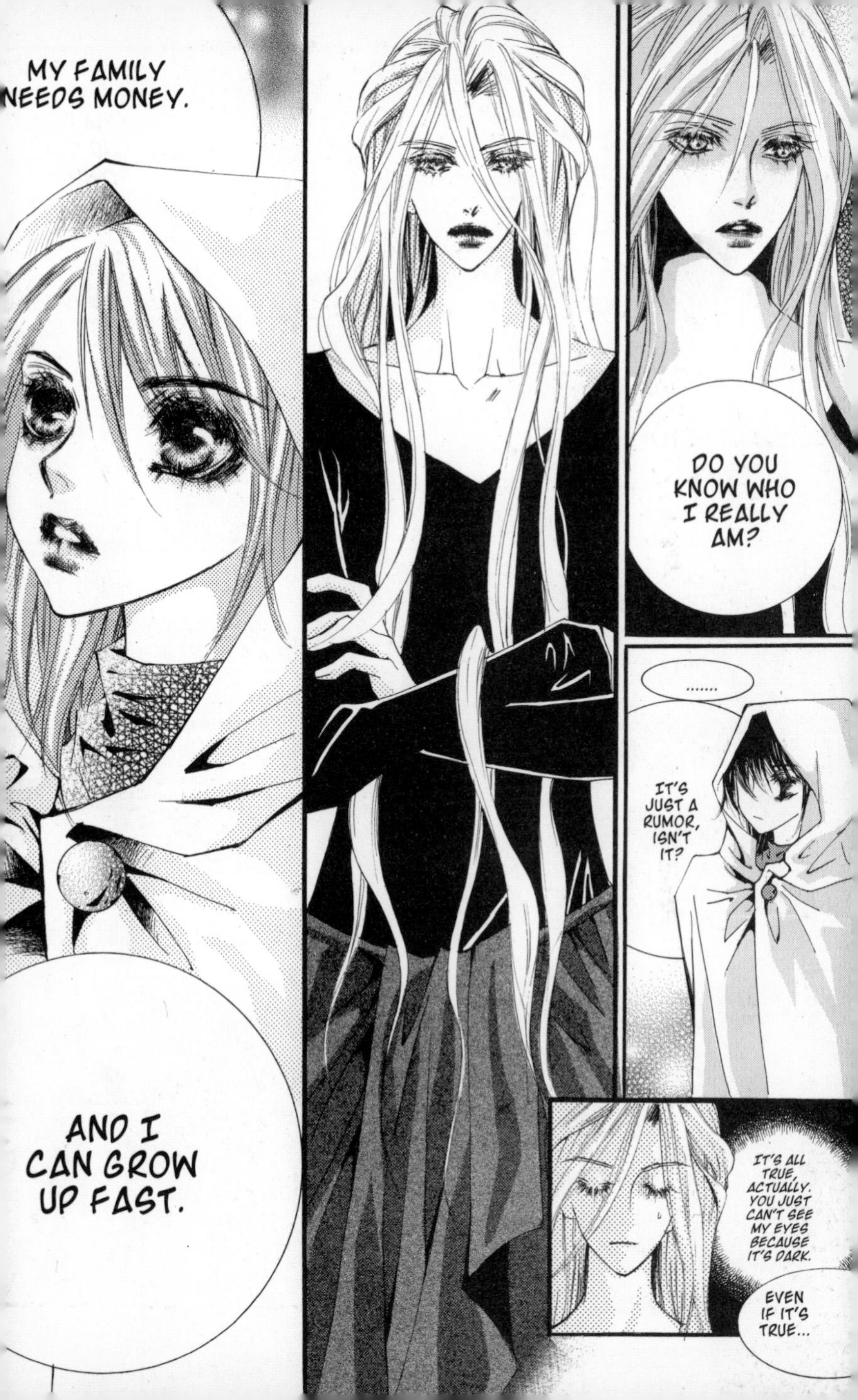
MY FAMILY NEEDS MONEY.
AND I CAN GROW UP FAST.
DO YOU KNOW WHO I REALLY AM?
....
IT'S JUST A RUMOR, ISN'T IT?
IT'S ALL TRUE, ACTUALLY. YOU JUST CAN'T SEE MY EYES BECAUSE IT'S DARK.
EVEN IF IT'S TRUE...

...IT CHANGES NOTHING.

I KNEW HUMANS WERE CAPABLE OF STRANGE THINGS, BUT THIS CHILD IS AN ENIGMA.

SOMETHING'S ODD, BUT I CAN'T QUITE FIGURE OUT WHAT IT IS.

THEN AGAIN, I AM BUYING A BRIDE WITH MONEY.

Give up

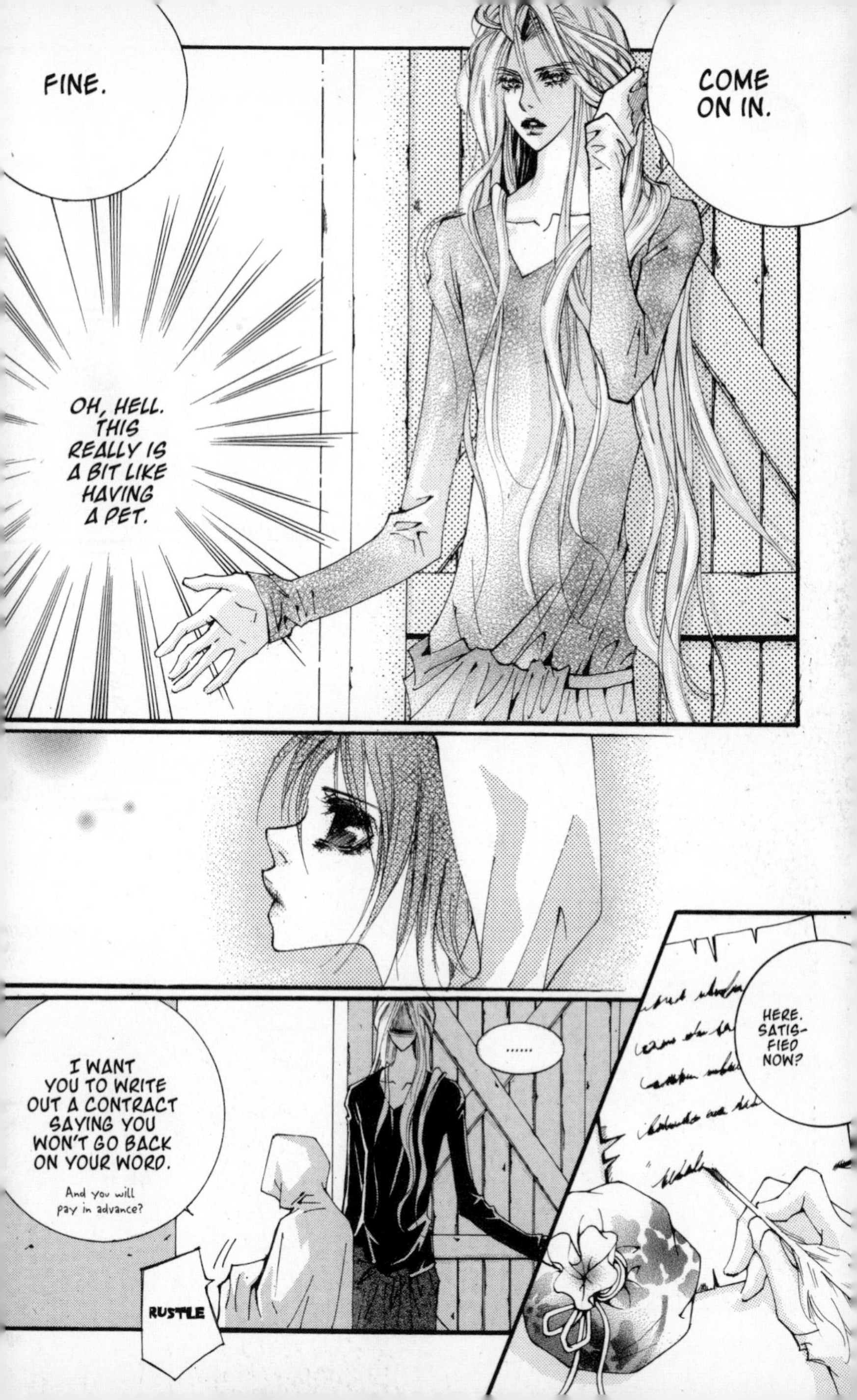
FINE.
OH, HELL. THIS REALLY IS A BIT LIKE HAVING A PET.
COME ON IN.
I WANT YOU TO WRITE OUT A CONTRACT SAYING YOU WON'T GO BACK ON YOUR WORD.
And you will pay in advance?
RUSTLE
......
HERE. SATIS-FIED NOW?

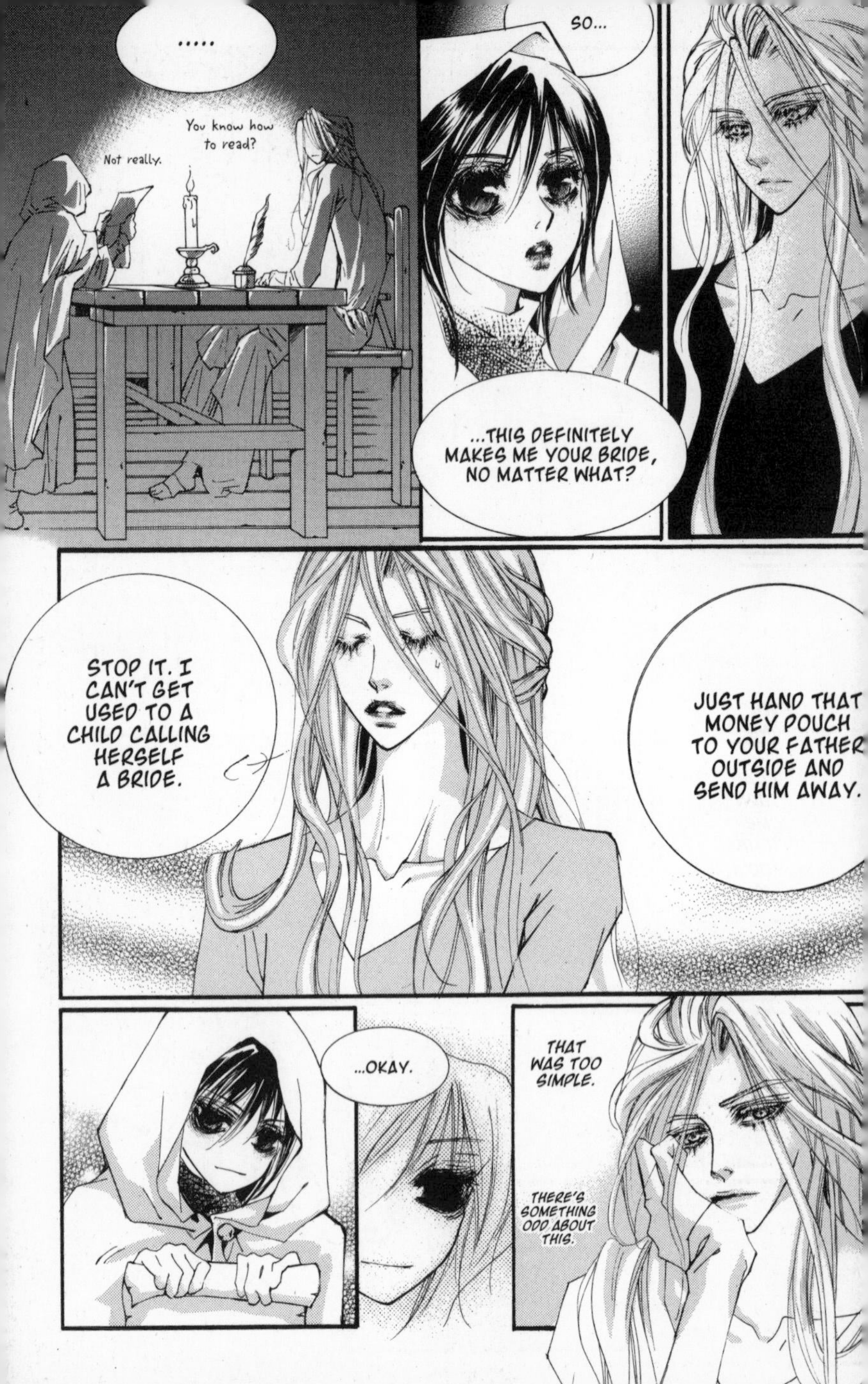
......
You know how to read?
Not really.
SO...
...THIS DEFINITELY MAKES ME YOUR BRIDE, NO MATTER WHAT?
STOP IT. I CAN'T GET USED TO A CHILD CALLING HERSELF A BRIDE.
JUST HAND THAT MONEY POUCH TO YOUR FATHER OUTSIDE AND SEND HIM AWAY.
...OKAY.
THAT WAS TOO SIMPLE.
THERE'S SOMETHING ODD ABOUT THIS.

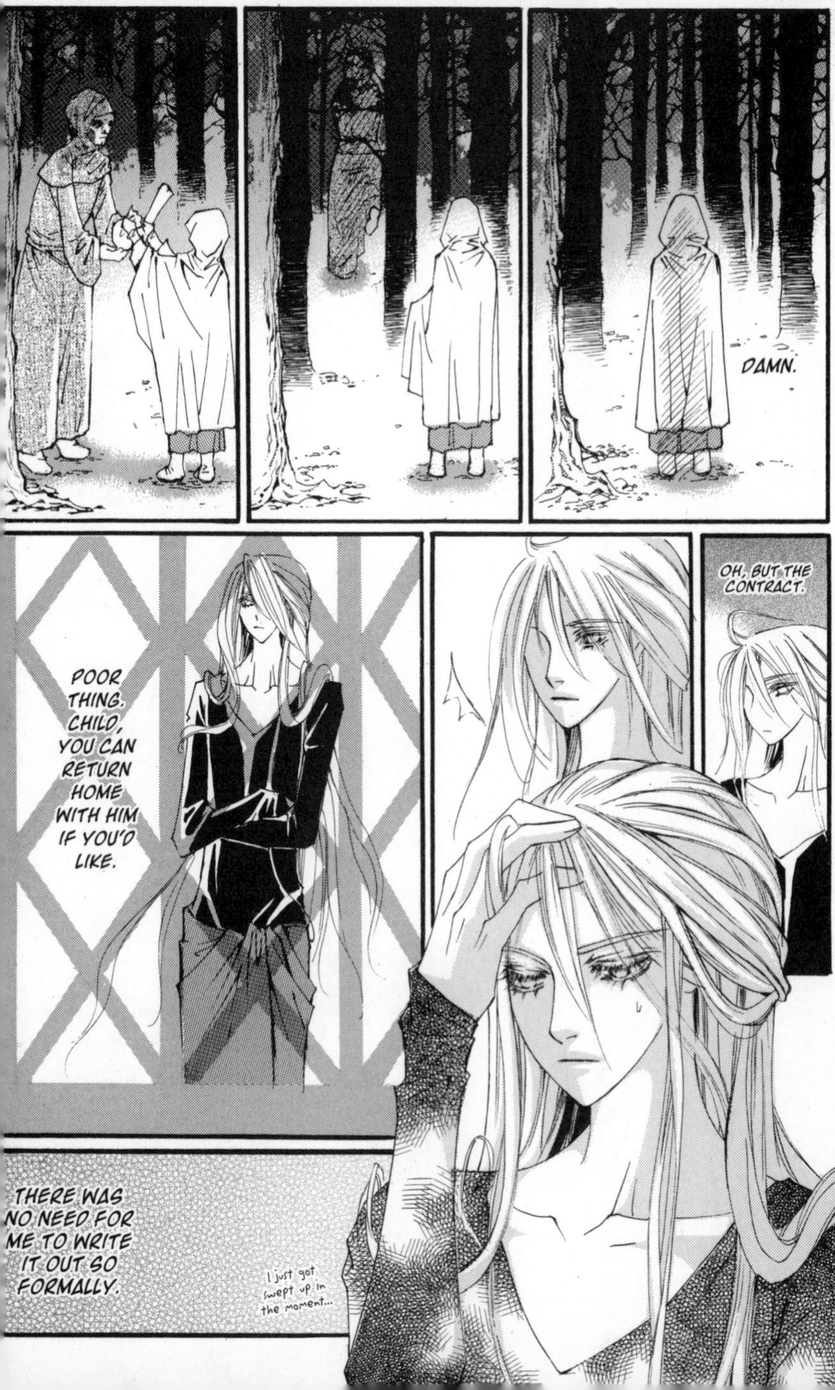
DAMN.
POOR THING. CHILD, YOU CAN RETURN HOME WITH HIM IF YOU'D LIKE.
OH, BUT THE CONTRACT.
THERE WAS NO NEED FOR ME TO WRITE IT OUT SO FORMALLY.
I just got swept up in the moment...

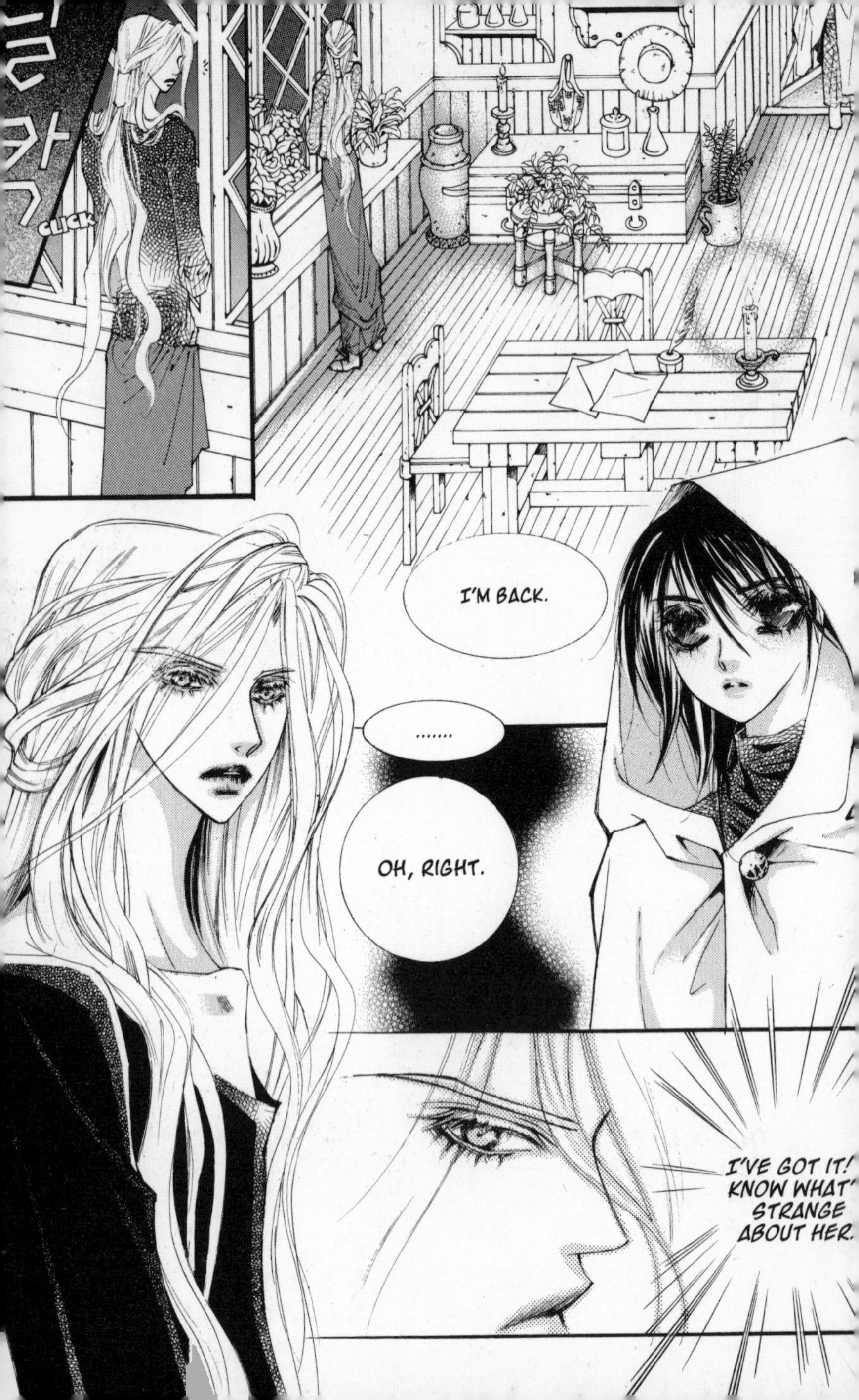
CLICK
I'M BACK.
....
OH, RIGHT.
I'VE GOT IT! KNOW WHAT' STRANGE ABOUT HER.

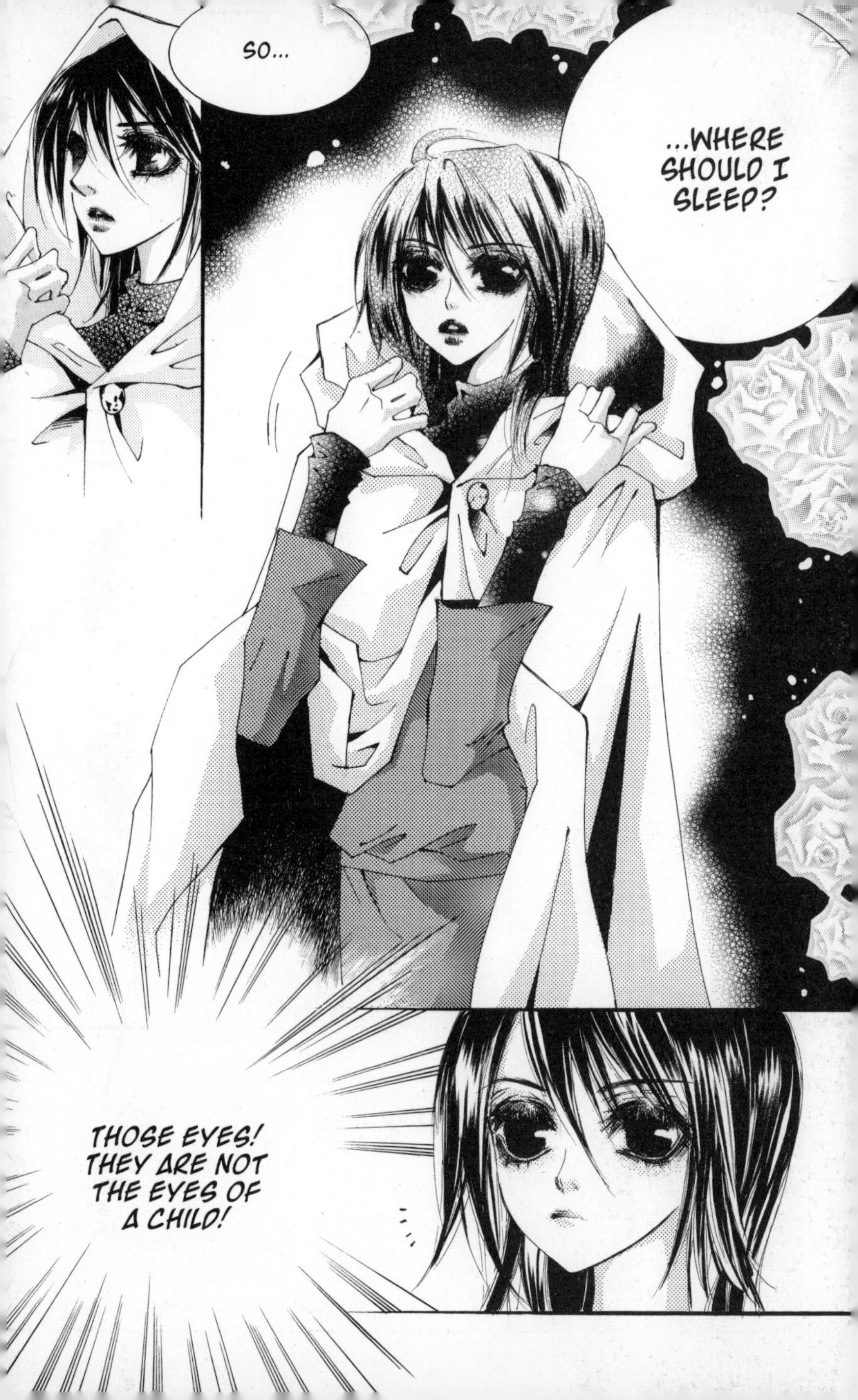
SO...
...WHERE SHOULD I SLEEP?
THOSE EYES! THEY ARE NOT THE EYES OF A CHILD!

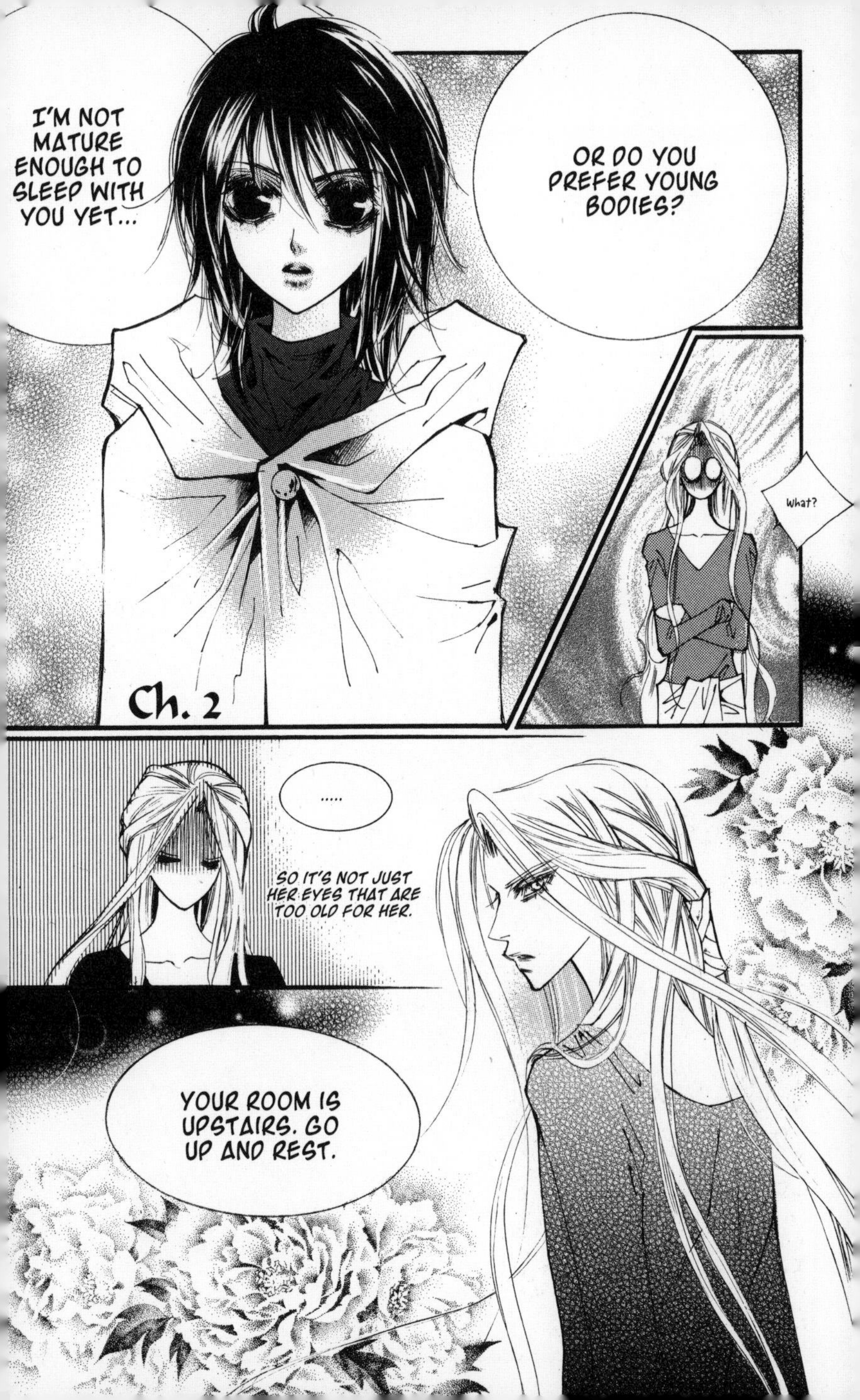
I'M NOT MATURE ENOUGH TO SLEEP WITH YOU YET...
OR DO YOU PREFER YOUNG BODIES?
Ch. 2
What?
.....
SO IT'S NOT JUST HER EYES THAT ARE TOO OLD FOR HER.
YOUR ROOM IS UPSTAIRS. GO UP AND REST.

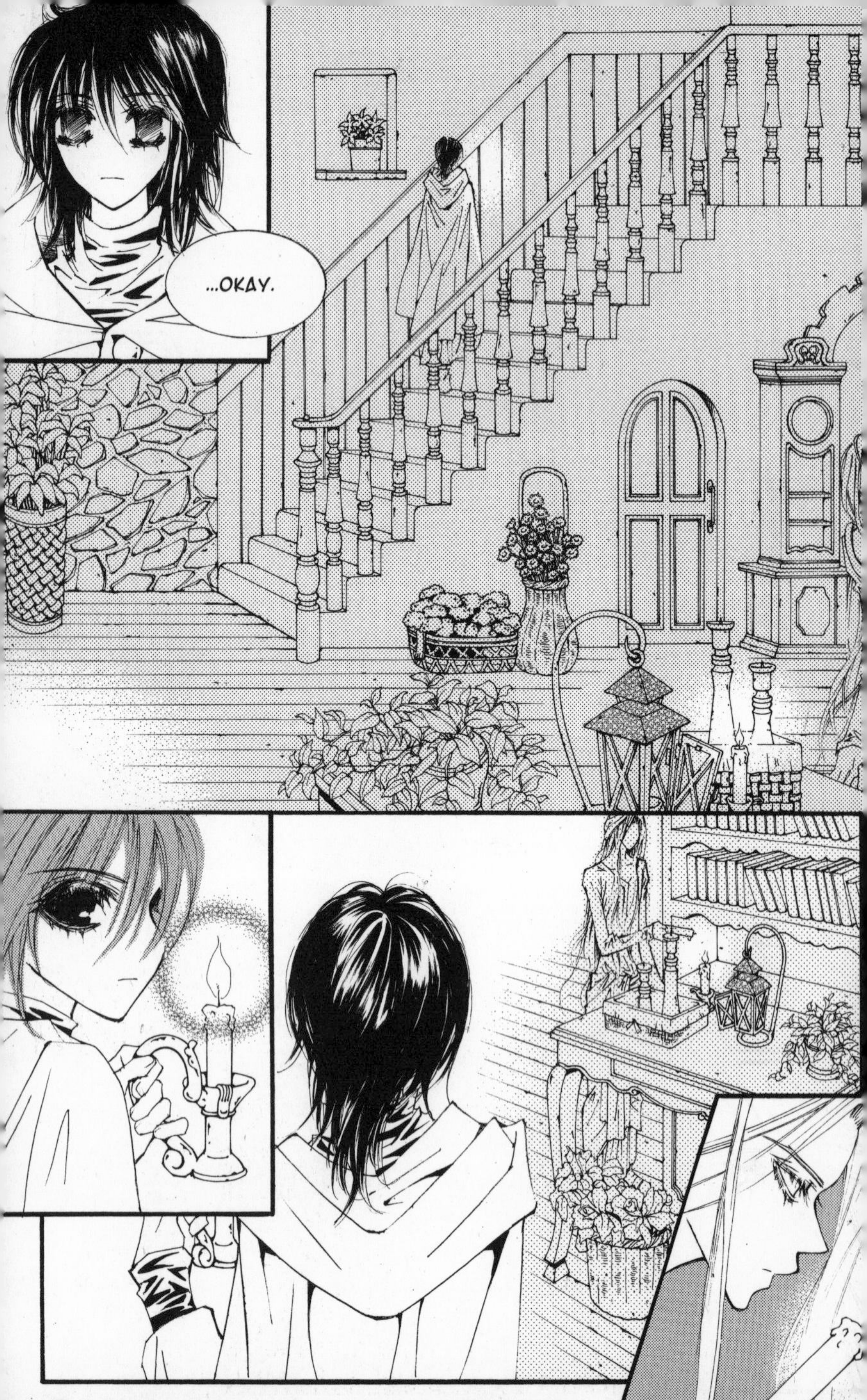
...OKAY.

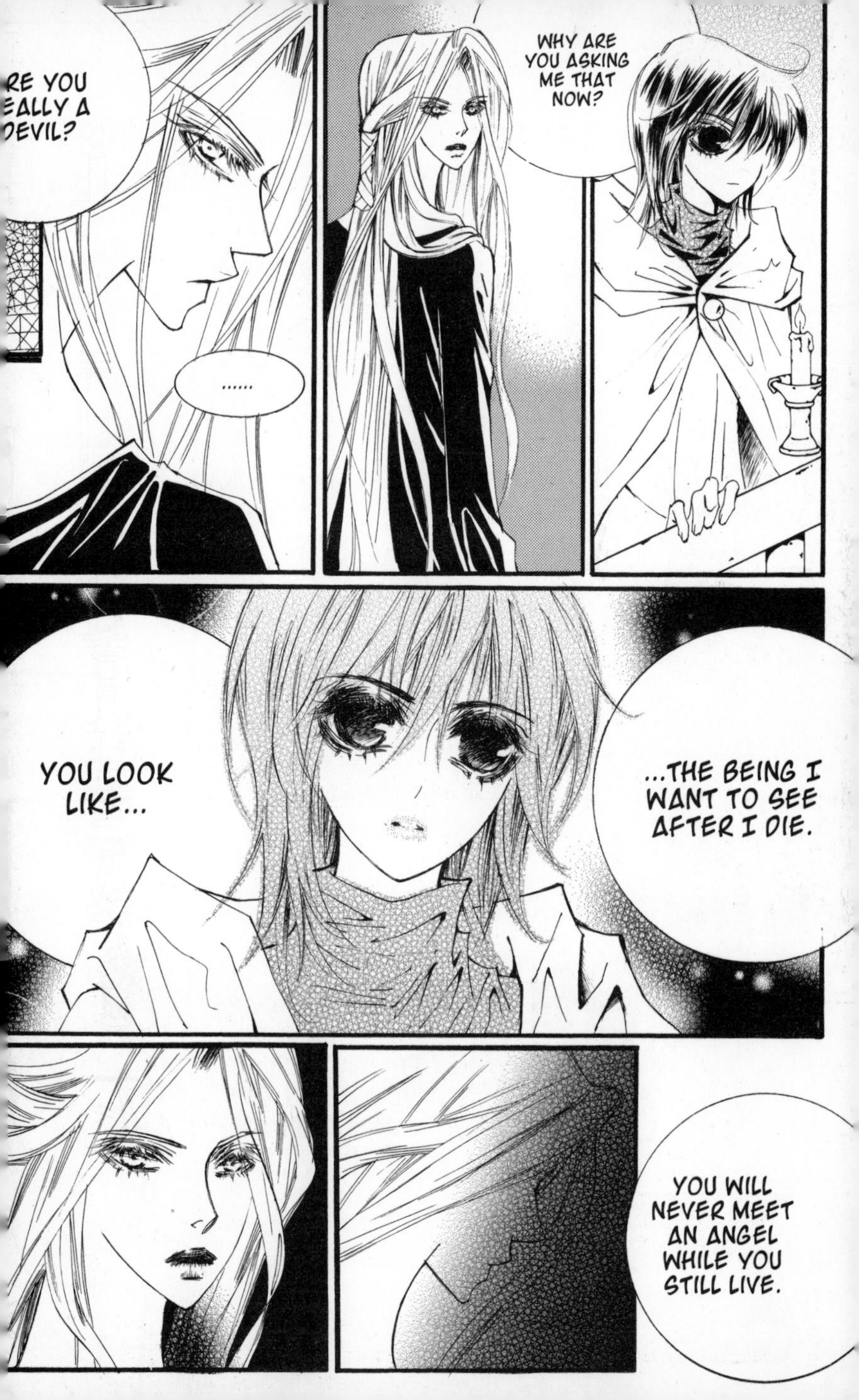
RE YOU EALLY A DEVIL?
......
WHY ARE YOU ASKING ME THAT NOW?
YOU LOOK LIKE...
...THE BEING I WANT TO SEE AFTER I DIE.
YOU WILL NEVER MEET AN ANGEL WHILE YOU STILL LIVE.

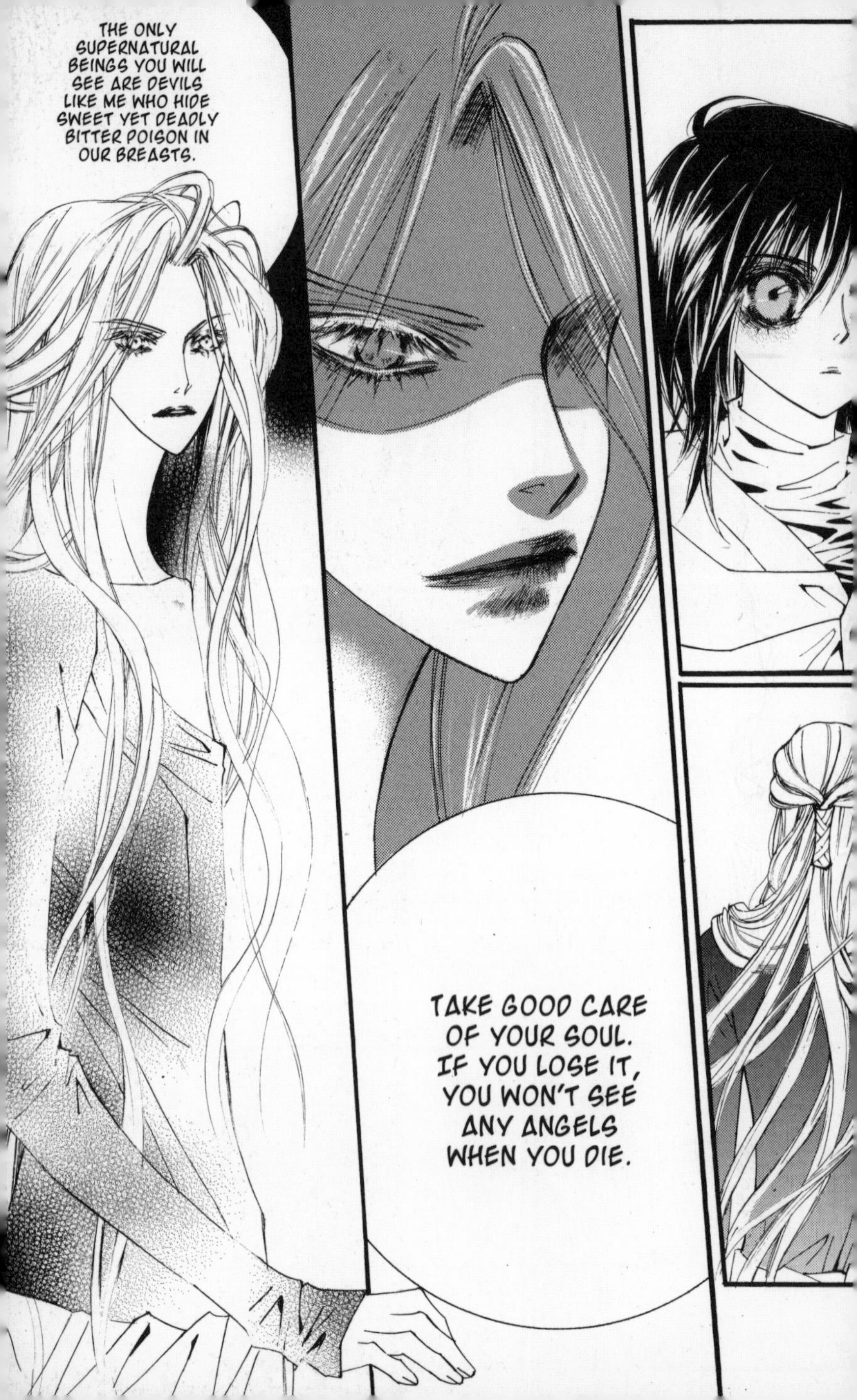
THE ONLY SUPERNATURAL BEINGS YOU WILL SEE ARE DEVILS LIKE ME WHO HIDE SWEET YET DEADLY BITTER POISON IN OUR BREASTS.
TAKE GOOD CARE OF YOUR SOUL. IF YOU LOSE IT, YOU WON'T SEE ANY ANGELS WHEN YOU DIE.

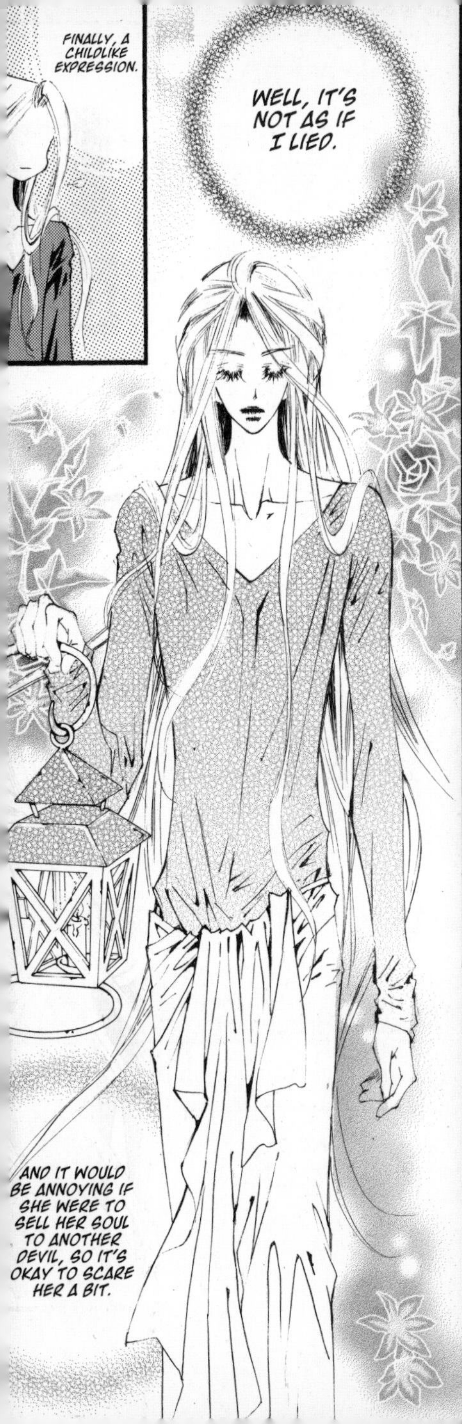
FINALLY, A CHILDLIKE EXPRESSION.
WELL, IT'S NOT AS IF I LIED.
AND IT WOULD BE ANNOYING IF SHE WERE TO SELL HER SOUL TO ANOTHER DEVIL, SO IT'S OKAY TO SCARE HER A BIT.
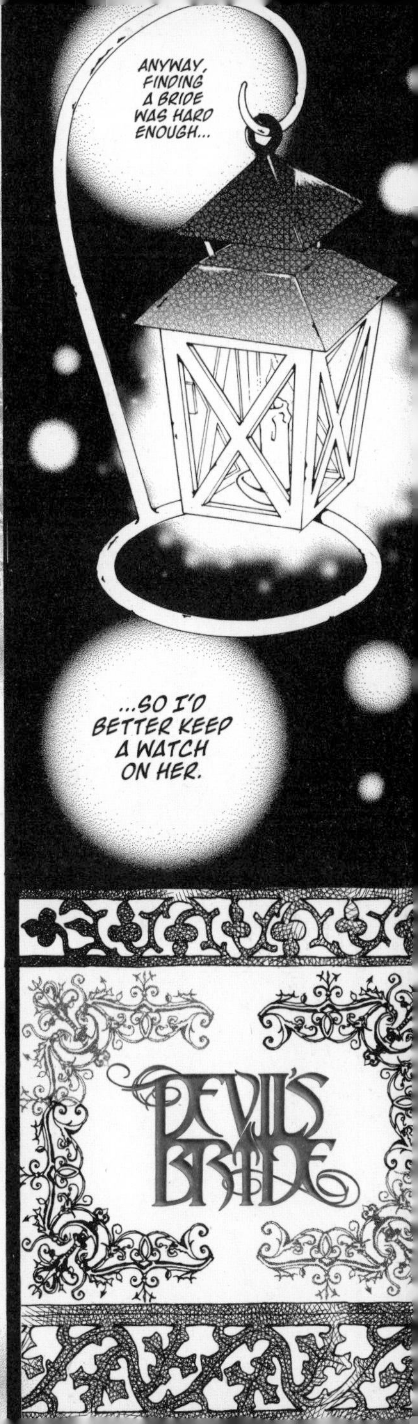
ANYWAY, FINDING A BRIDE WAS HARD ENOUGH...
...SO I'D BETTER KEEP A WATCH ON HER.
DEVIL'S BRIDE

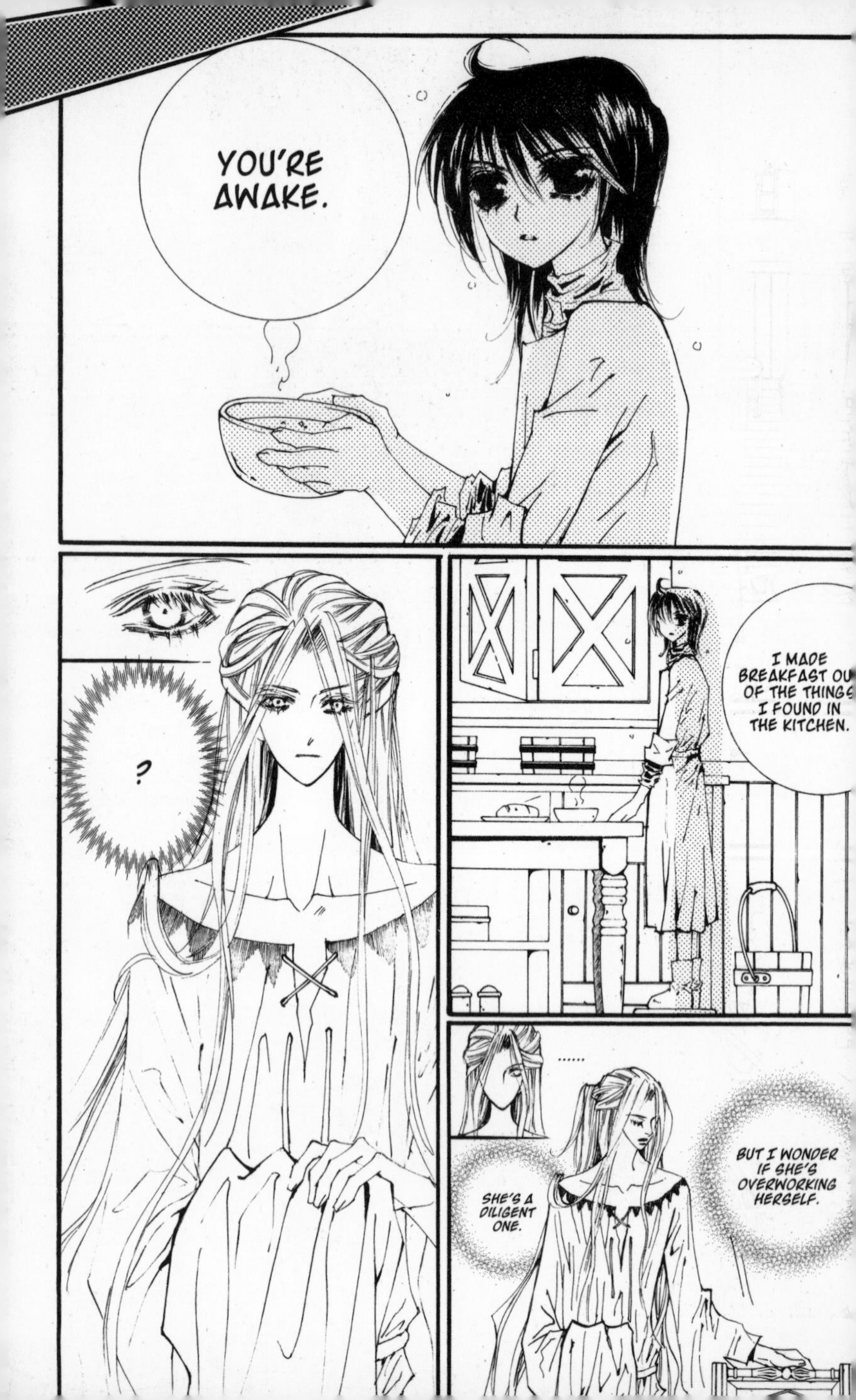
YOU'RE AWAKE.
?
I MADE BREAKFAST OU OF THE THINGS I FOUND IN THE KITCHEN.
......
SHE'S A DILIGENT ONE.
BUT I WONDER IF SHE'S OVERWORKING HERSELF.

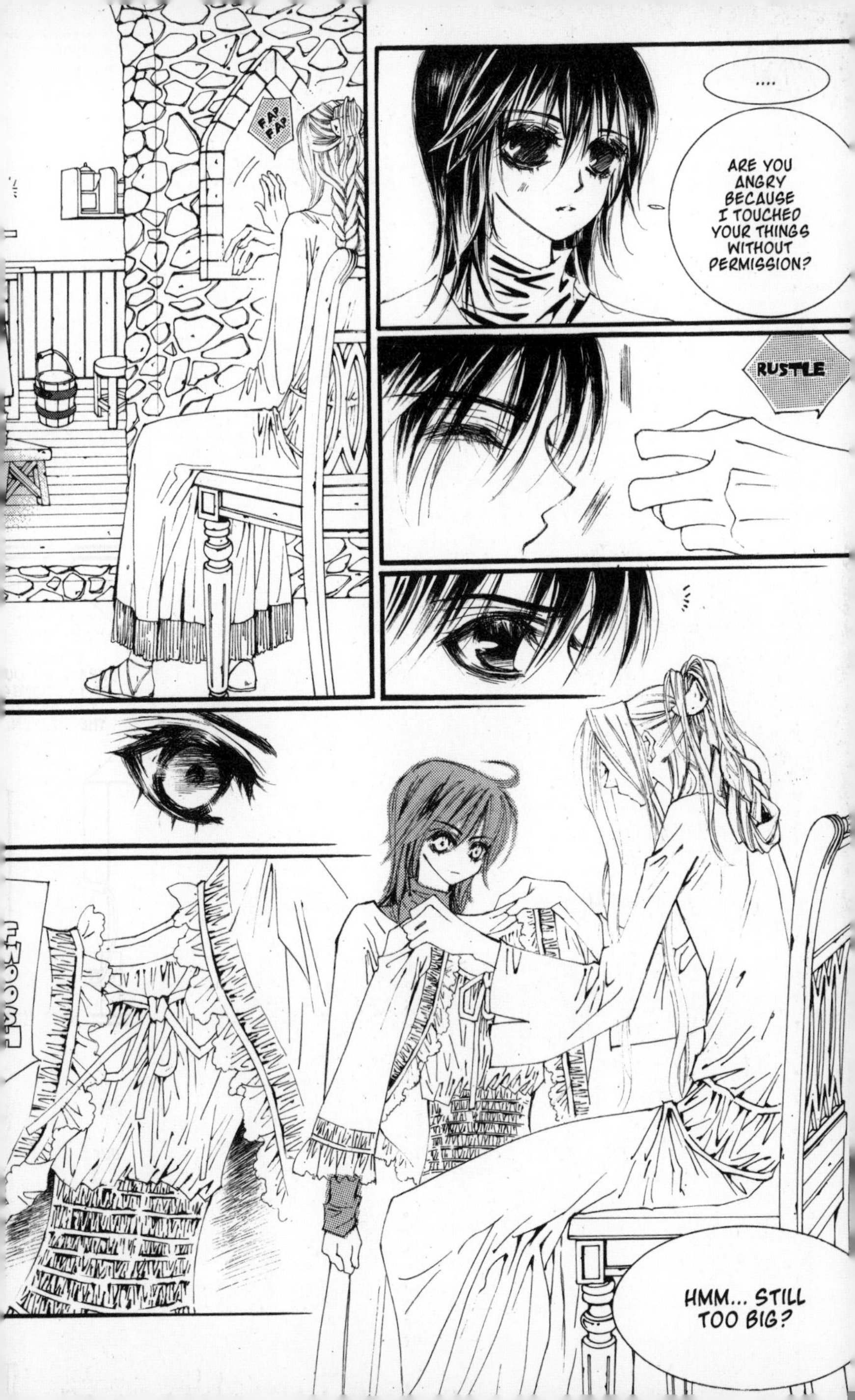
FAP FAP
....
ARE YOU ANGRY BECAUSE I TOUCHED YOUR THINGS WITHOUT PERMISSION?
RUSTLE
HMM... STILL TOO BIG?

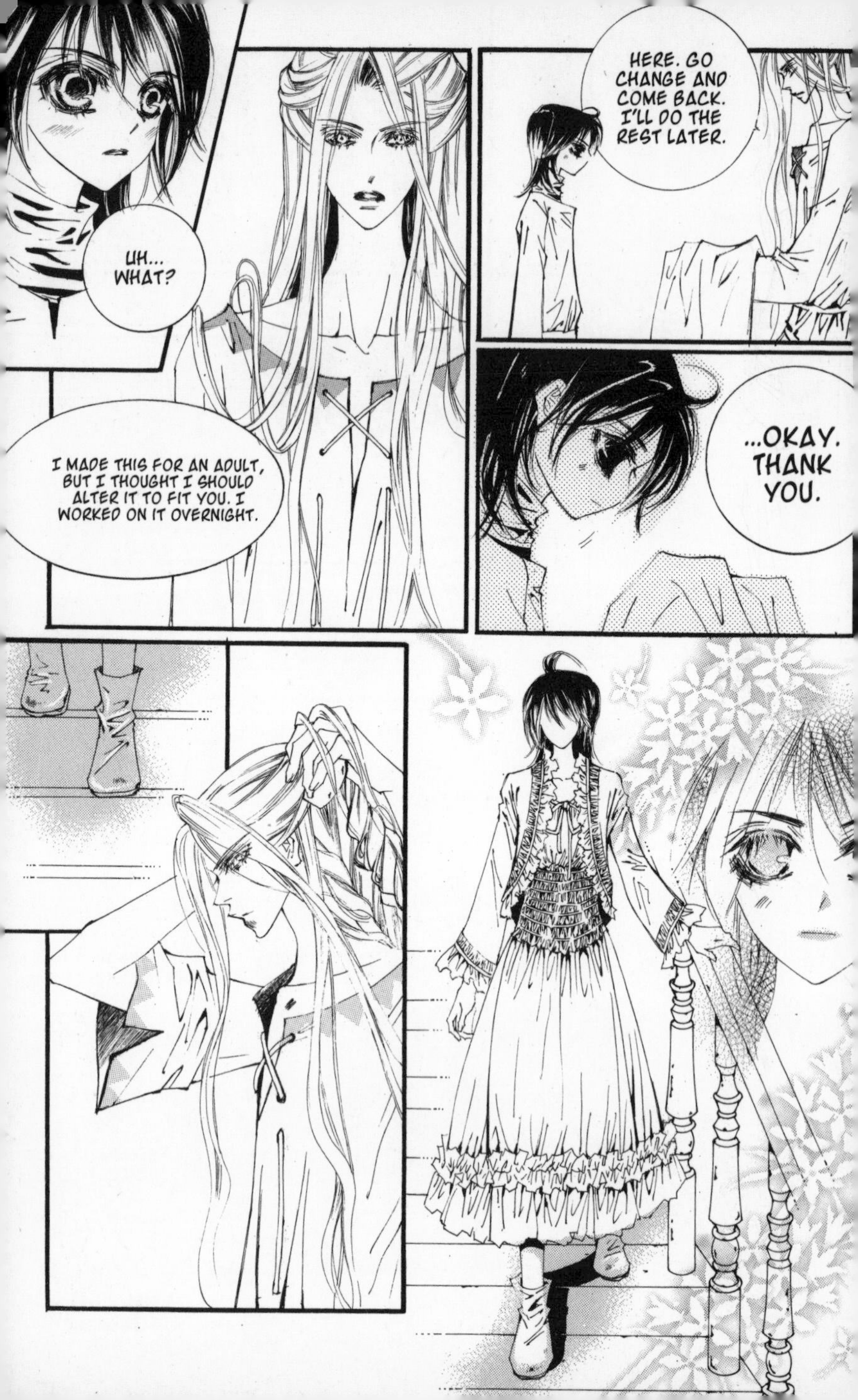
UH... WHAT?
I MADE THIS FOR AN ADULT, BUT I THOUGHT I SHOULD ALTER IT TO FIT YOU. I WORKED ON IT OVERNIGHT.
HERE. GO CHANGE AND COME BACK. I'LL DO THE REST LATER.
...OKAY. THANK YOU.

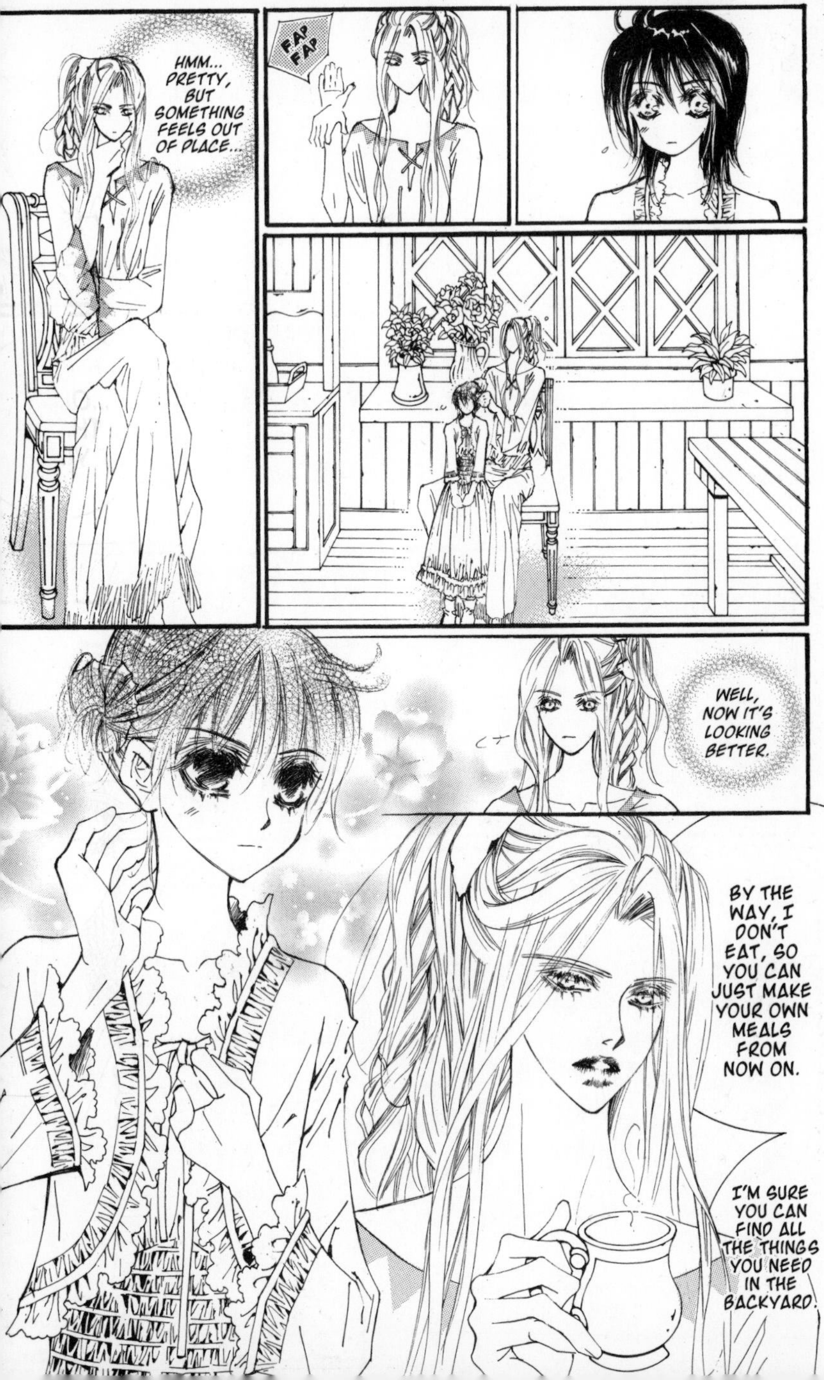
HMM... PRETTY, BUT SOMETHING FEELS OUT OF PLACE...
FAP FAP
WELL, NOW IT'S LOOKING BETTER.
BY THE WAY, I DON'T EAT, SO YOU CAN JUST MAKE YOUR OWN MEALS FROM NOW ON.
I'M SURE YOU CAN FIND ALL THE THINGS YOU NEED IN THE BACKYARD.

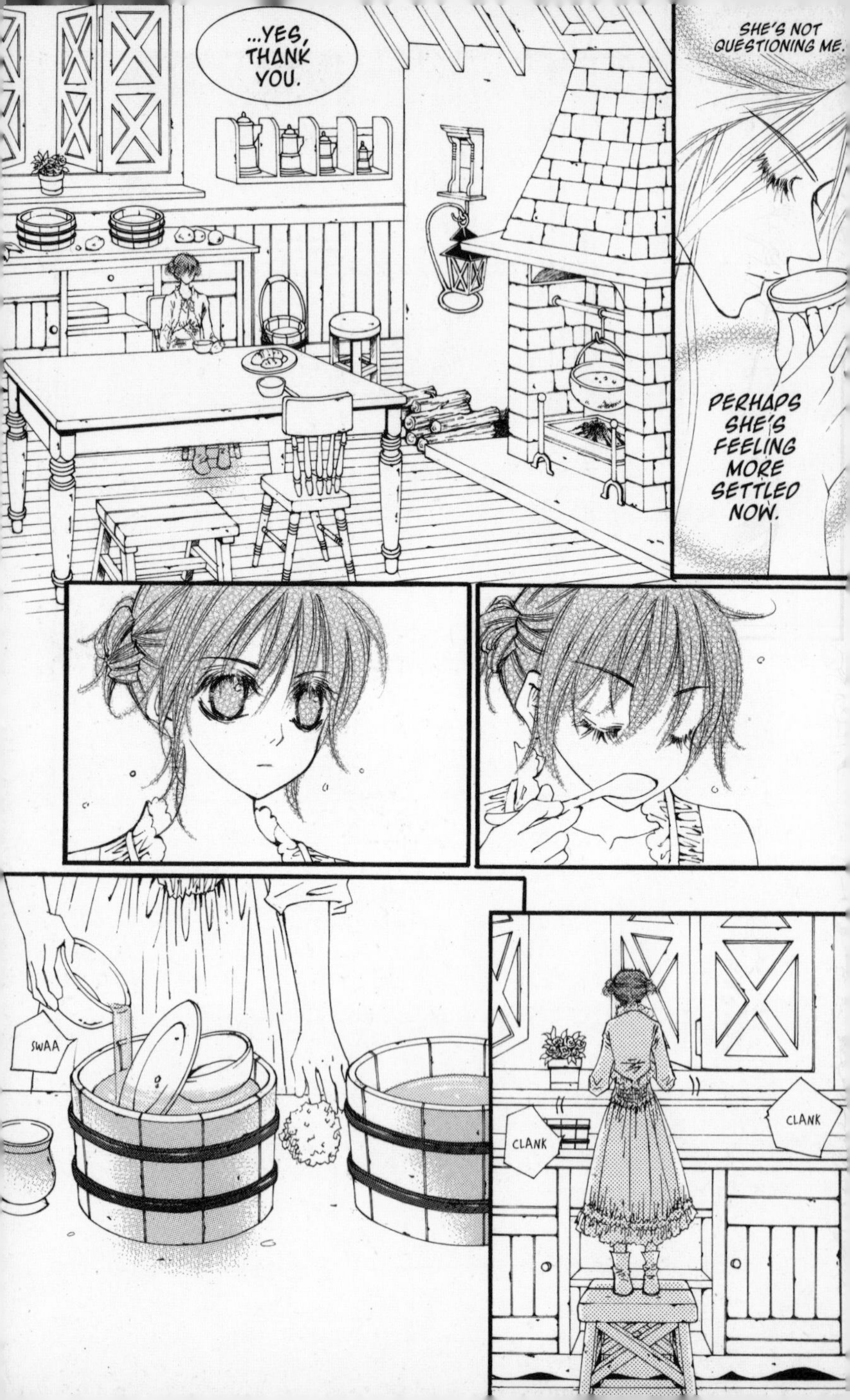
...YES, THANK YOU.
SHE'S NOT QUESTIONING ME.
PERHAPS SHE'S FEELING MORE SETTLED NOW.
SWAA
CLANK
CLANK

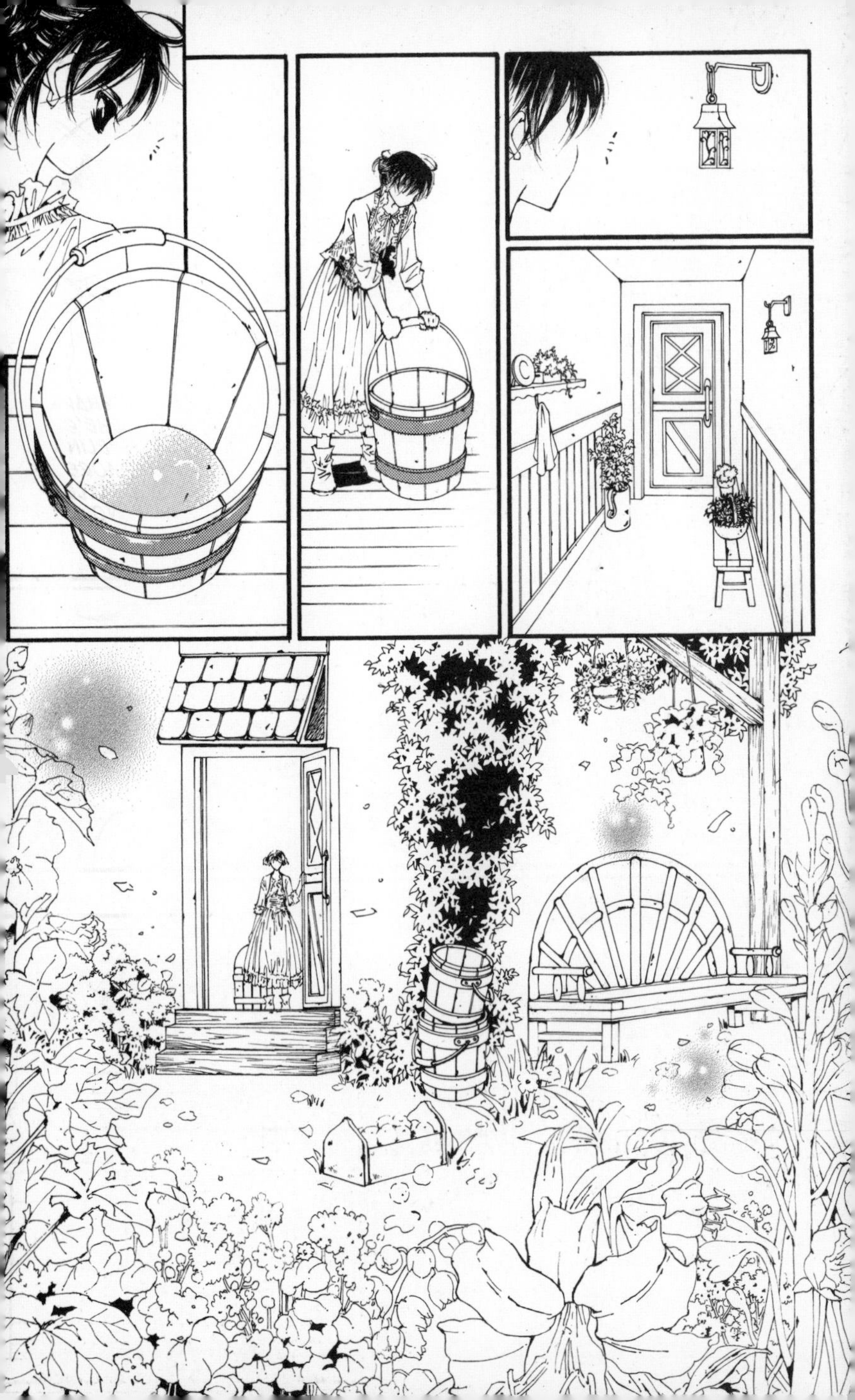

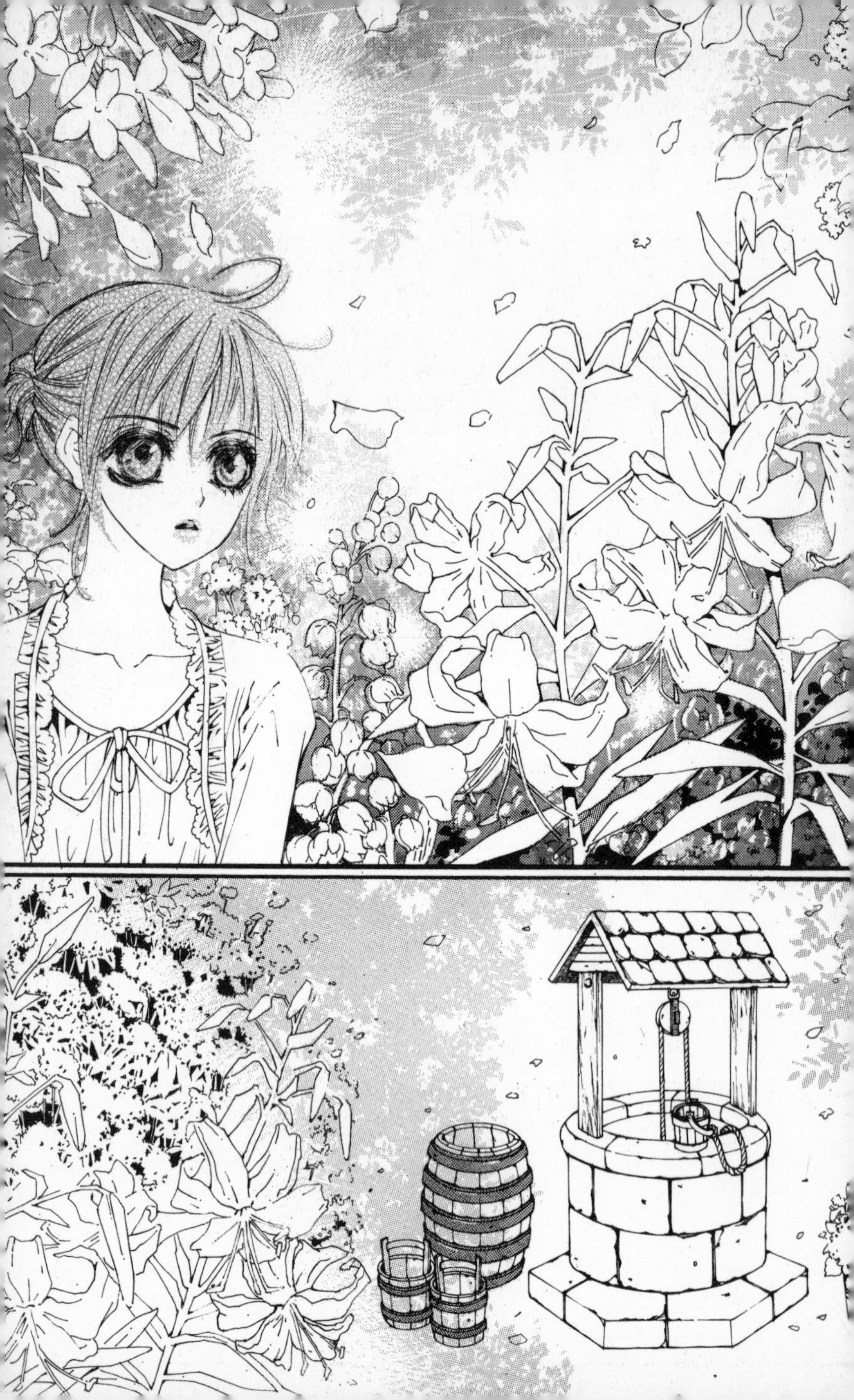

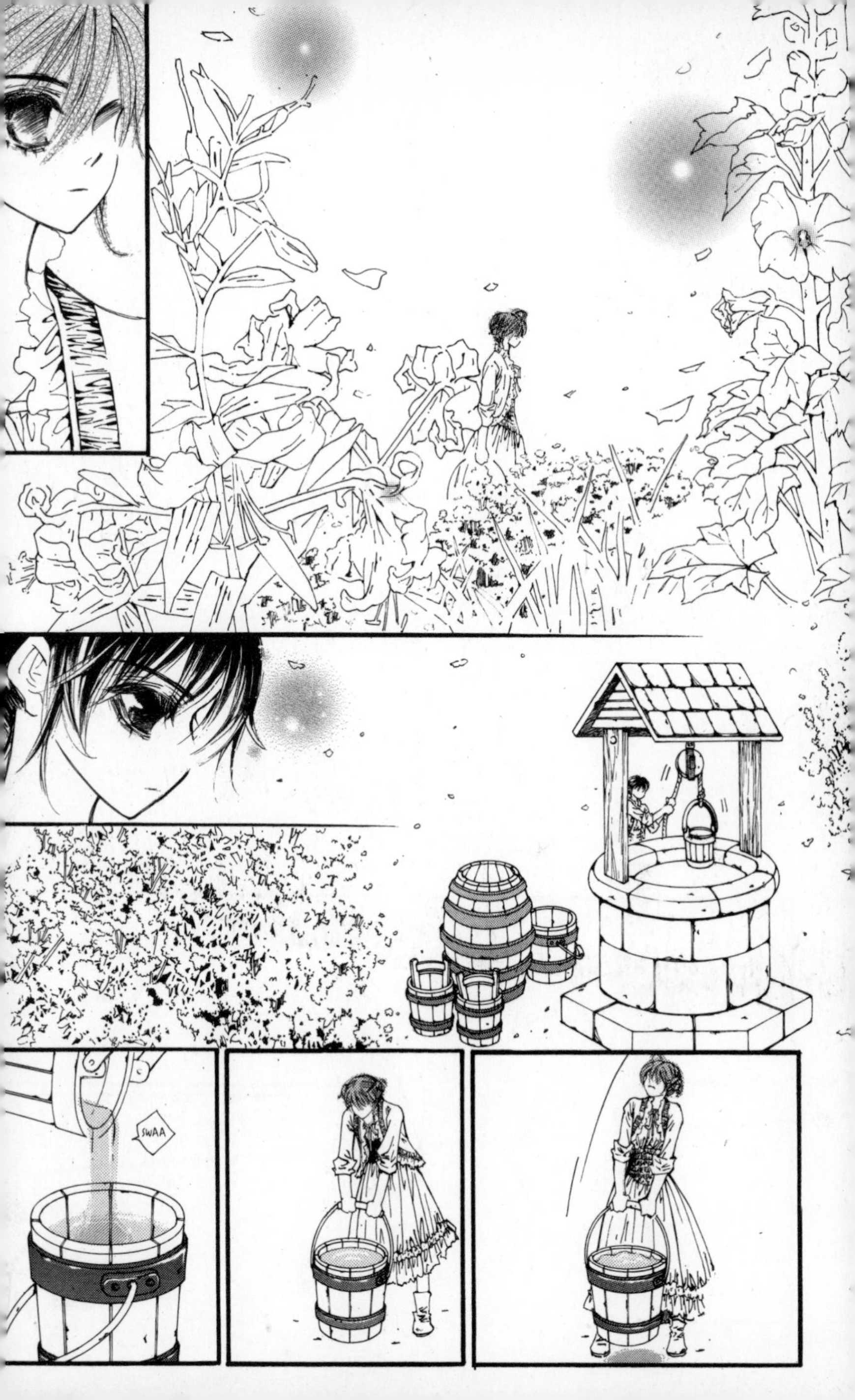
SWAA

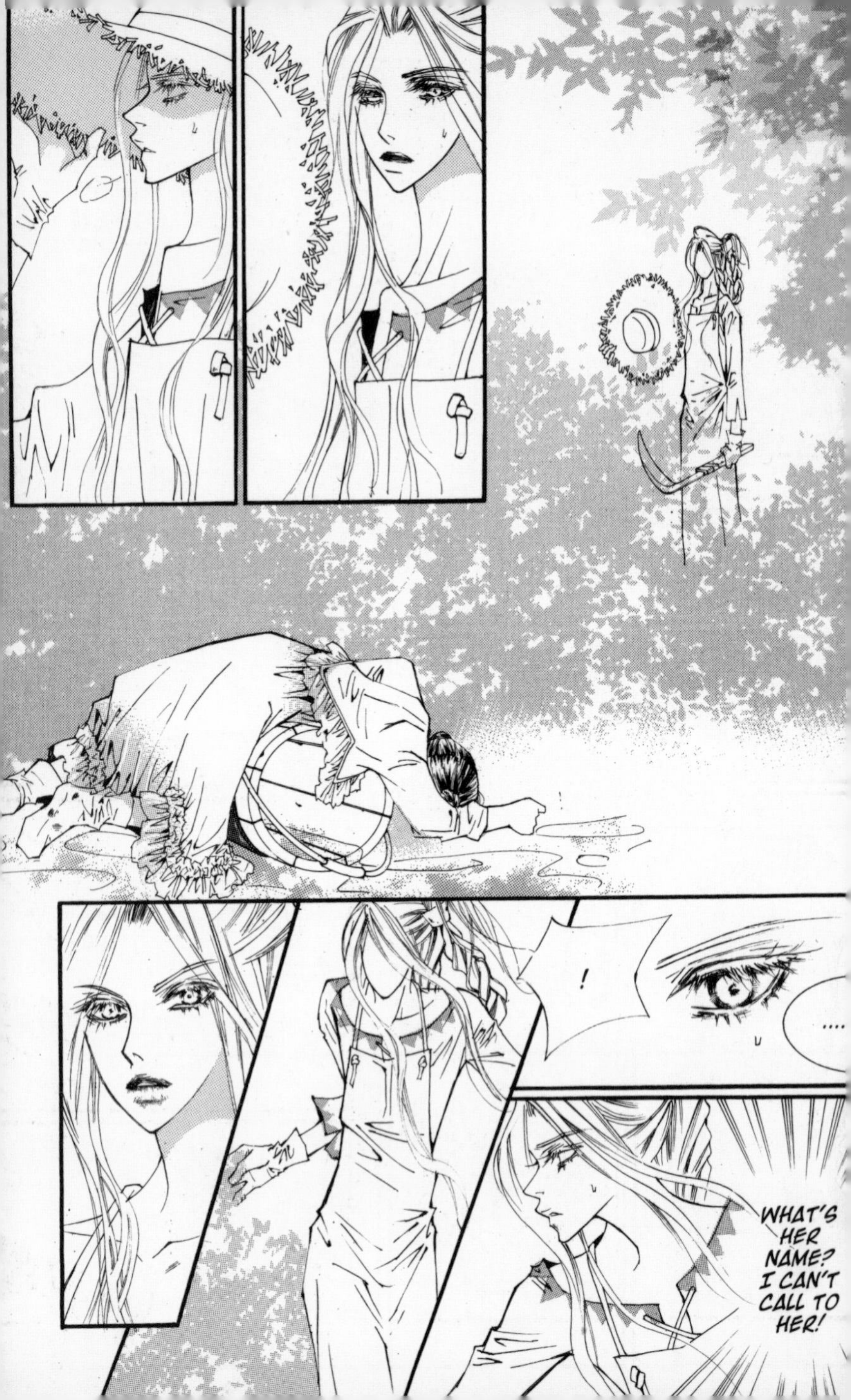
!
!
....
WHAT'S HER NAME? I CAN'T CALL TO HER!

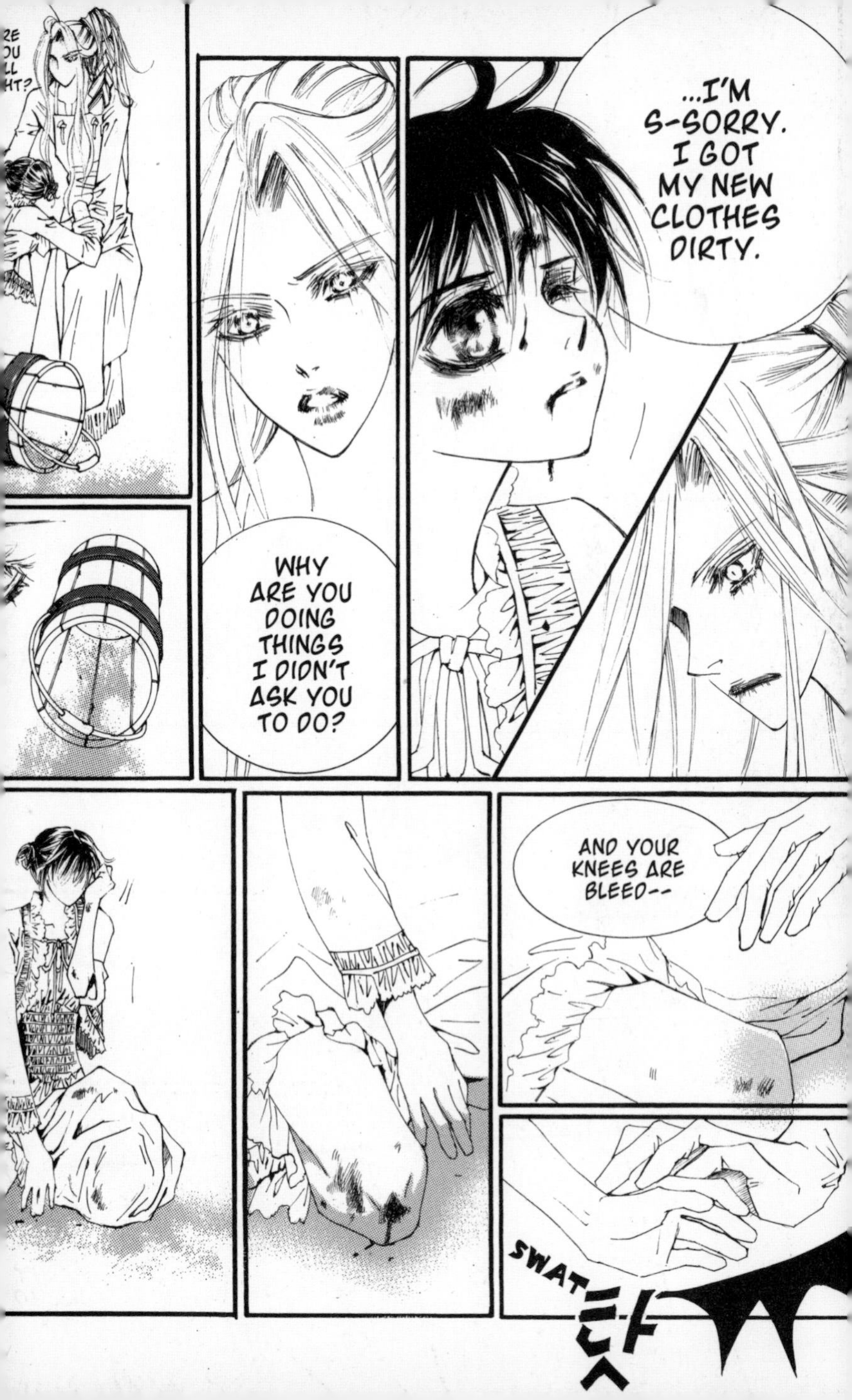

RE OU LL HT?
WHY ARE YOU DOING THINGS I DIDN'T ASK YOU TO DO?
...I'M S-SORRY. I GOT MY NEW CLOTHES DIRTY.
AND YOUR KNEES ARE BLEED--
SWAT

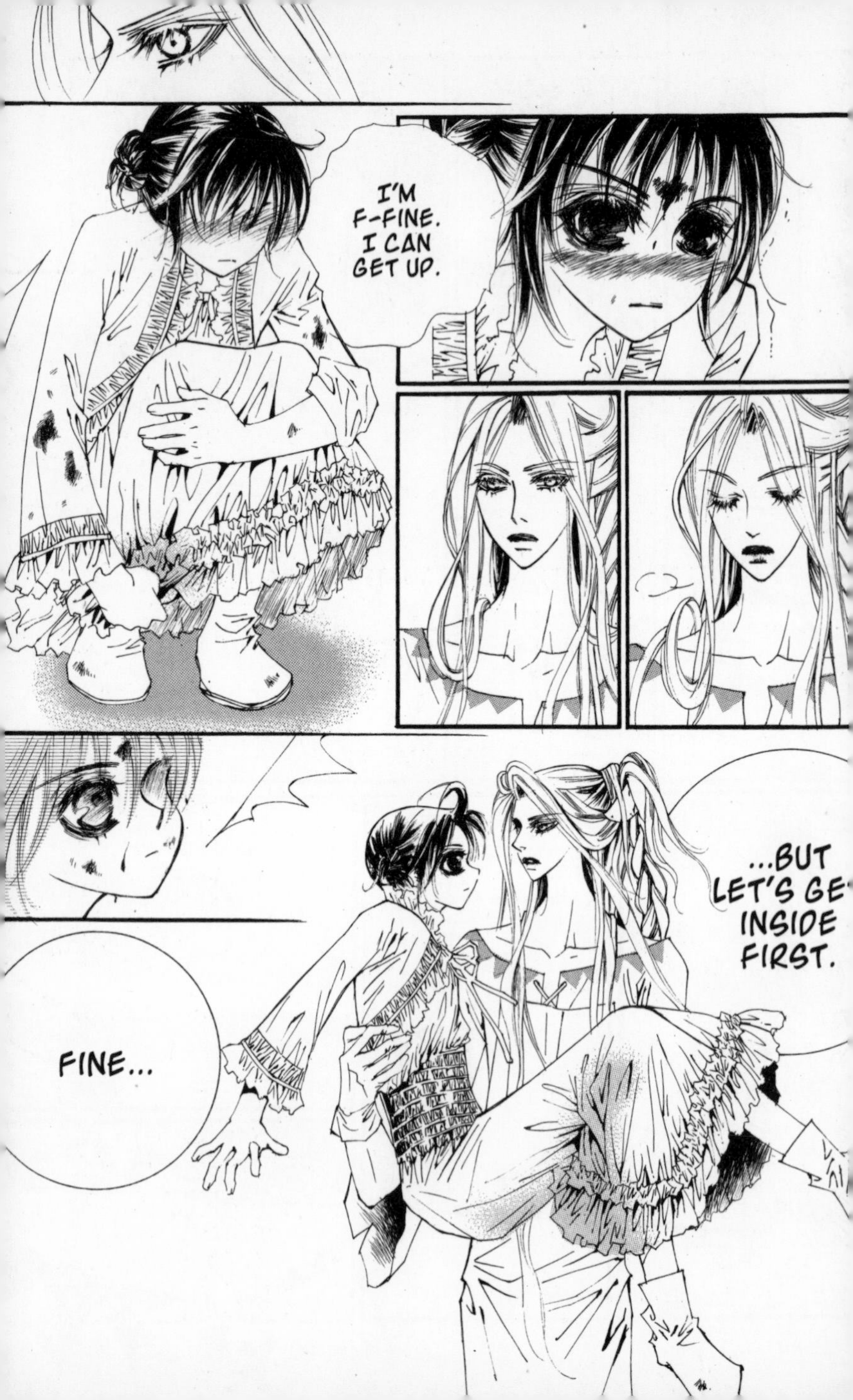
I'M F-FINE. I CAN GET UP.
...BUT LET'S GE- INSIDE FIRST.
FINE...

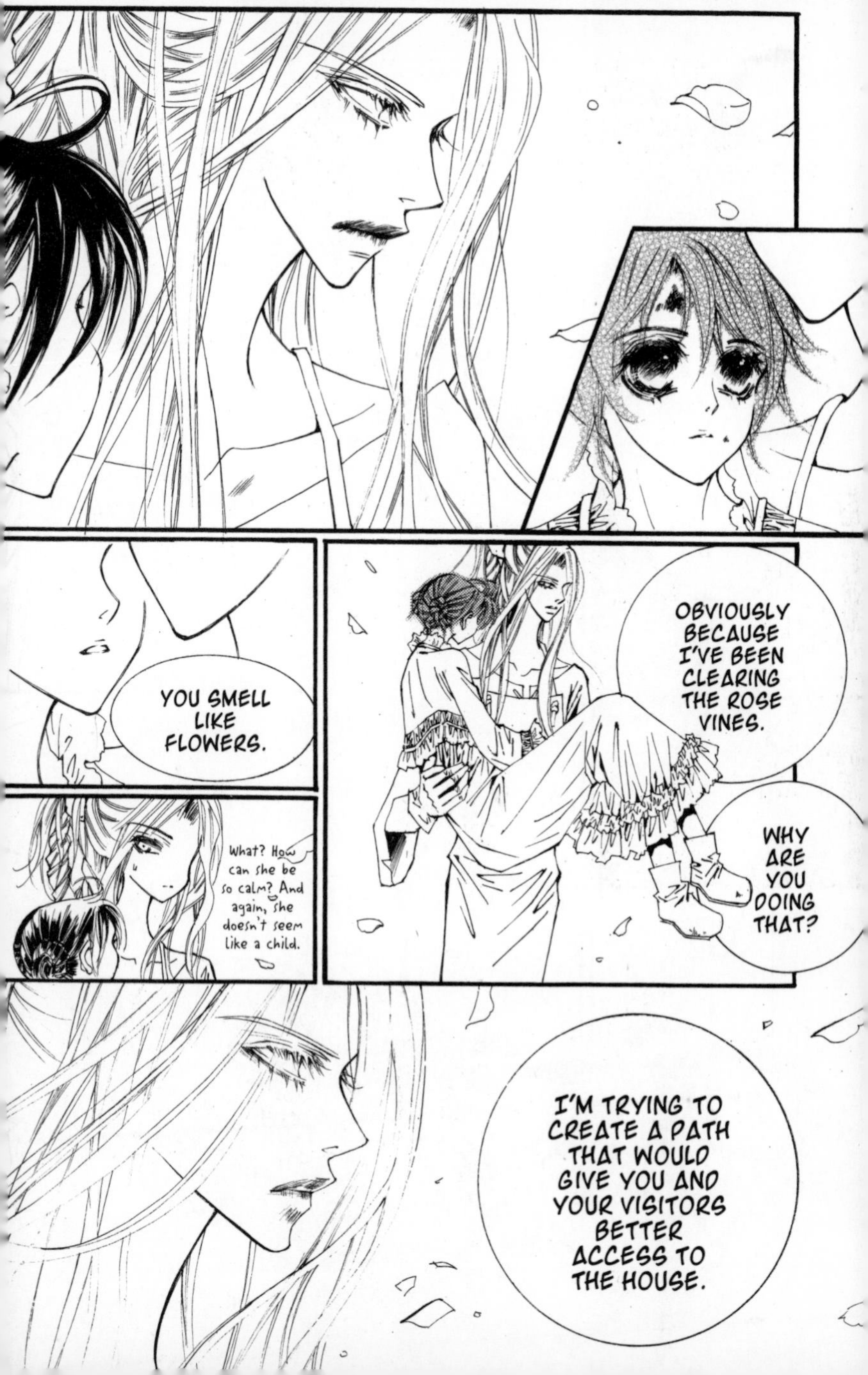
YOU SMELL LIKE FLOWERS.
What? How can she be so calm? And again, she doesn't seem like a child.
OBVIOUSLY BECAUSE I'VE BEEN CLEARING THE ROSE VINES.
WHY ARE YOU DOING THAT?
I'M TRYING TO CREATE A PATH THAT WOULD GIVE YOU AND YOUR VISITORS BETTER ACCESS TO THE HOUSE.

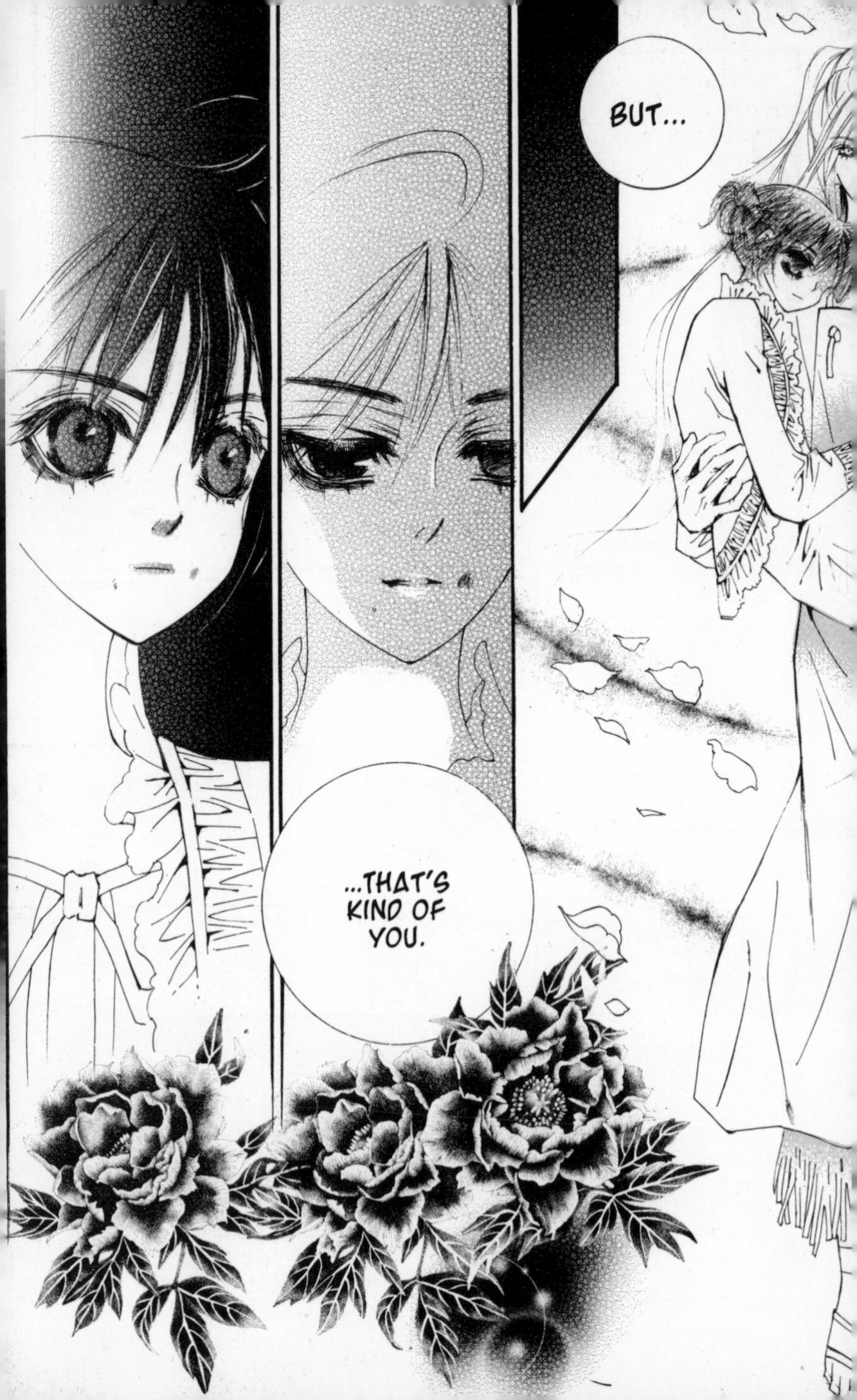

...THAT'S KIND OF YOU.
BUT...

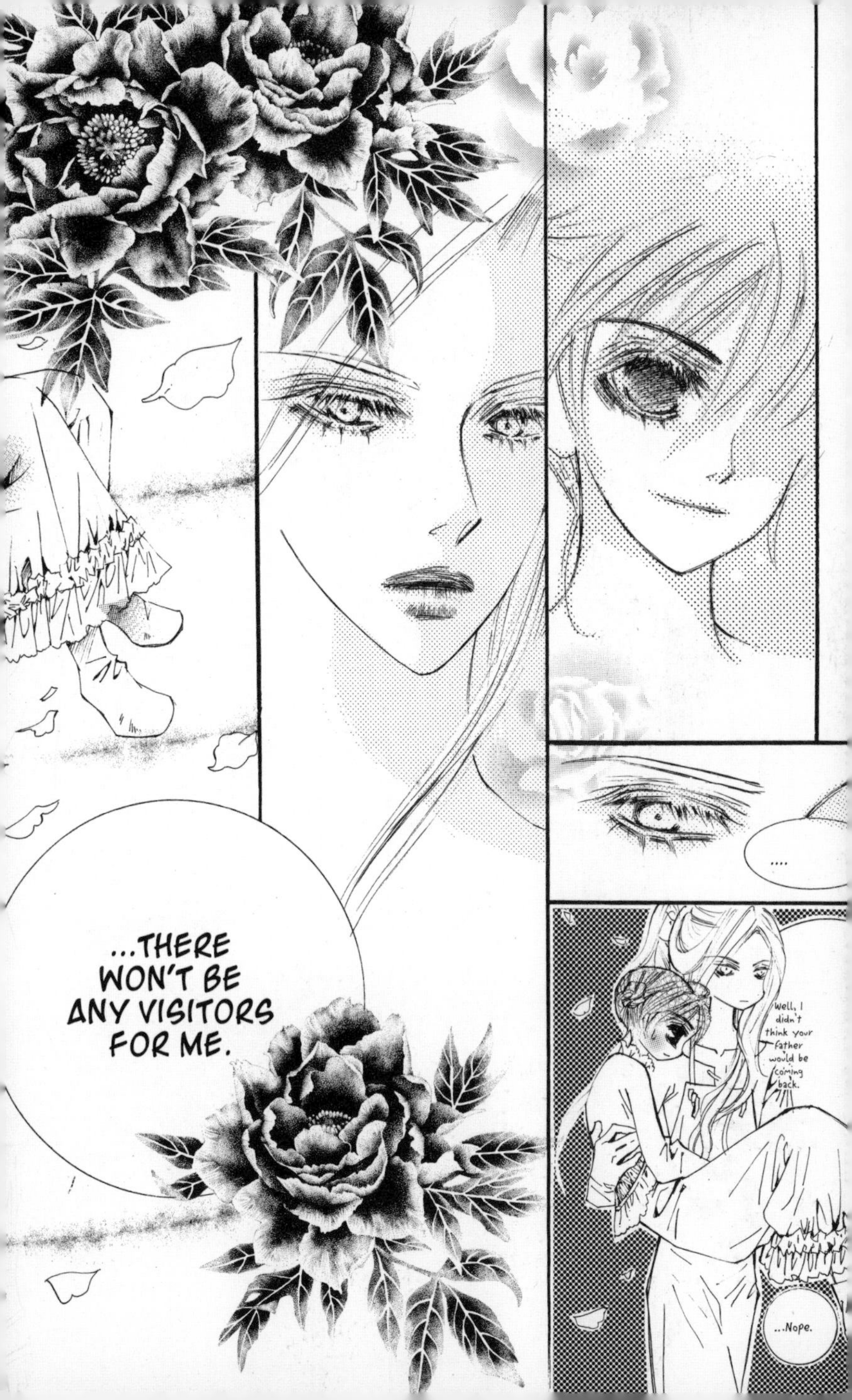
...THERE WON'T BE ANY VISITORS FOR ME.
...
Well, I didn't think your father would be coming back.
...Nope.

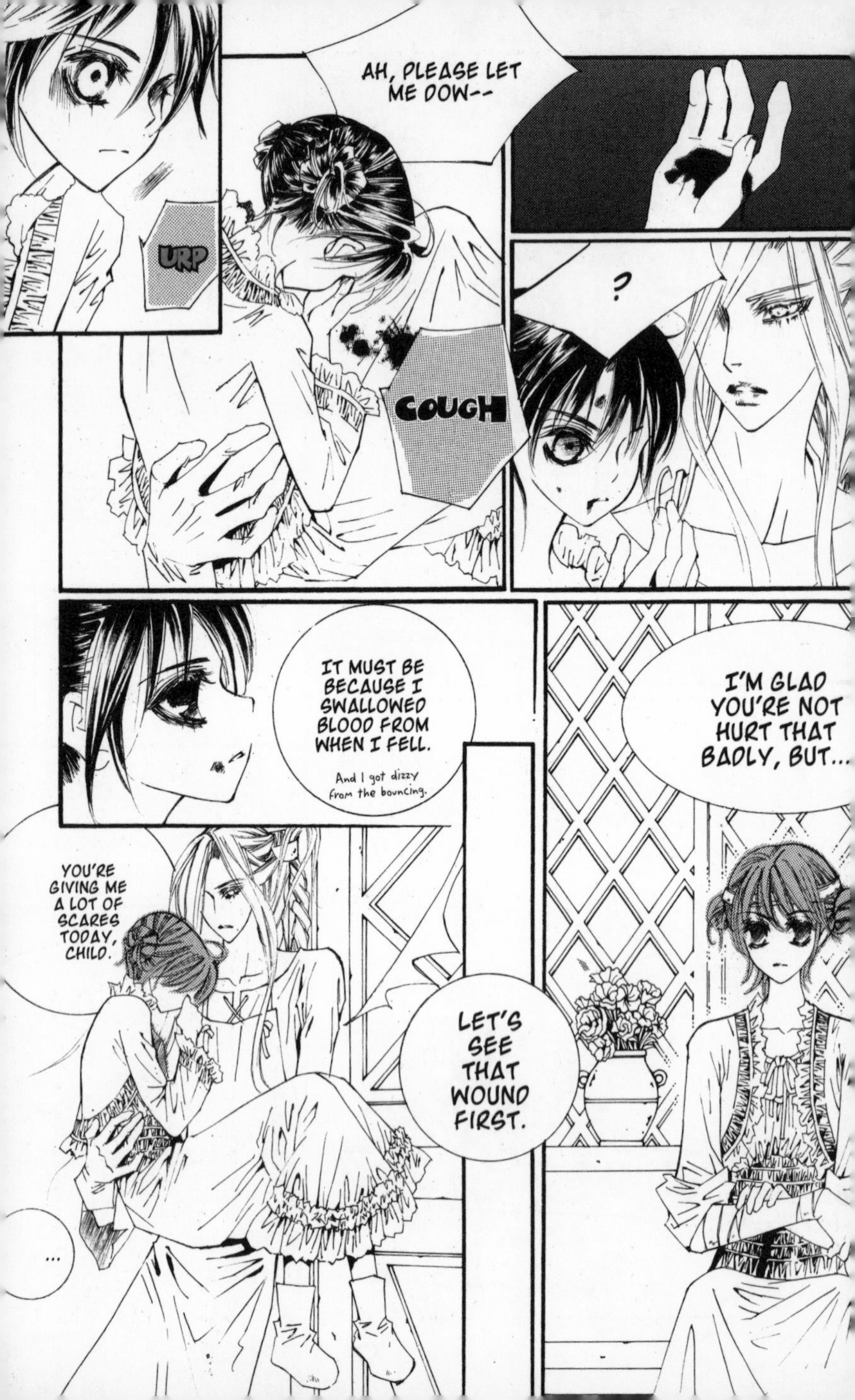
URP
AH, PLEASE LET ME DOW--
COUGH
?
IT MUST BE BECAUSE I SWALLOWED BLOOD FROM WHEN I FELL.
And I got dizzy from the bouncing.
YOU'RE GIVING ME A LOT OF SCARES TODAY, CHILD.
LET'S SEE THAT WOUND FIRST.
...
I'M GLAD YOU'RE NOT HURT THAT BADLY, BUT...

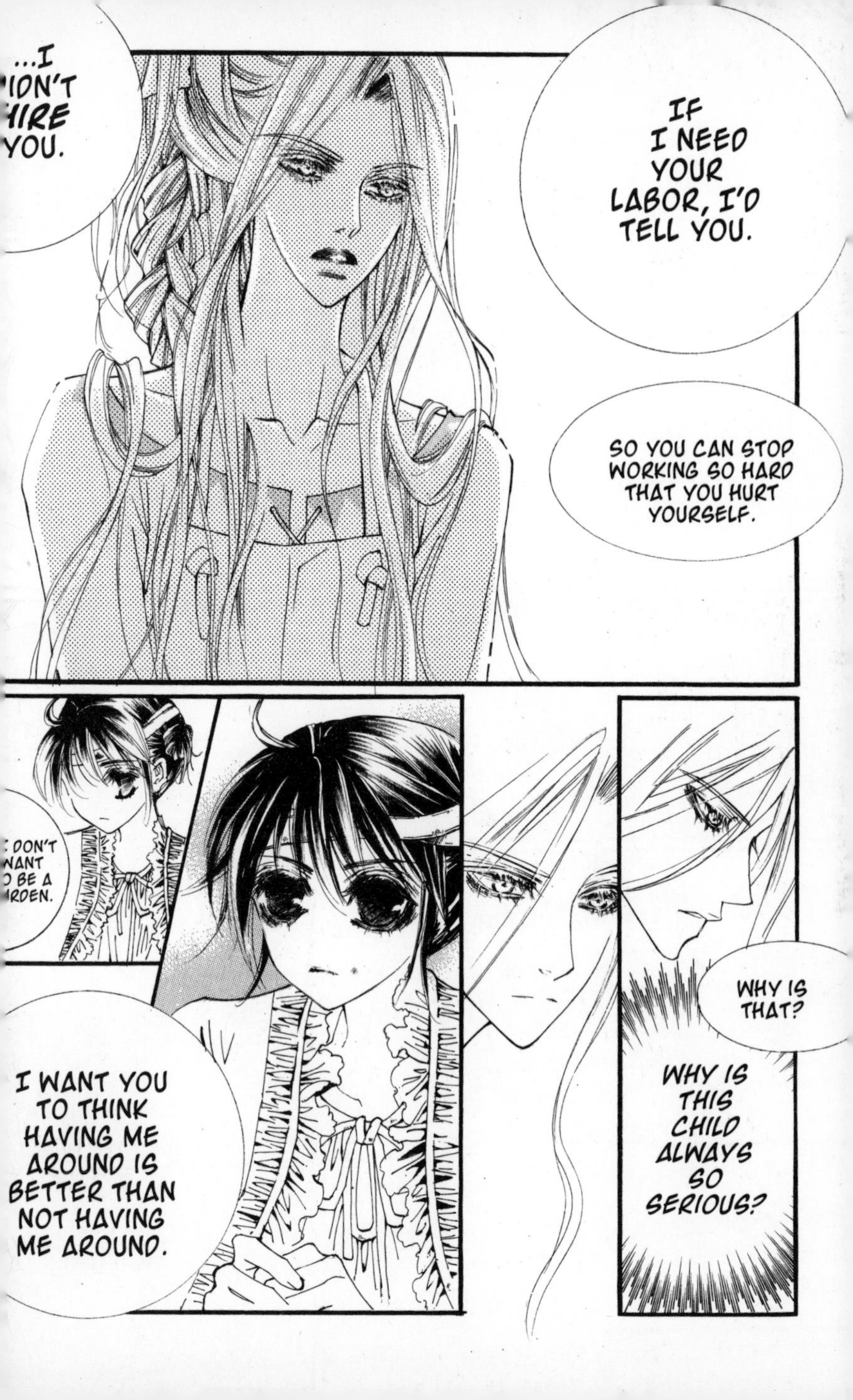
...I IDN'T HIRE YOU.
IF I NEED YOUR LABOR, I'D TELL YOU.
SO YOU CAN STOP WORKING SO HARD THAT YOU HURT YOURSELF.
DON'T WANT BE A RDEN.
I WANT YOU TO THINK HAVING ME AROUND IS BETTER THAN NOT HAVING ME AROUND.
WHY IS THAT?
WHY IS THIS CHILD ALWAYS SO SERIOUS?

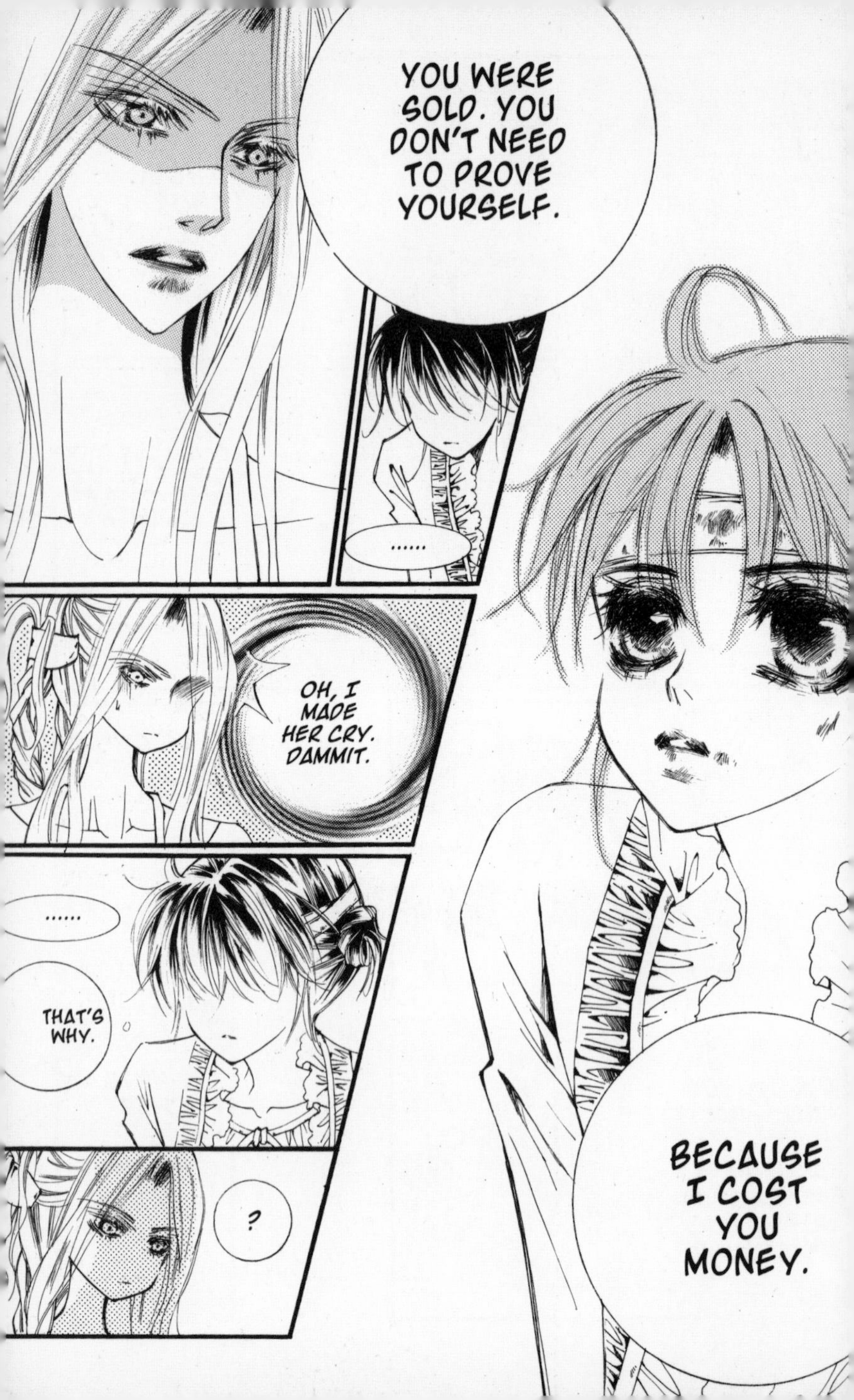
YOU WERE SOLD. YOU DON'T NEED TO PROVE YOURSELF.
......
OH, I MADE HER CRY. DAMMIT.
......
THAT'S WHY.
?
BECAUSE I COST YOU MONEY.

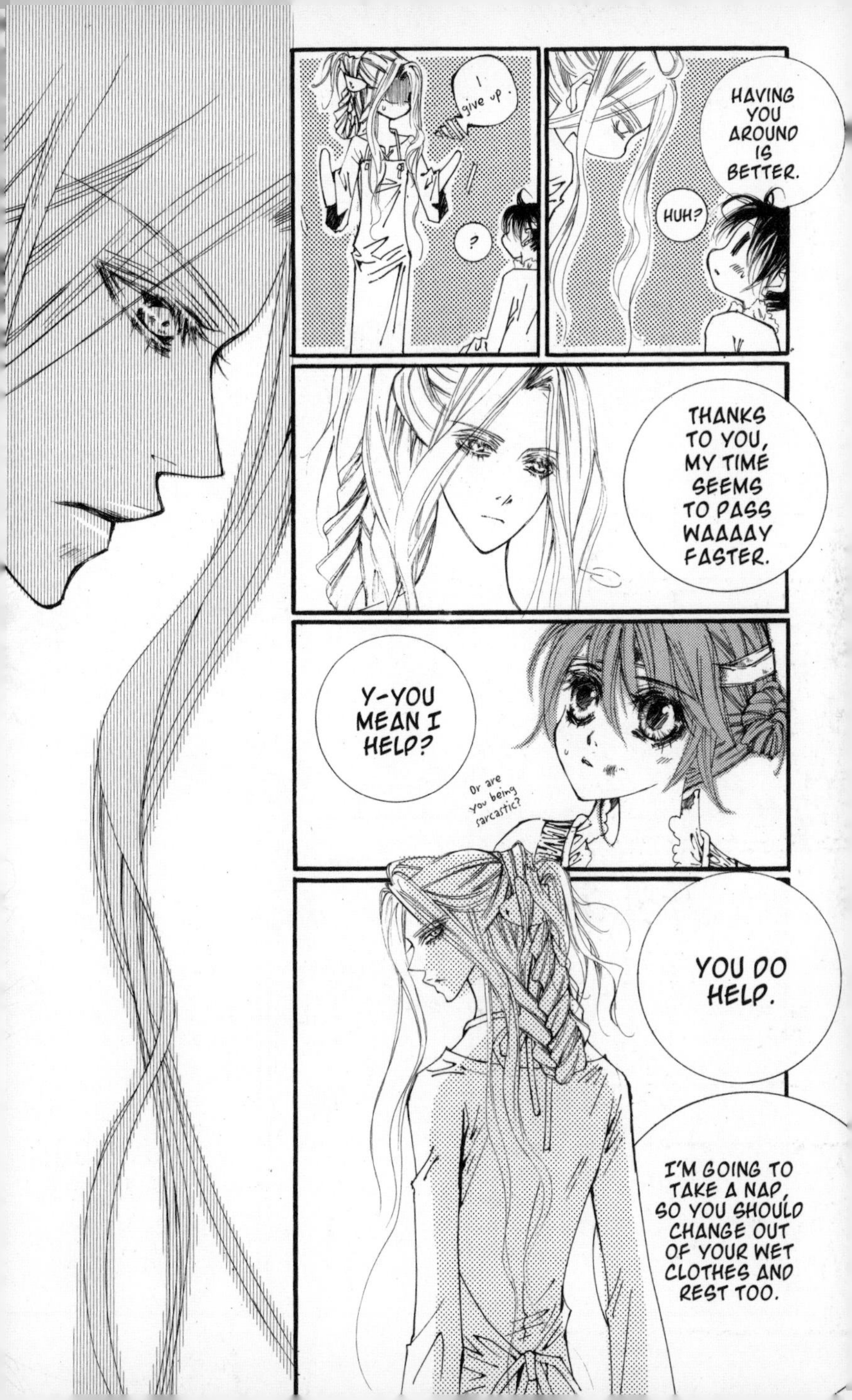
I give up.
?
HAVING YOU AROUND IS BETTER.
HUH?
THANKS TO YOU, MY TIME SEEMS TO PASS WAAAAY FASTER.
Y-YOU MEAN I HELP?
Or are you being sarcastic?
YOU DO HELP.
I'M GOING TO TAKE A NAP, SO YOU SHOULD CHANGE OUT OF YOUR WET CLOTHES AND REST TOO.

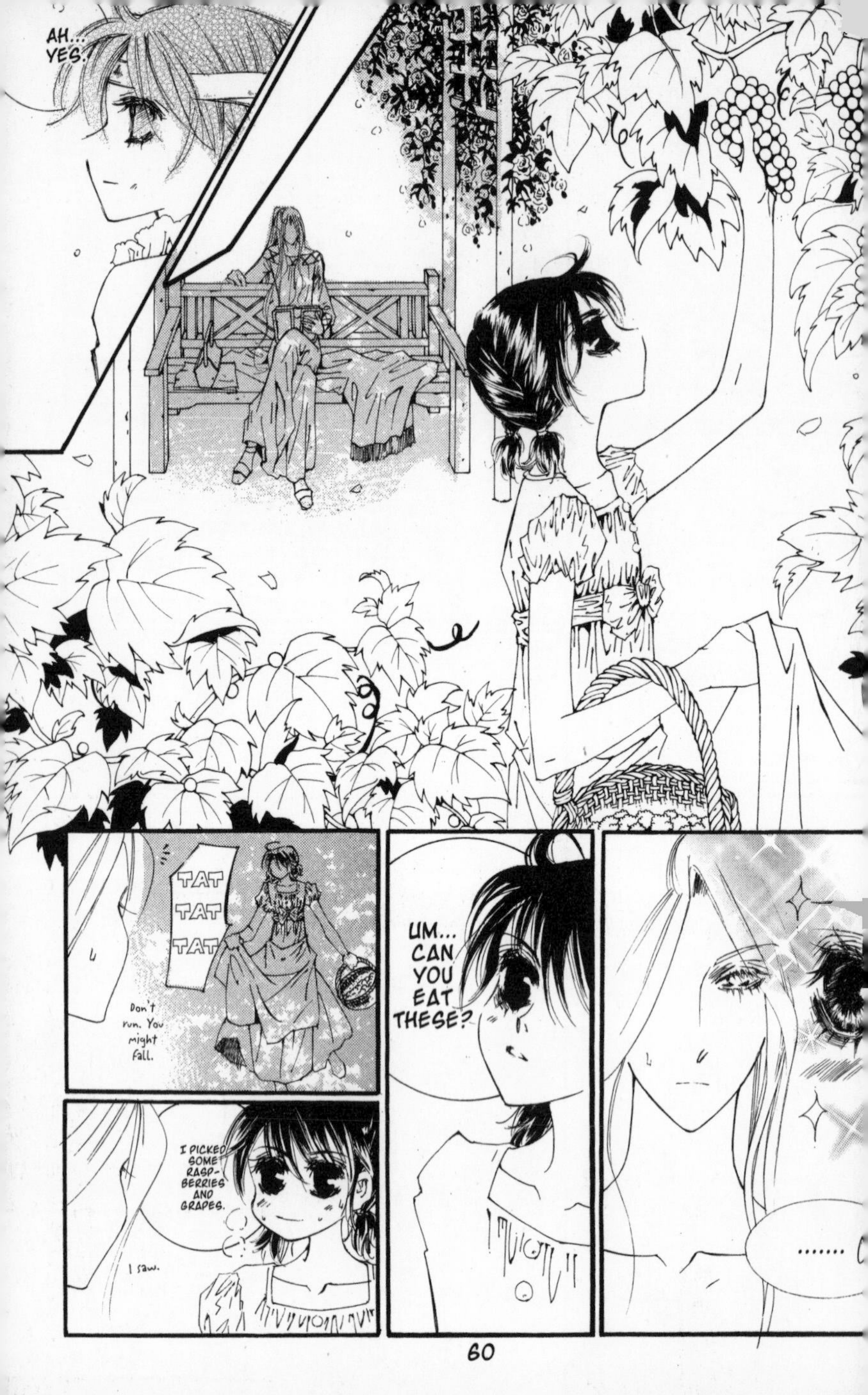
AH... YES.
TAT TAT TAT
Don't run. You might fall.
UM... CAN YOU EAT THESE?
....
I PICKED SOME RASP-BERRIES AND GRAPES.
I saw.

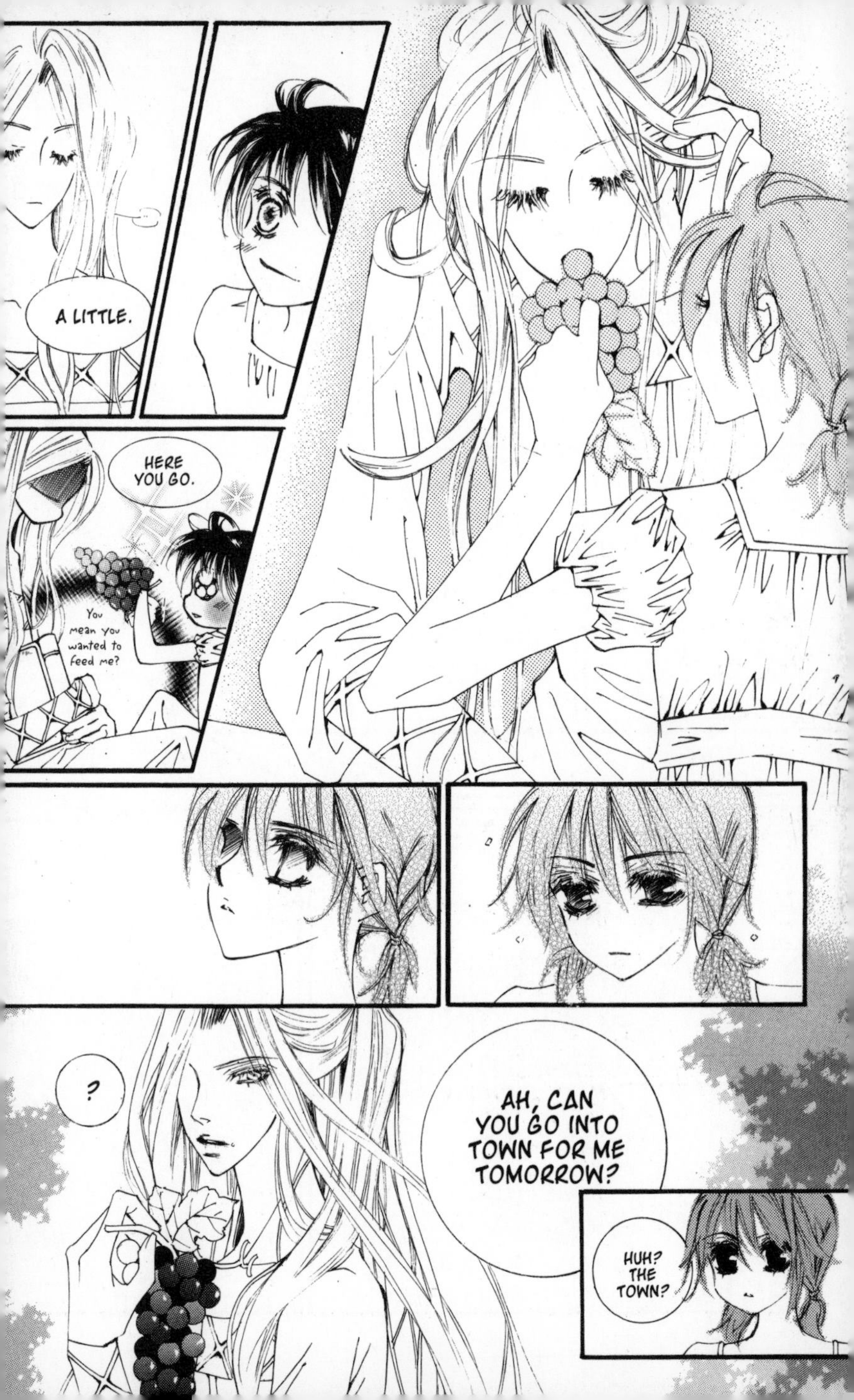
A LITTLE.
HERE YOU GO.
You mean you wanted to feed me?
?
AH, CAN YOU GO INTO TOWN FOR ME TOMORROW?
HUH? THE TOWN?

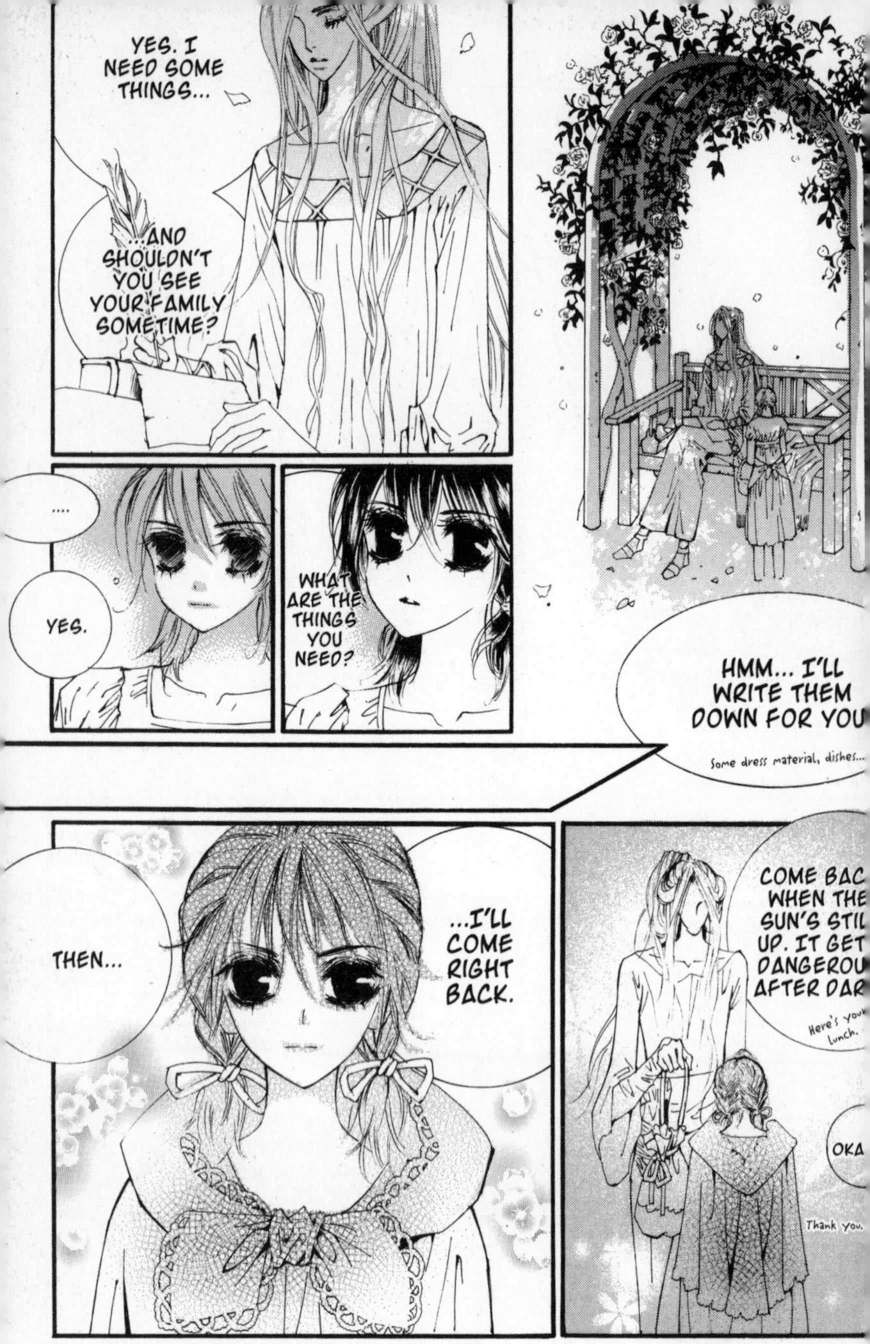
YES. I NEED SOME THINGS...
...AND SHOULDN'T YOU SEE YOUR FAMILY SOMETIME?
....
YES.
WHAT ARE THE THINGS YOU NEED?
HMM... I'LL WRITE THEM DOWN FOR YOU
Some dress material, dishes...
THEN...
...I'LL COME RIGHT BACK.
COME BAC WHEN THE SUN'S STIL UP. IT GET DANGEROU AFTER DAR
Here's you lunch.
OKA
Thank you.

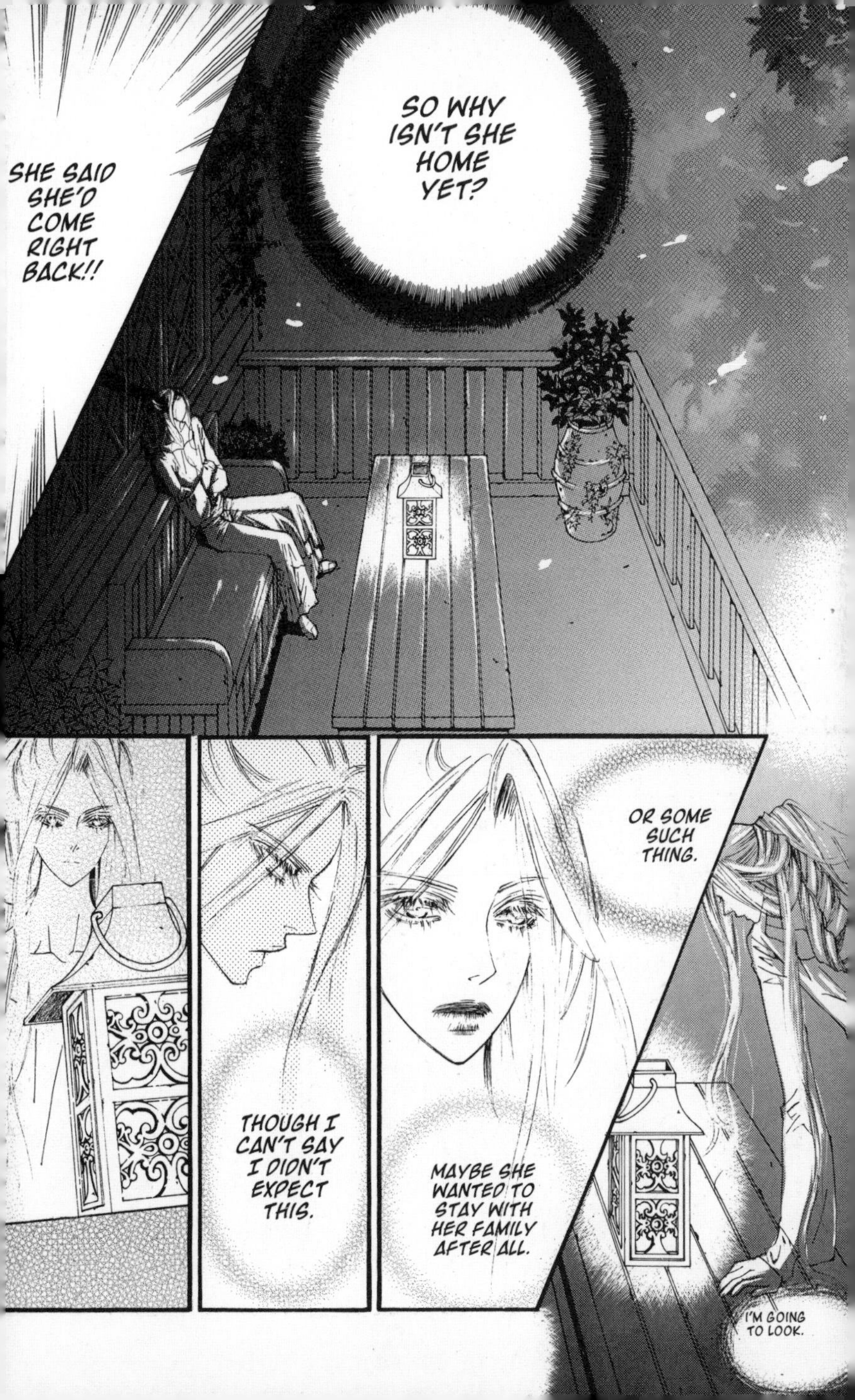
SHE SAID SHE'D COME RIGHT BACK!!
SO WHY ISN'T SHE HOME YET?
THOUGH I CAN'T SAY I DIDN'T EXPECT THIS.
MAYBE SHE WANTED TO STAY WITH HER FAMILY AFTER ALL.
OR SOME SUCH THING.
I'M GOING TO LOOK.

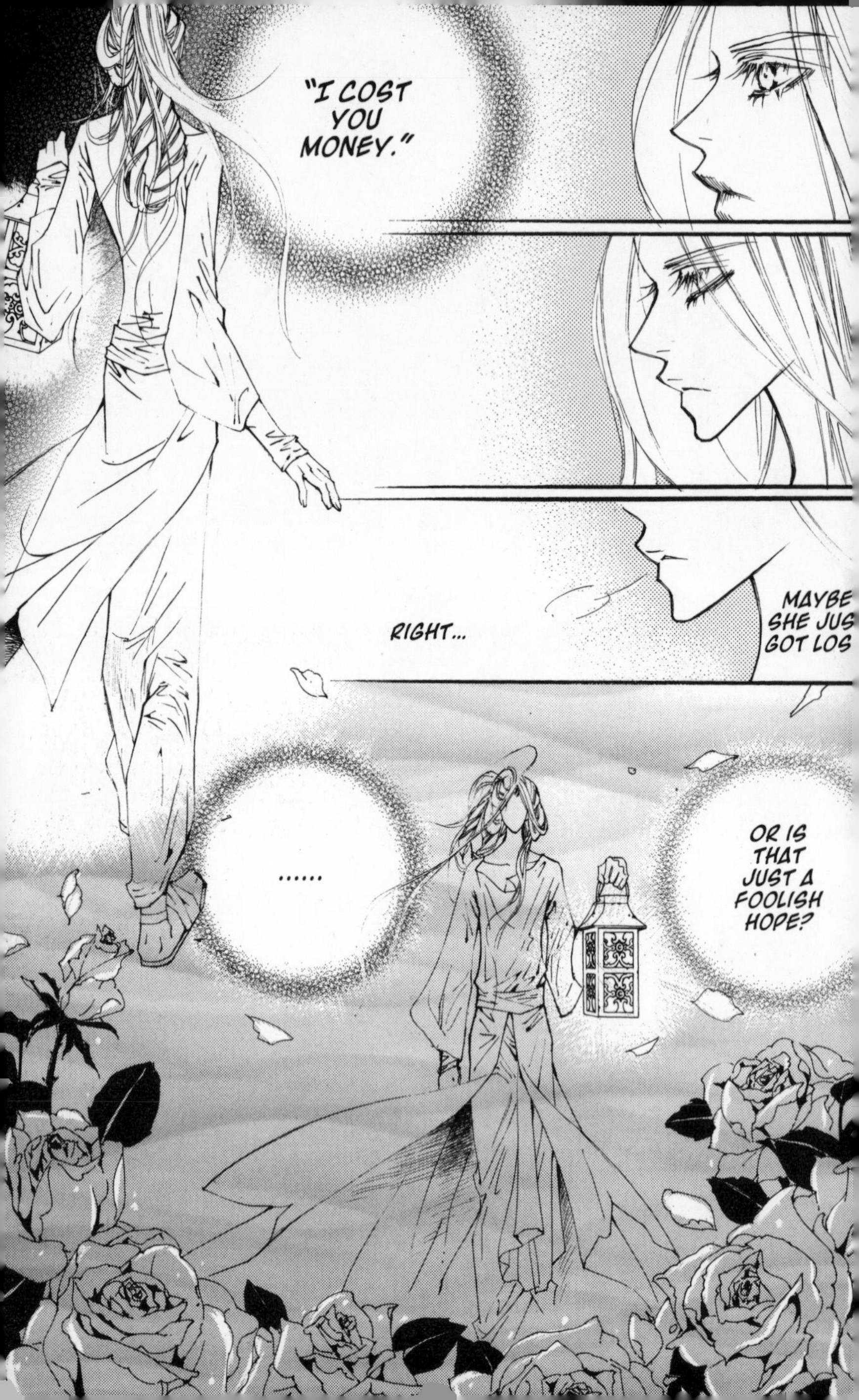
"I COST YOU MONEY."
RIGHT...
MAYBE SHE JUS GOT LOS
......
OR IS THAT JUST A FOOLISH HOPE?

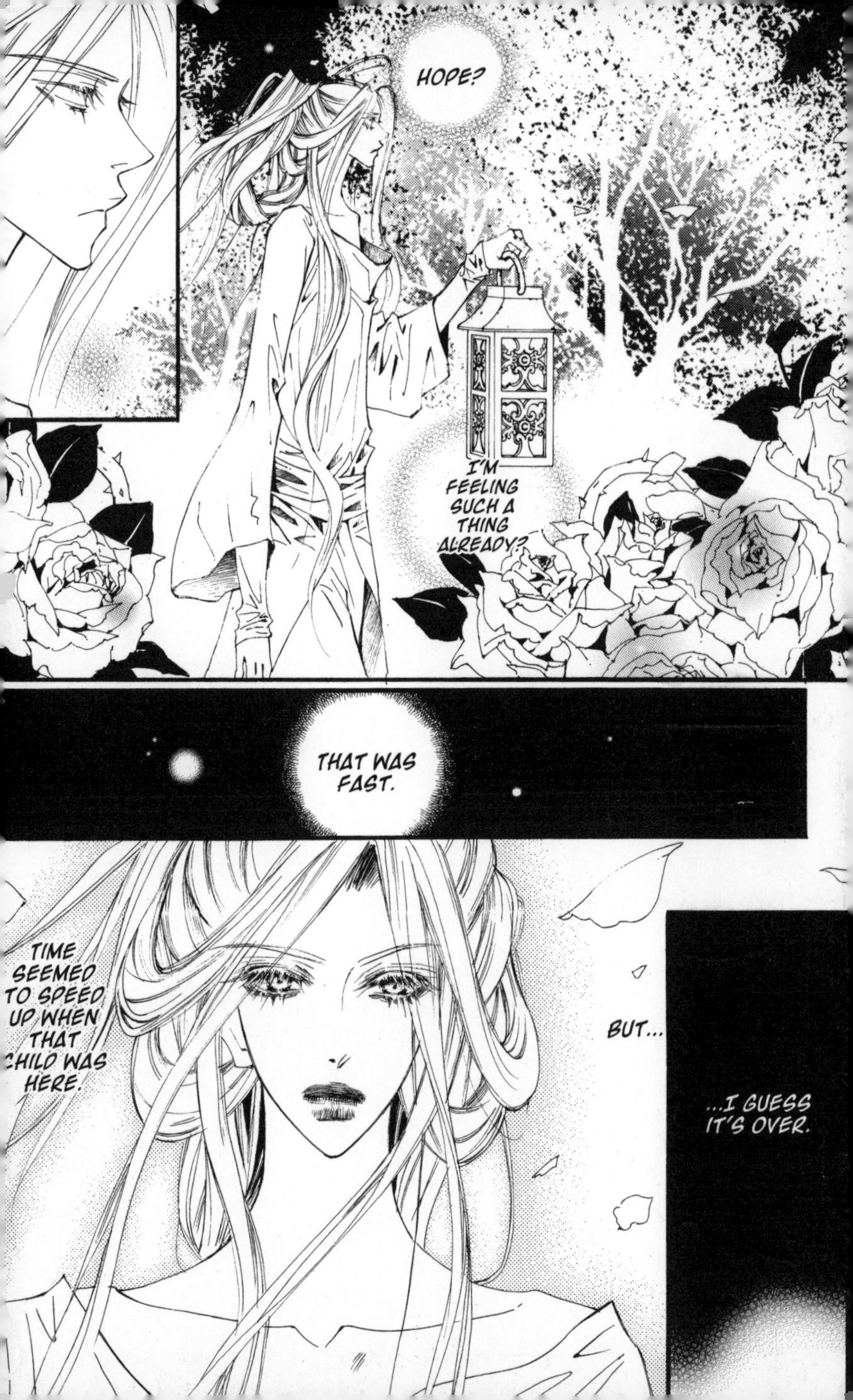
HOPE?
I'M FEELING SUCH A THING ALREADY?
THAT WAS FAST.
TIME SEEMED TO SPEED UP WHEN THAT CHILD WAS HERE.
BUT...
...I GUESS IT'S OVER.

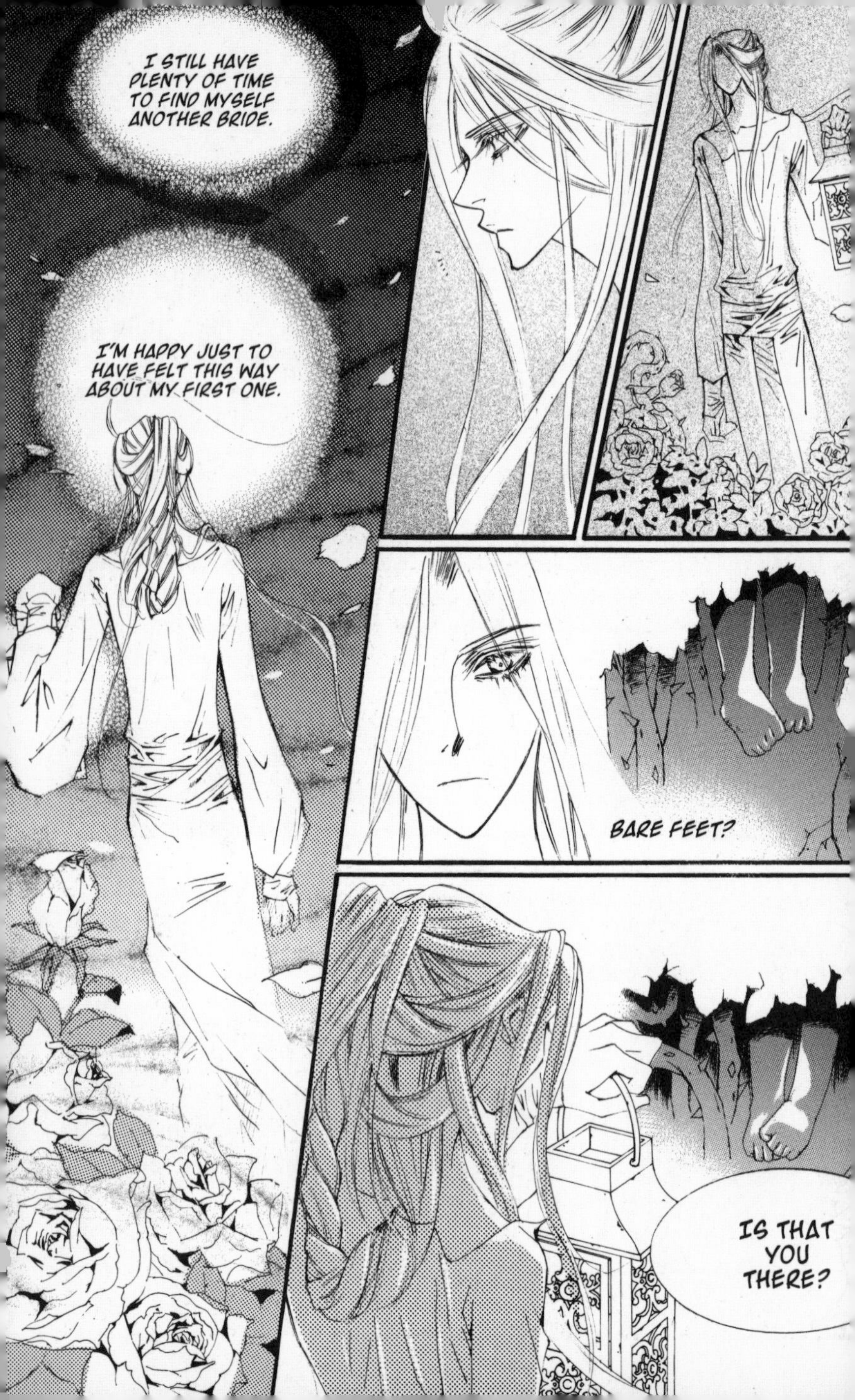
I STILL HAVE PLENTY OF TIME TO FIND MYSELF ANOTHER BRIDE.
I'M HAPPY JUST TO HAVE FELT THIS WAY ABOUT MY FIRST ONE.
BARE FEET?
IS THAT YOU THERE?

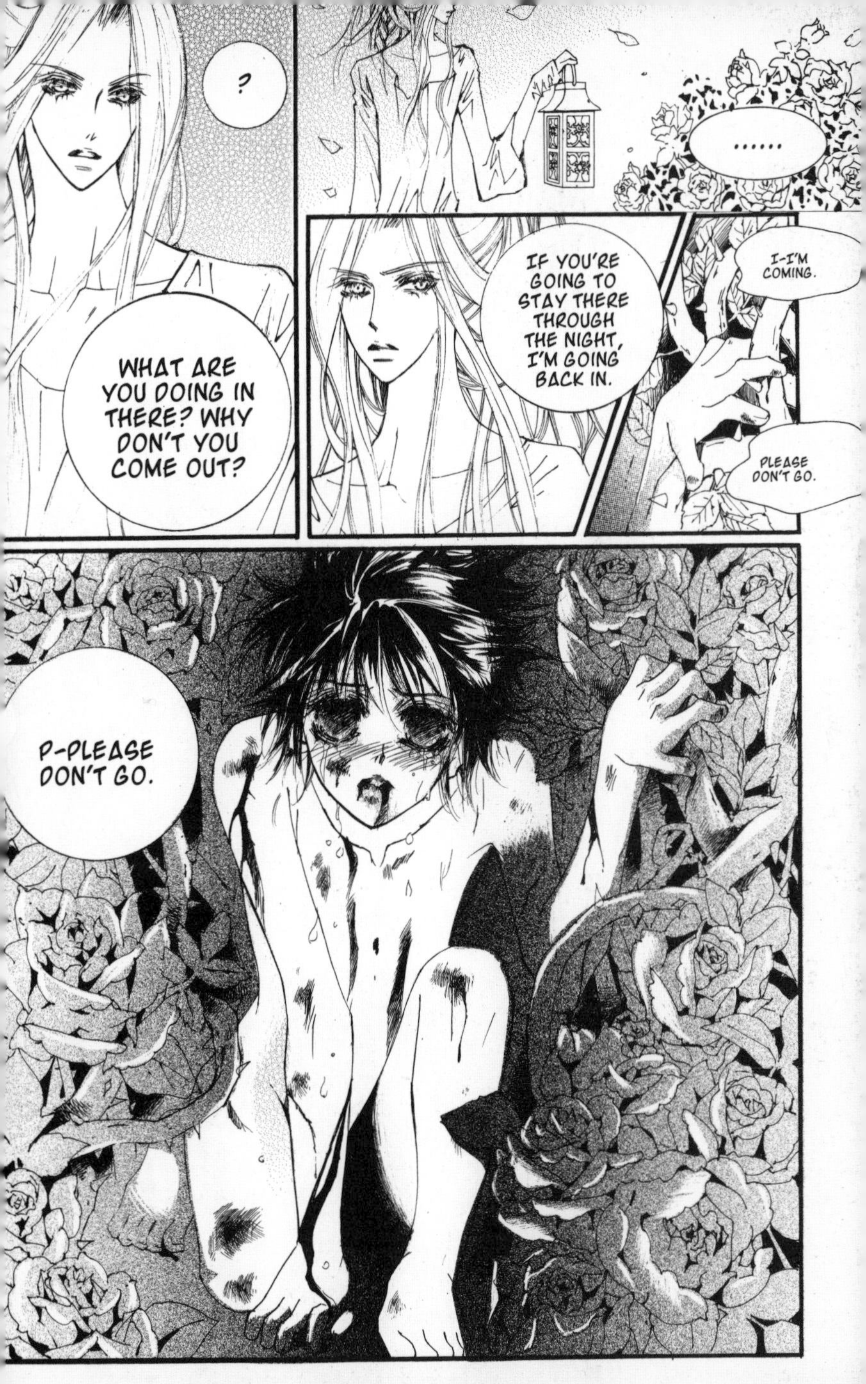
?
......
WHAT ARE YOU DOING IN THERE? WHY DON'T YOU COME OUT?
IF YOU'RE GOING TO STAY THERE THROUGH THE NIGHT, I'M GOING BACK IN.
I-I'M COMING.
PLEASE DON'T GO.
P-PLEASE DON'T GO.

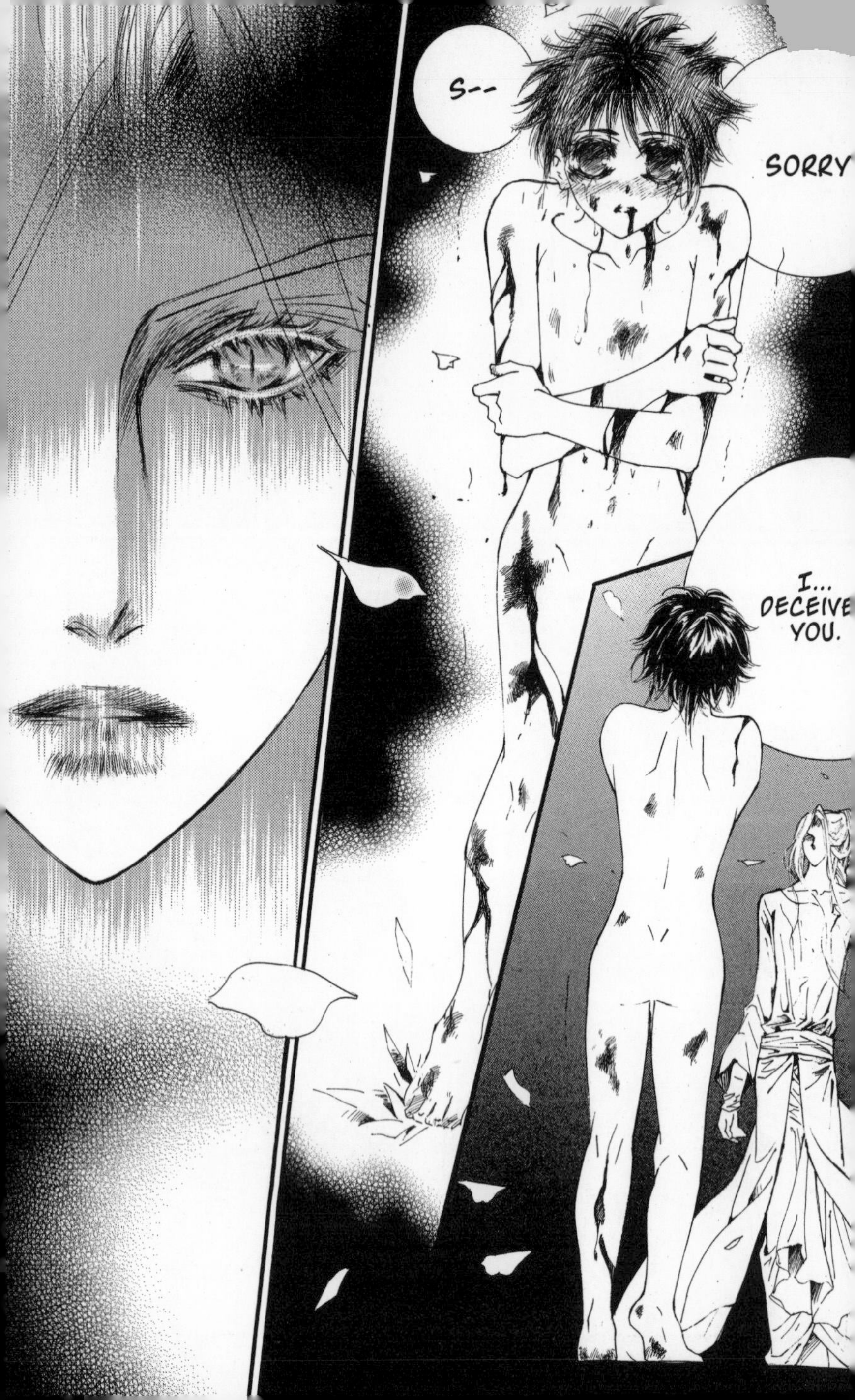
S--
SORRY
I... DECEIVE YOU.

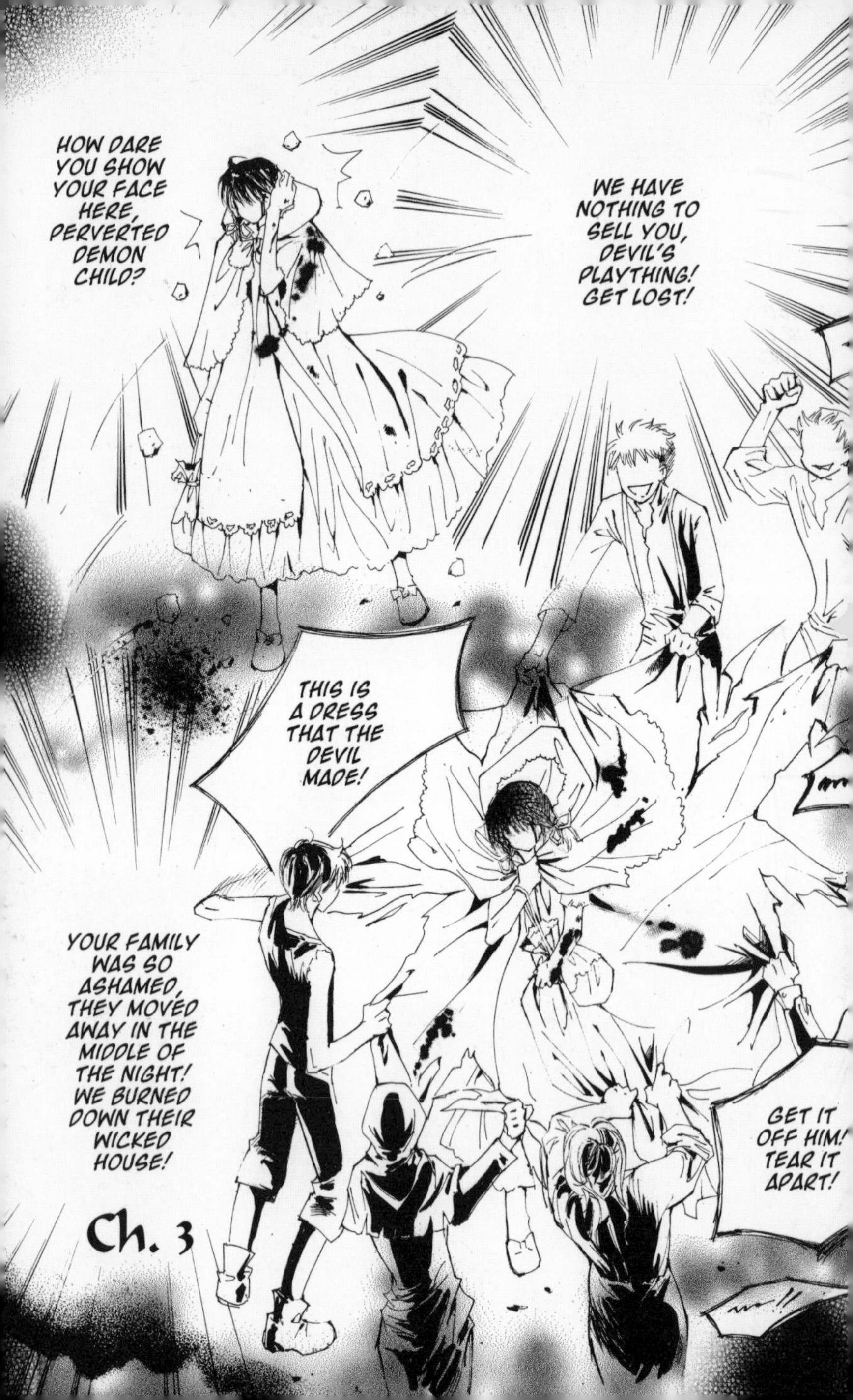
HOW DARE YOU SHOW YOUR FACE HERE, PERVERTED DEMON CHILD?
WE HAVE NOTHING TO SELL YOU, DEVIL'S PLAYTHING! GET LOST!
THIS IS A DRESS THAT THE DEVIL MADE!
YOUR FAMILY WAS SO ASHAMED, THEY MOVED AWAY IN THE MIDDLE OF THE NIGHT! WE BURNED DOWN THEIR WICKED HOUSE!
GET IT OFF HIM! TEAR IT APART!
Ch. 3

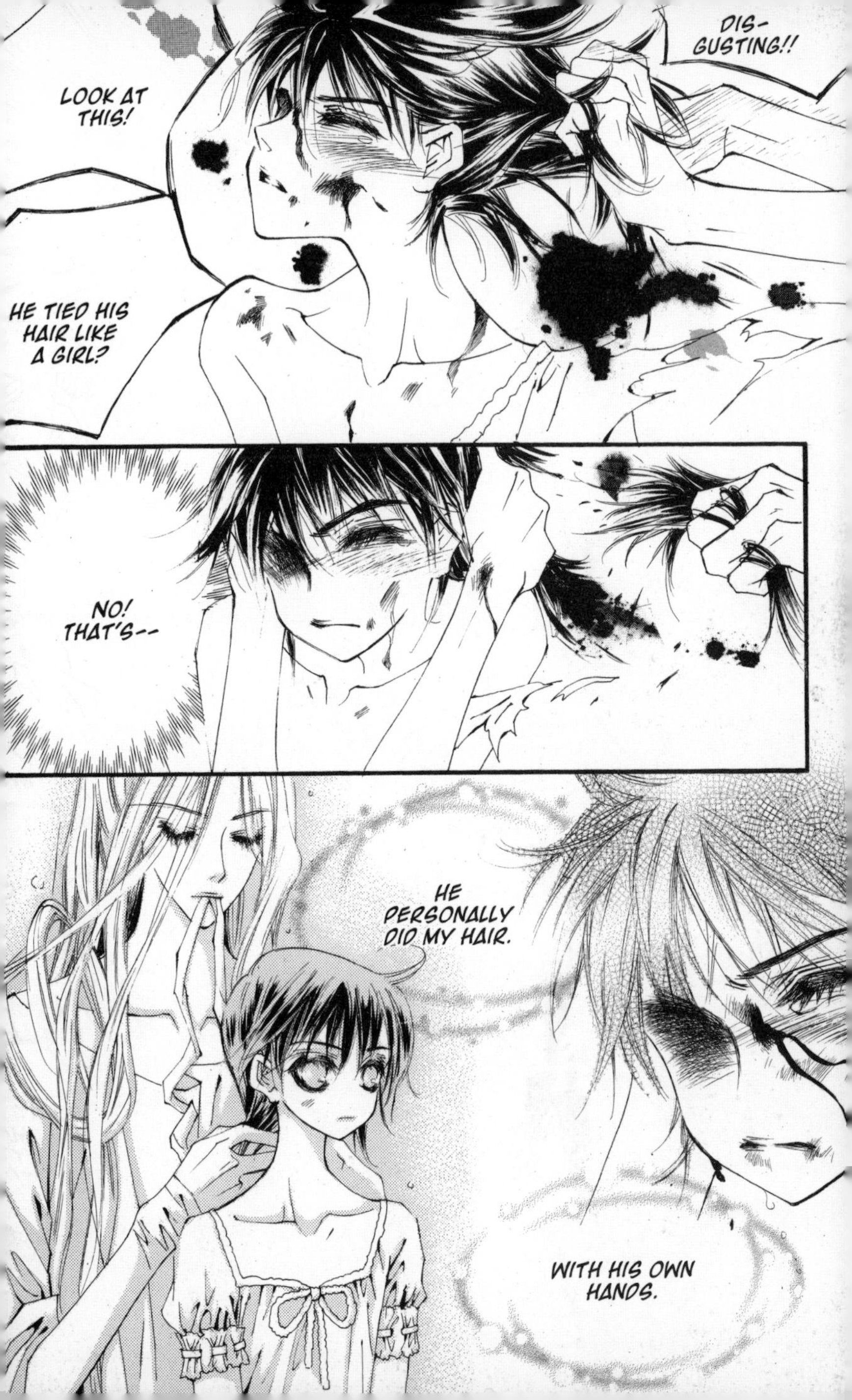

LOOK AT THIS!
HE TIED HIS HAIR LIKE A GIRL?
DIS-GUSTING!!
NO! THAT'S--
HE PERSONALLY DID MY HAIR.
WITH HIS OWN HANDS.

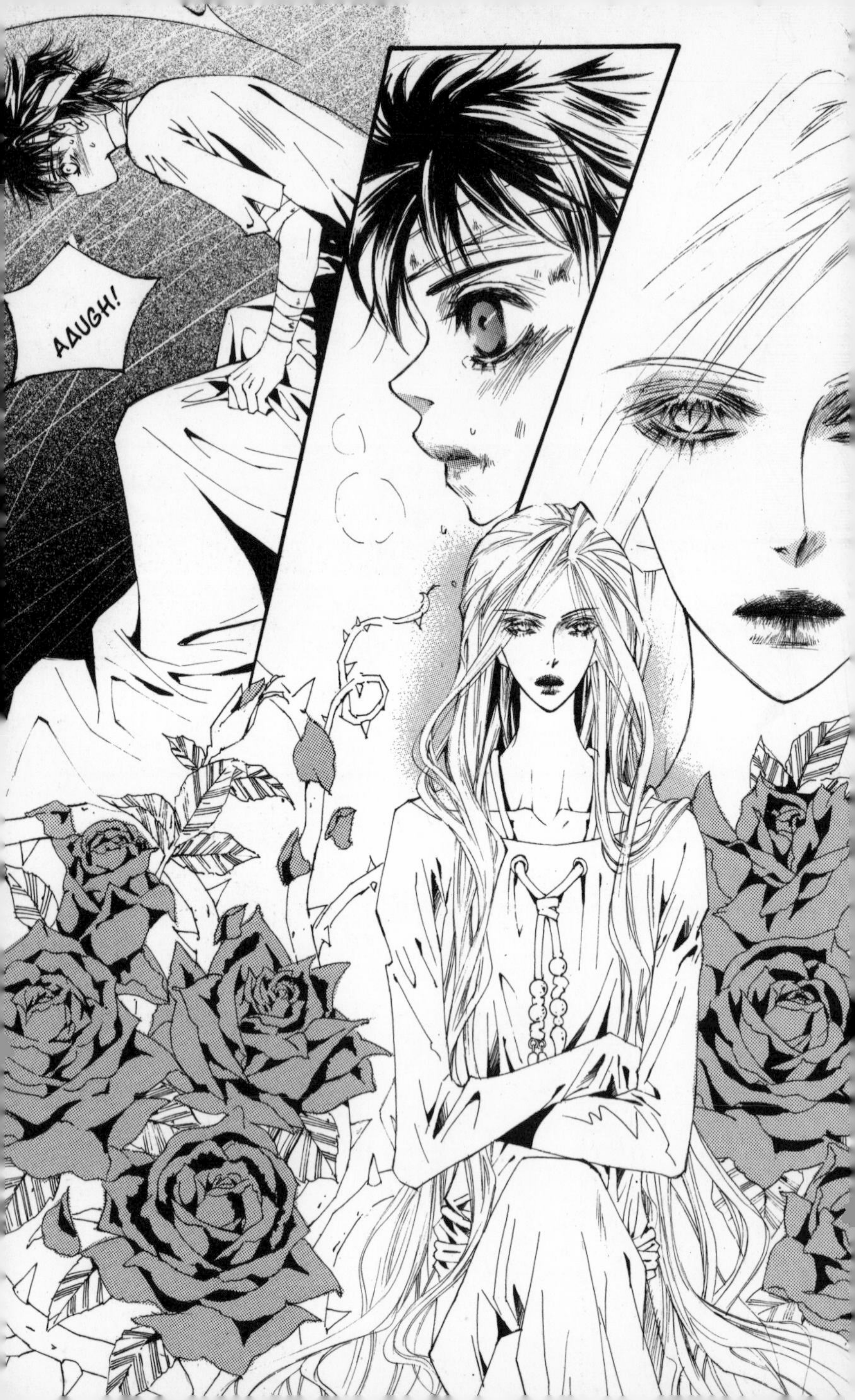
AAUGH!

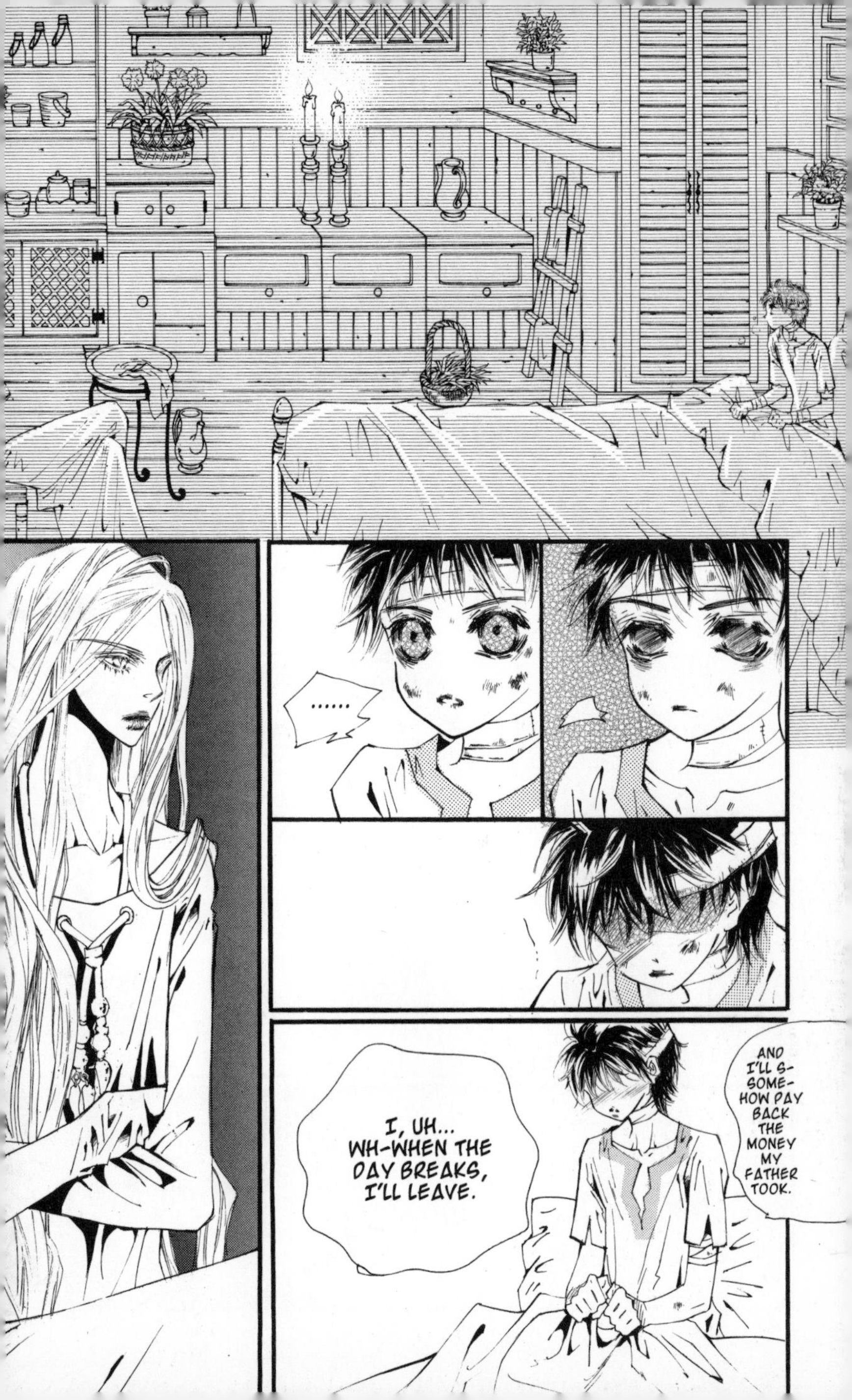
......
I, UH... WH-WHEN THE DAY BREAKS, I'LL LEAVE.
AND I'LL S-SOME-HOW PAY BACK THE MONEY MY FATHER TOOK.

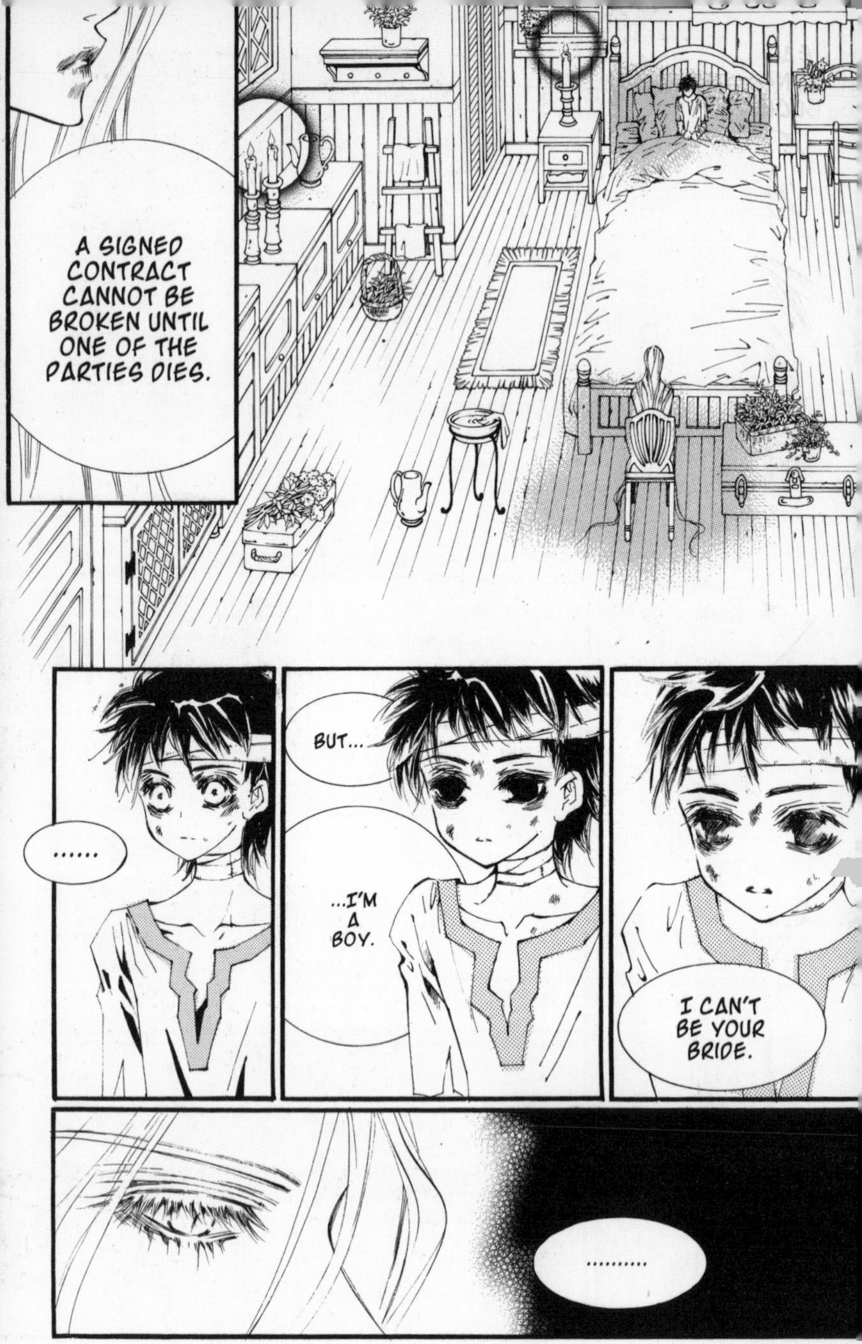
A SIGNED CONTRACT CANNOT BE BROKEN UNTIL ONE OF THE PARTIES DIES.
......
BUT...
...I'M A BOY.
I CAN'T BE YOUR BRIDE.
....

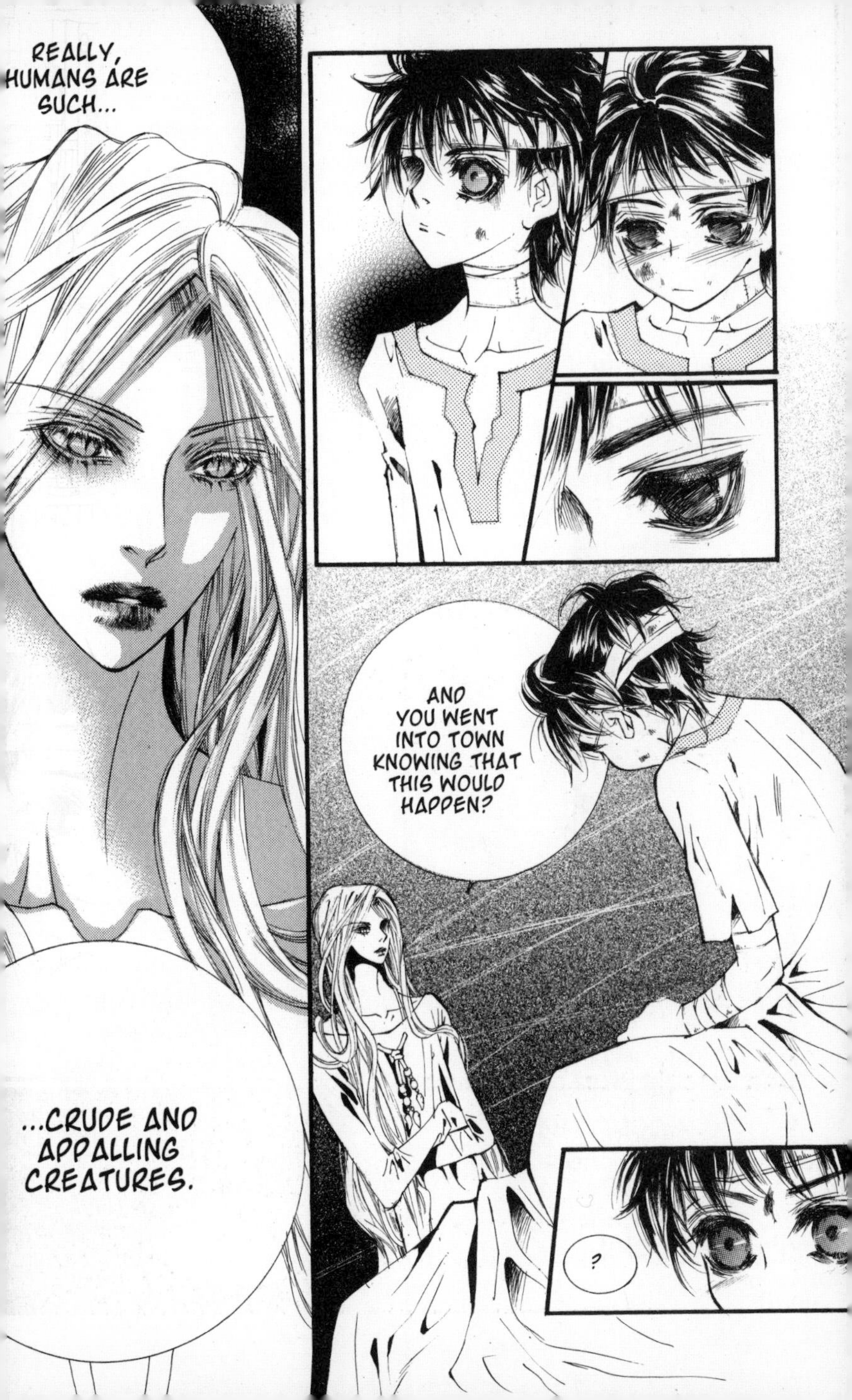
REALLY, HUMANS ARE SUCH...
...CRUDE AND APPALLING CREATURES.
AND YOU WENT INTO TOWN KNOWING THAT THIS WOULD HAPPEN?
?

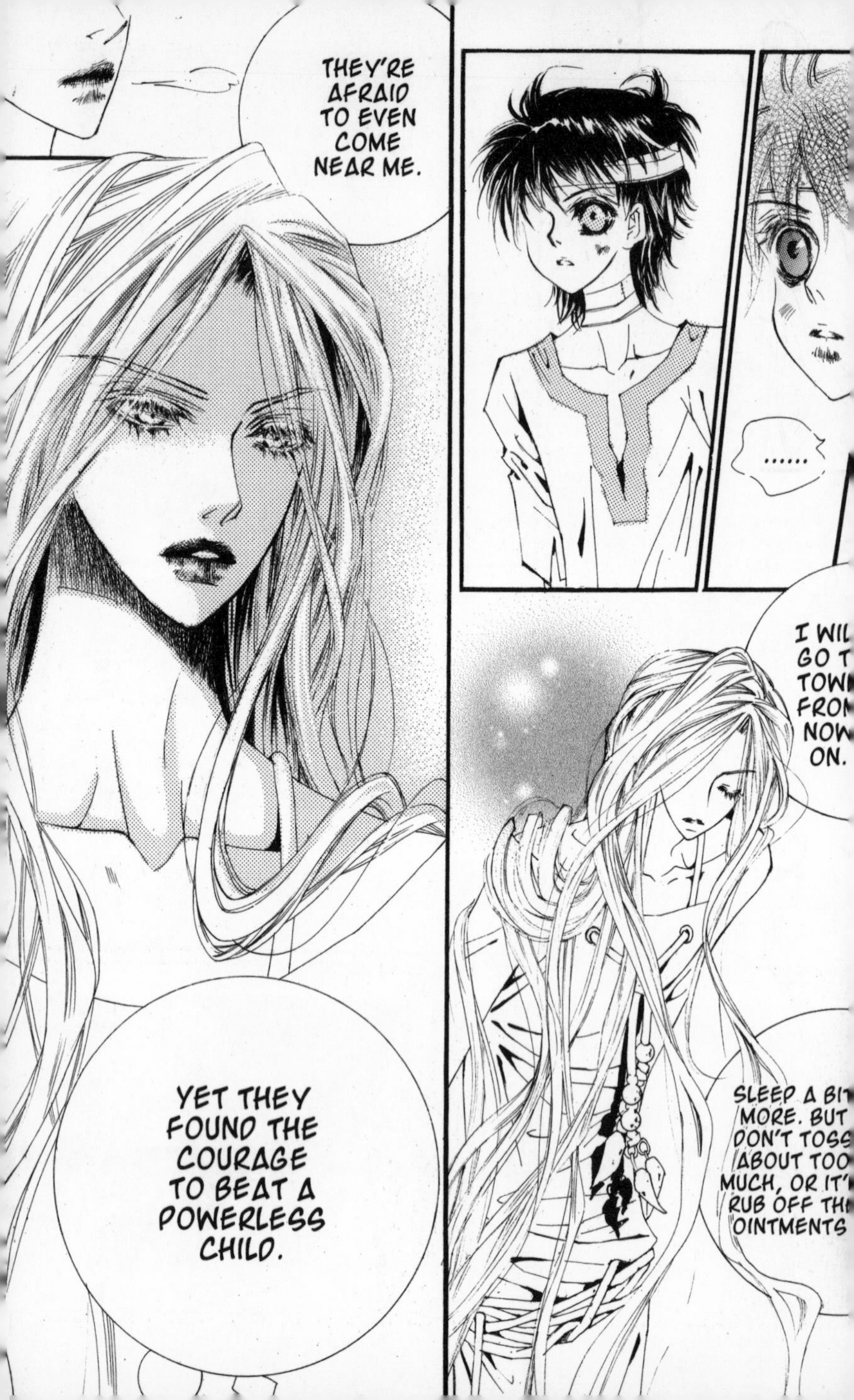
THEY'RE AFRAID TO EVEN COME NEAR ME.
YET THEY FOUND THE COURAGE TO BEAT A POWERLESS CHILD.
......
I WIL GO T TOW FRO NOW ON.
SLEEP A BI MORE. BUT DON'T TOSS ABOUT TOO MUCH, OR IT' RUB OFF TH OINTMENTS

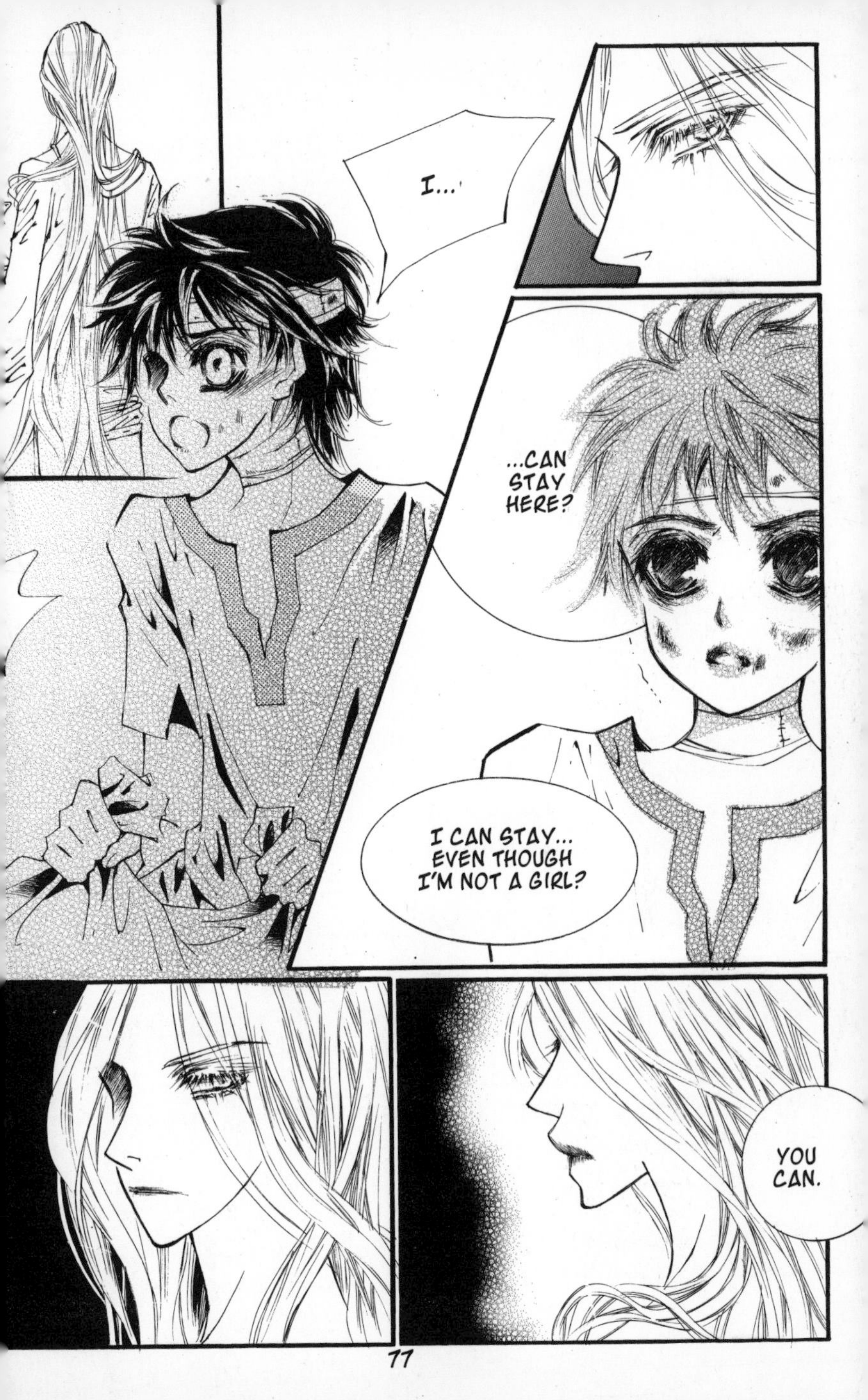
I...
...CAN STAY HERE?
I CAN STAY... EVEN THOUGH I'M NOT A GIRL?
YOU CAN.

Closet

DAMN. I'LL HAVE T' ALTER THOSE CLOTHE AGAIN.

And boys' clothes aren't even pretty.

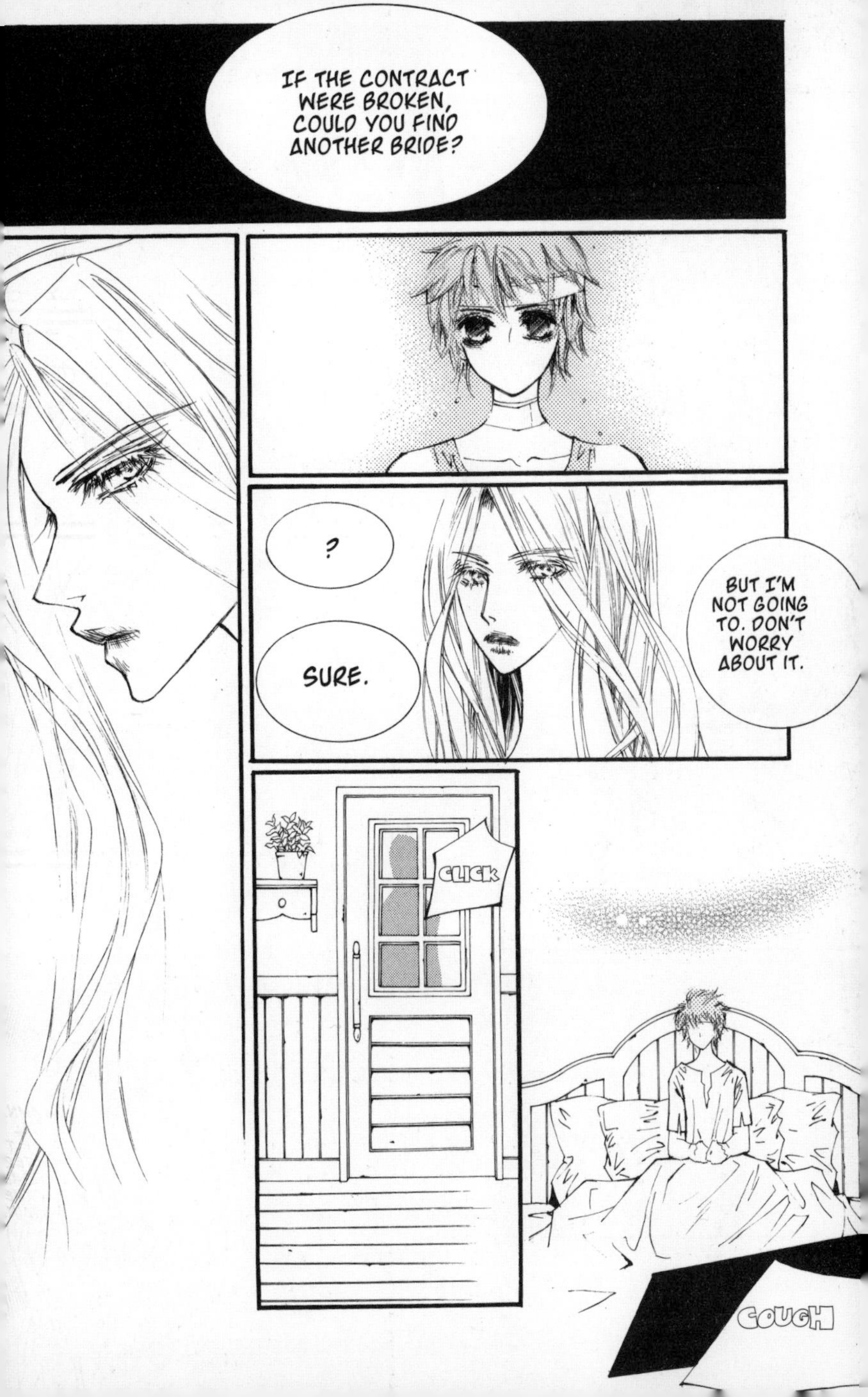
IF THE CONTRACT WERE BROKEN, COULD YOU FIND ANOTHER BRIDE?
?
SURE.
BUT I'M NOT GOING TO. DON'T WORRY ABOUT IT.
CLICK
COUGH

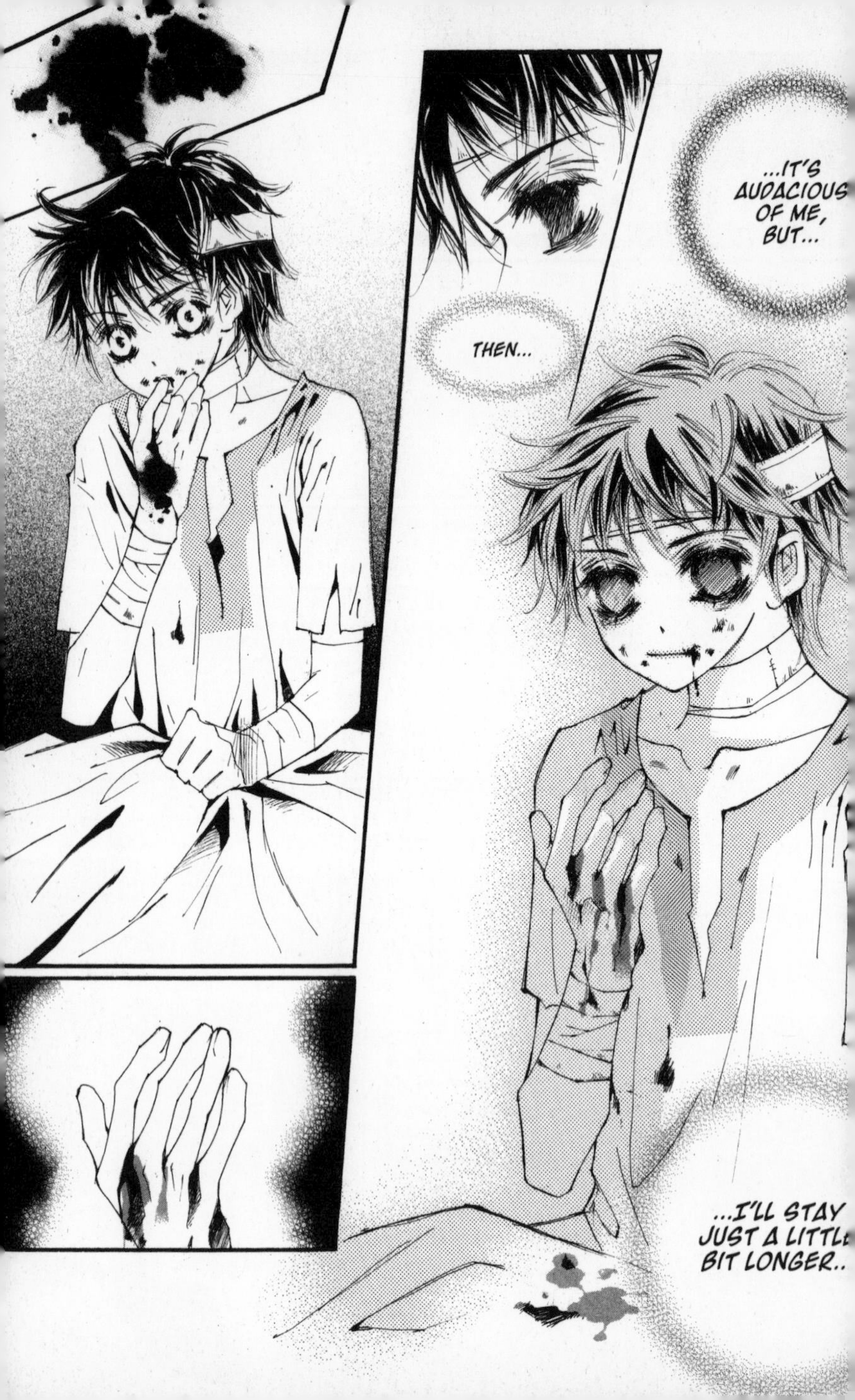
THEN...
...IT'S AUDACIOUS OF ME, BUT...
...I'LL STAY JUST A LITTLE BIT LONGER..

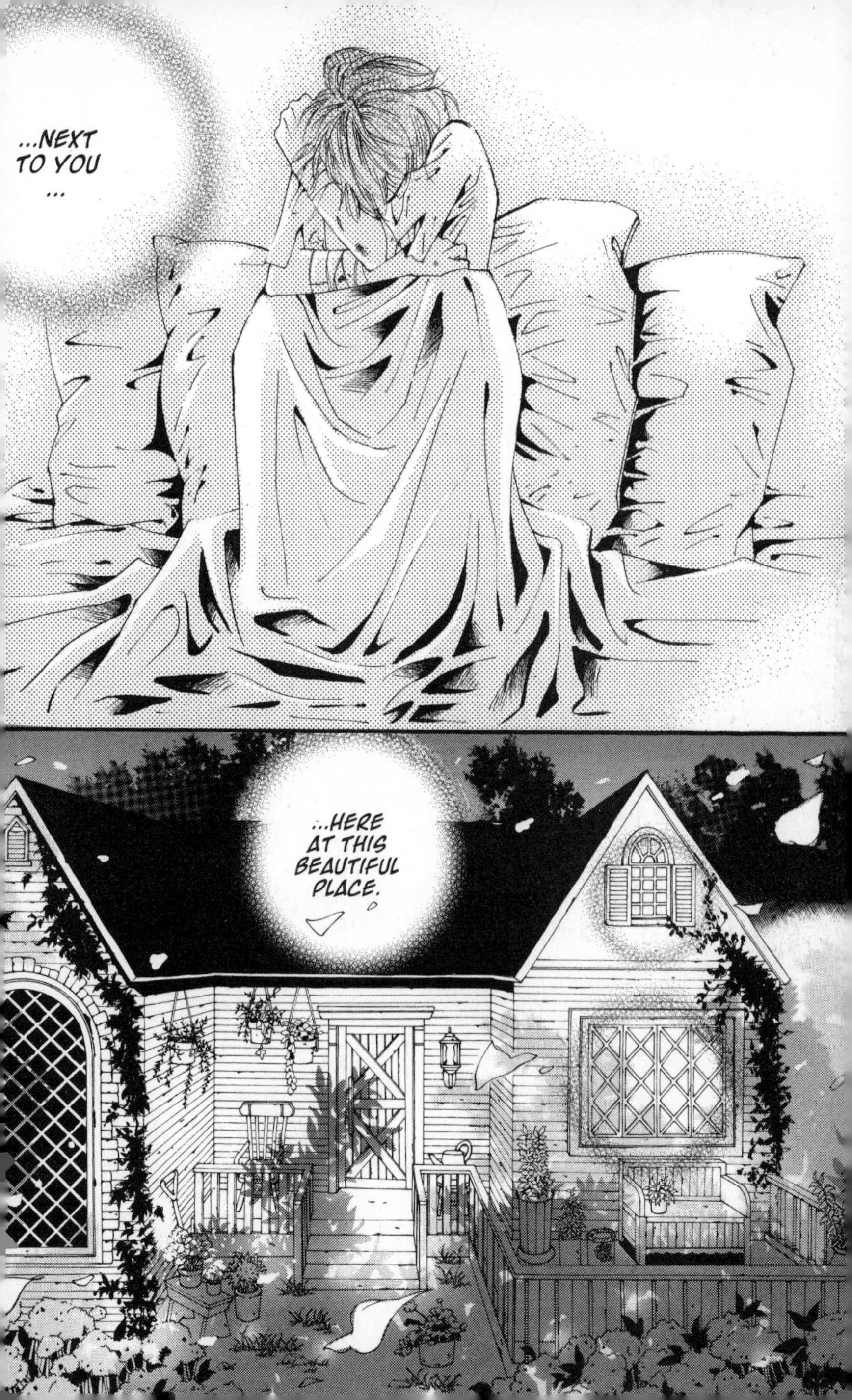
...NEXT TO YOU ...
...HERE AT THIS BEAUTIFUL PLACE.

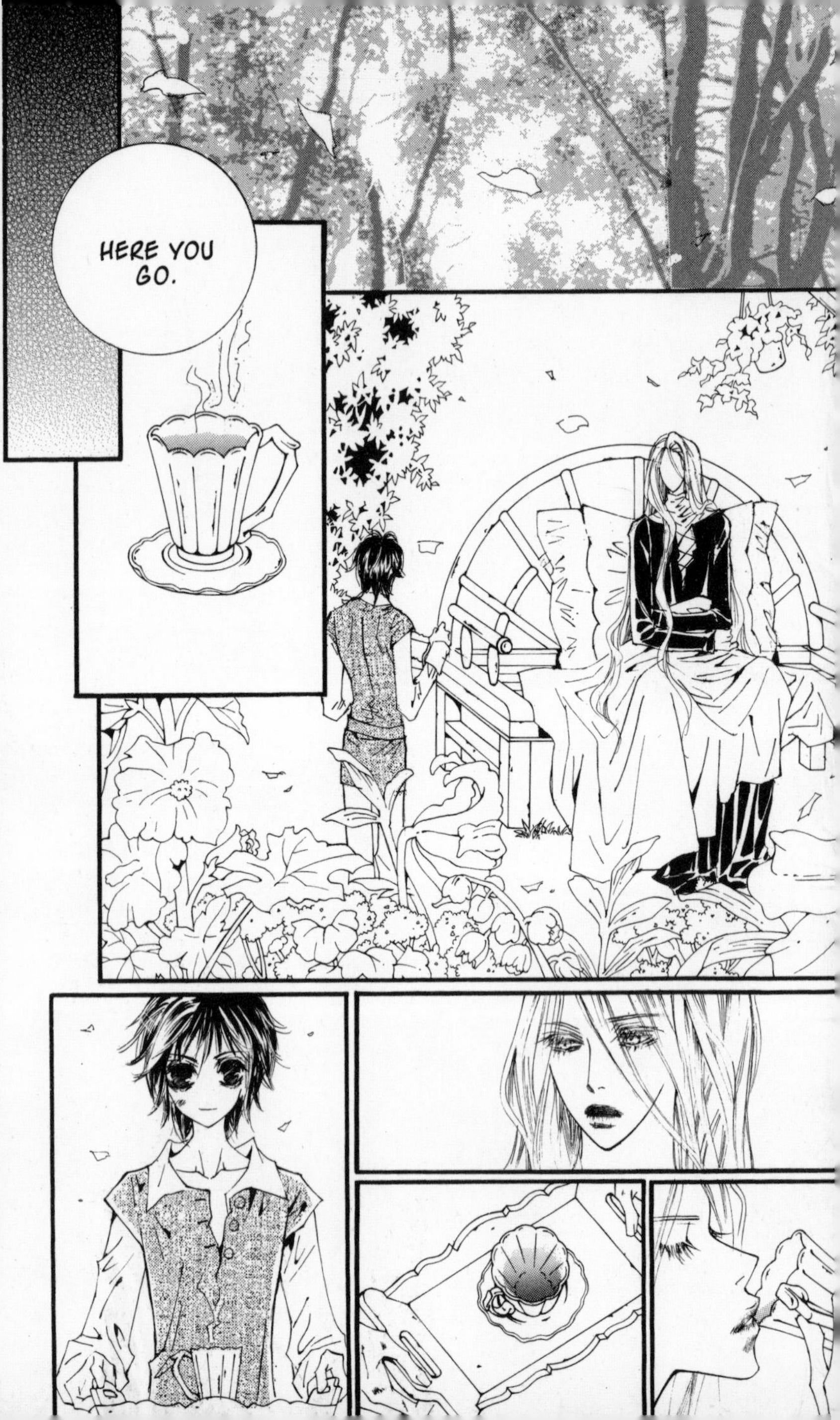
HERE YOU GO.

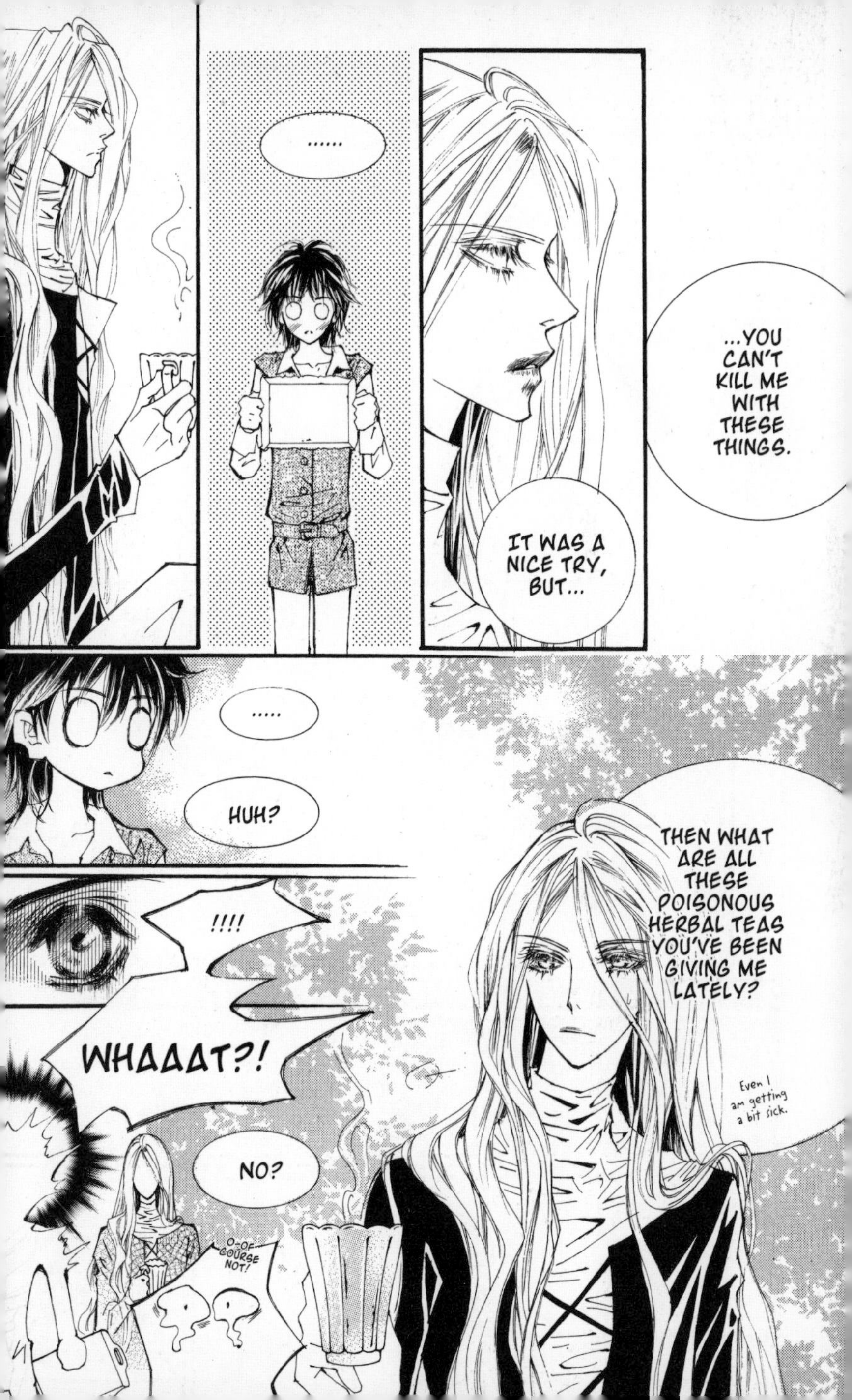

......
IT WAS A NICE TRY, BUT...
...YOU CAN'T KILL ME WITH THESE THINGS.
.....
HUH?
!!!!
WHAAAT?!
NO?
O-OF COURSE NOT!
THEN WHAT ARE ALL THESE POISONOUS HERBAL TEAS YOU'VE BEEN GIVING ME LATELY?
Even I am getting a bit sick.

......

...BREW YOU SOME TEA WITH NEW HERBS FOUND

But they all looked alike

I THOUGHT YOU LOOKED TIRED LATELY, SO I WANTED TO...

......

SO THAT'S WHY YOUR HANDS ARE IN THAT STATE.

BECAUSE YOU'VE BEEN MESSIN' AROUND IN THE FOREST.

Too late to hide them now...

HOW LONG DO YOU THINK I'VE LIVED?

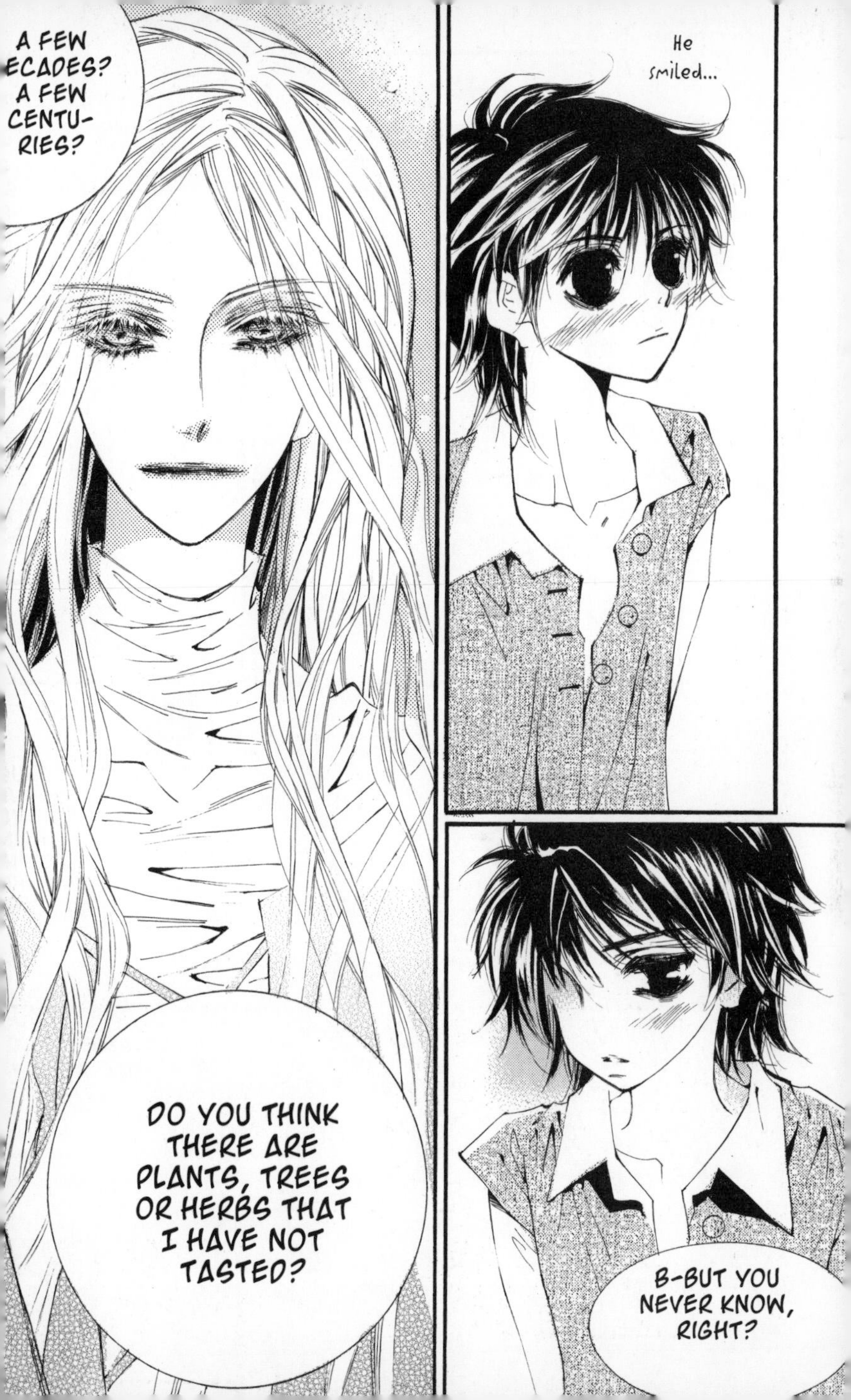
A FEW ECADES? A FEW CENTU-RIES?
DO YOU THINK THERE ARE PLANTS, TREES OR HERBS THAT I HAVE NOT TASTED?
He smiled...
B-BUT YOU NEVER KNOW, RIGHT?

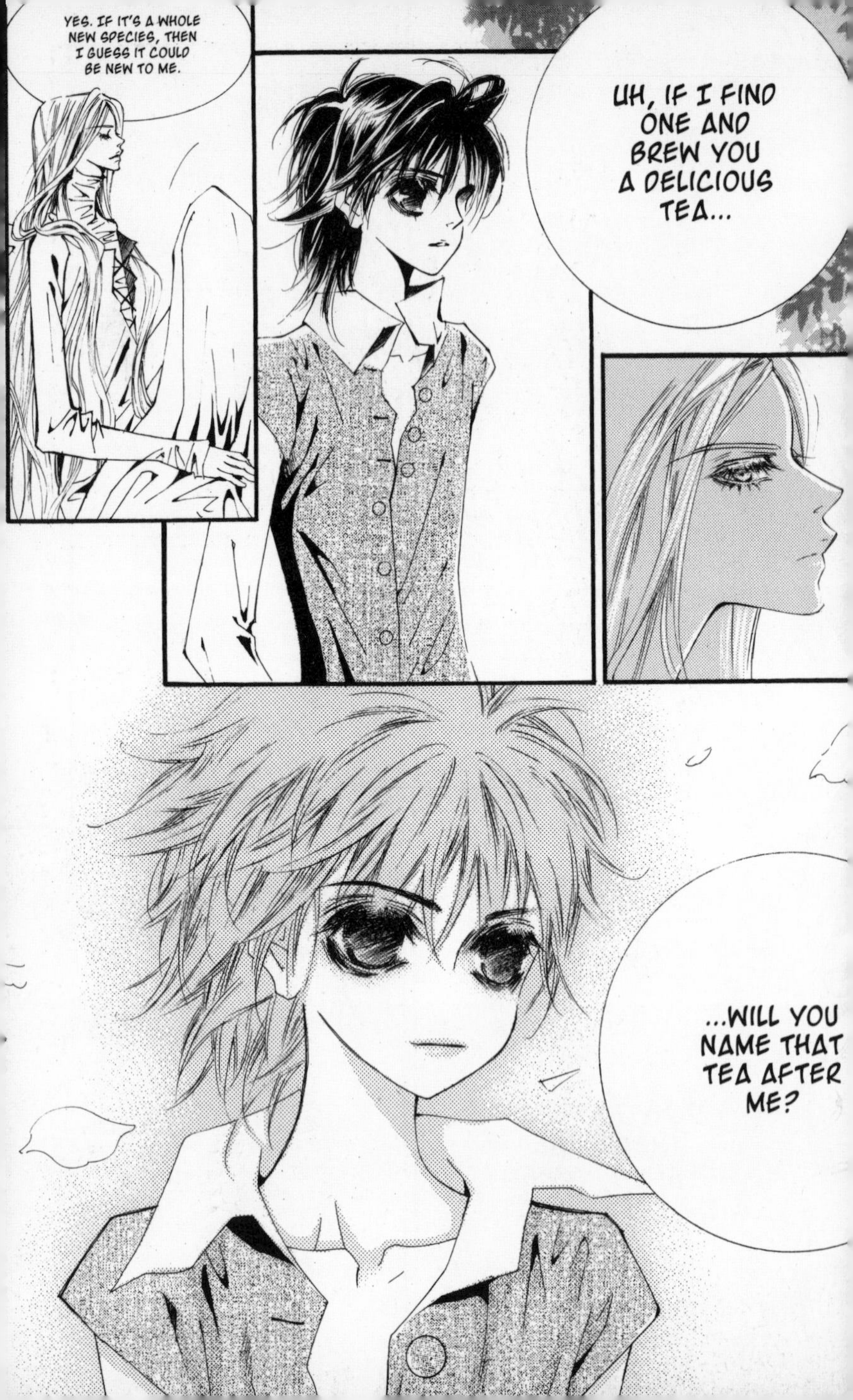
YES. IF IT'S A WHOLE NEW SPECIES, THEN I GUESS IT COULD BE NEW TO ME.
UH, IF I FIND ONE AND BREW YOU A DELICIOUS TEA...
...WILL YOU NAME THAT TEA AFTER ME?

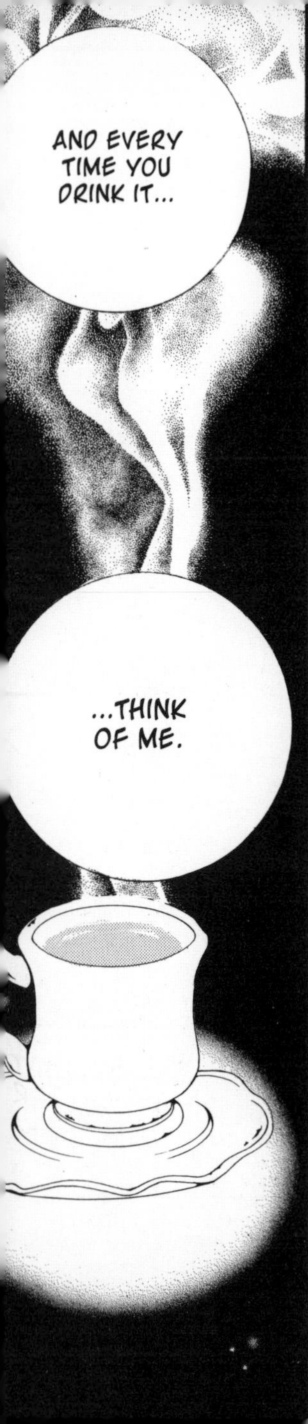
AND EVERY TIME YOU DRINK IT...
...THINK OF ME.

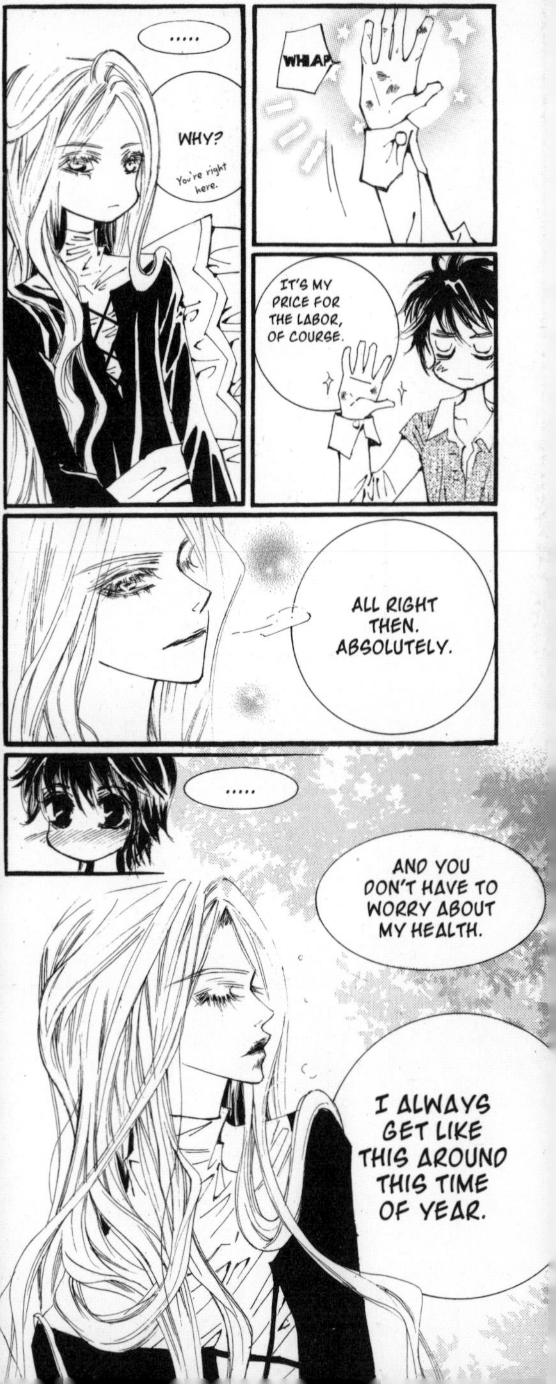
.....
WHY?
You're right here.
WHIAP
IT'S MY PRICE FOR THE LABOR, OF COURSE.
ALL RIGHT THEN. ABSOLUTELY.
.....
AND YOU DON'T HAVE TO WORRY ABOUT MY HEALTH.
I ALWAYS GET LIKE THIS AROUND THIS TIME OF YEAR.

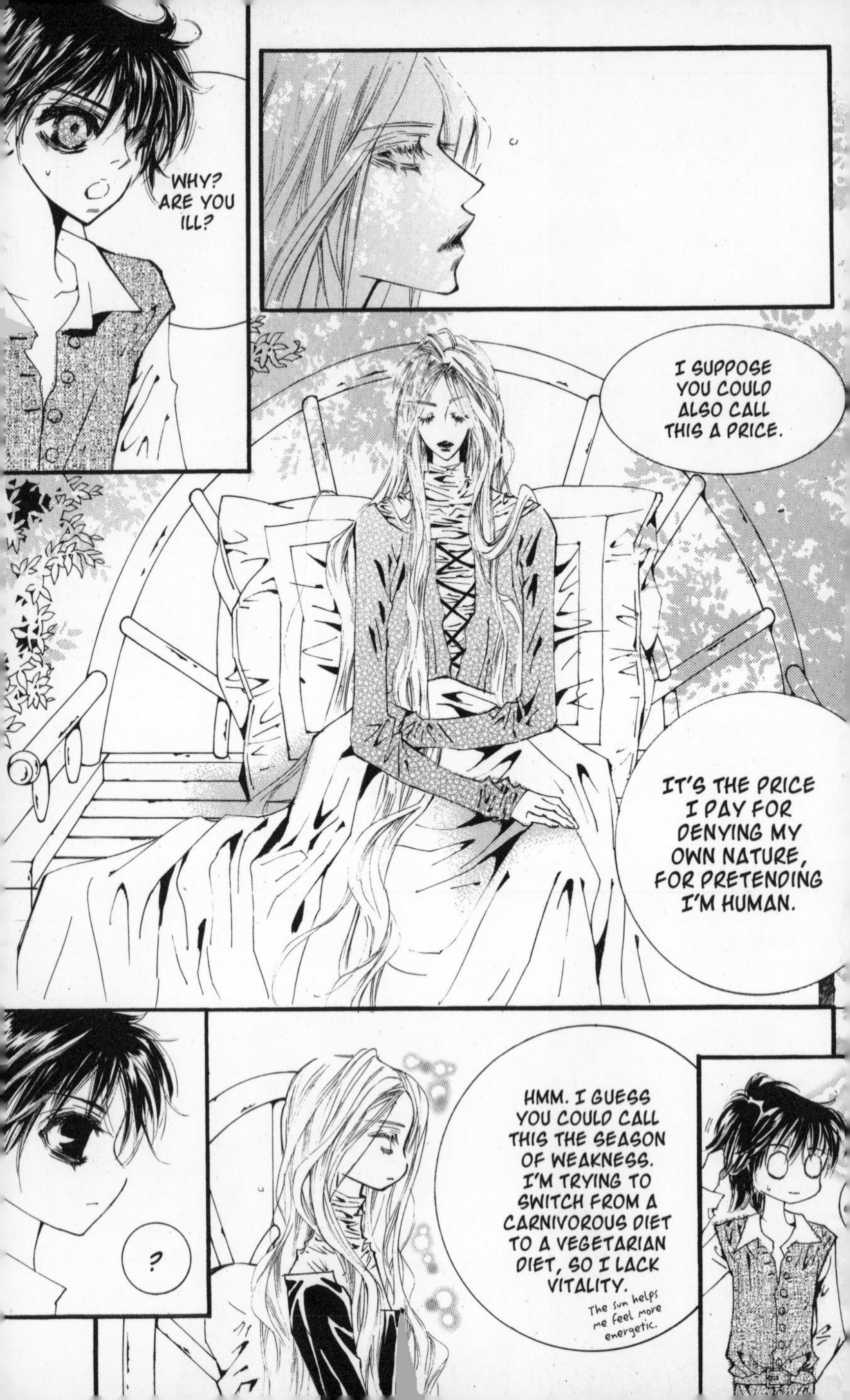
WHY? ARE YOU ILL?
I SUPPOSE YOU COULD ALSO CALL THIS A PRICE.
IT'S THE PRICE I PAY FOR DENYING MY OWN NATURE, FOR PRETENDING I'M HUMAN.
?
HMM. I GUESS YOU COULD CALL THIS THE SEASON OF WEAKNESS. I'M TRYING TO SWITCH FROM A CARNIVOROUS DIET TO A VEGETARIAN DIET, SO I LACK VITALITY.
The sun helps me feel more energetic.

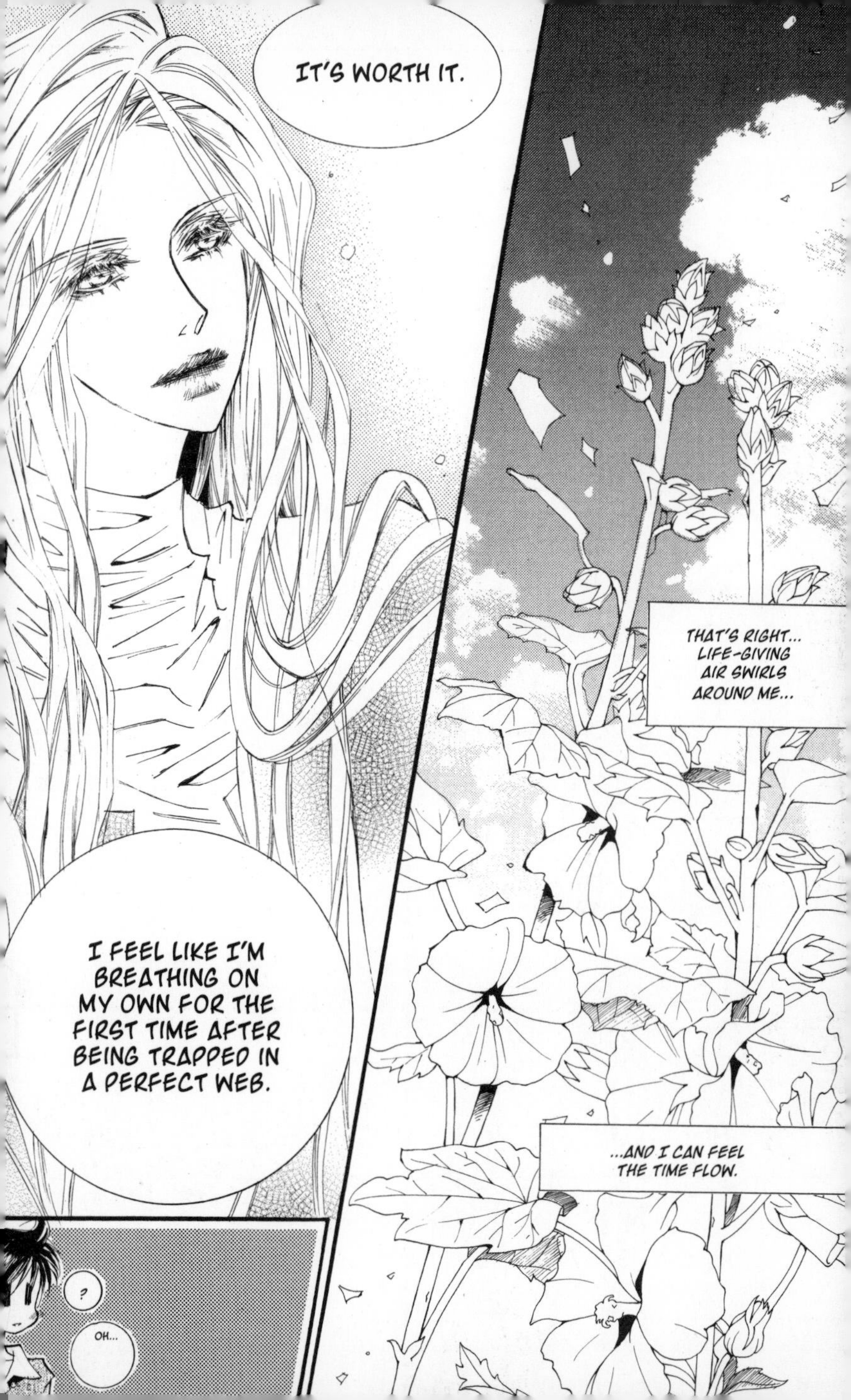
IT'S WORTH IT.
I FEEL LIKE I'M BREATHING ON MY OWN FOR THE FIRST TIME AFTER BEING TRAPPED IN A PERFECT WEB.
?
OH...
THAT'S RIGHT... LIFE-GIVING AIR SWIRLS AROUND ME...
...AND I CAN FEEL THE TIME FLOW.

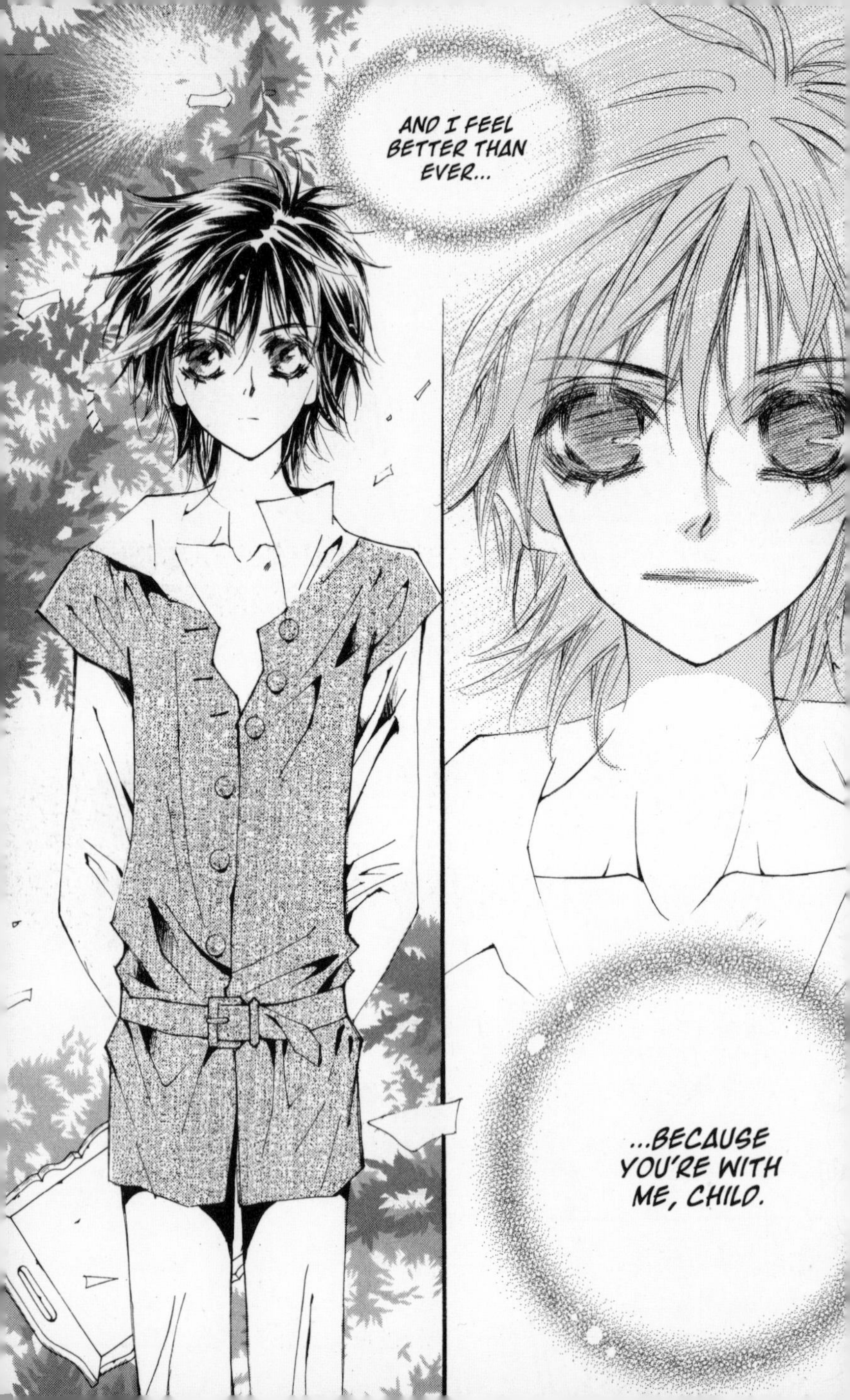
AND I FEEL BETTER THAN EVER...
...BECAUSE YOU'RE WITH ME, CHILD.

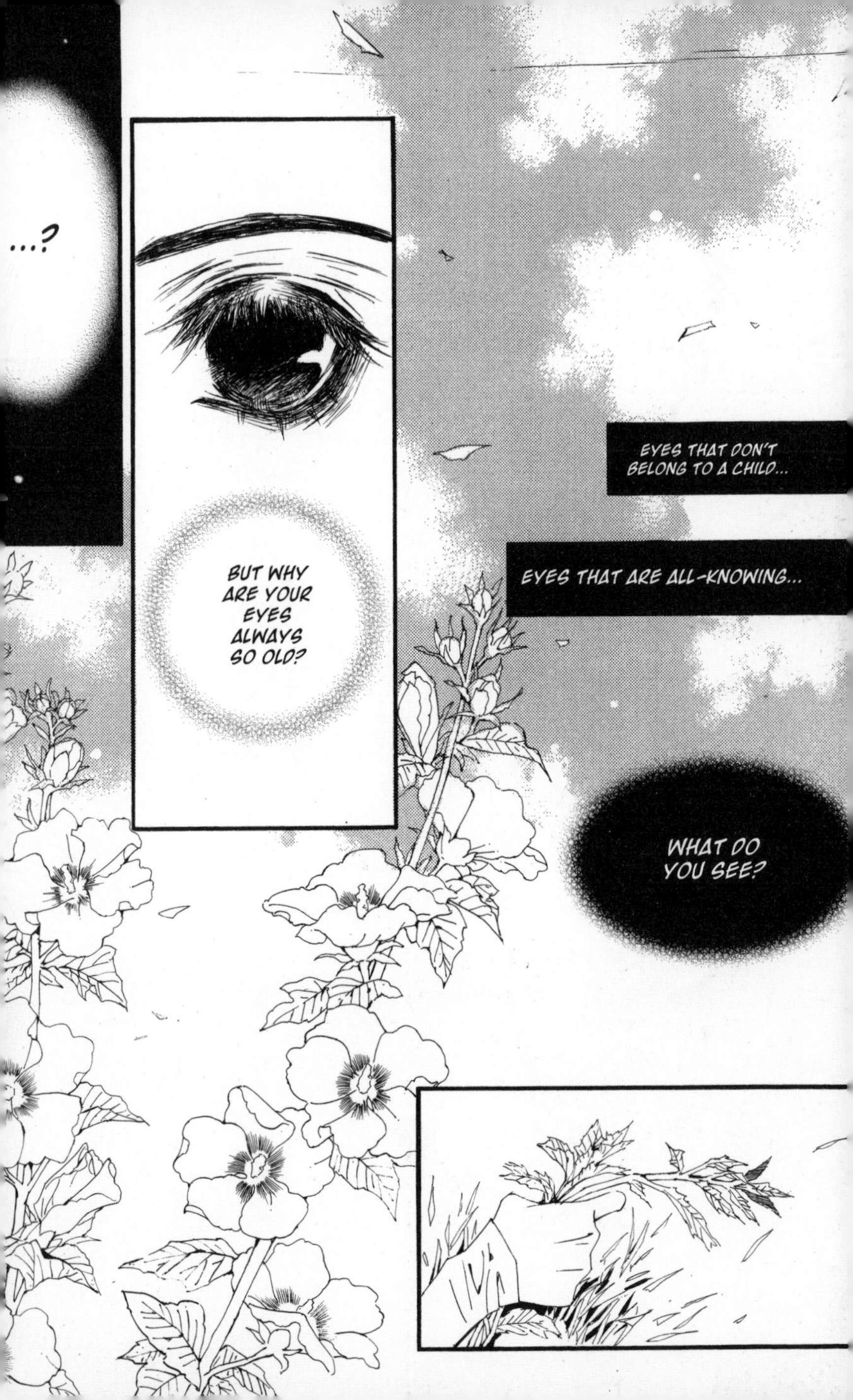
...?
BUT WHY ARE YOUR EYES ALWAYS SO OLD?
EYES THAT DON'T BELONG TO A CHILD...
EYES THAT ARE ALL-KNOWING...
WHAT DO YOU SEE?

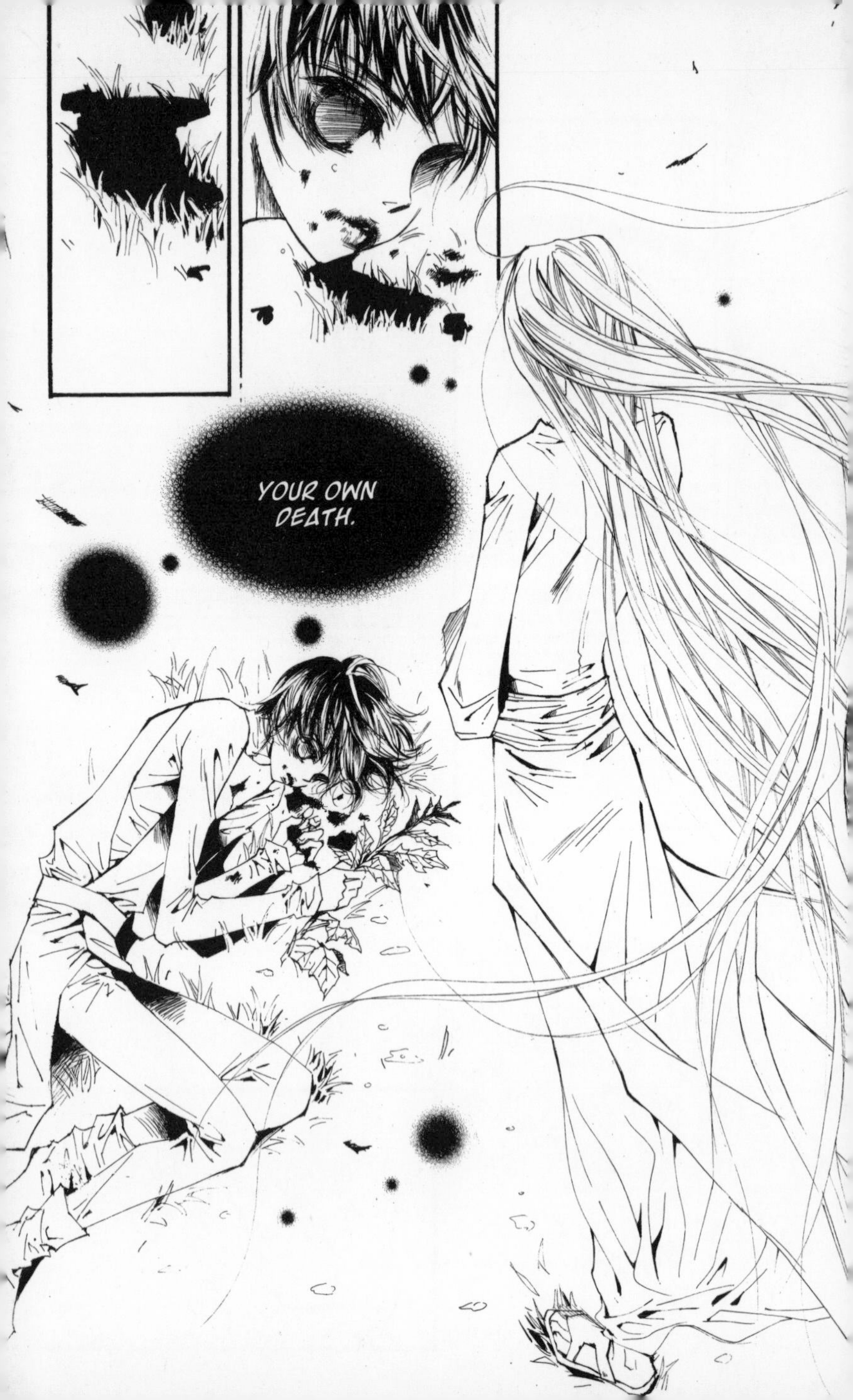
YOUR OWN DEATH.

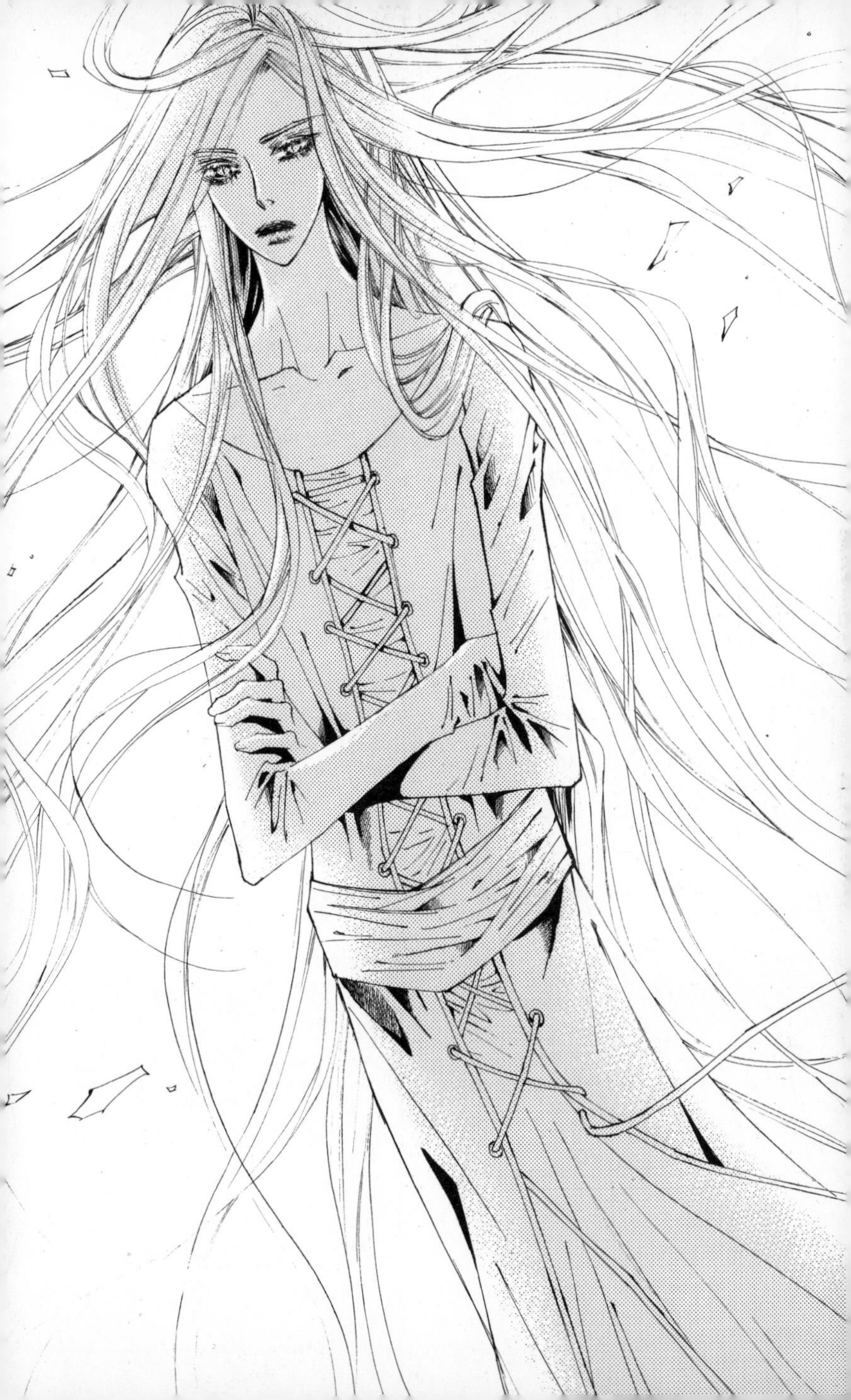

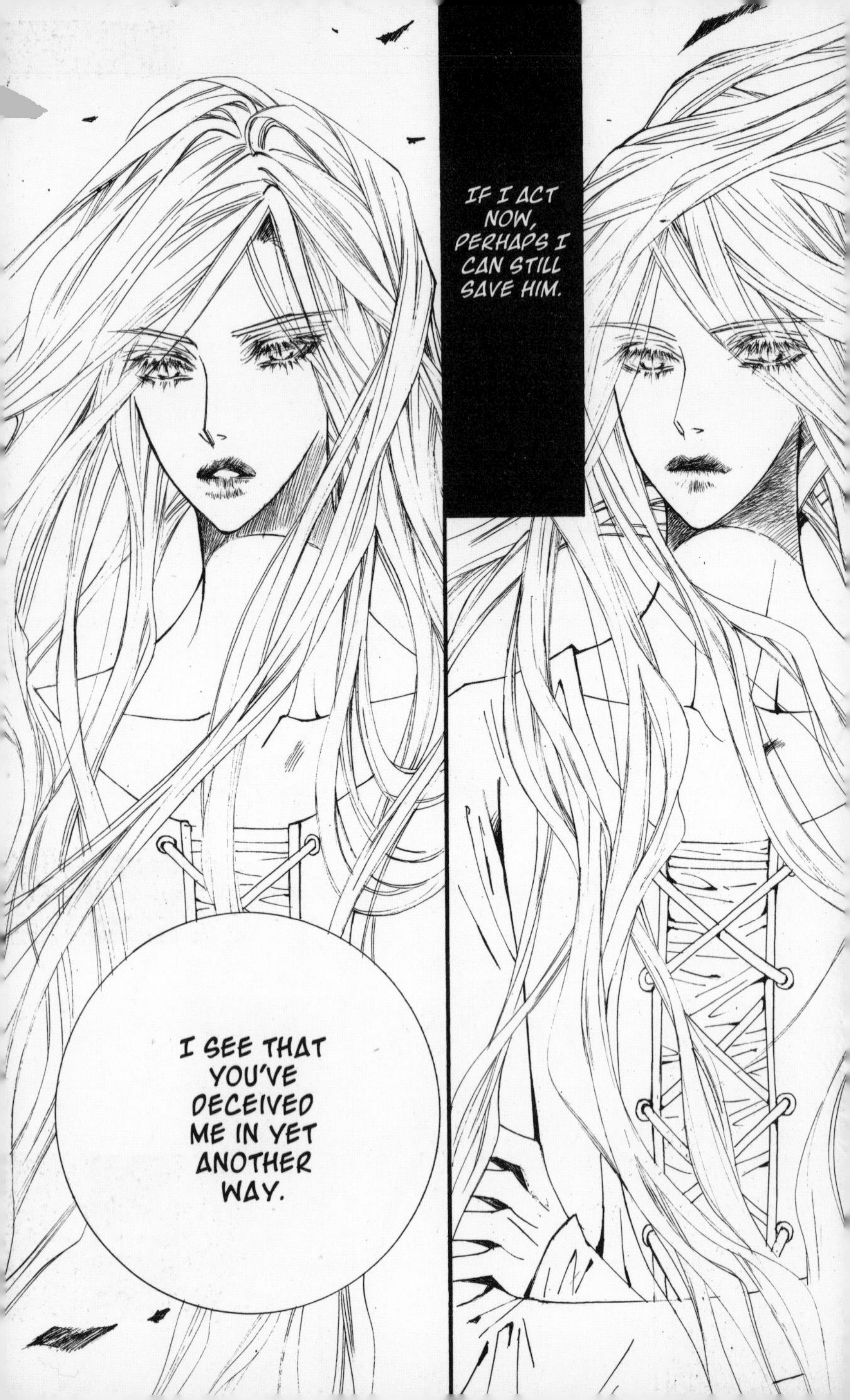
I SEE THAT YOU'VE DECEIVED ME IN YET ANOTHER WAY.
IF I ACT NOW, PERHAPS I CAN STILL SAVE HIM.

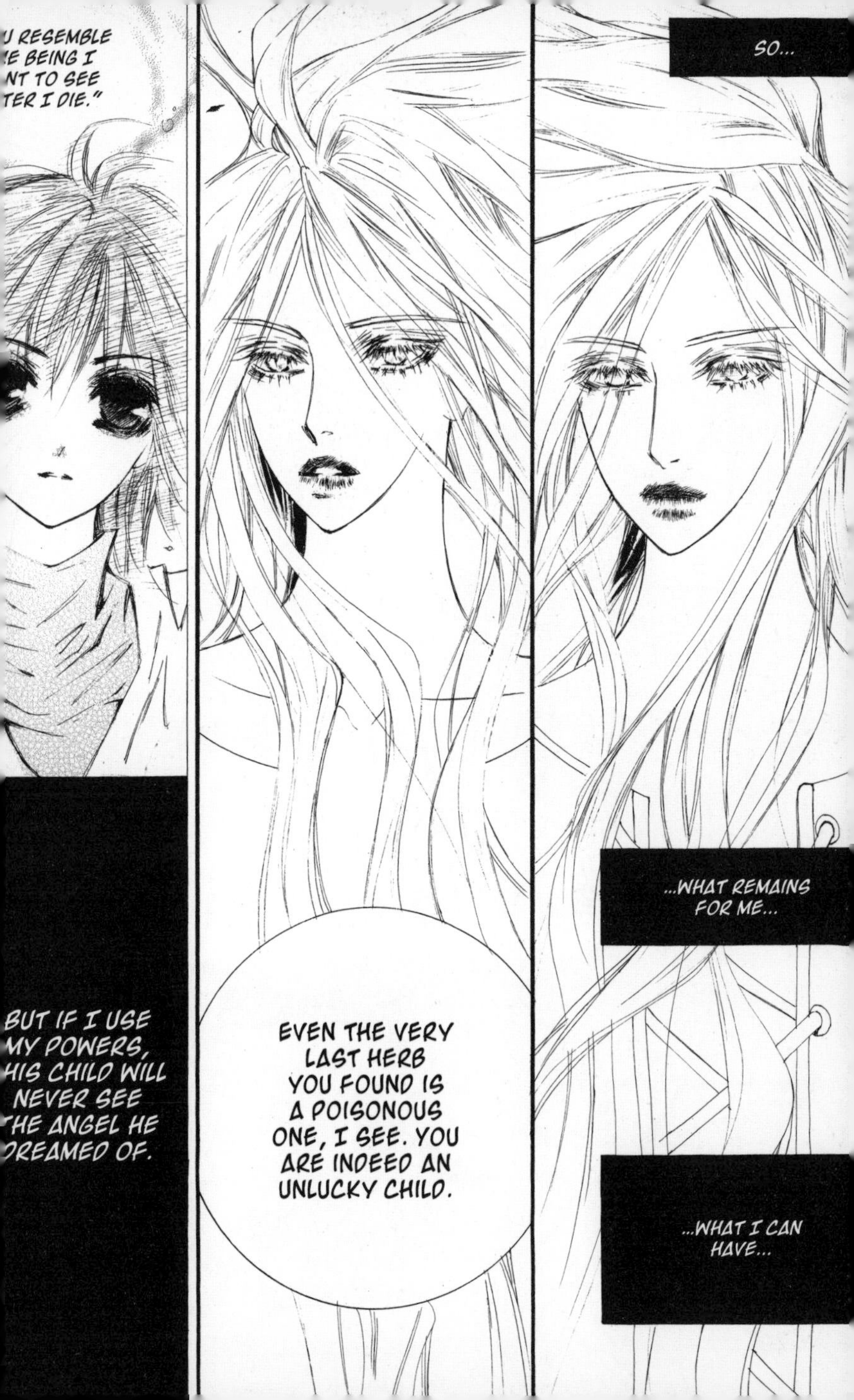
U RESEMBLE E BEING I NT TO SEE TER I DIE."
BUT IF I USE MY POWERS, HIS CHILD WILL NEVER SEE THE ANGEL HE DREAMED OF.
EVEN THE VERY LAST HERB YOU FOUND IS A POISONOUS ONE, I SEE. YOU ARE INDEED AN UNLUCKY CHILD.
SO...
...WHAT REMAINS FOR ME...
...WHAT I CAN HAVE...

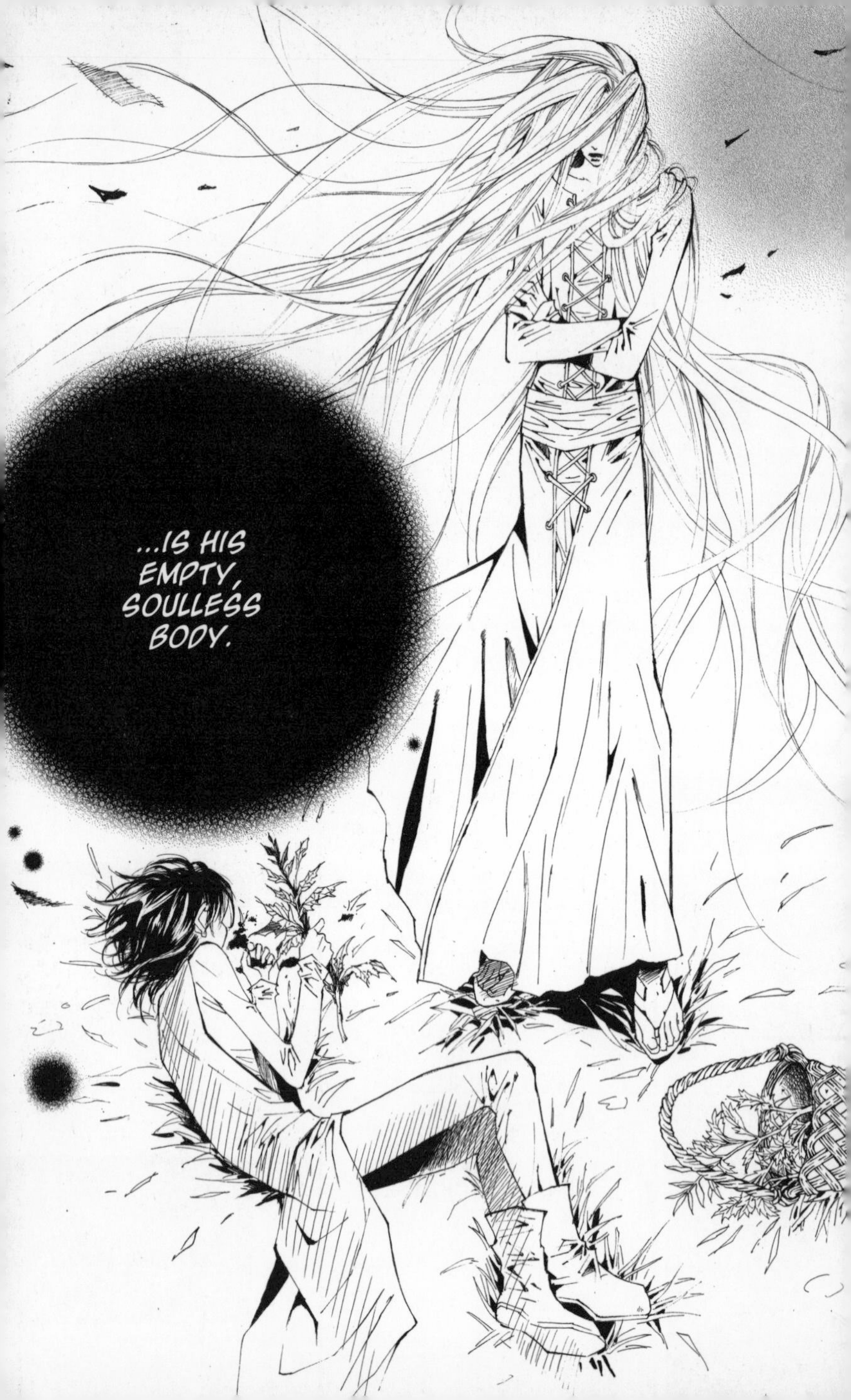
...IS HIS EMPTY, SOULLESS BODY.

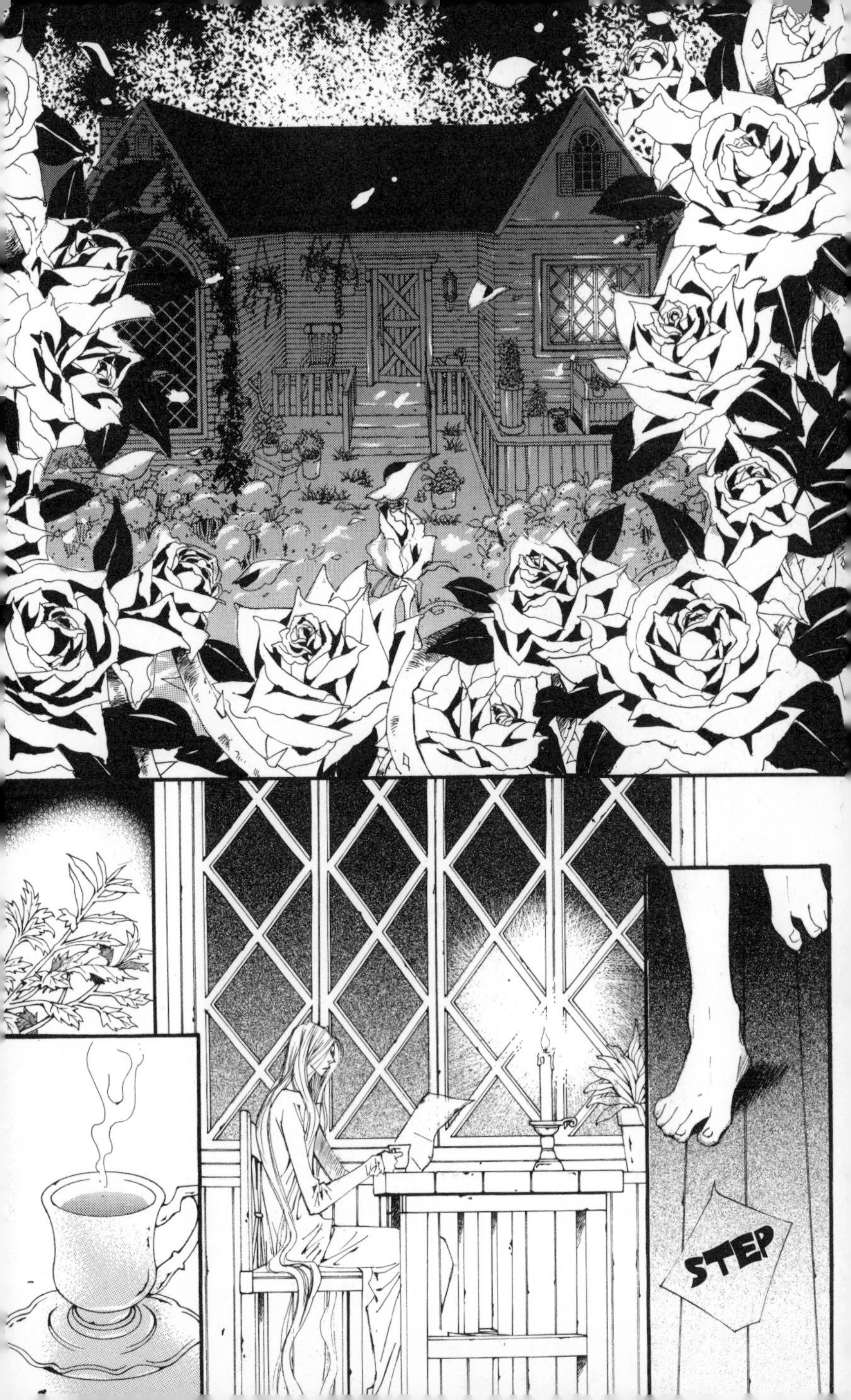
STEP

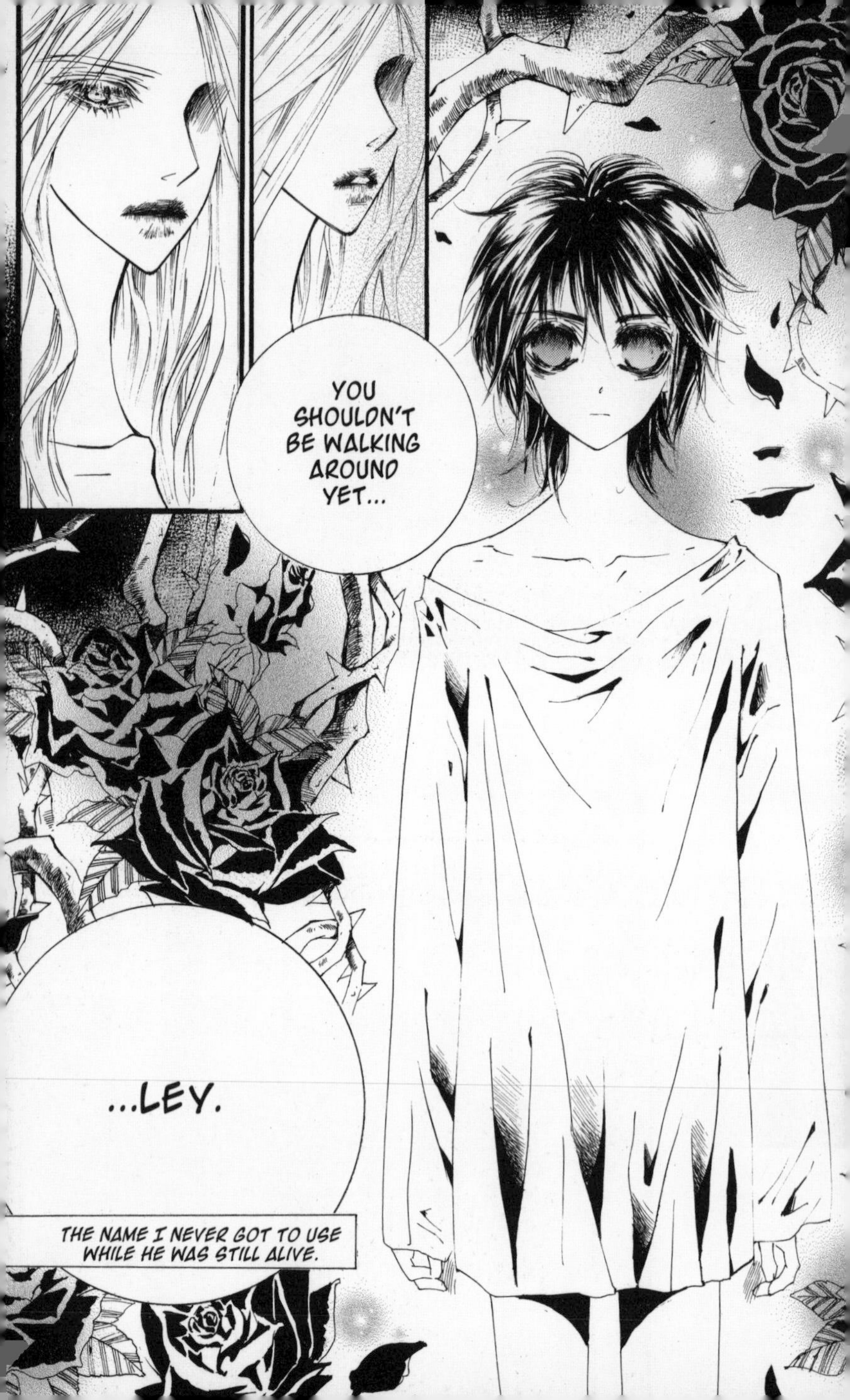
YOU SHOULDN'T BE WALKING AROUND YET...
...LEY.
THE NAME I NEVER GOT TO USE WHILE HE WAS STILL ALIVE.

COLD AND STIFF BODY.

EMPTY EYES THAT DON'T SEE ANYTHING.

A DEAD CHILD.

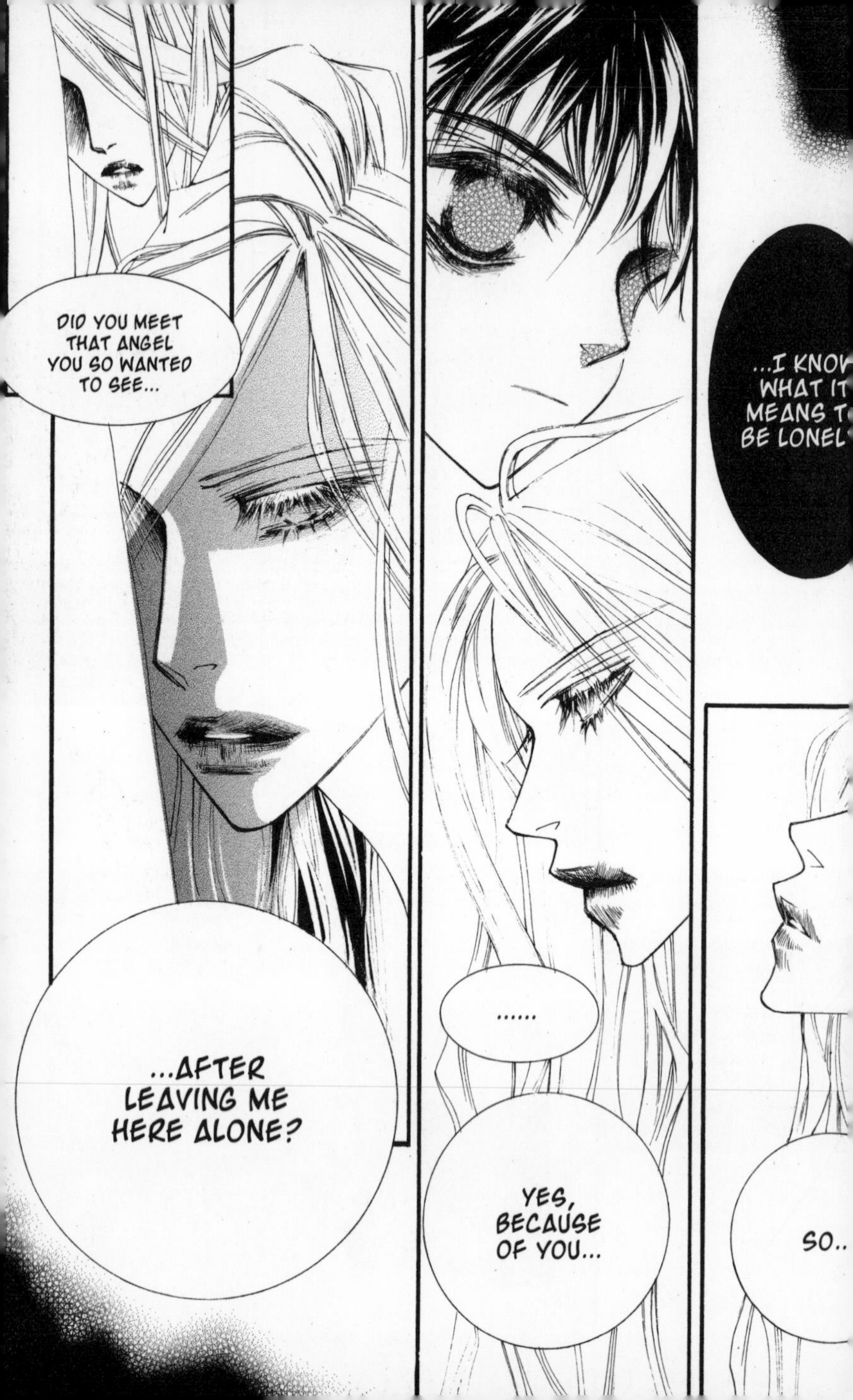
DID YOU MEET THAT ANGEL YOU SO WANTED TO SEE...
...AFTER LEAVING ME HERE ALONE?
......
YES, BECAUSE OF YOU...
...I KNOW WHAT IT MEANS T BE LONEL
SO..

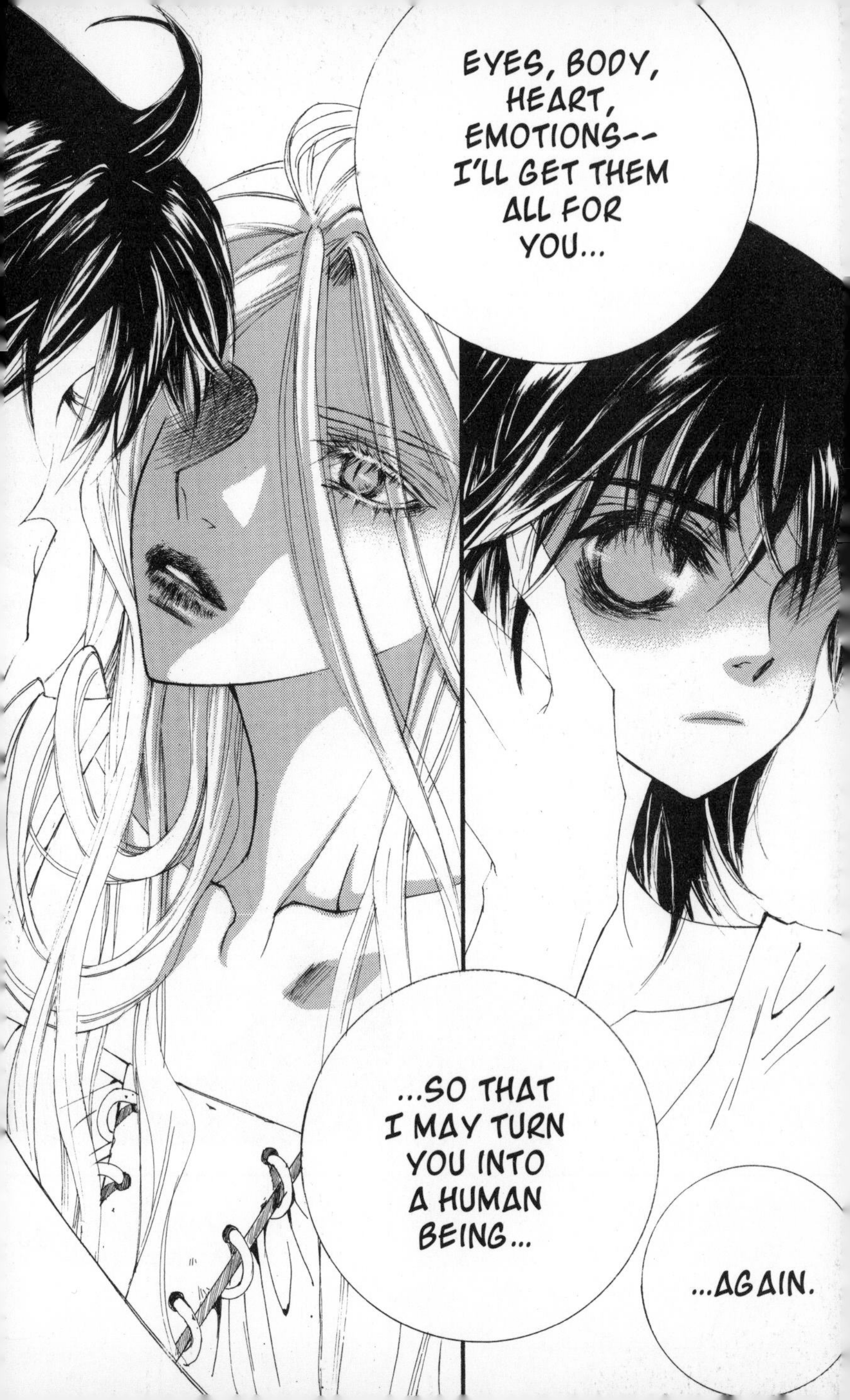
EYES, BODY, HEART, EMOTIONS-- I'LL GET THEM ALL FOR YOU...
...SO THAT I MAY TURN YOU INTO A HUMAN BEING...
...AGAIN.

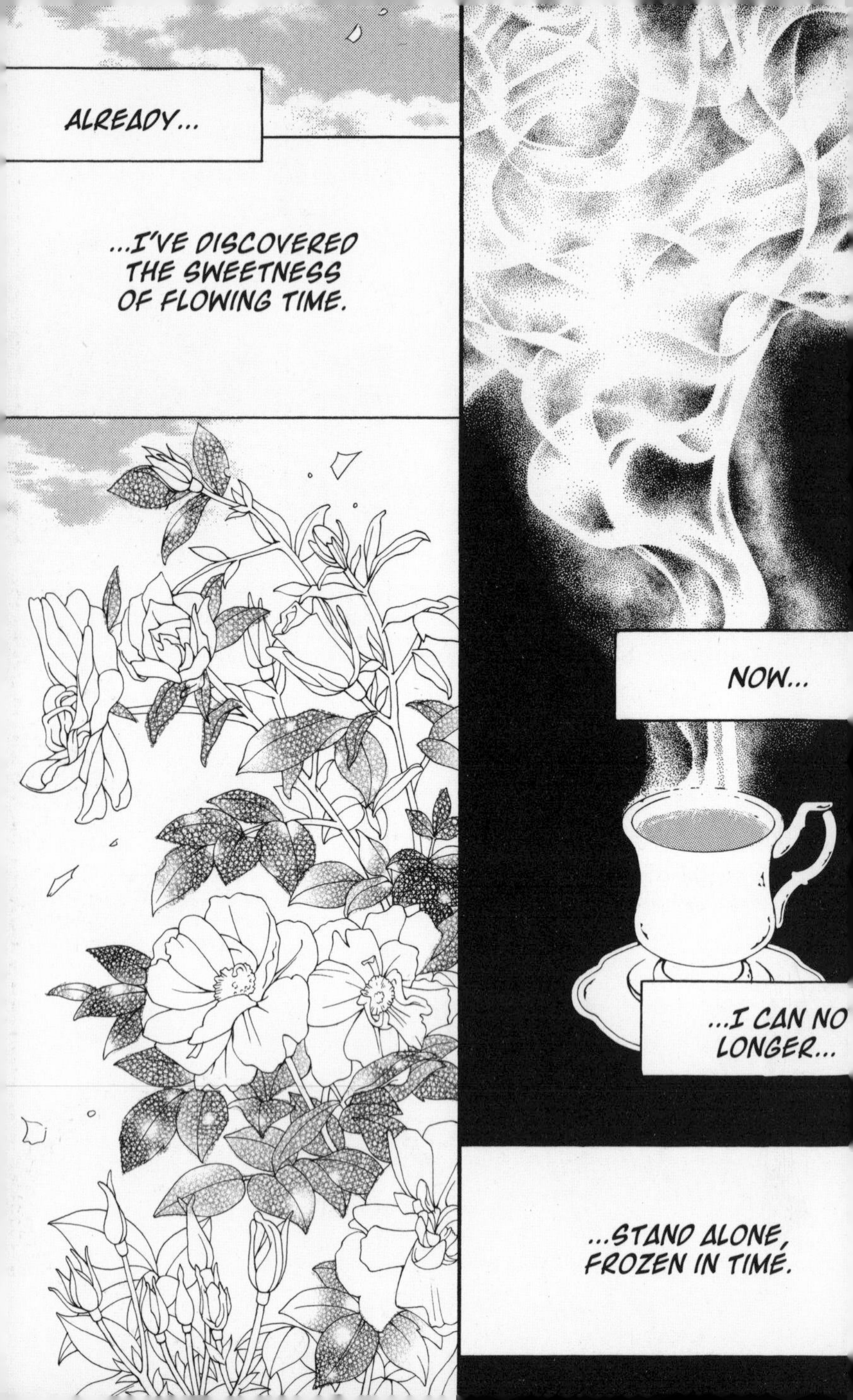
ALREADY...
...I'VE DISCOVERED THE SWEETNESS OF FLOWING TIME.
NOW...
...I CAN NO LONGER...
...STAND ALONE, FROZEN IN TIME.

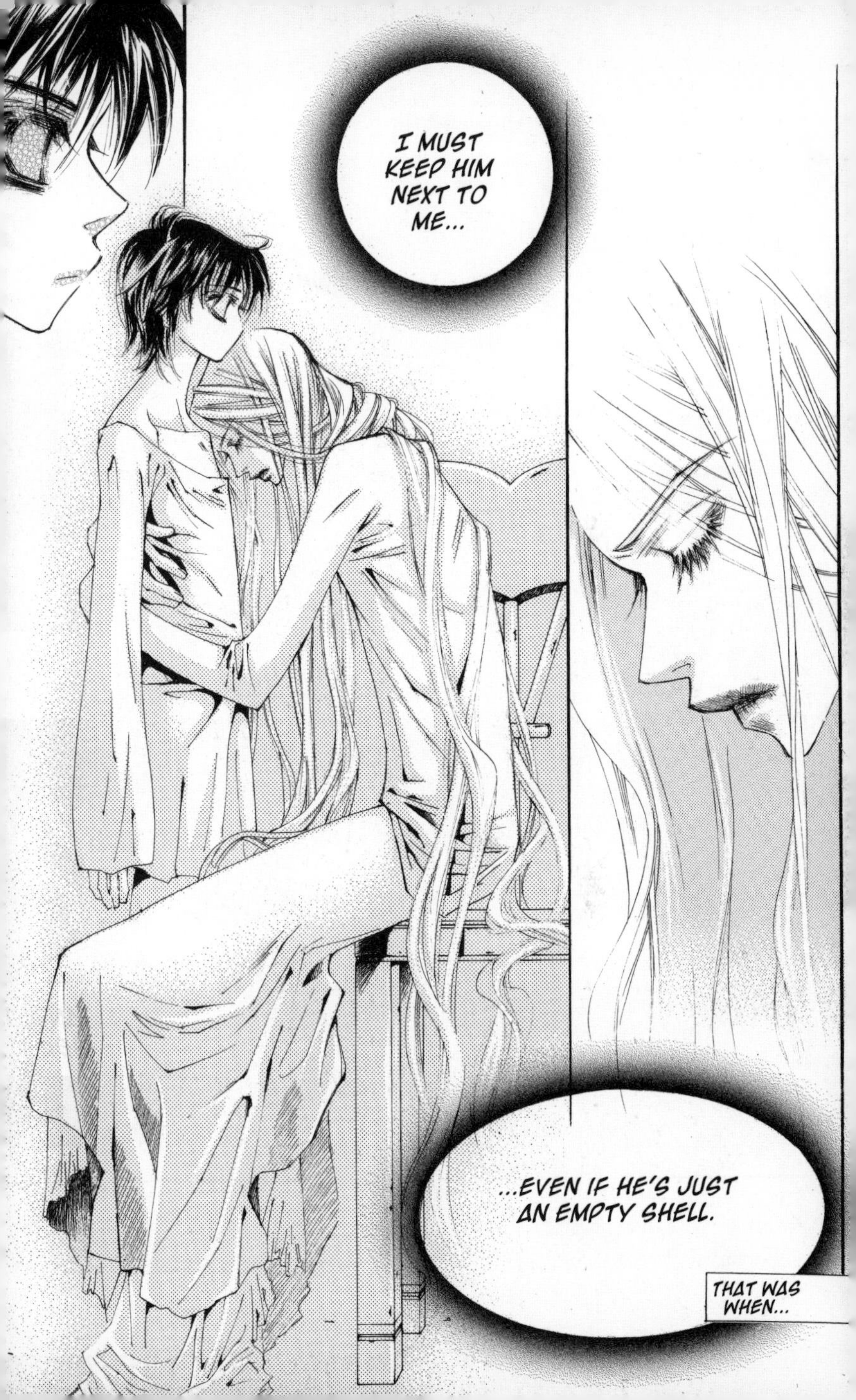
I MUST KEEP HIM NEXT TO ME...
...EVEN IF HE'S JUST AN EMPTY SHELL.
THAT WAS WHEN...

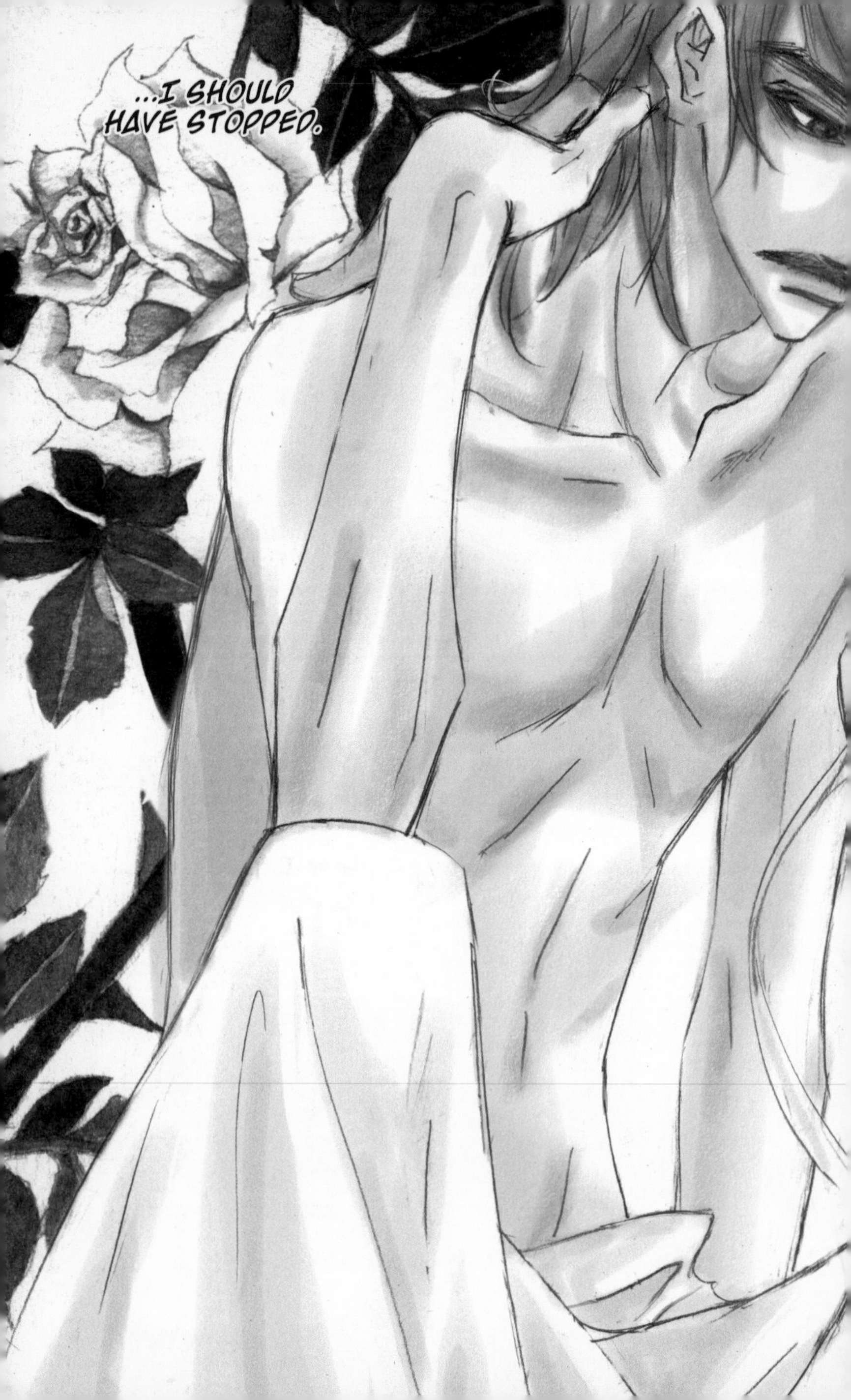
...I SHOULD HAVE STOPPED.

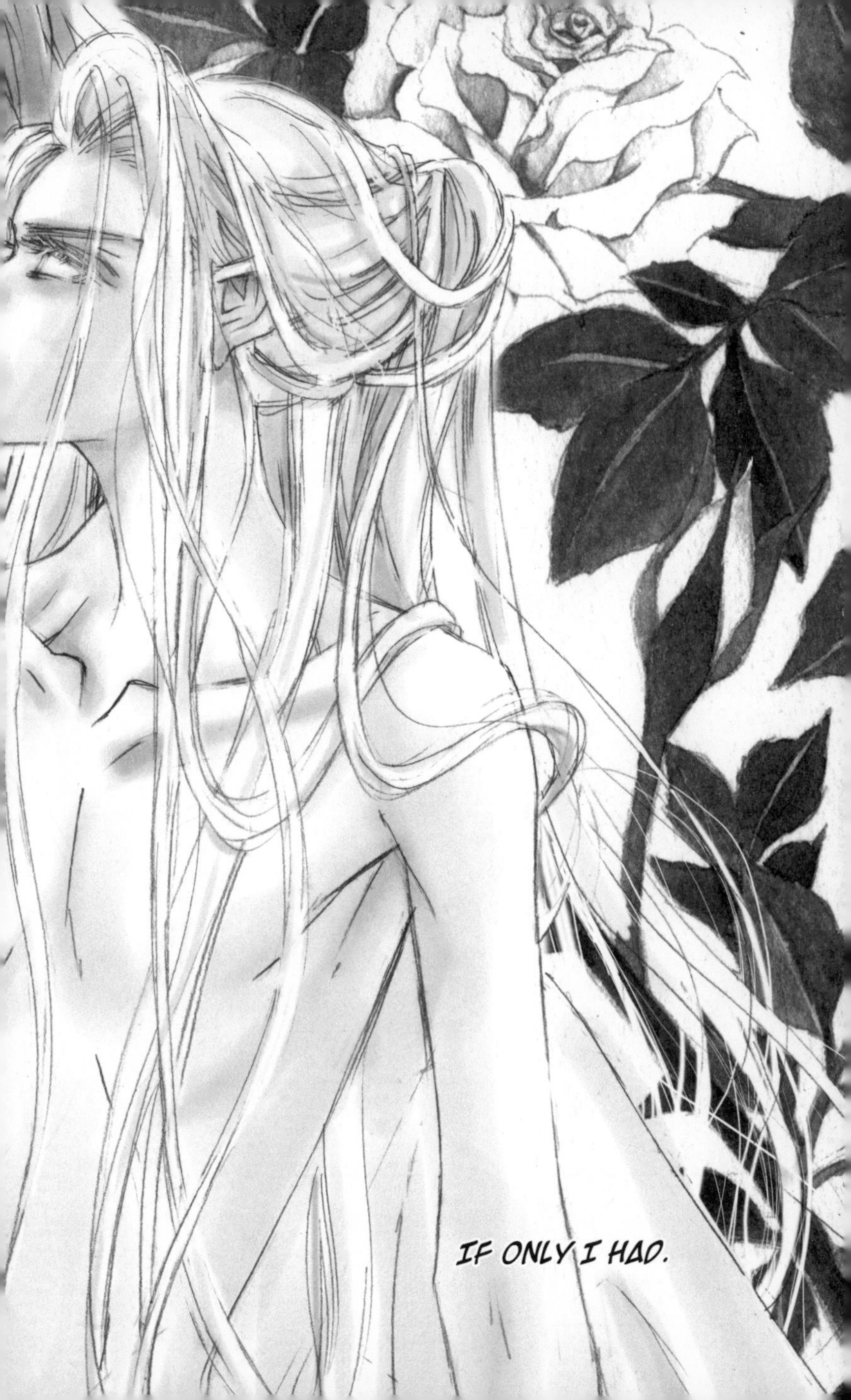
IF ONLY I HAD.

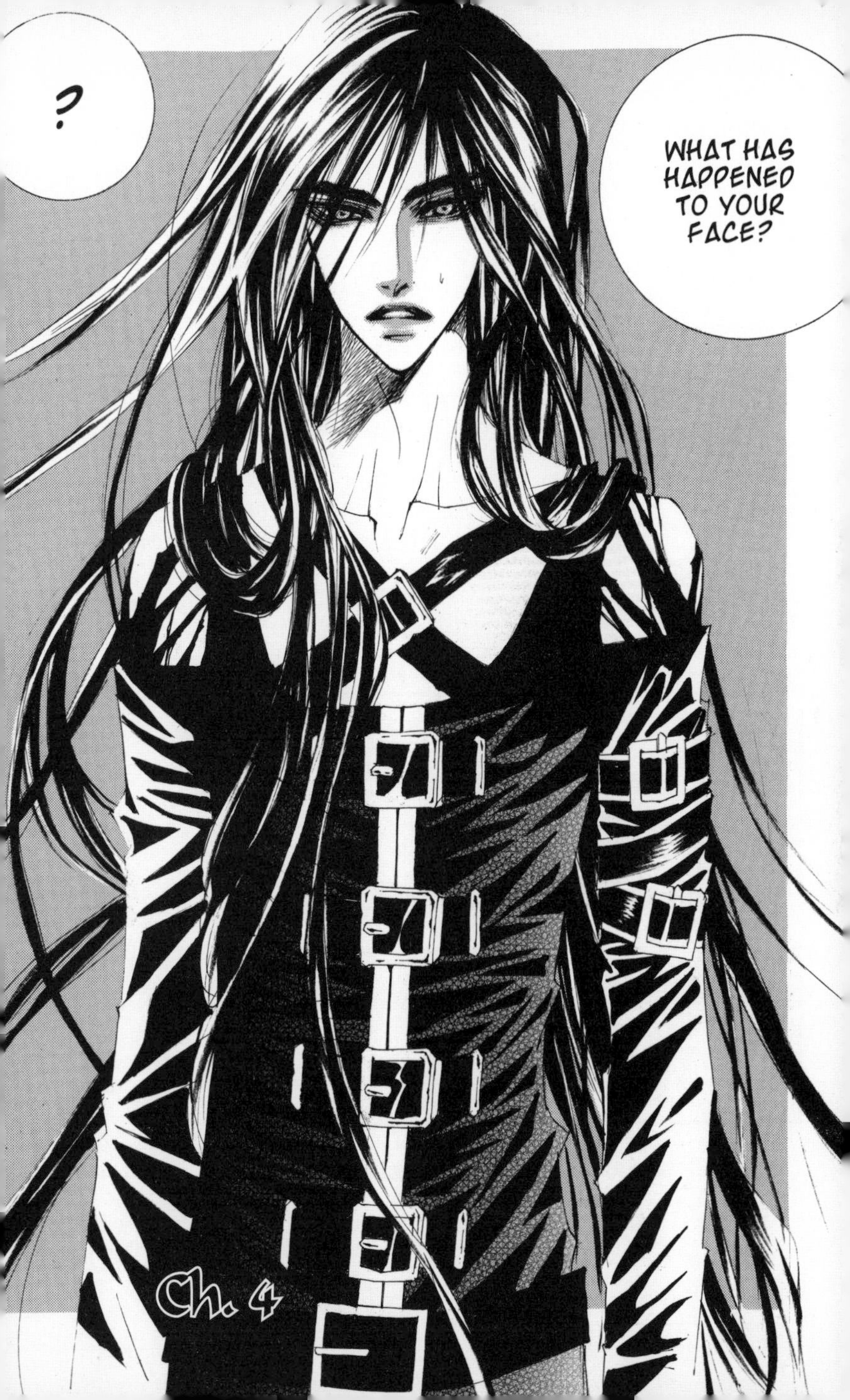
?
WHAT HAS HAPPENED TO YOUR FACE?
Ch. 4

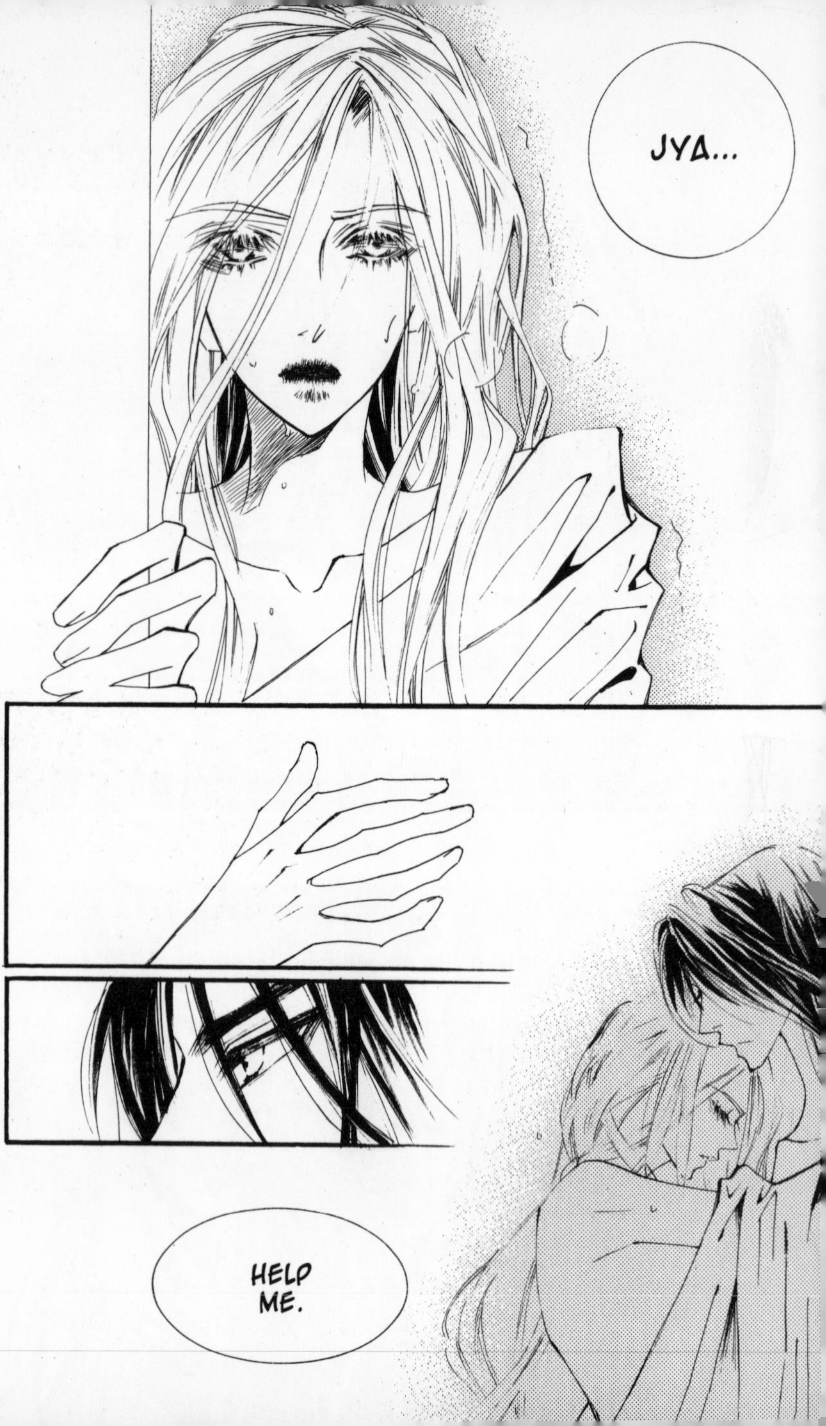
JYA...
HELP ME.

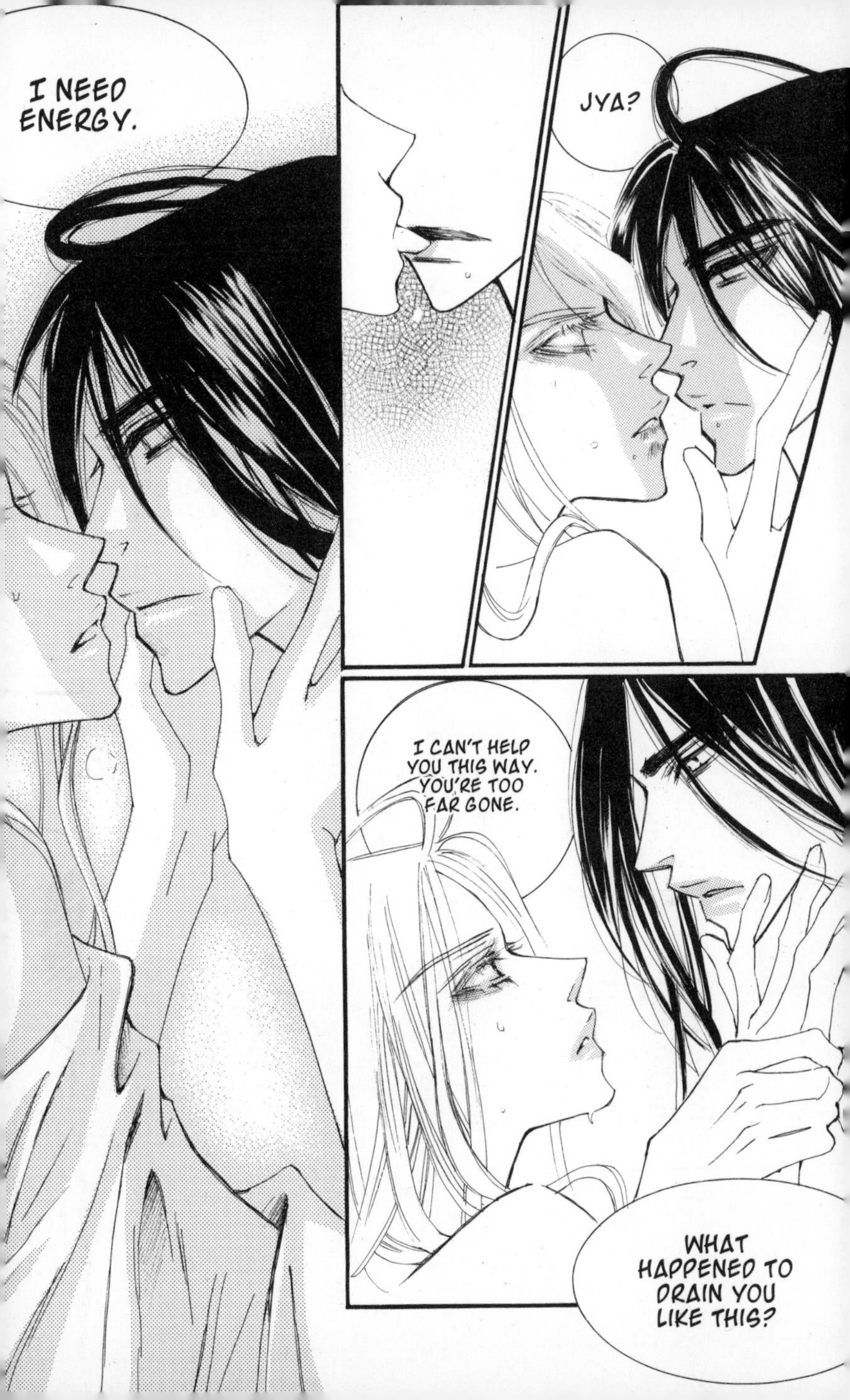
I NEED ENERGY.
JYA?
I CAN'T HELP YOU THIS WAY. YOU'RE TOO FAR GONE.
WHAT HAPPENED TO DRAIN YOU LIKE THIS?

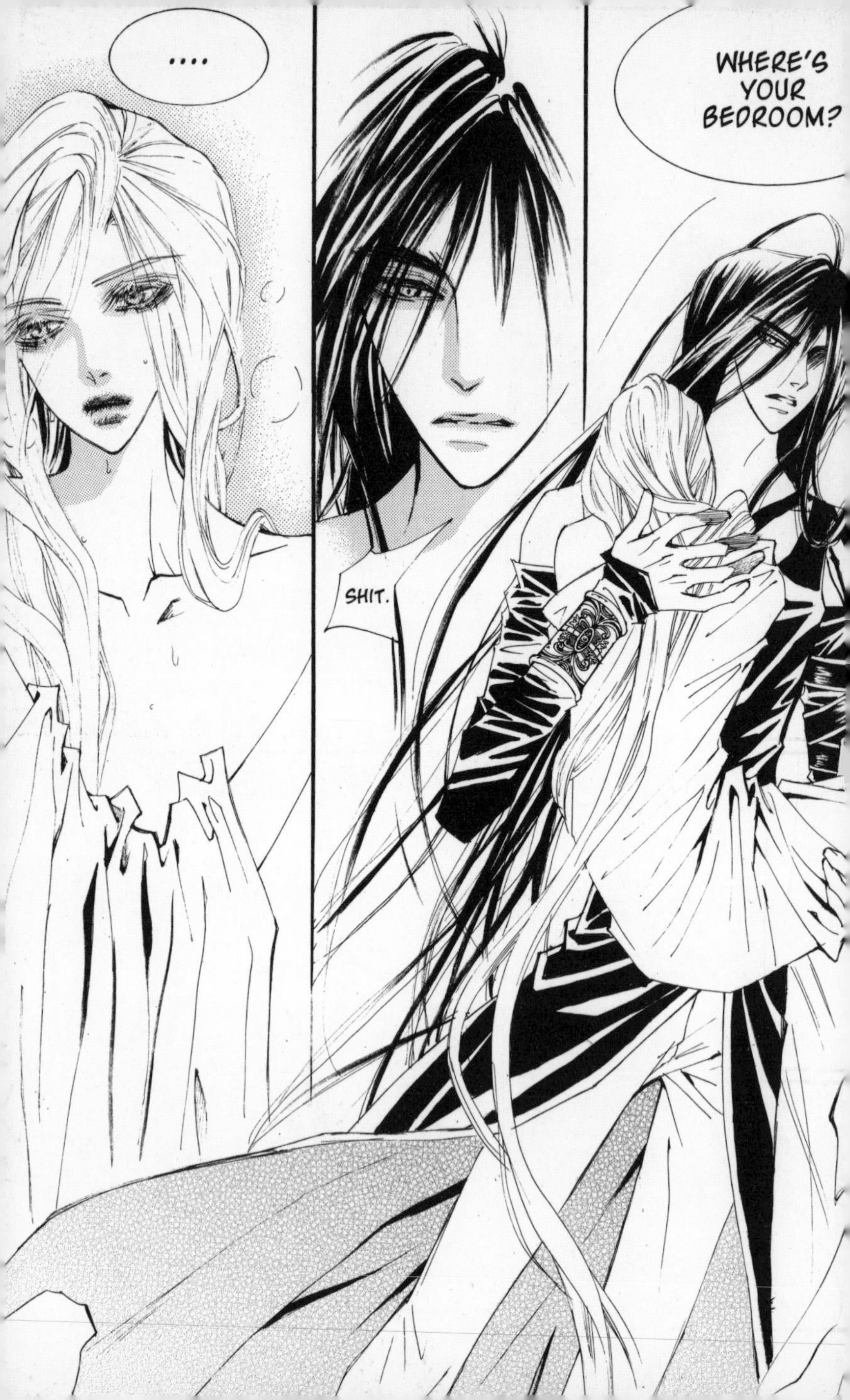
....
SHIT.
WHERE'S YOUR BEDROOM?

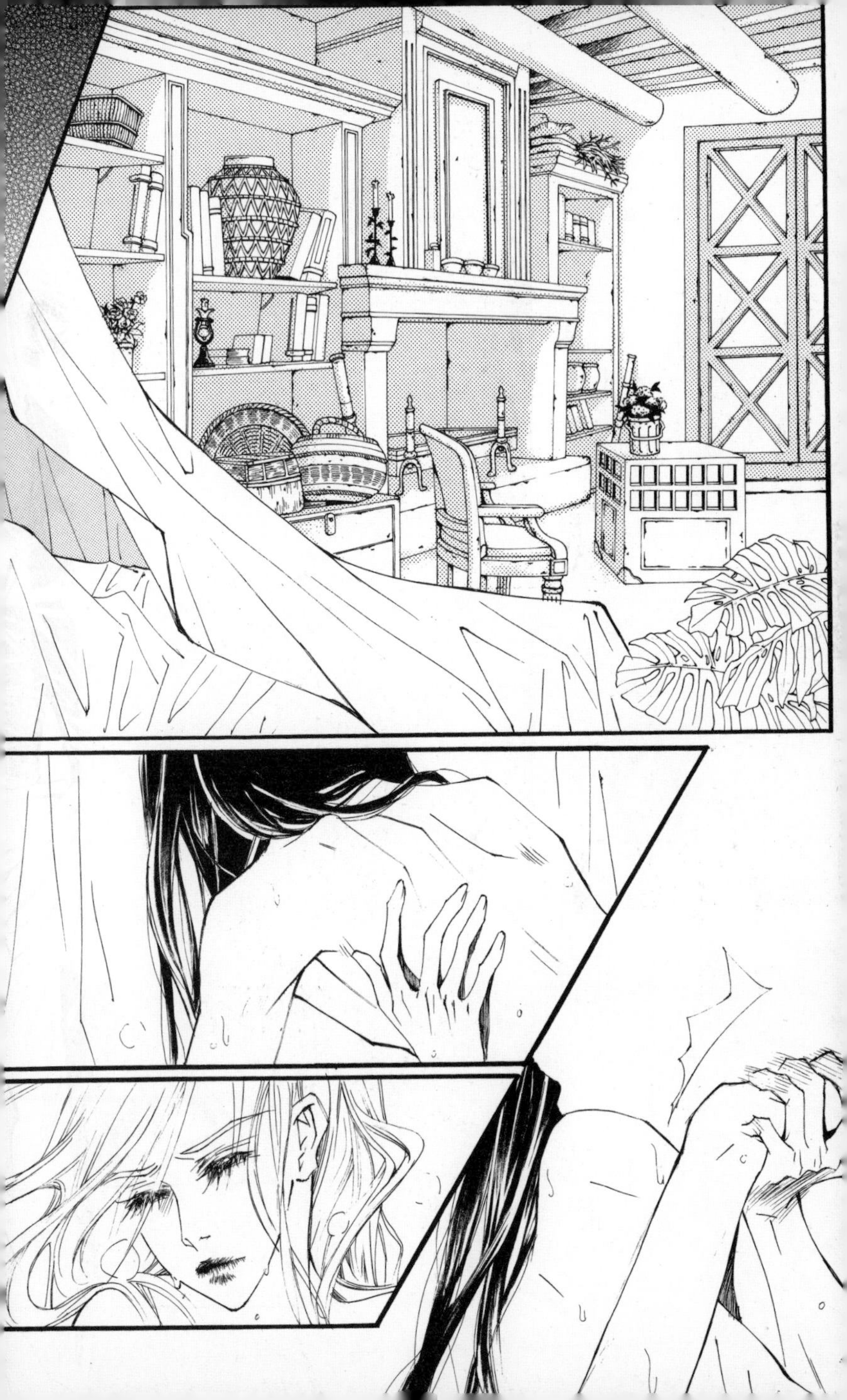

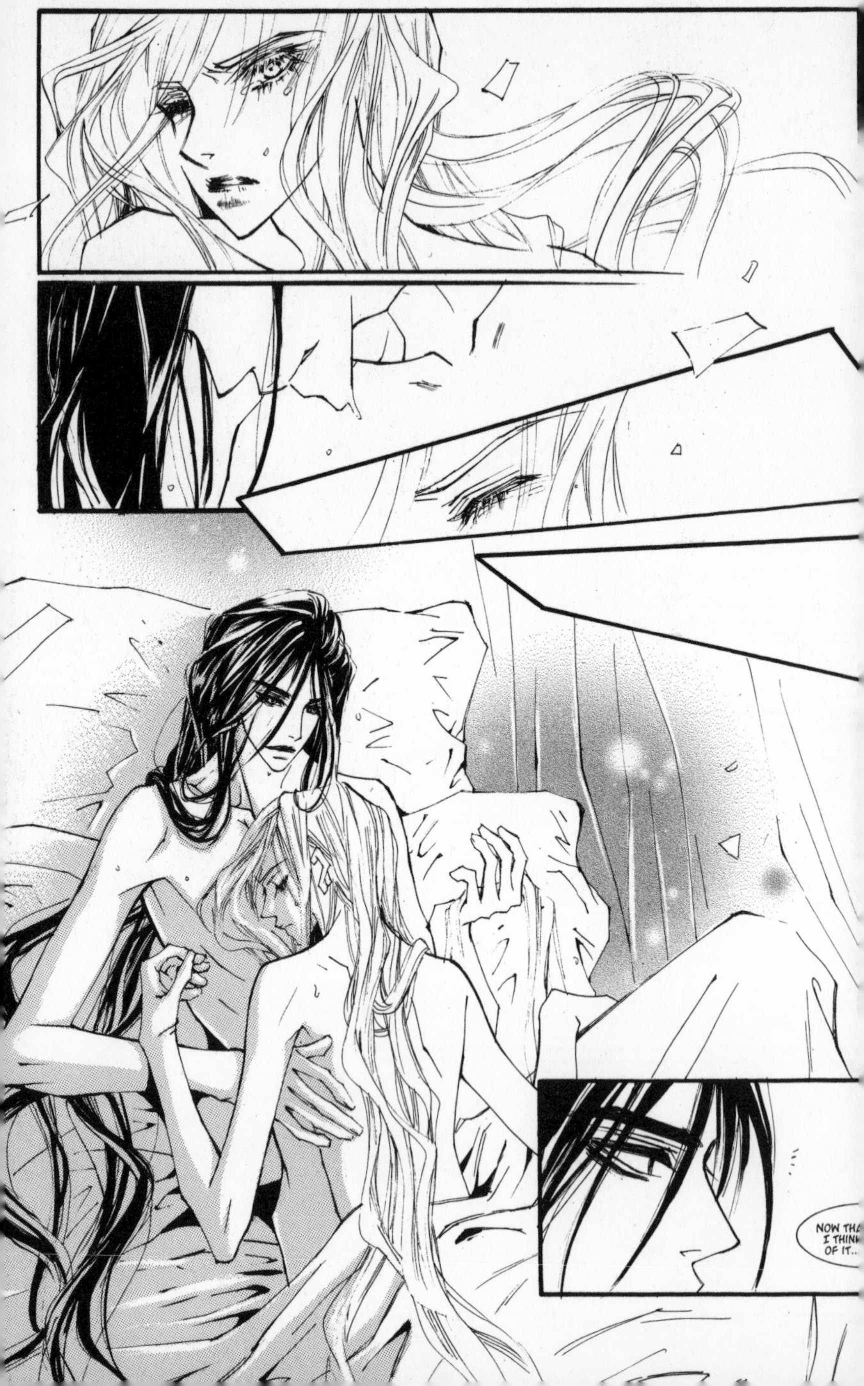
NOW THA
I THINK
OF IT...

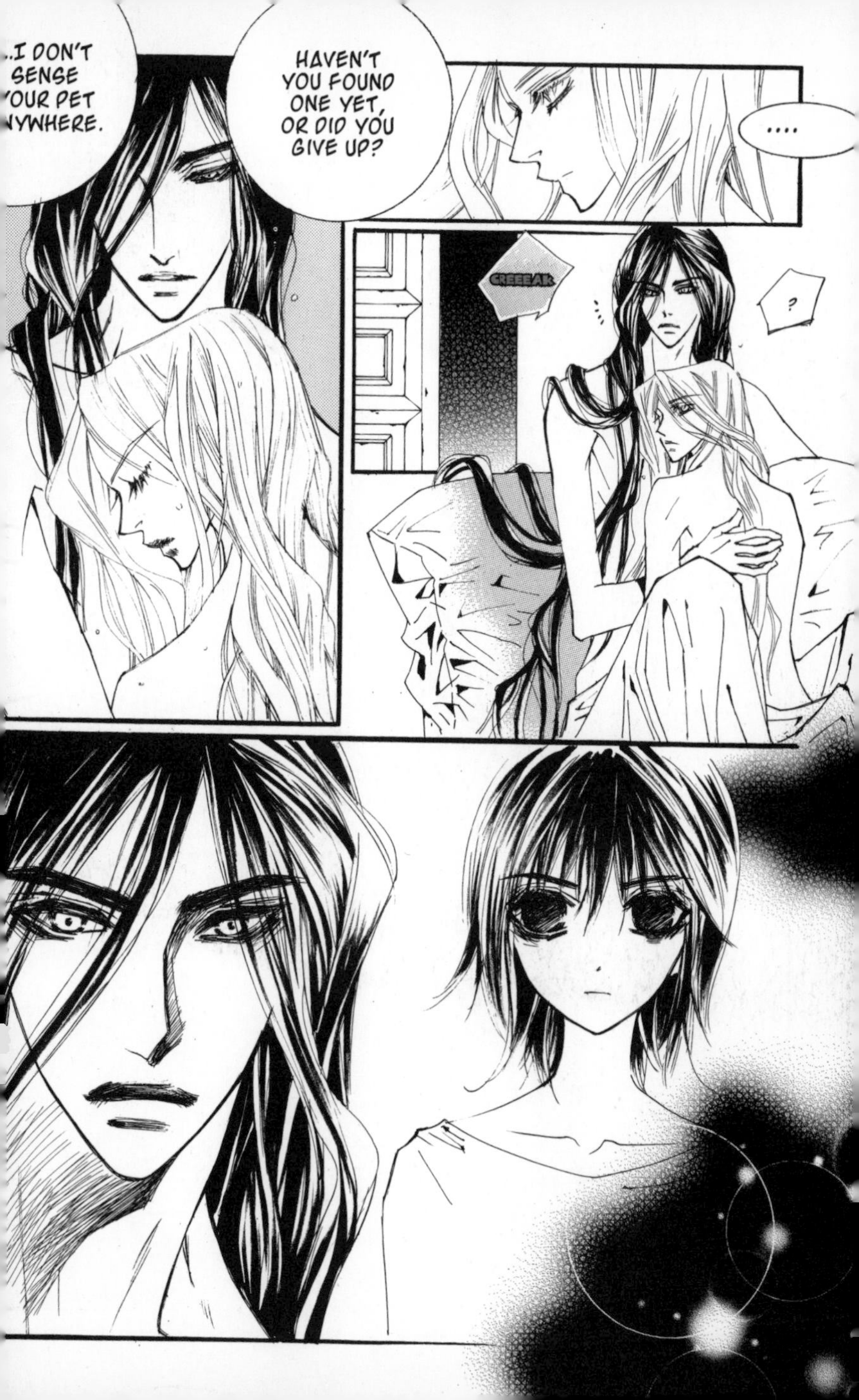
..I DON'T SENSE 'OUR PET NYWHERE.
HAVEN'T YOU FOUND ONE YET, OR DID YOU GIVE UP?
....
CREEEAK
?

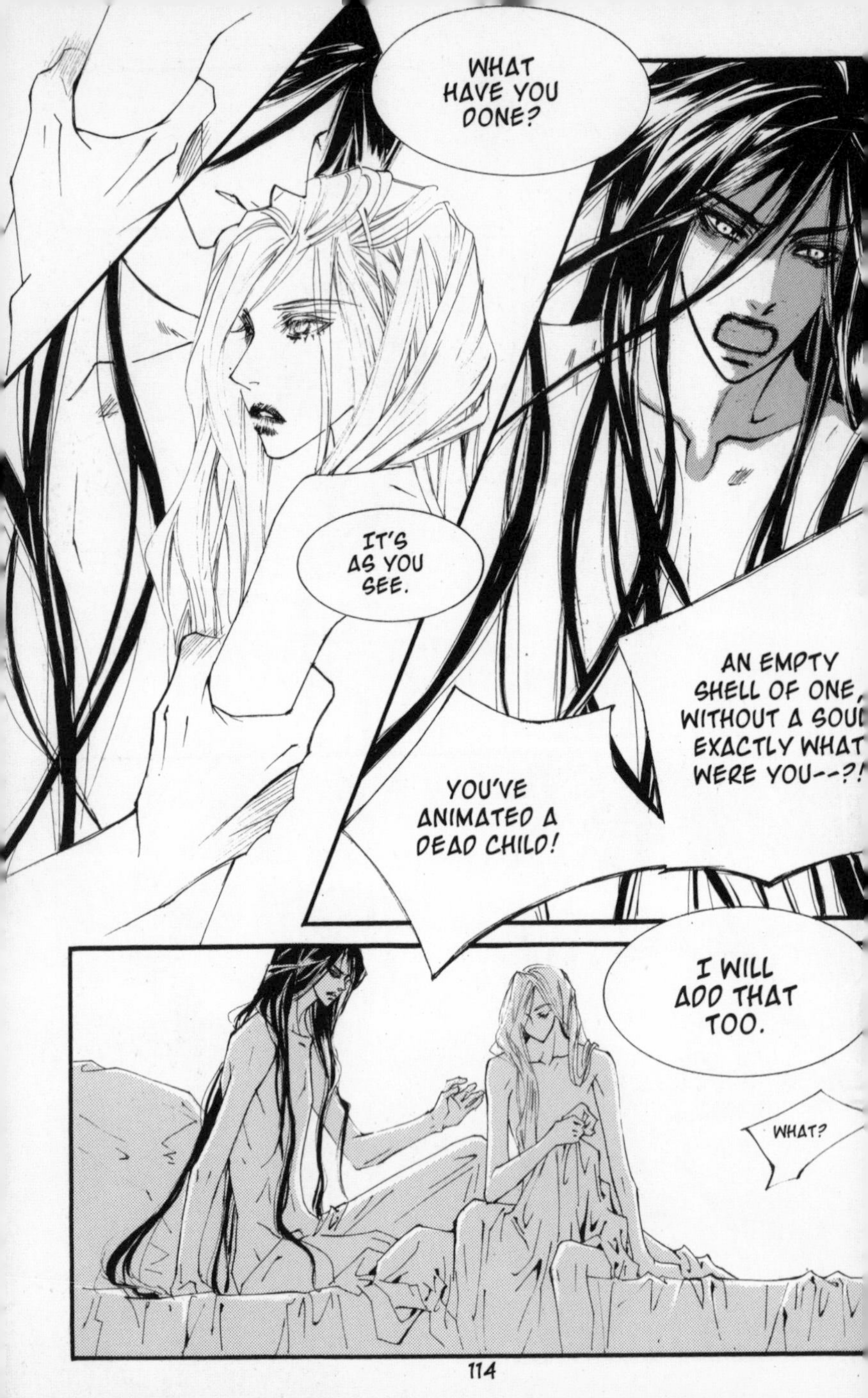
WHAT HAVE YOU DONE?
IT'S AS YOU SEE.
YOU'VE ANIMATED A DEAD CHILD!
AN EMPTY SHELL OF ONE, WITHOUT A SOUL EXACTLY WHAT WERE YOU--?!
I WILL ADD THAT TOO.
WHAT?

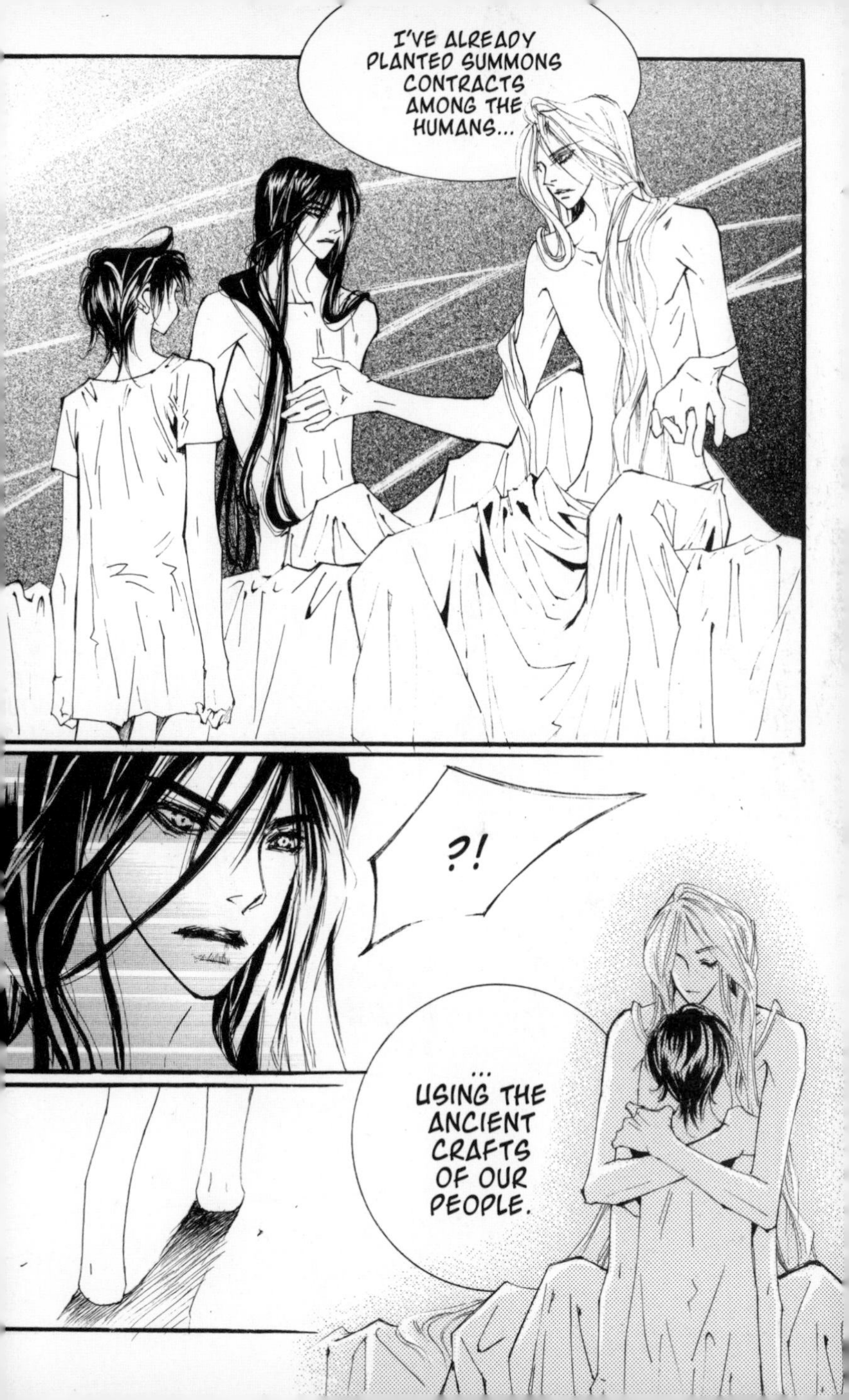
I'VE ALREADY PLANTED SUMMONS CONTRACTS AMONG THE HUMANS...
?!
... USING THE ANCIENT CRAFTS OF OUR PEOPLE.

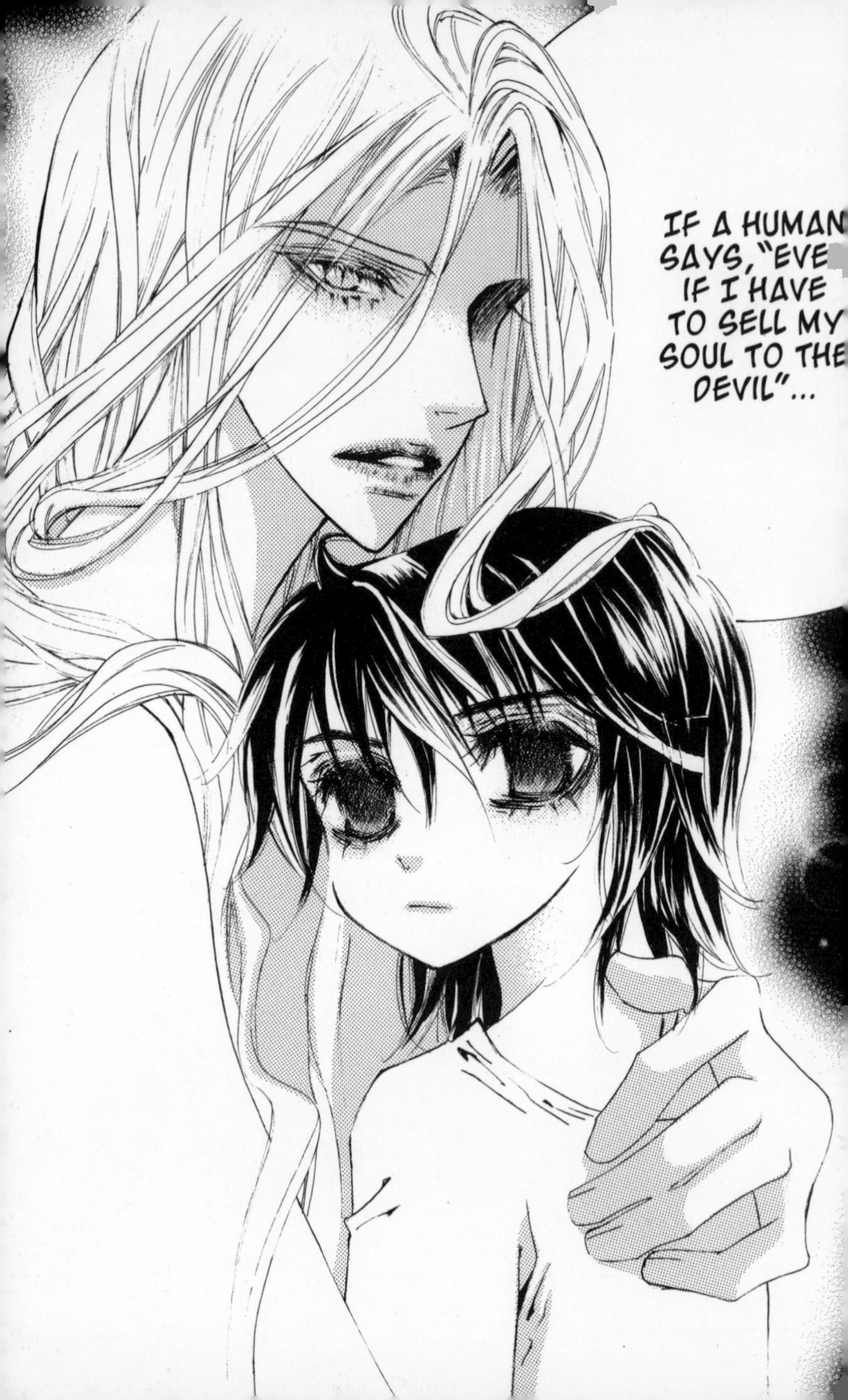
IF A HUMAN SAYS, "EVE IF I HAVE TO SELL MY SOUL TO THE DEVIL"...

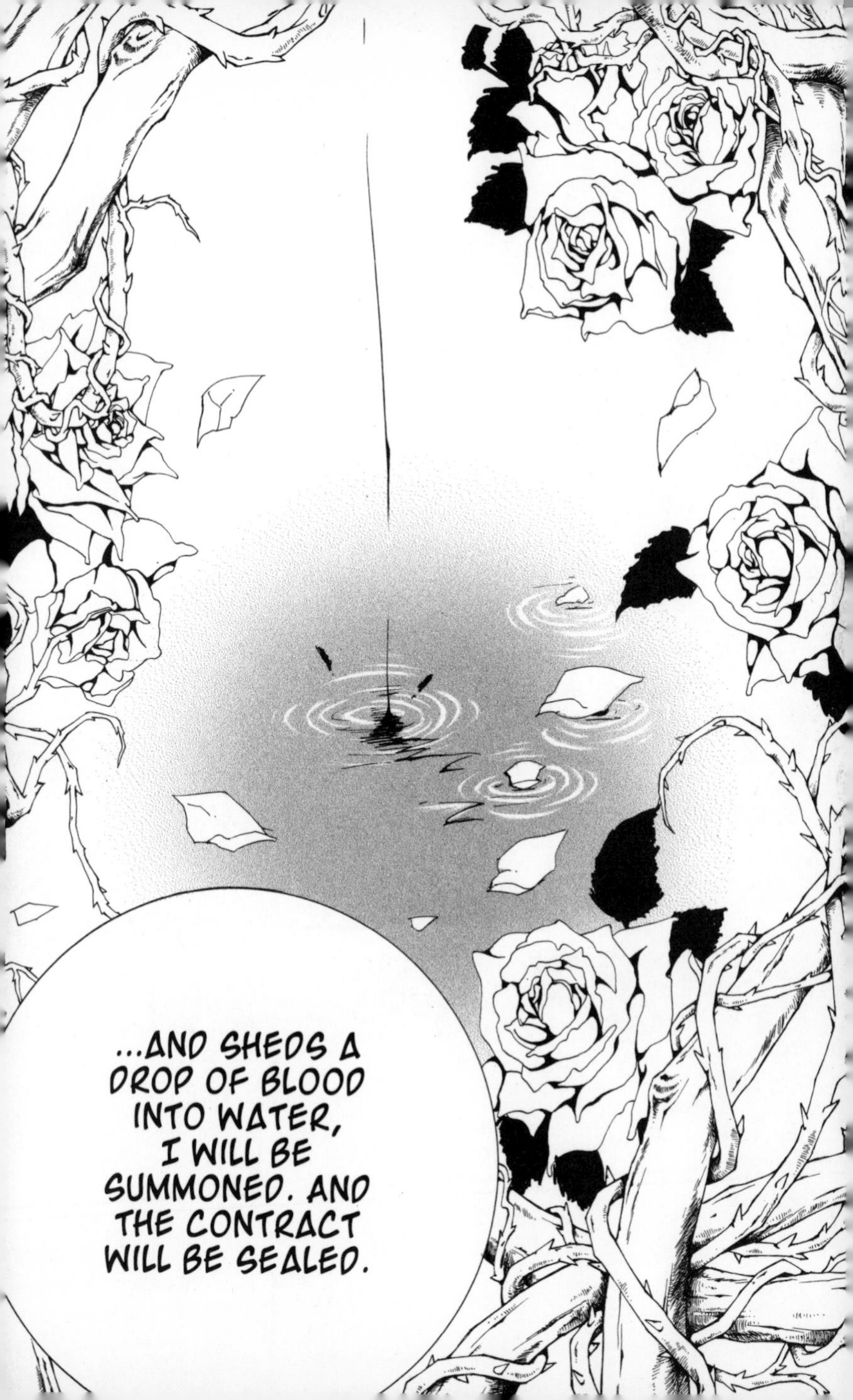
...AND SHEDS A DROP OF BLOOD INTO WATER, I WILL BE SUMMONED. AND THE CONTRACT WILL BE SEALED.

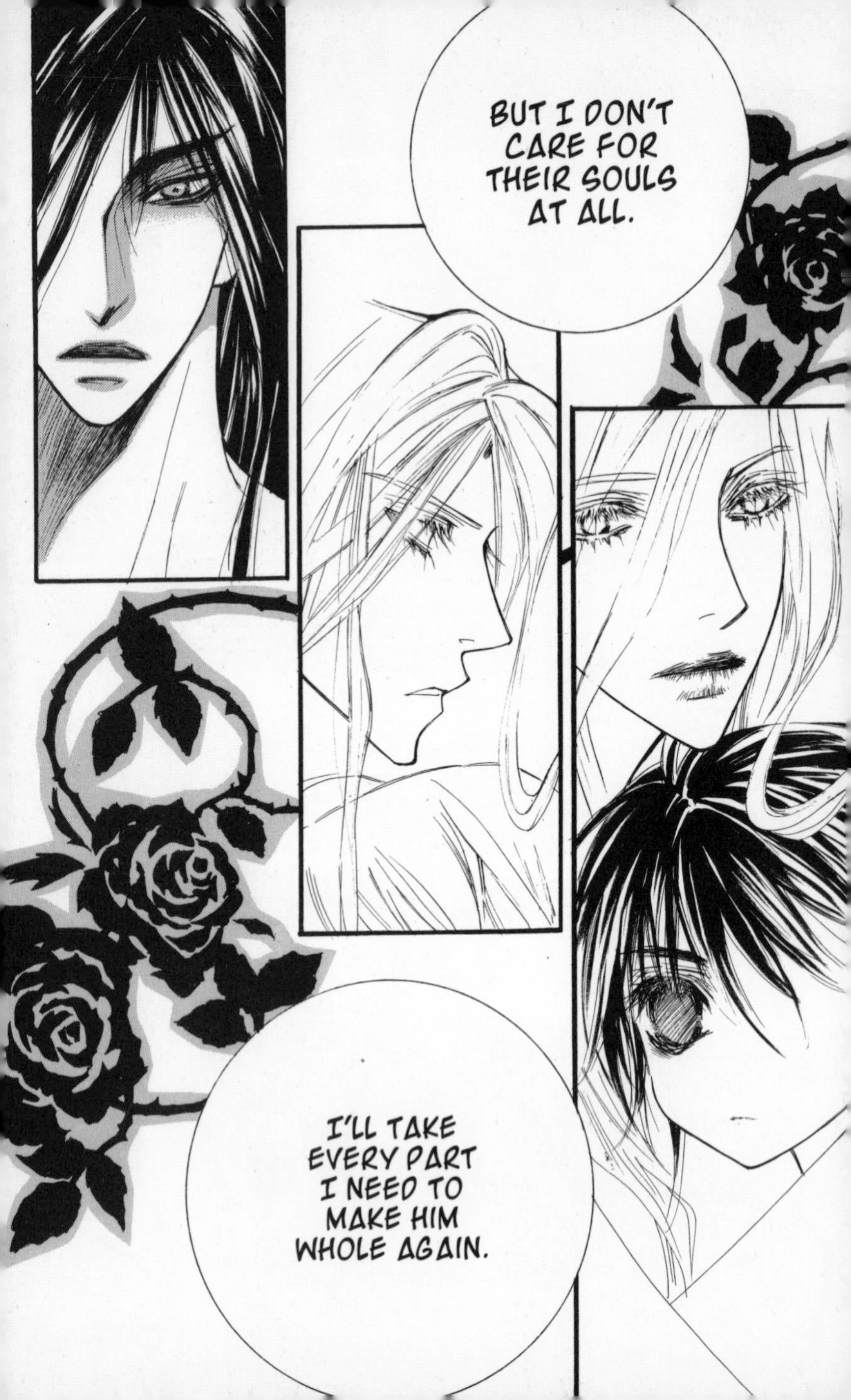
BUT I DON'T CARE FOR THEIR SOULS AT ALL.
I'LL TAKE EVERY PART I NEED TO MAKE HIM WHOLE AGAIN.

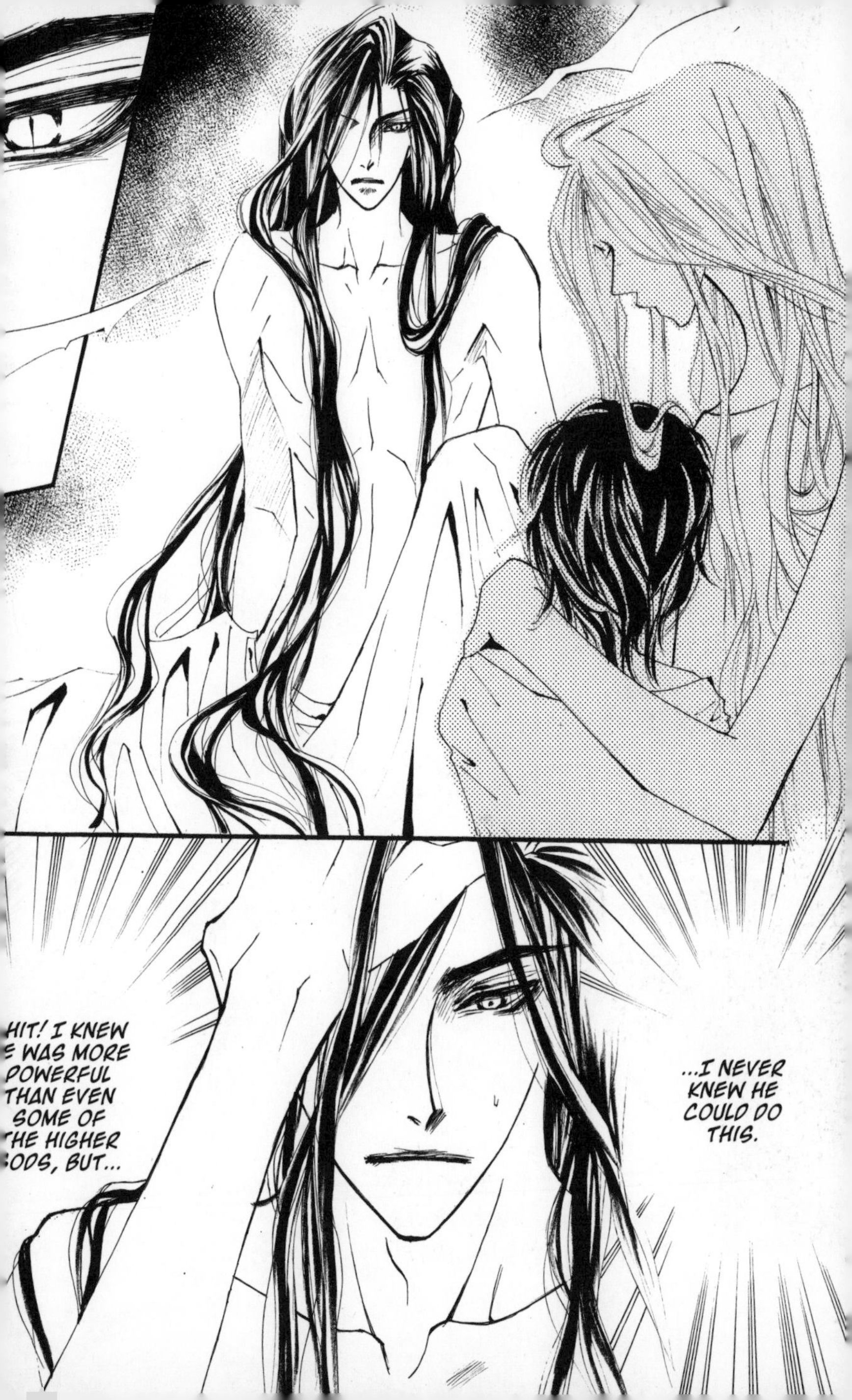
HIT! I KNEW
E WAS MORE
POWERFUL
THAN EVEN
SOME OF
THE HIGHER
ODS, BUT...
...I NEVER
KNEW HE
COULD DO
THIS.

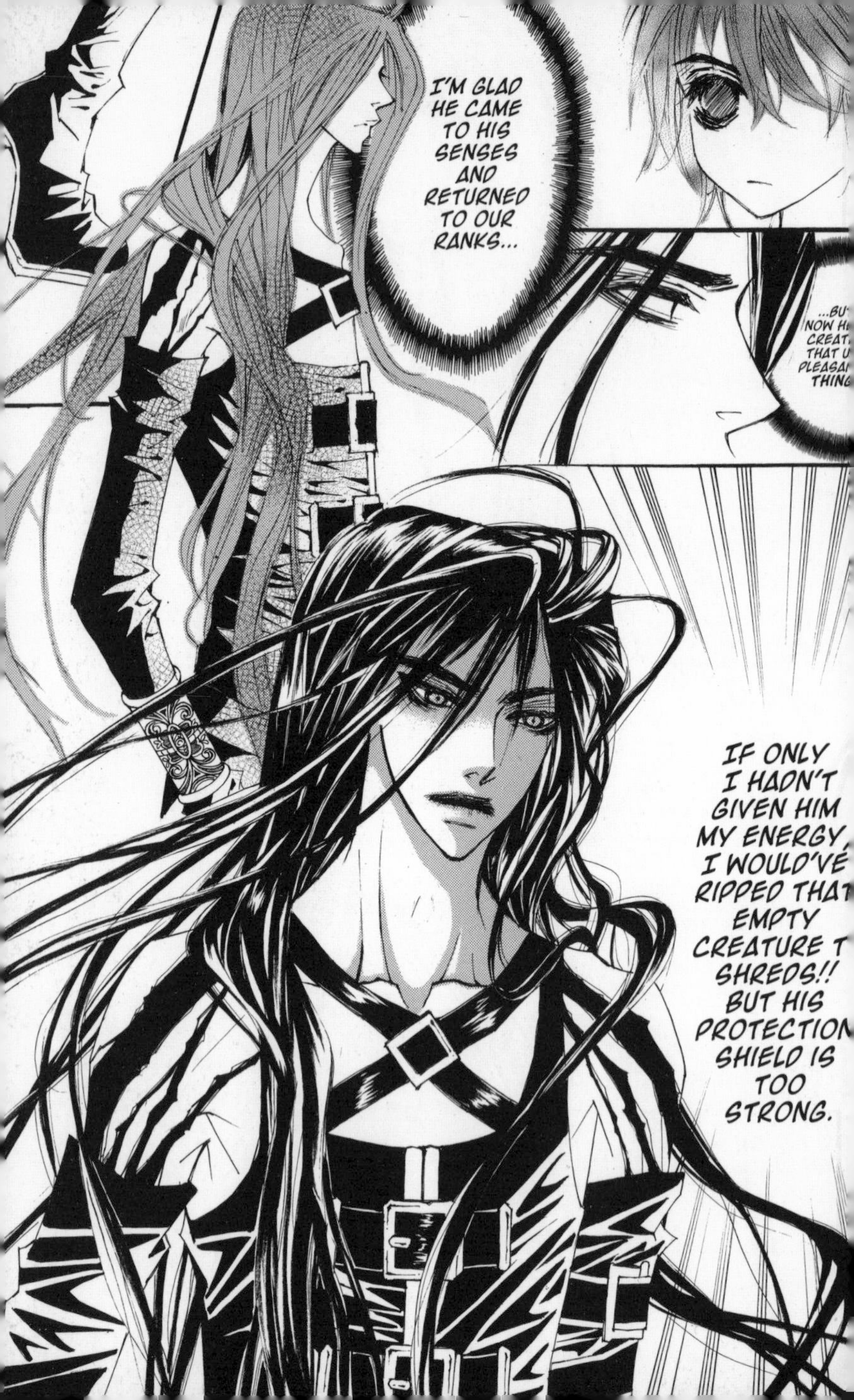
I'M GLAD HE CAME TO HIS SENSES AND RETURNED TO OUR RANKS...
...BUT NOW HI CREAT THAT U PLEASAN THING
IF ONLY I HADN'T GIVEN HIM MY ENERGY, I WOULD'VE RIPPED THAT EMPTY CREATURE T SHREDS!! BUT HIS PROTECTION SHIELD IS TOO STRONG.

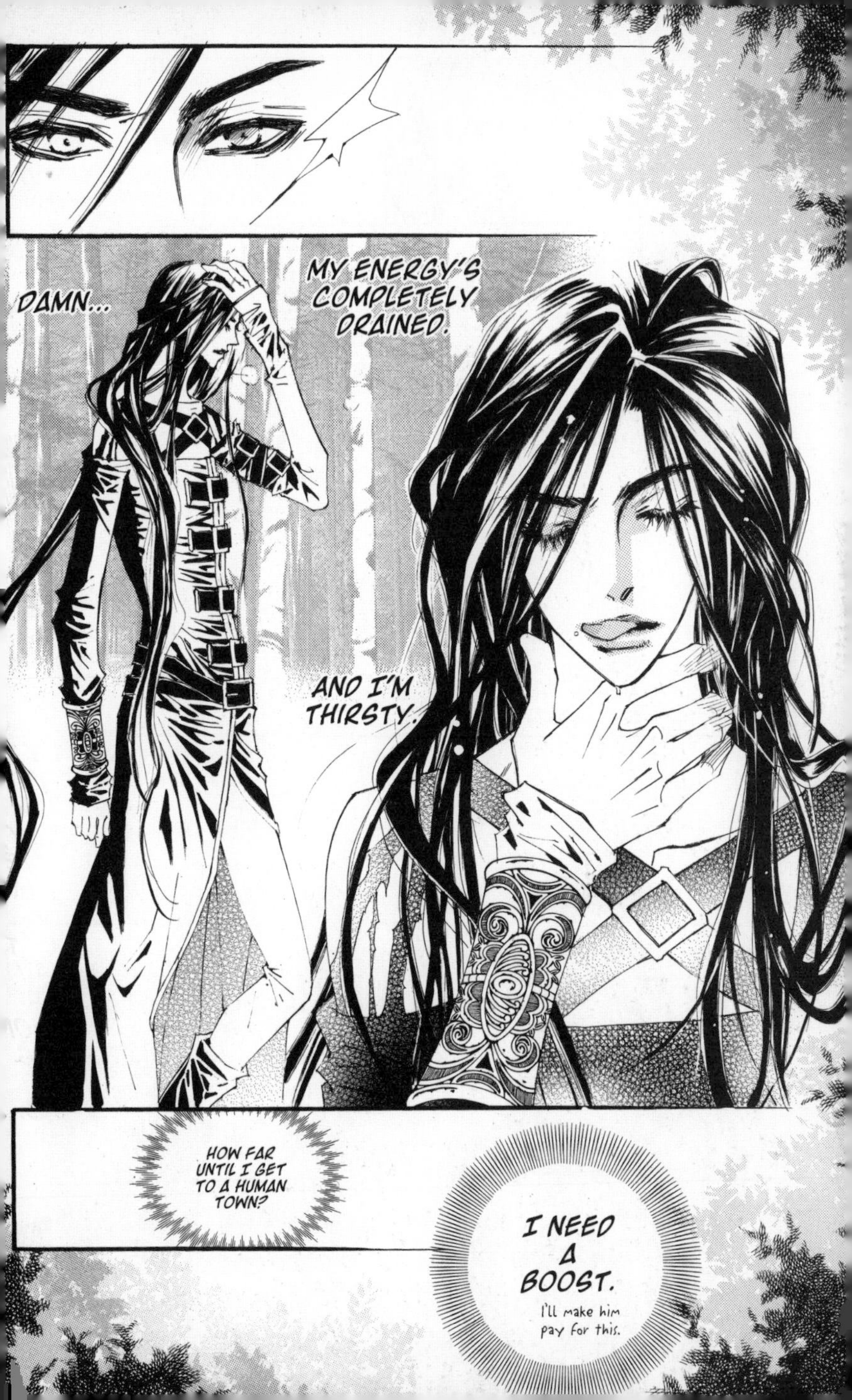
DAMN...
MY ENERGY'S COMPLETELY DRAINED.
AND I'M THIRSTY.
HOW FAR UNTIL I GET TO A HUMAN TOWN?
I NEED A BOOST.
I'll make him pay for this.

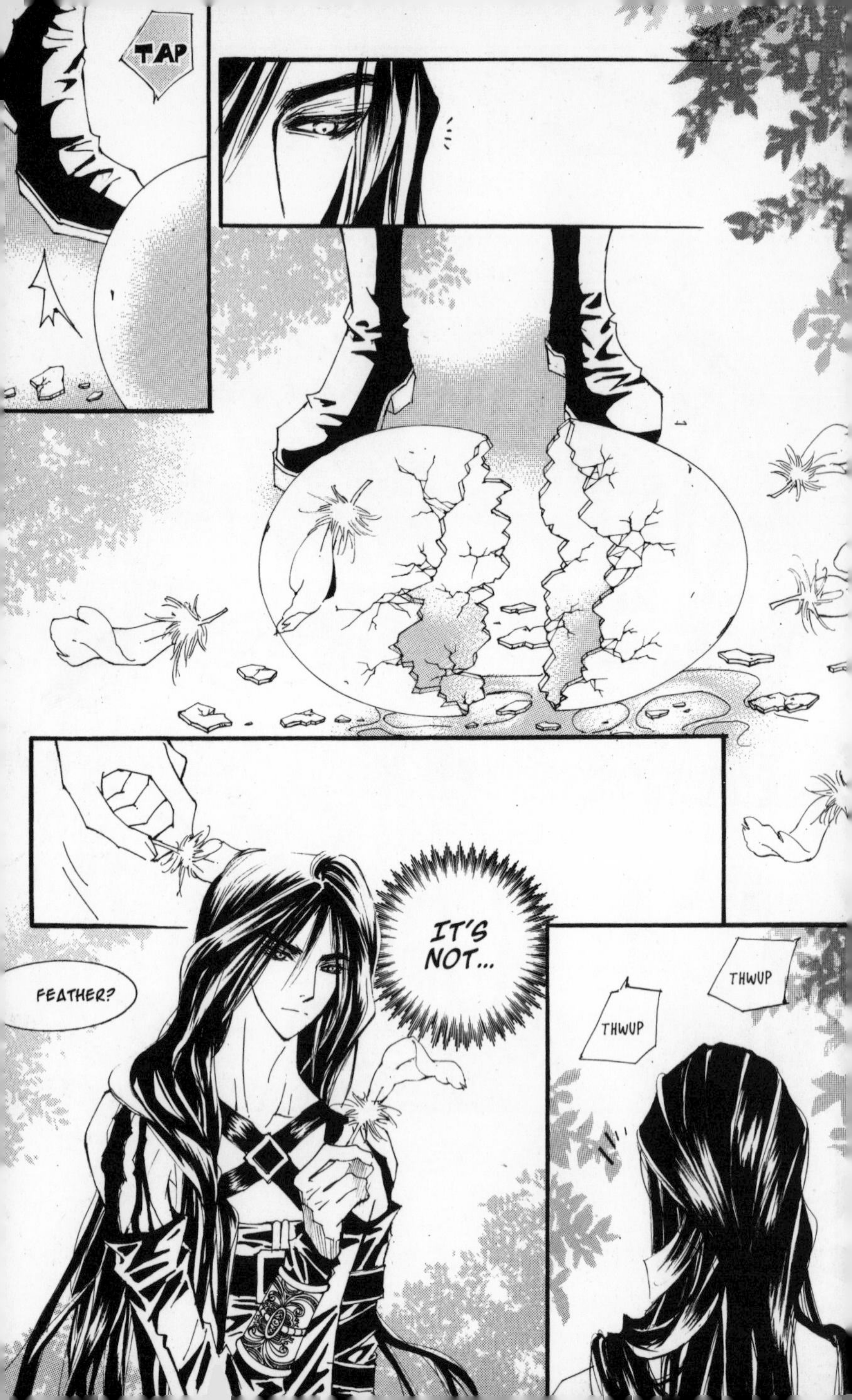
TAP
IT'S NOT...
FEATHER?
THWUP
THWUP

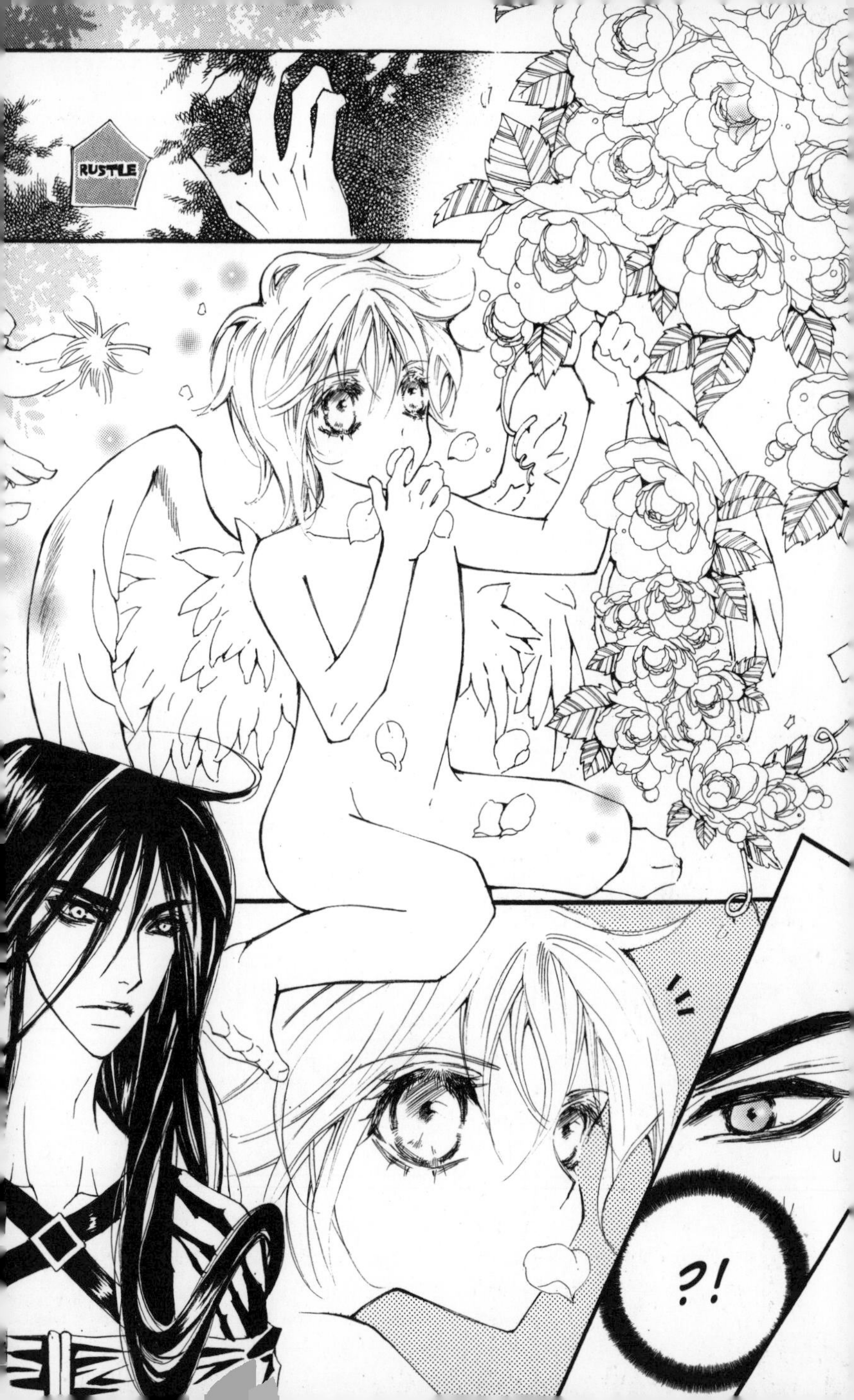
RUSTLE
?!

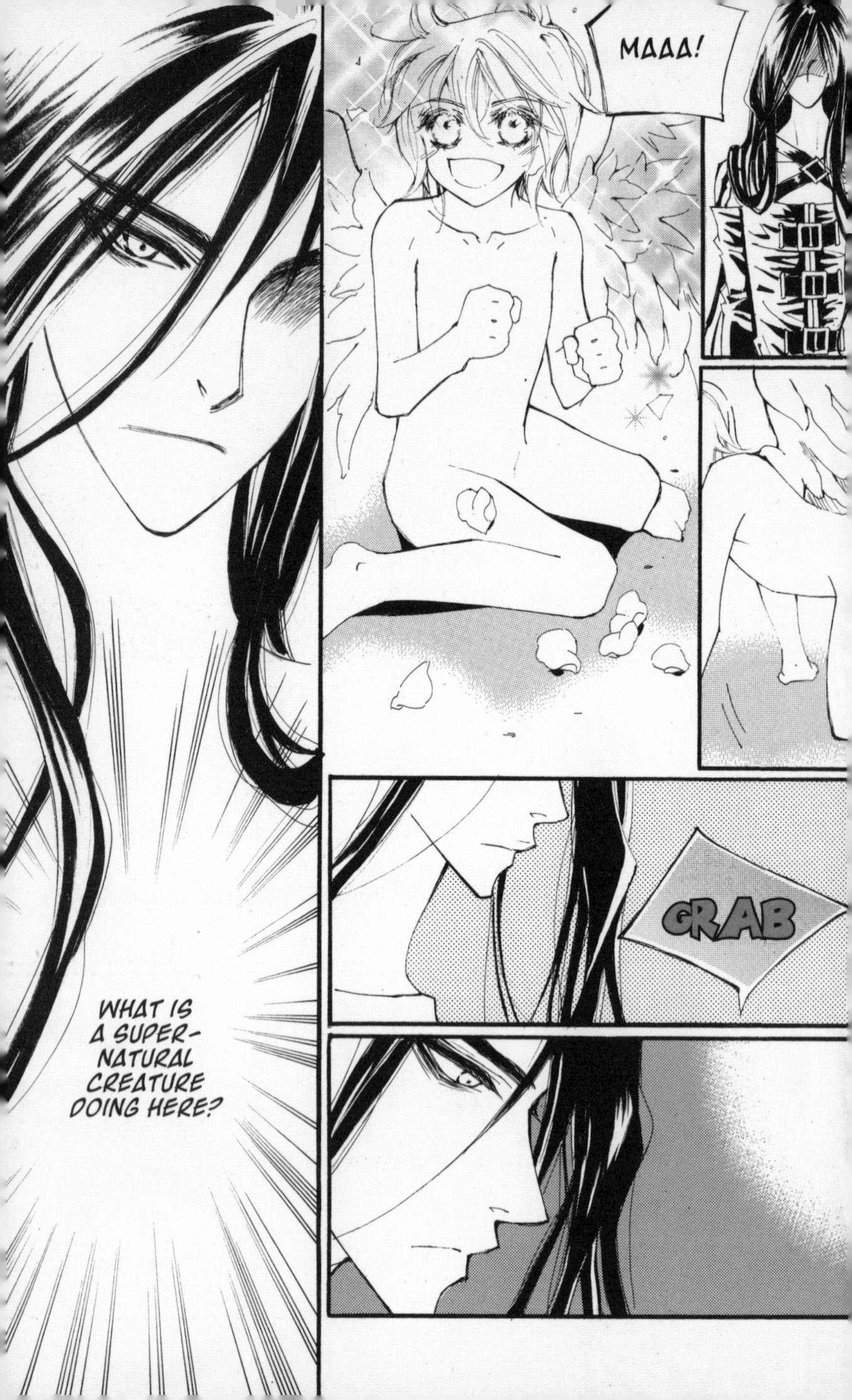
MAAA!
GRAB
WHAT IS A SUPER-NATURAL CREATURE DOING HERE?

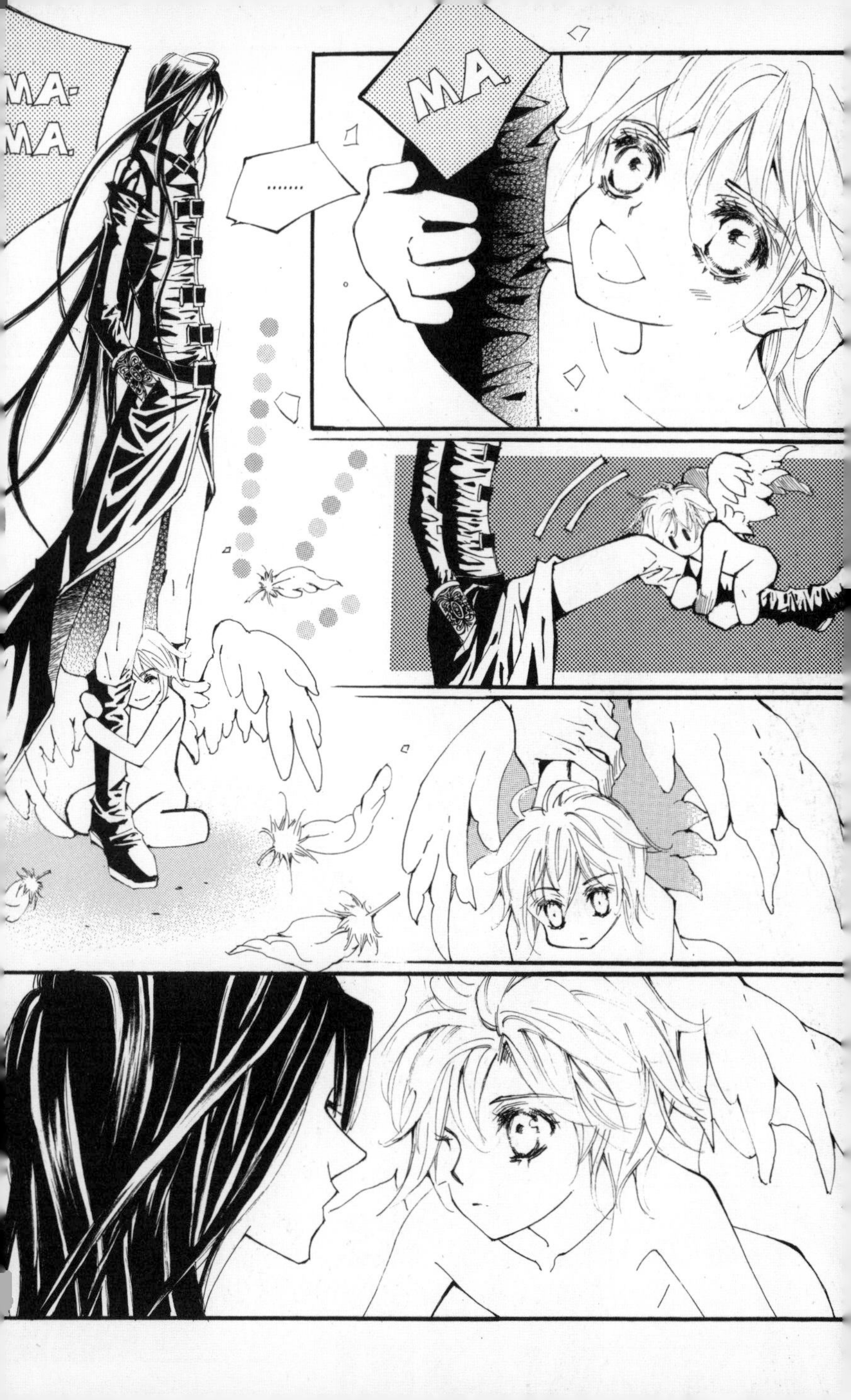
MA-
MA.
......
MA.

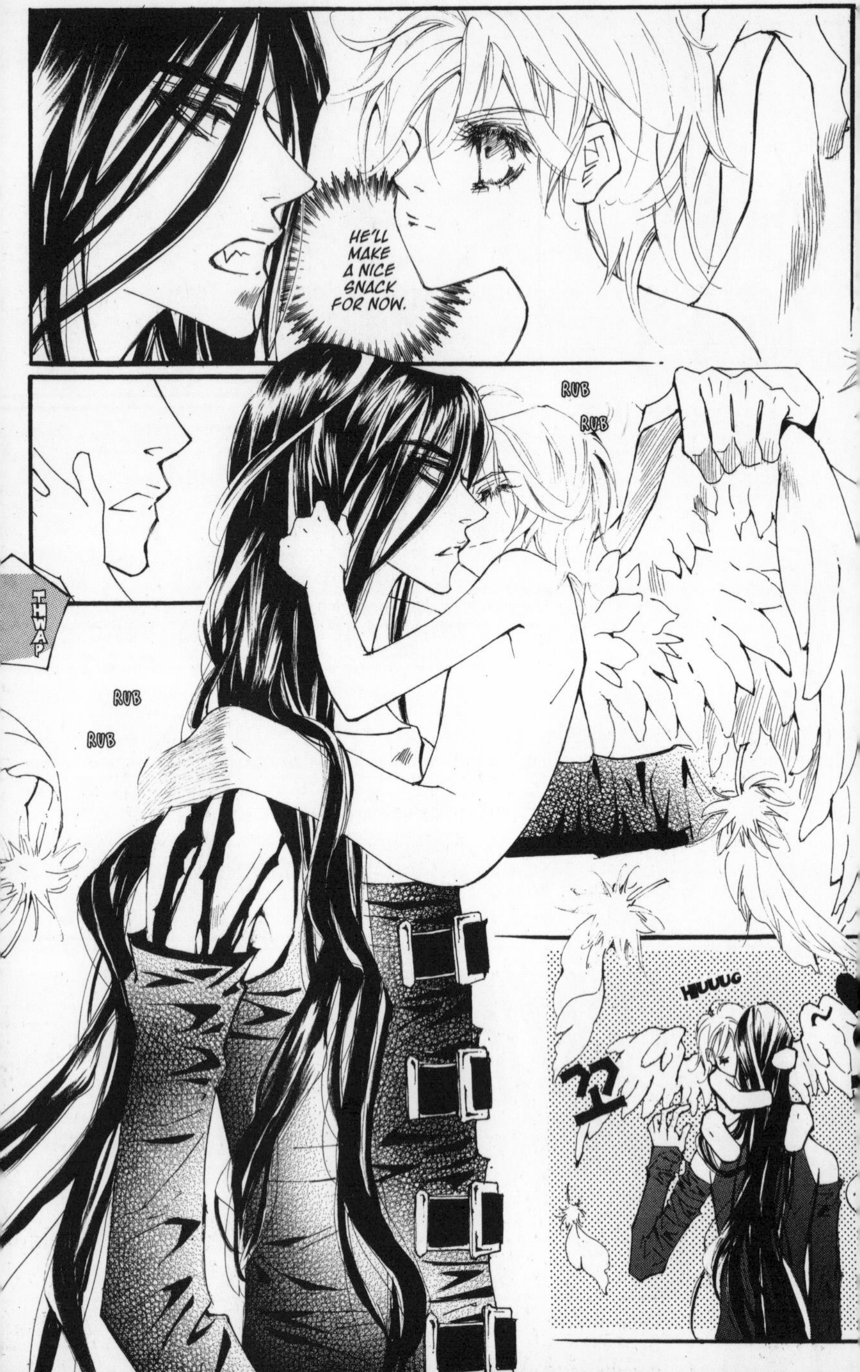
HE'LL MAKE A NICE SNACK FOR NOW.
THWAP
RUB
RUB
RUB
RUB
HUUUG

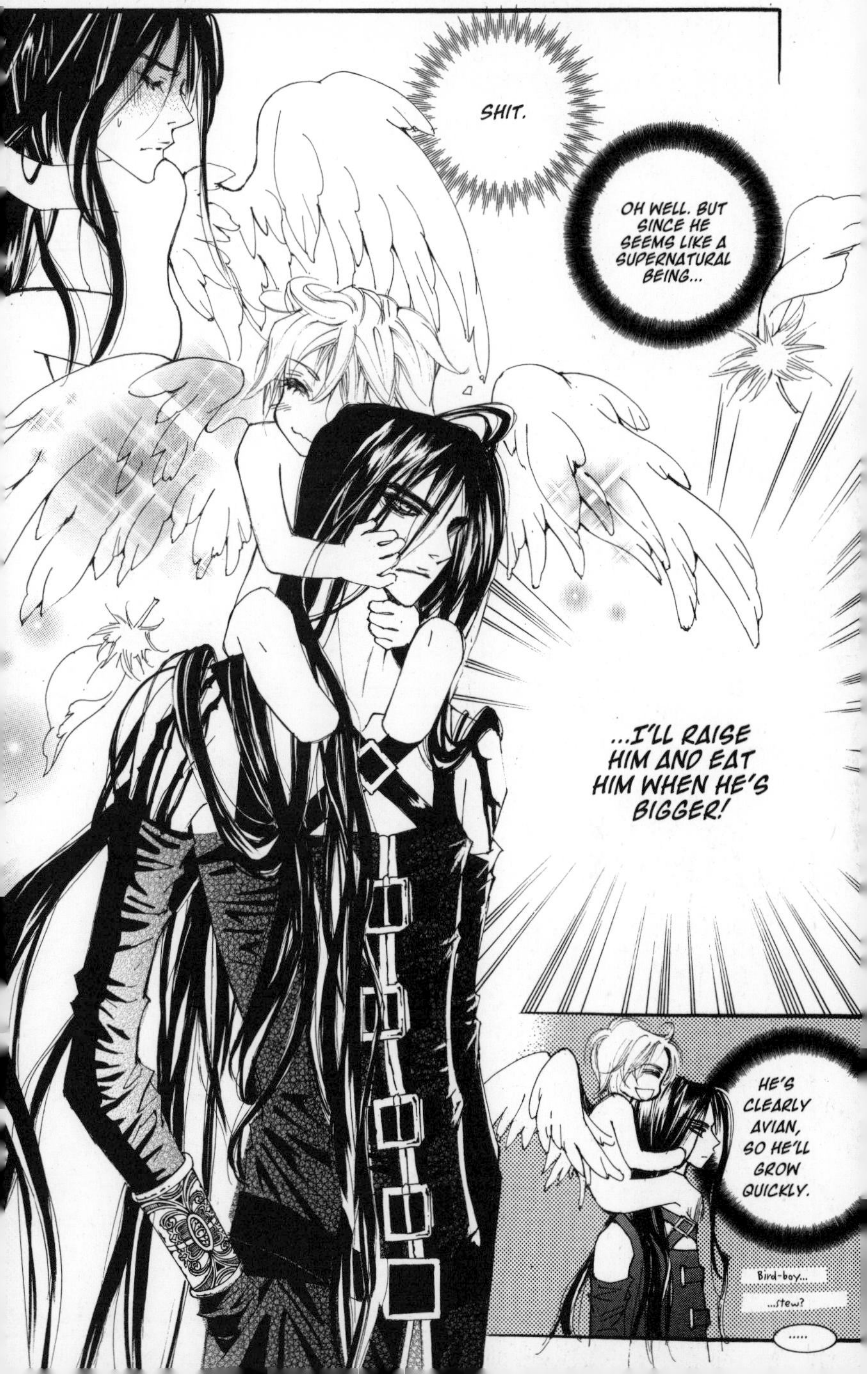
SHIT.
OH WELL. BUT SINCE HE SEEMS LIKE A SUPERNATURAL BEING...
...I'LL RAISE HIM AND EAT HIM WHEN HE'S BIGGER!
HE'S CLEARLY AVIAN, SO HE'LL GROW QUICKLY.
Bird-boy...
...stew?
.....

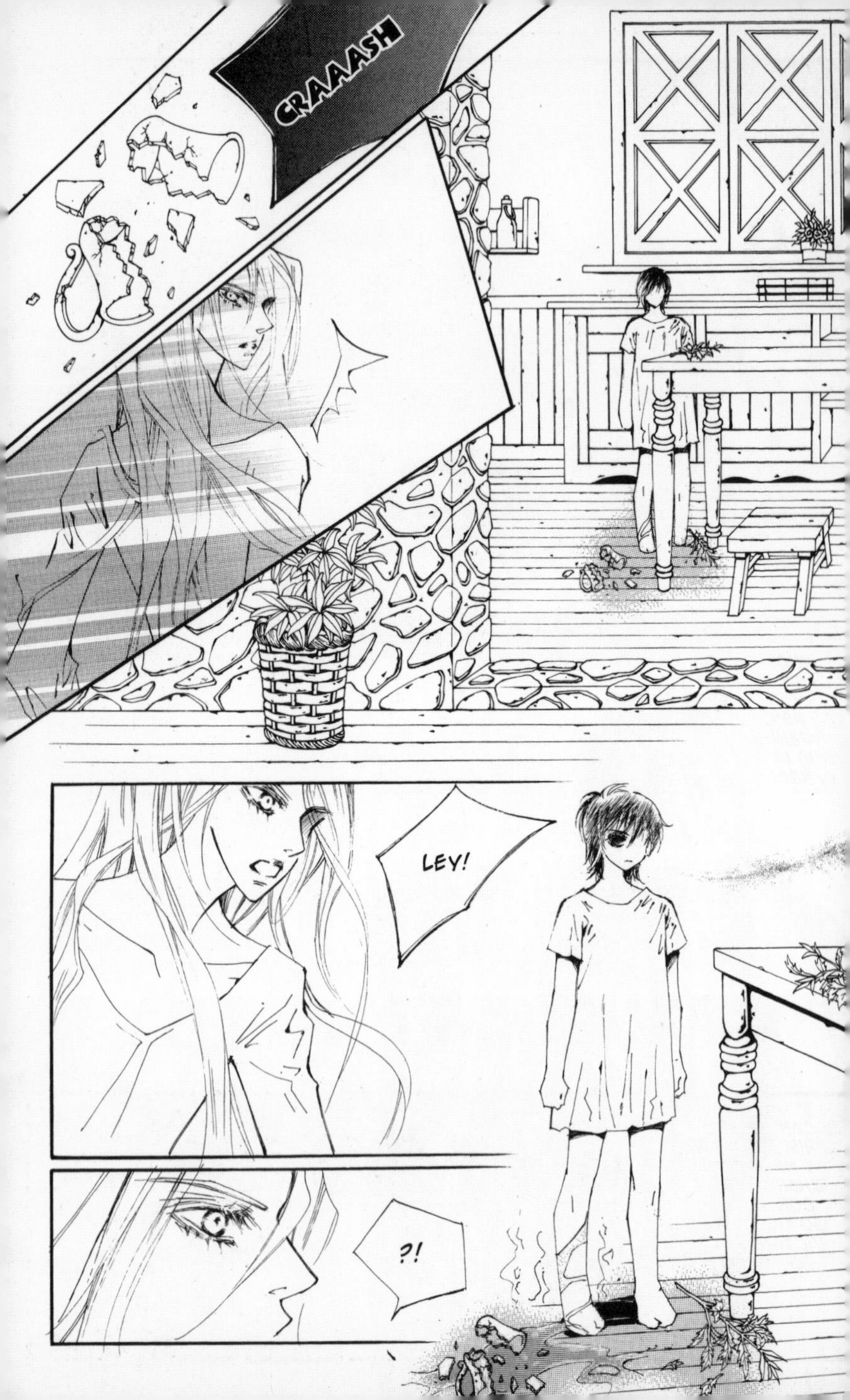
CRAAASH
LEY!
?!

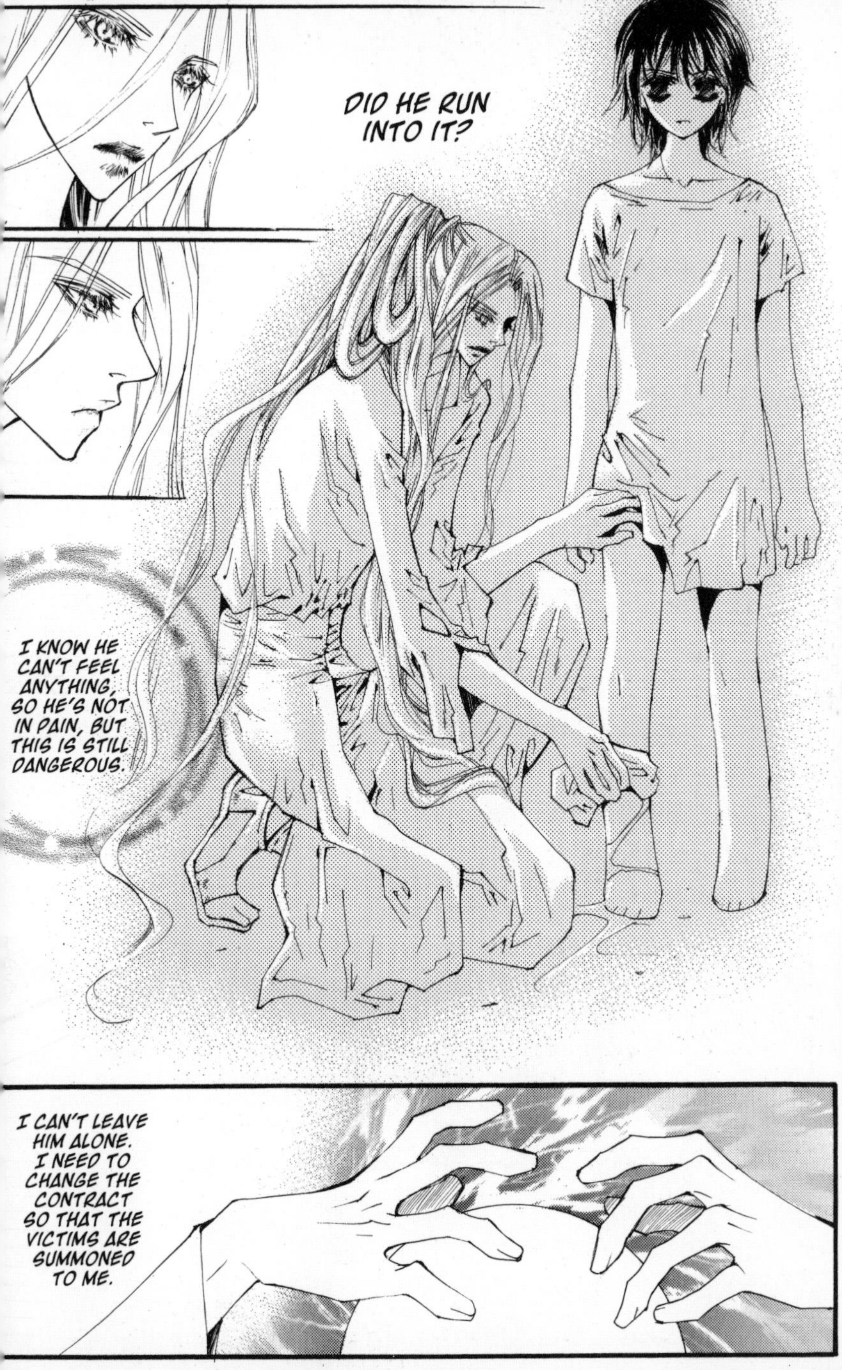
DID HE RUN INTO IT?
I KNOW HE CAN'T FEEL ANYTHING, SO HE'S NOT IN PAIN, BUT THIS IS STILL DANGEROUS.
I CAN'T LEAVE HIM ALONE. I NEED TO CHANGE THE CONTRACT SO THAT THE VICTIMS ARE SUMMONED TO ME.

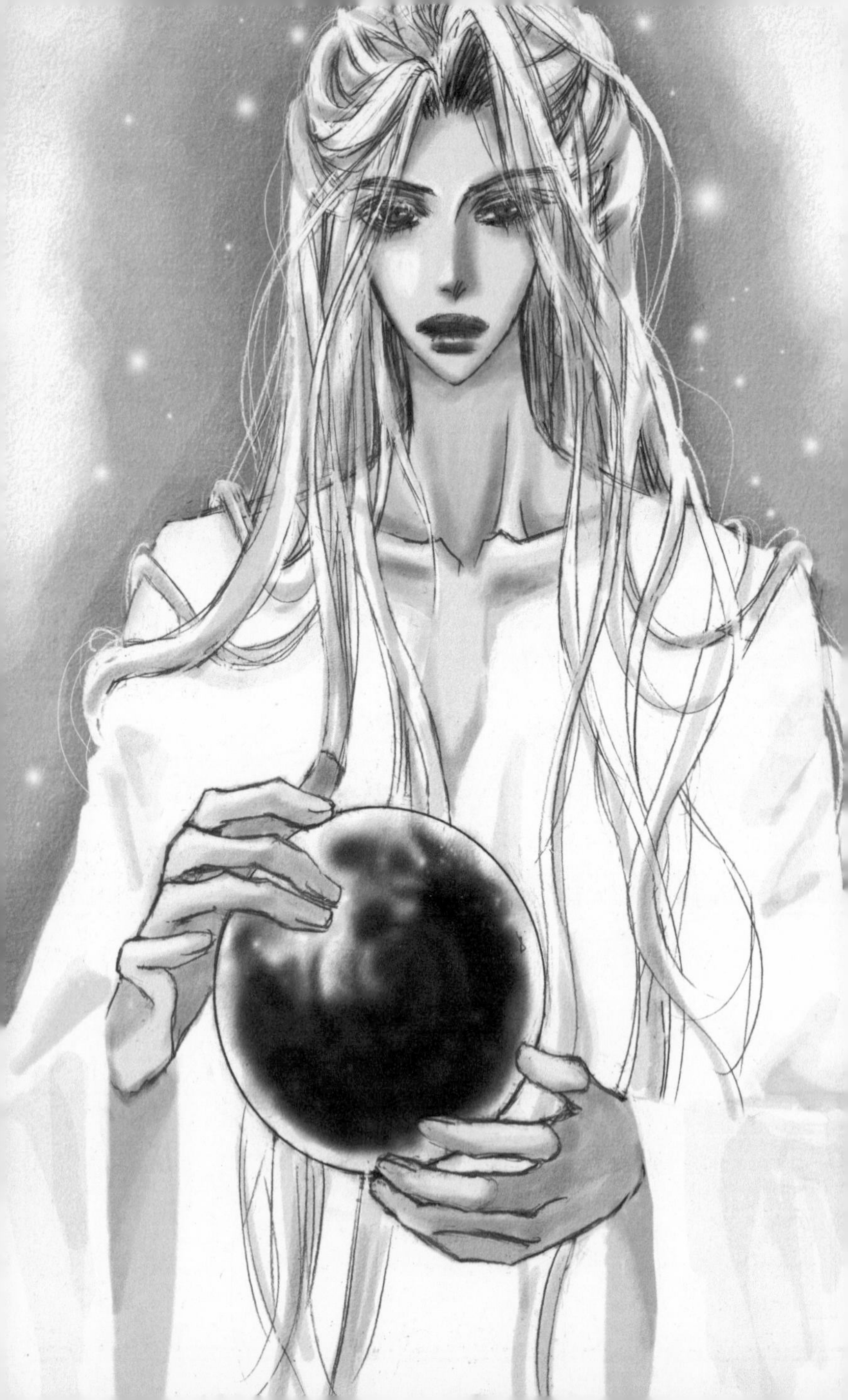

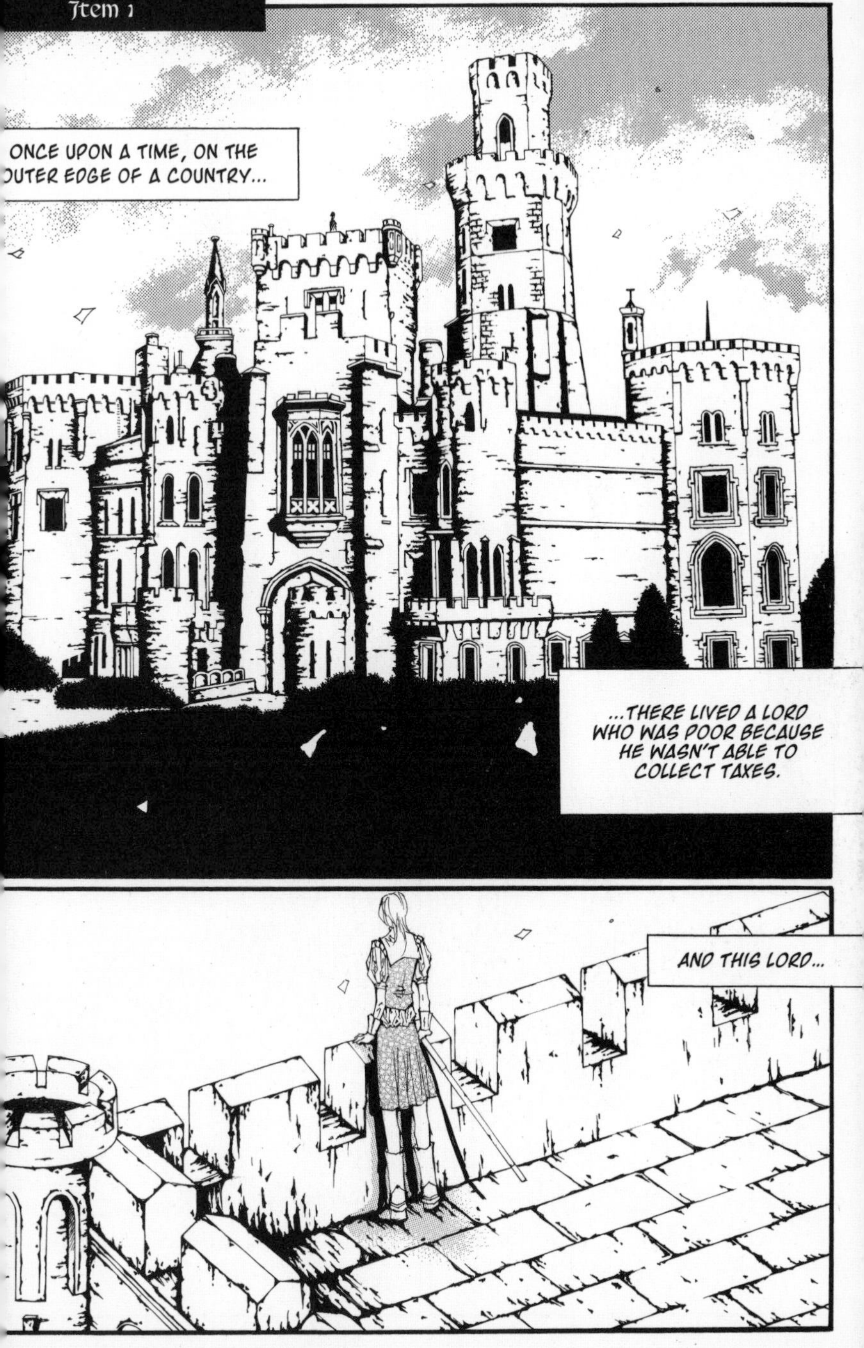
ONCE UPON A TIME, ON THE OUTER EDGE OF A COUNTRY...
...THERE LIVED A LORD WHO WAS POOR BECAUSE HE WASN'T ABLE TO COLLECT TAXES.
AND THIS LORD...

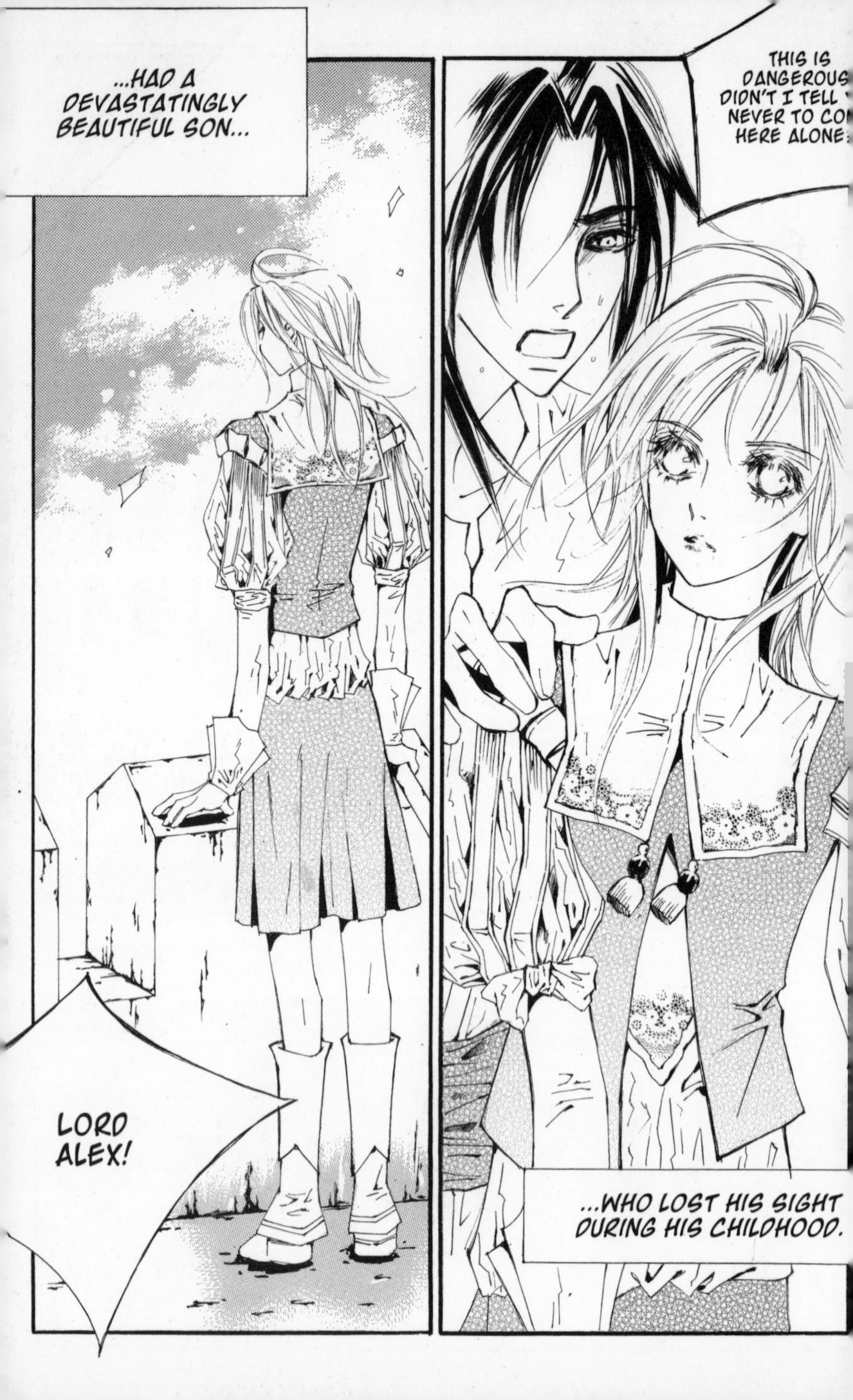
...HAD A DEVASTATINGLY BEAUTIFUL SON...
LORD ALEX!
THIS IS DANGEROUS DIDN'T I TELL NEVER TO CO HERE ALONE
...WHO LOST HIS SIGHT DURING HIS CHILDHOOD.

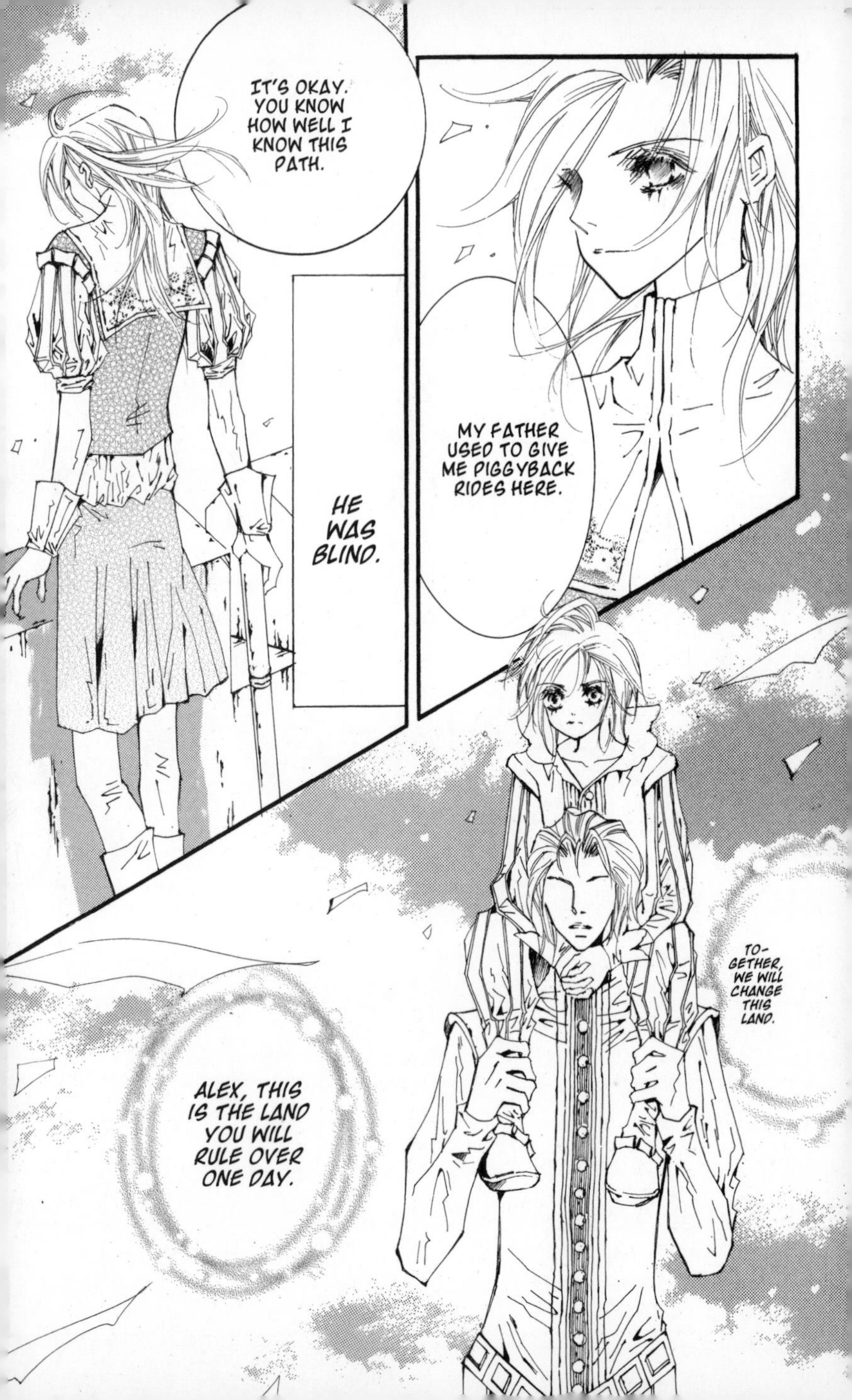
IT'S OKAY. YOU KNOW HOW WELL I KNOW THIS PATH.
HE WAS BLIND.
MY FATHER USED TO GIVE ME PIGGYBACK RIDES HERE.
ALEX, THIS IS THE LAND YOU WILL RULE OVER ONE DAY.
TO-GETHER, WE WILL CHANGE THIS LAND.

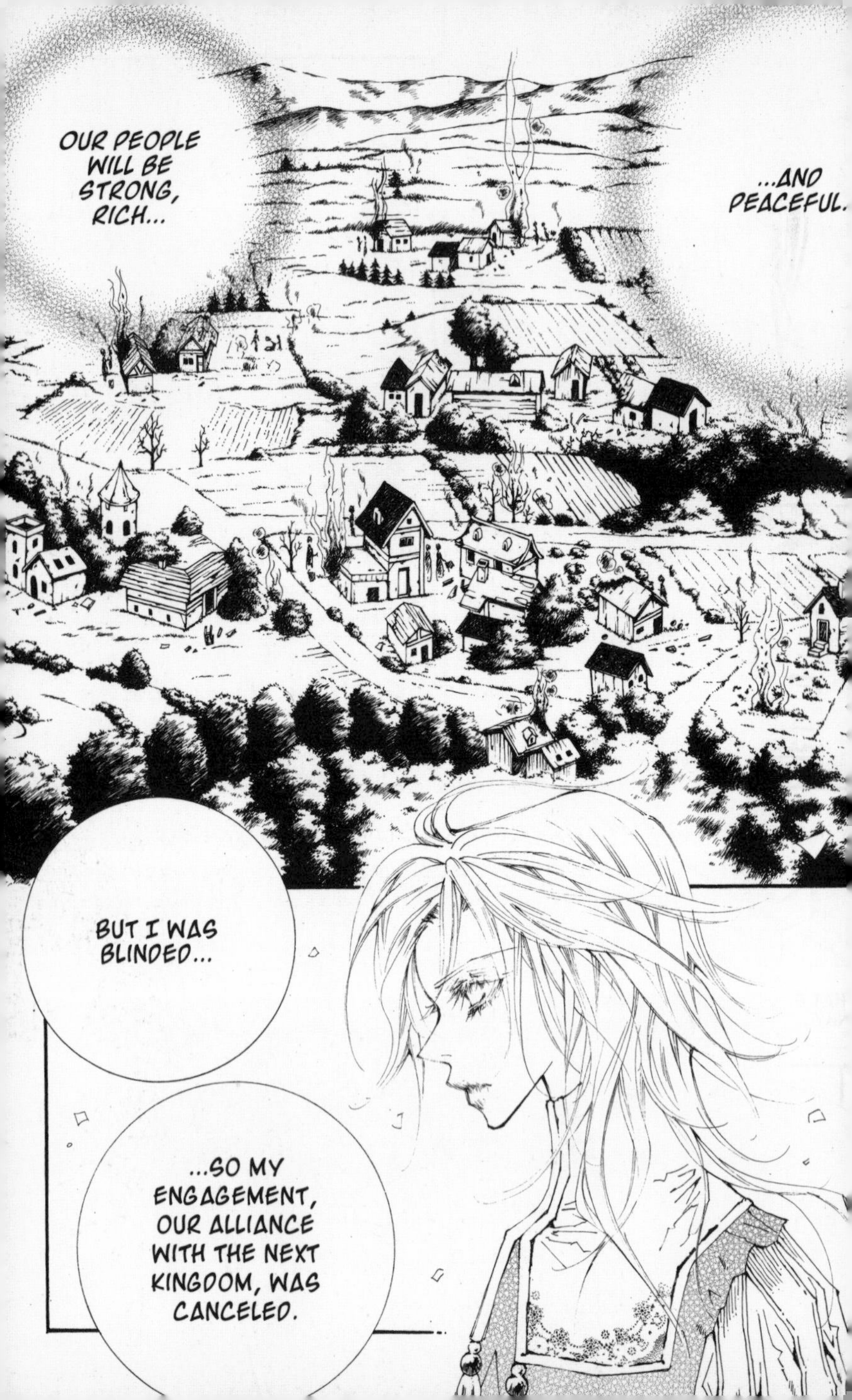
OUR PEOPLE WILL BE STRONG, RICH...
...AND PEACEFUL.
BUT I WAS BLINDED...
...SO MY ENGAGEMENT, OUR ALLIANCE WITH THE NEXT KINGDOM, WAS CANCELED.

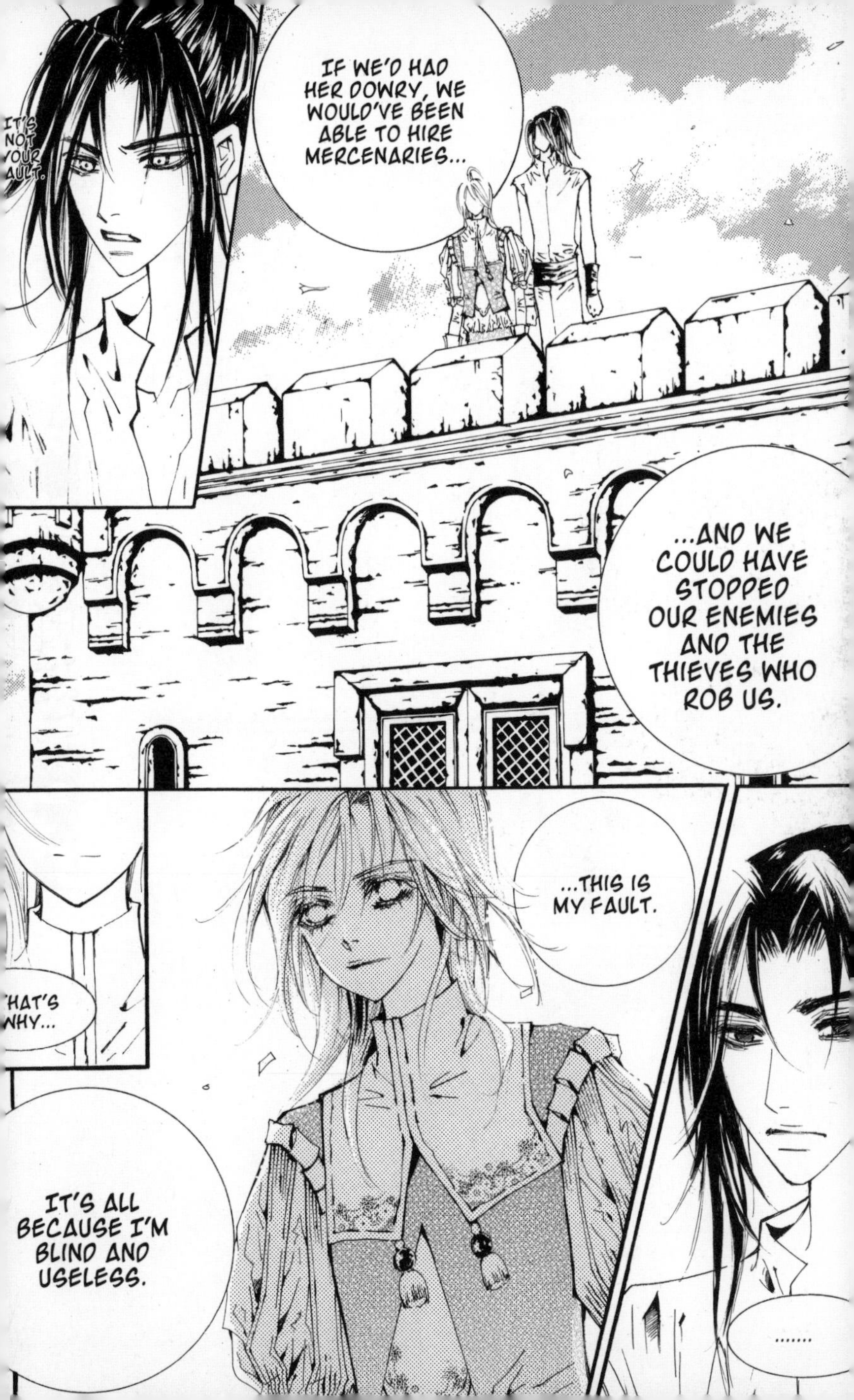
IT'S NOT YOUR AULT.
IF WE'D HAD HER DOWRY, WE WOULD'VE BEEN ABLE TO HIRE MERCENARIES...
...AND WE COULD HAVE STOPPED OUR ENEMIES AND THE THIEVES WHO ROB US.
HAT'S WHY...
...THIS IS MY FAULT.
IT'S ALL BECAUSE I'M BLIND AND USELESS.
......

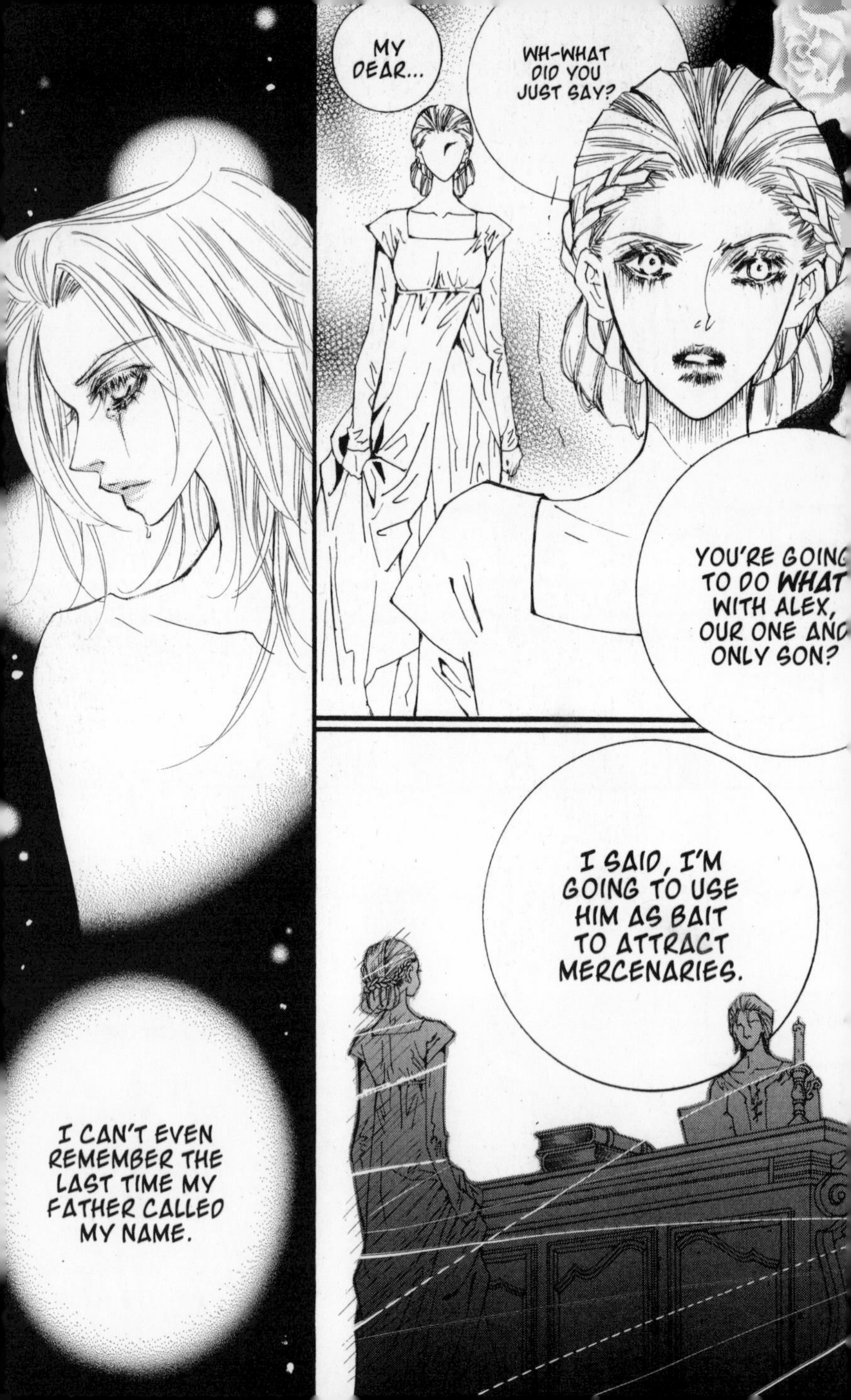
I CAN'T EVEN REMEMBER THE LAST TIME MY FATHER CALLED MY NAME.
MY DEAR...
WH-WHAT DID YOU JUST SAY?
YOU'RE GOING TO DO **WHAT** WITH ALEX, OUR ONE AND ONLY SON?
I SAID, I'M GOING TO USE HIM AS BAIT TO ATTRACT MERCENARIES.

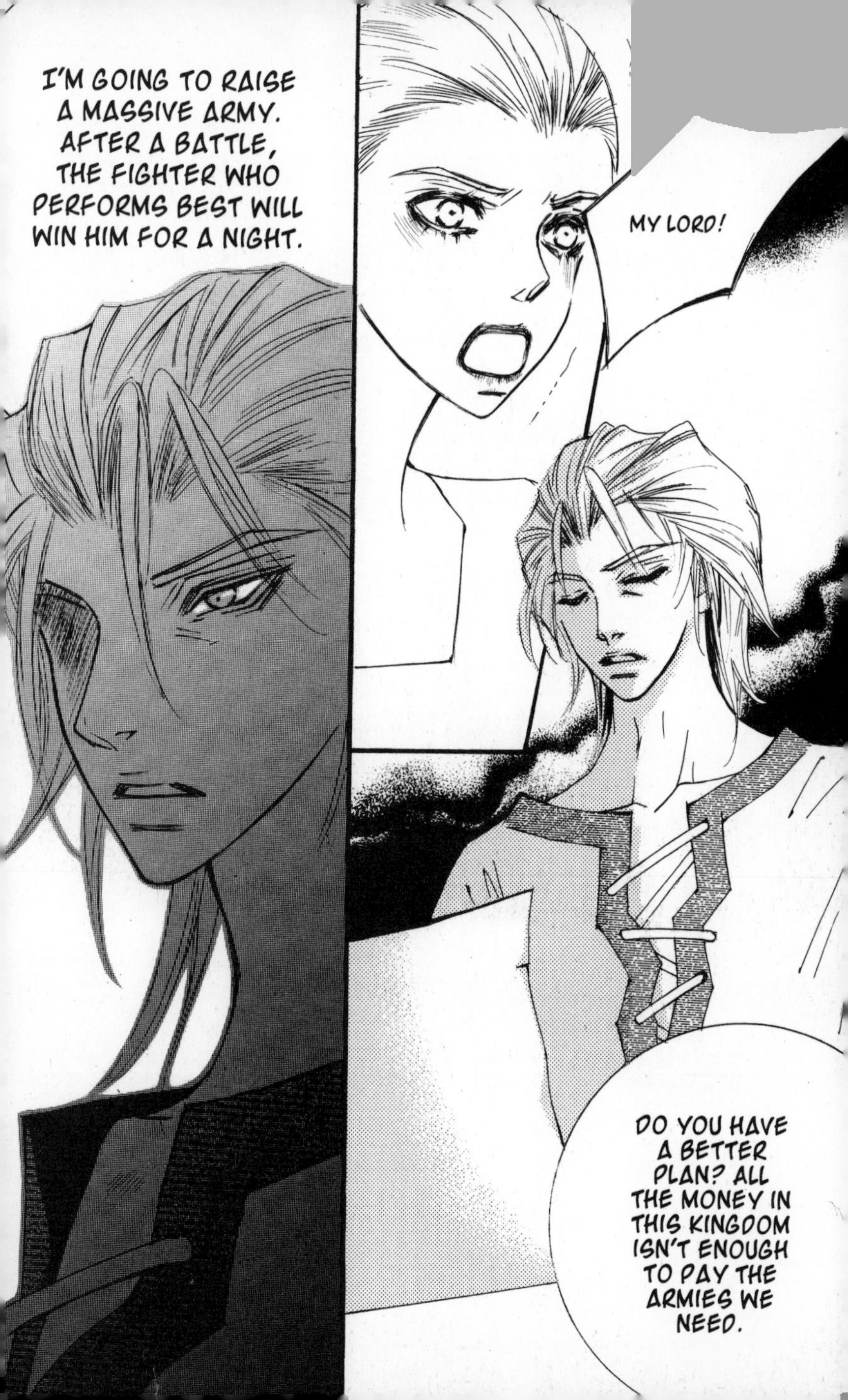
I'M GOING TO RAISE A MASSIVE ARMY. AFTER A BATTLE, THE FIGHTER WHO PERFORMS BEST WILL WIN HIM FOR A NIGHT.
MY LORD!
DO YOU HAVE A BETTER PLAN? ALL THE MONEY IN THIS KINGDOM ISN'T ENOUGH TO PAY THE ARMIES WE NEED.

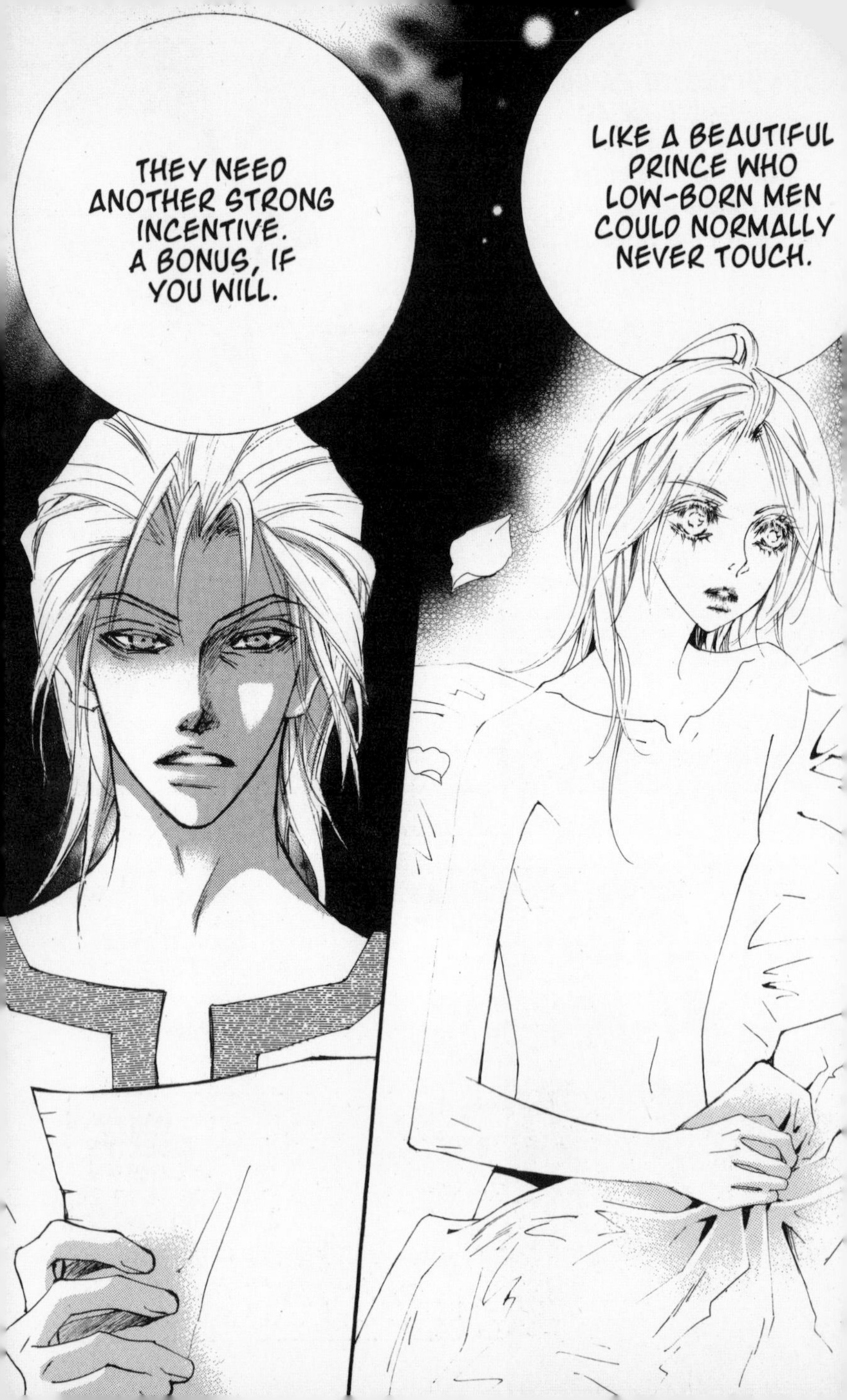
THEY NEED ANOTHER STRONG INCENTIVE. A BONUS, IF YOU WILL.
LIKE A BEAUTIFUL PRINCE WHO LOW-BORN MEN COULD NORMALLY NEVER TOUCH.

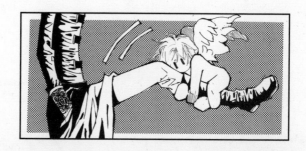

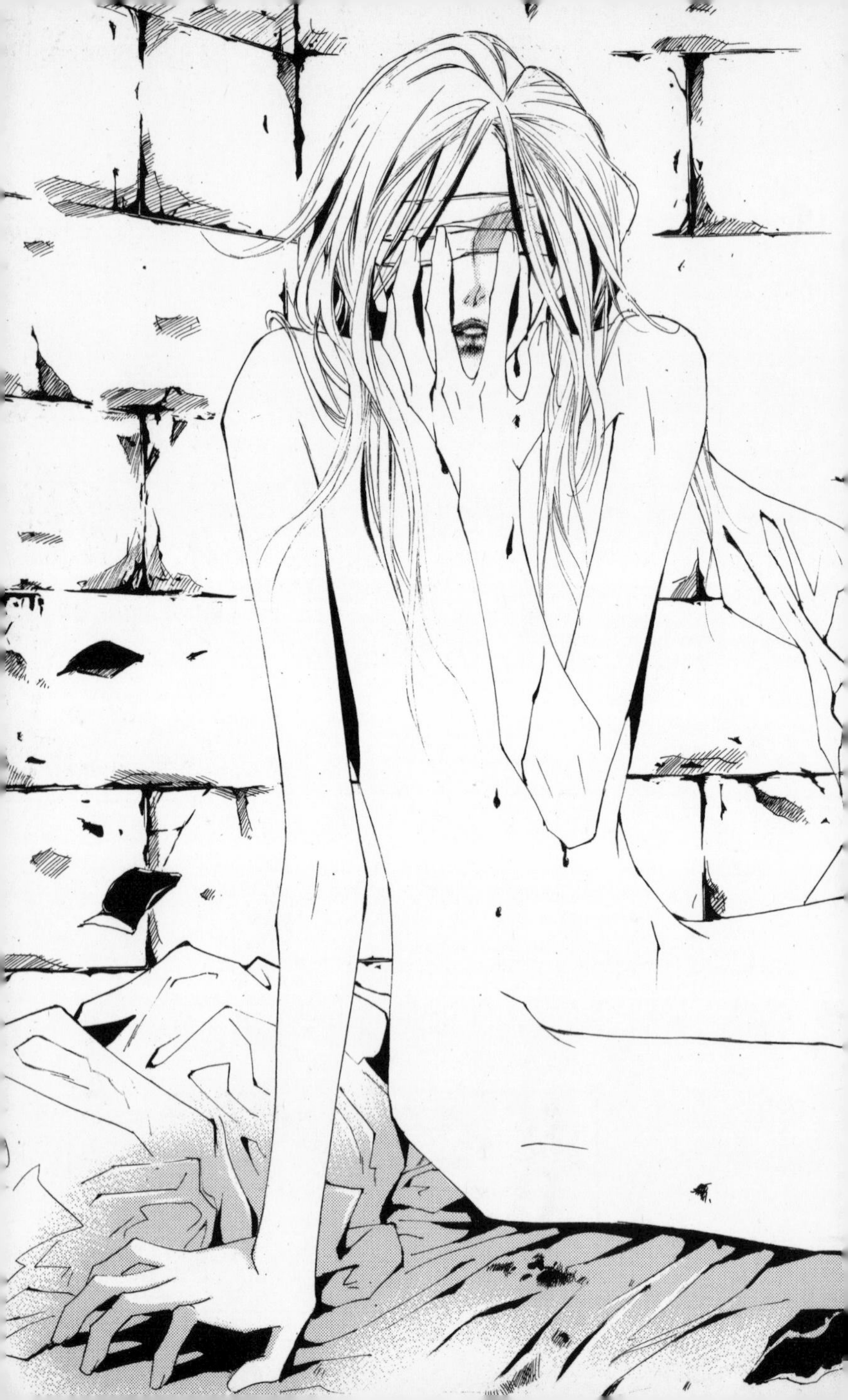

Ch. 5 Item 1: Eyes

Please Close My Eyes (Part 1)

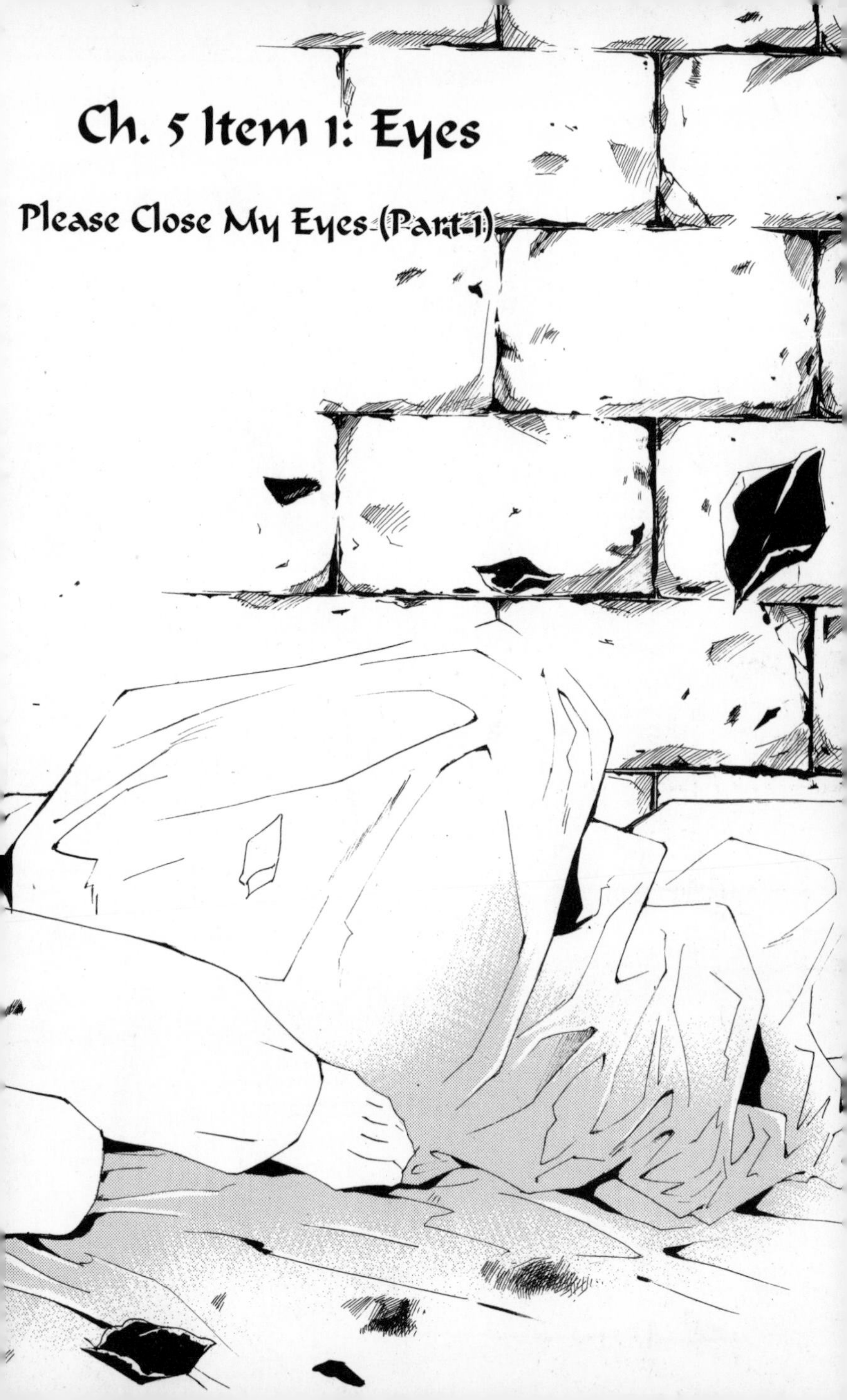

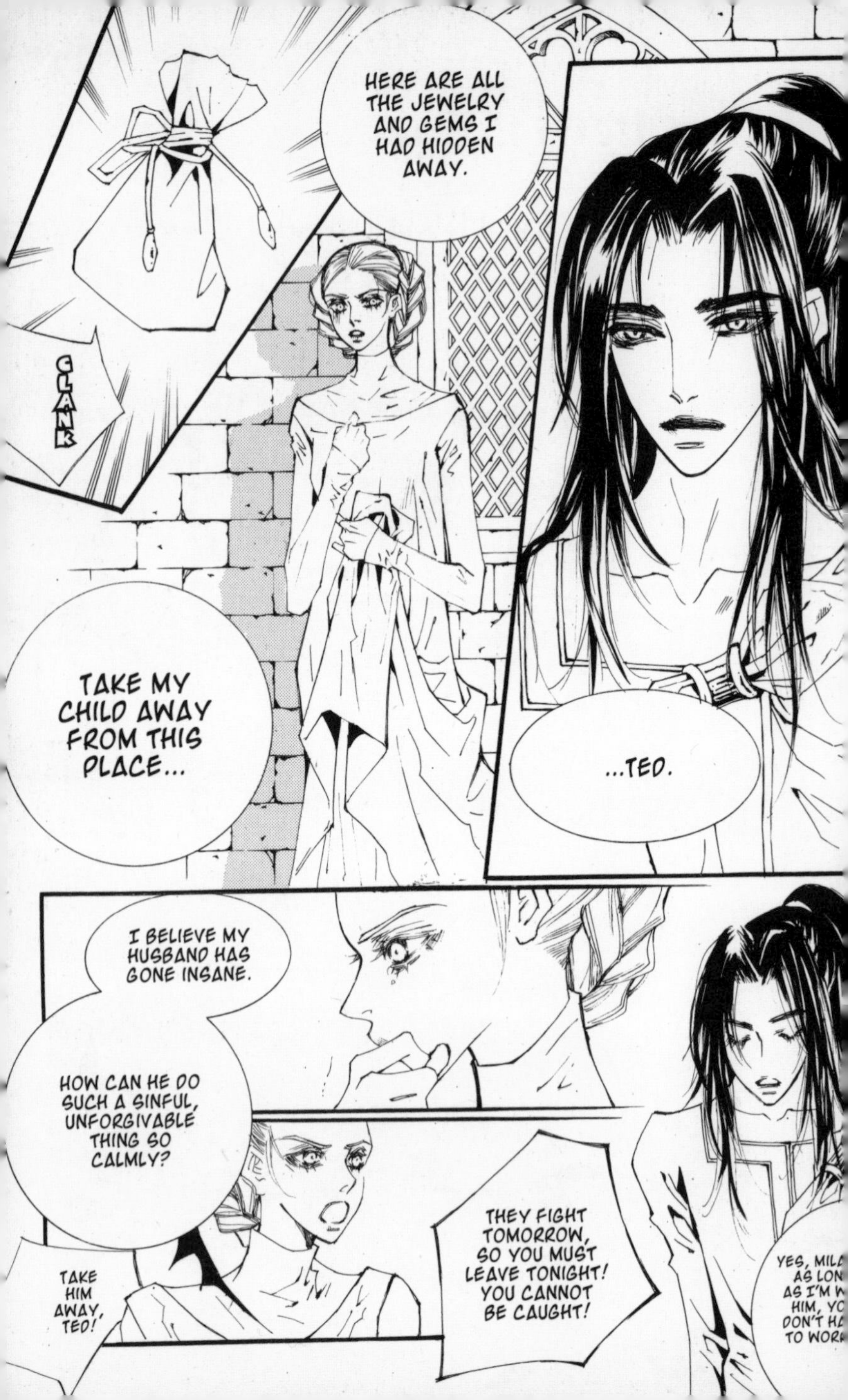
CLANK
HERE ARE ALL THE JEWELRY AND GEMS I HAD HIDDEN AWAY.
TAKE MY CHILD AWAY FROM THIS PLACE...
...TEO.
I BELIEVE MY HUSBAND HAS GONE INSANE.
HOW CAN HE DO SUCH A SINFUL, UNFORGIVABLE THING SO CALMLY?
TAKE HIM AWAY, TEO!
THEY FIGHT TOMORROW, SO YOU MUST LEAVE TONIGHT! YOU CANNOT BE CAUGHT!
YES, MILA AS LON AS I'M W HIM, YO DON'T HA TO WORR

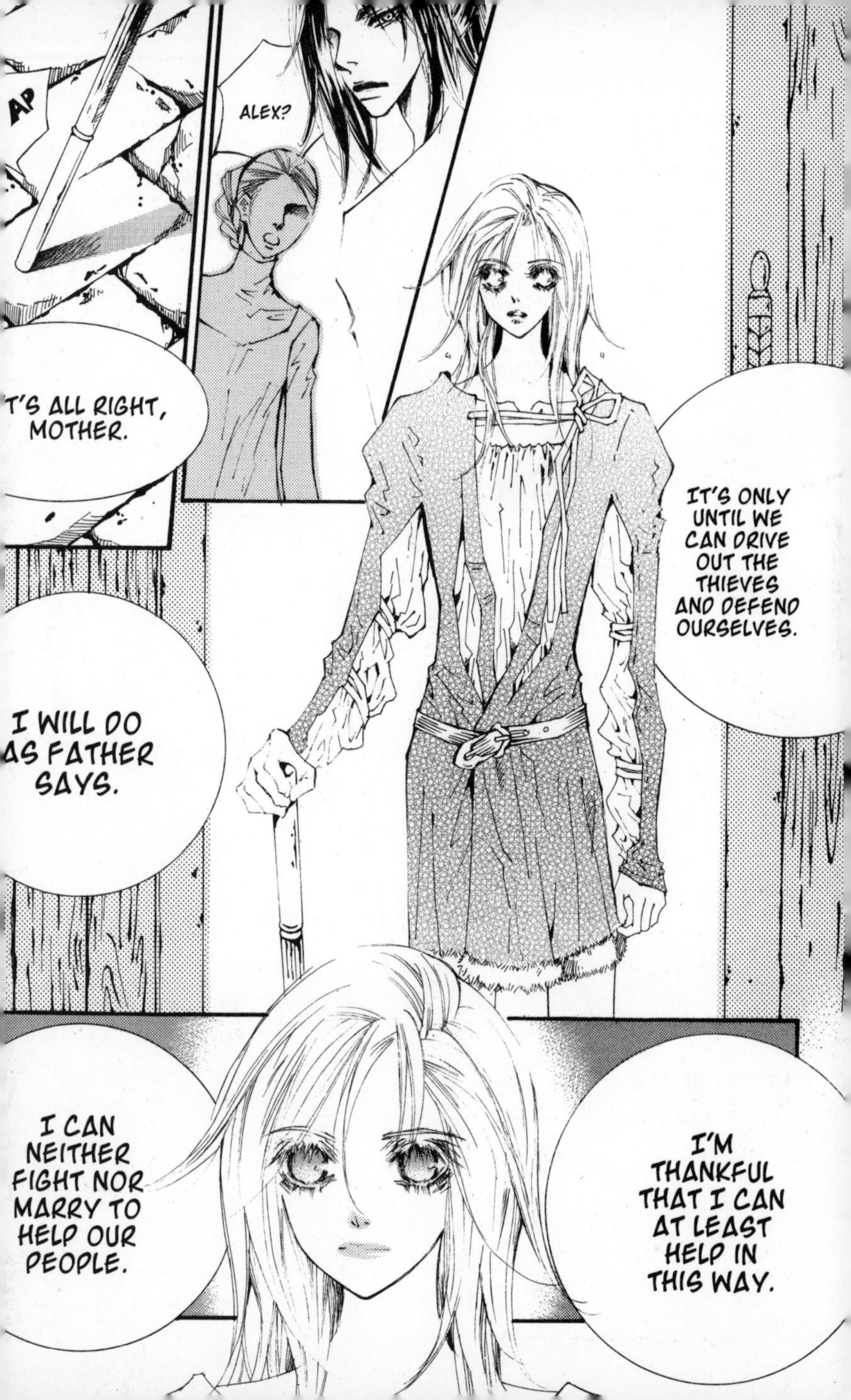
AP
ALEX?
T'S ALL RIGHT, MOTHER.
IT'S ONLY UNTIL WE CAN DRIVE OUT THE THIEVES AND DEFEND OURSELVES.
I WILL DO AS FATHER SAYS.
I CAN NEITHER FIGHT NOR MARRY TO HELP OUR PEOPLE.
I'M THANKFUL THAT I CAN AT LEAST HELP IN THIS WAY.

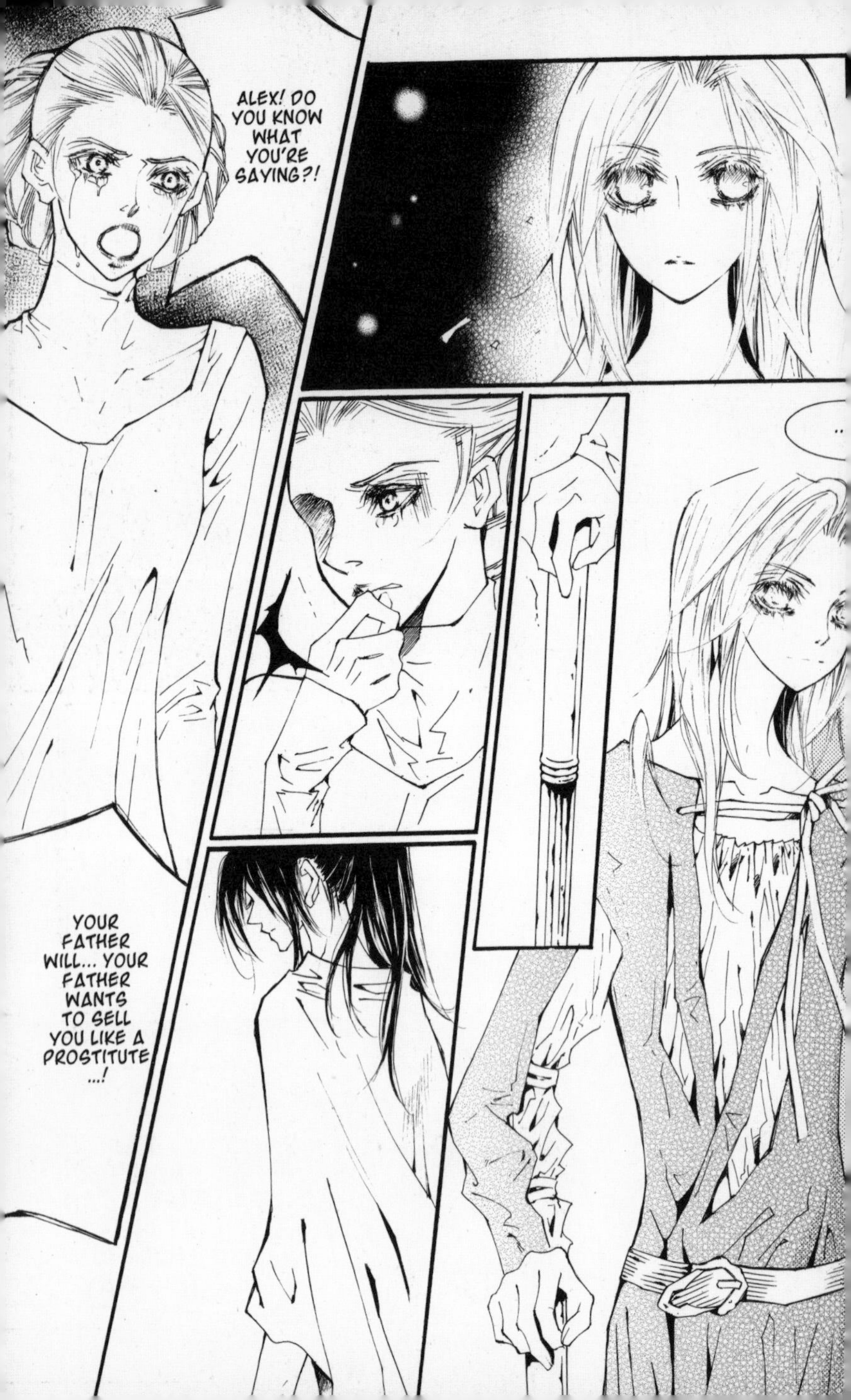
ALEX! DO YOU KNOW WHAT YOU'RE SAYING?!
...
YOUR FATHER WILL... YOUR FATHER WANTS TO SELL YOU LIKE A PROSTITUTE ...!

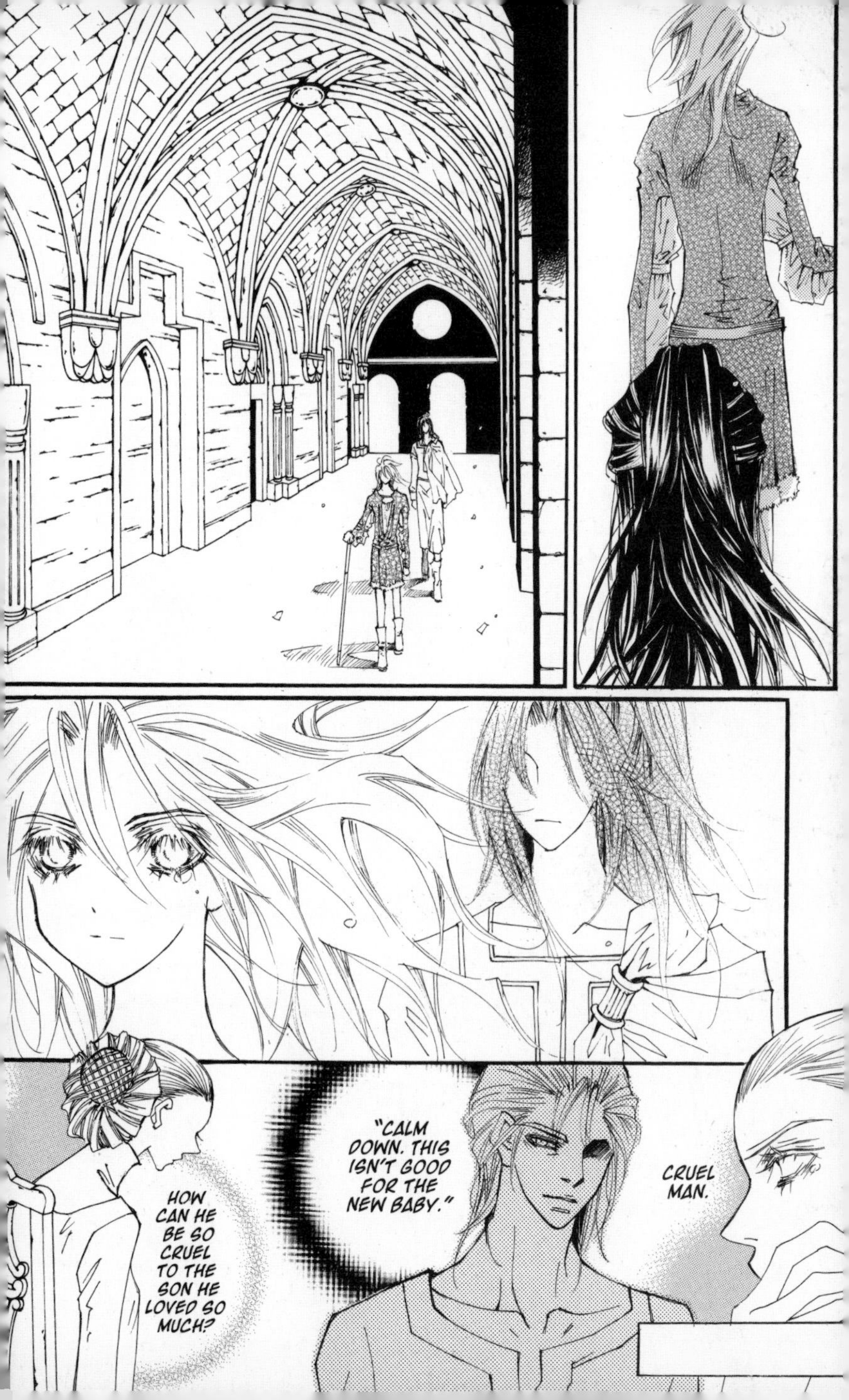
HOW CAN HE BE SO CRUEL TO THE SON HE LOVED SO MUCH?
"CALM DOWN. THIS ISN'T GOOD FOR THE NEW BABY."
CRUEL MAN.

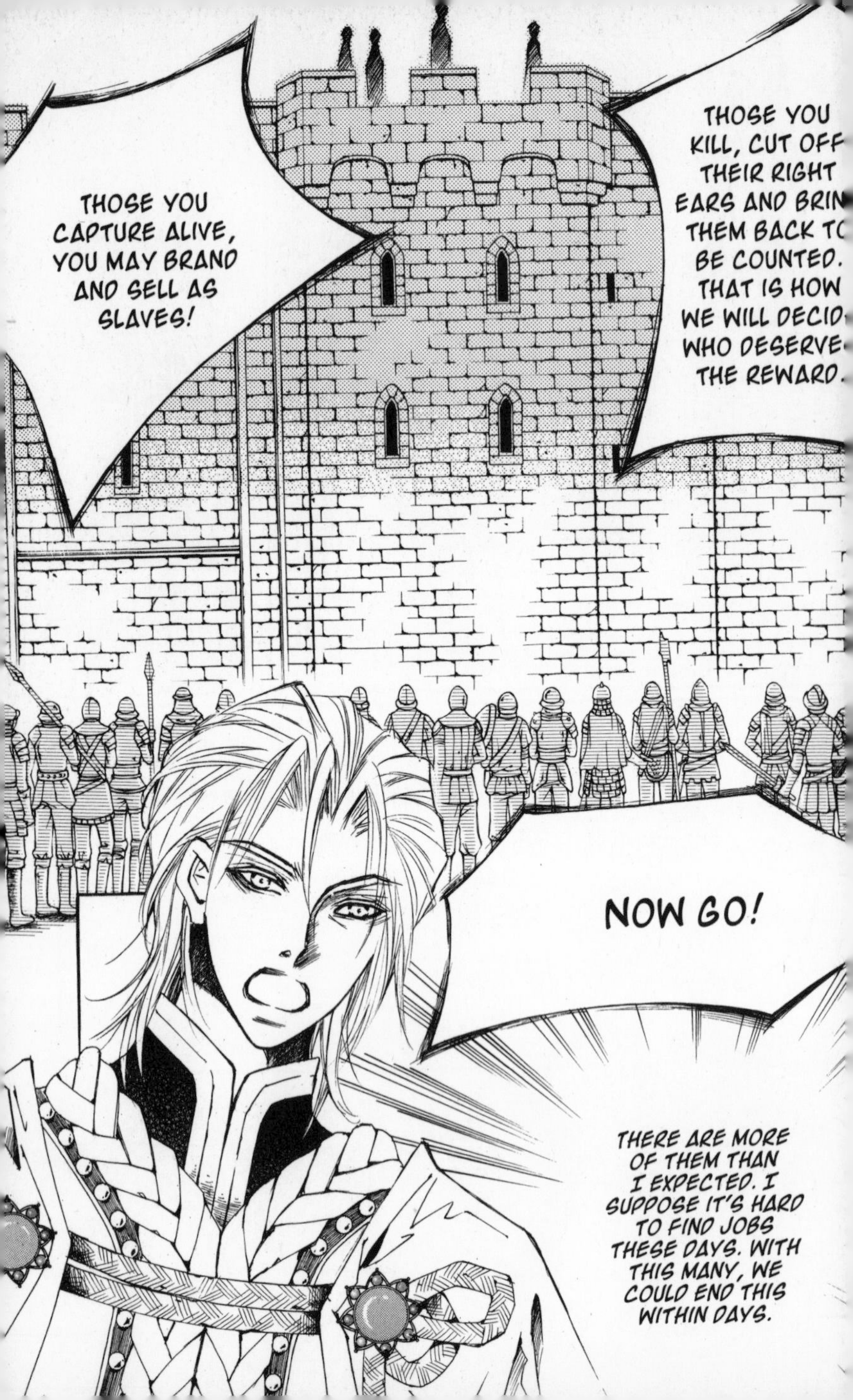
THOSE YOU CAPTURE ALIVE, YOU MAY BRAND AND SELL AS SLAVES!
THOSE YOU KILL, CUT OFF THEIR RIGHT EARS AND BRIN THEM BACK T BE COUNTED. THAT IS HOW WE WILL DECID WHO DESERVE THE REWARD.
NOW GO!
THERE ARE MORE OF THEM THAN I EXPECTED. I SUPPOSE IT'S HARD TO FIND JOBS THESE DAYS. WITH THIS MANY, WE COULD END THIS WITHIN DAYS.

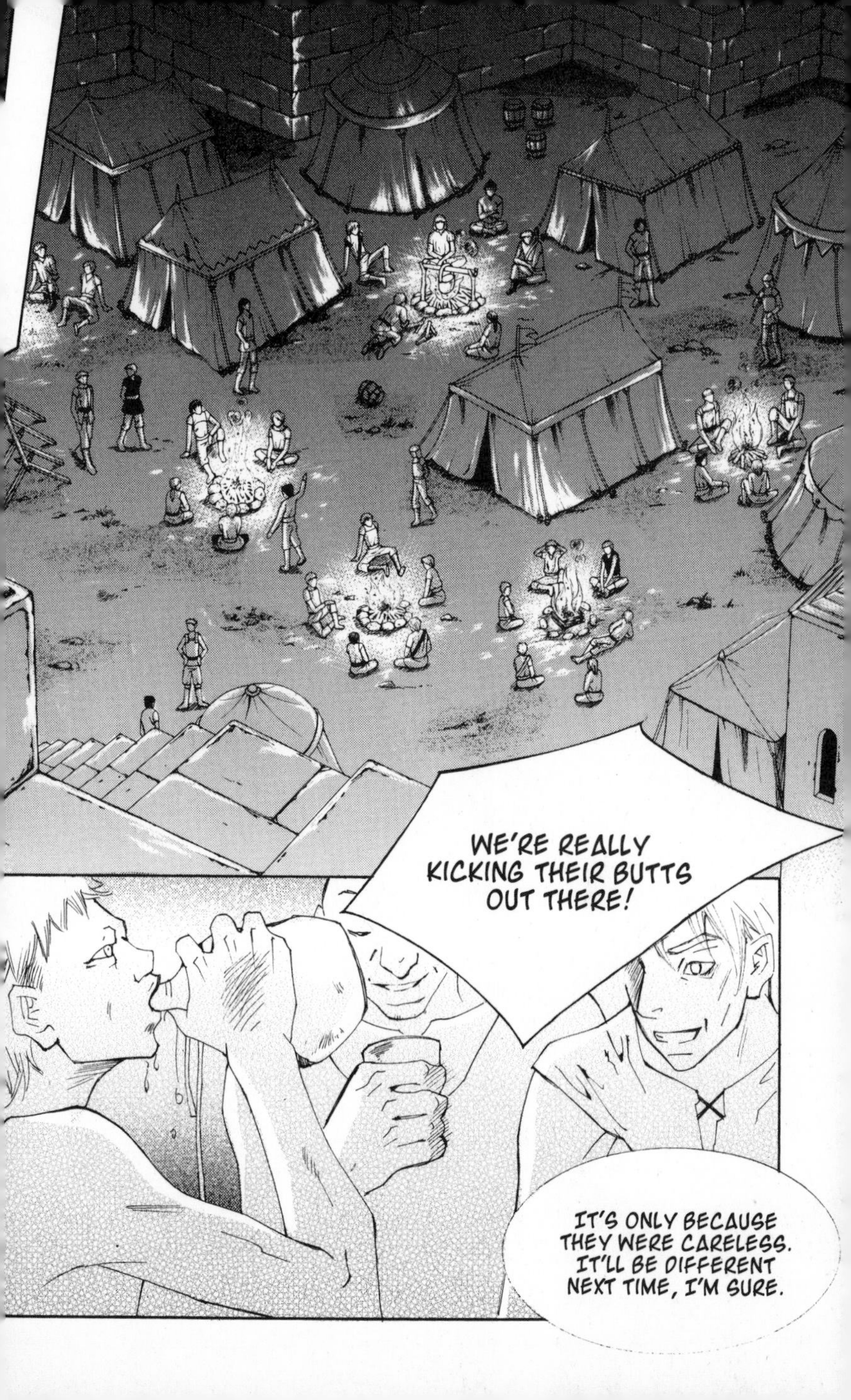
WE'RE REALLY KICKING THEIR BUTTS OUT THERE!
IT'S ONLY BECAUSE THEY WERE CARELESS. IT'LL BE DIFFERENT NEXT TIME, I'M SURE.

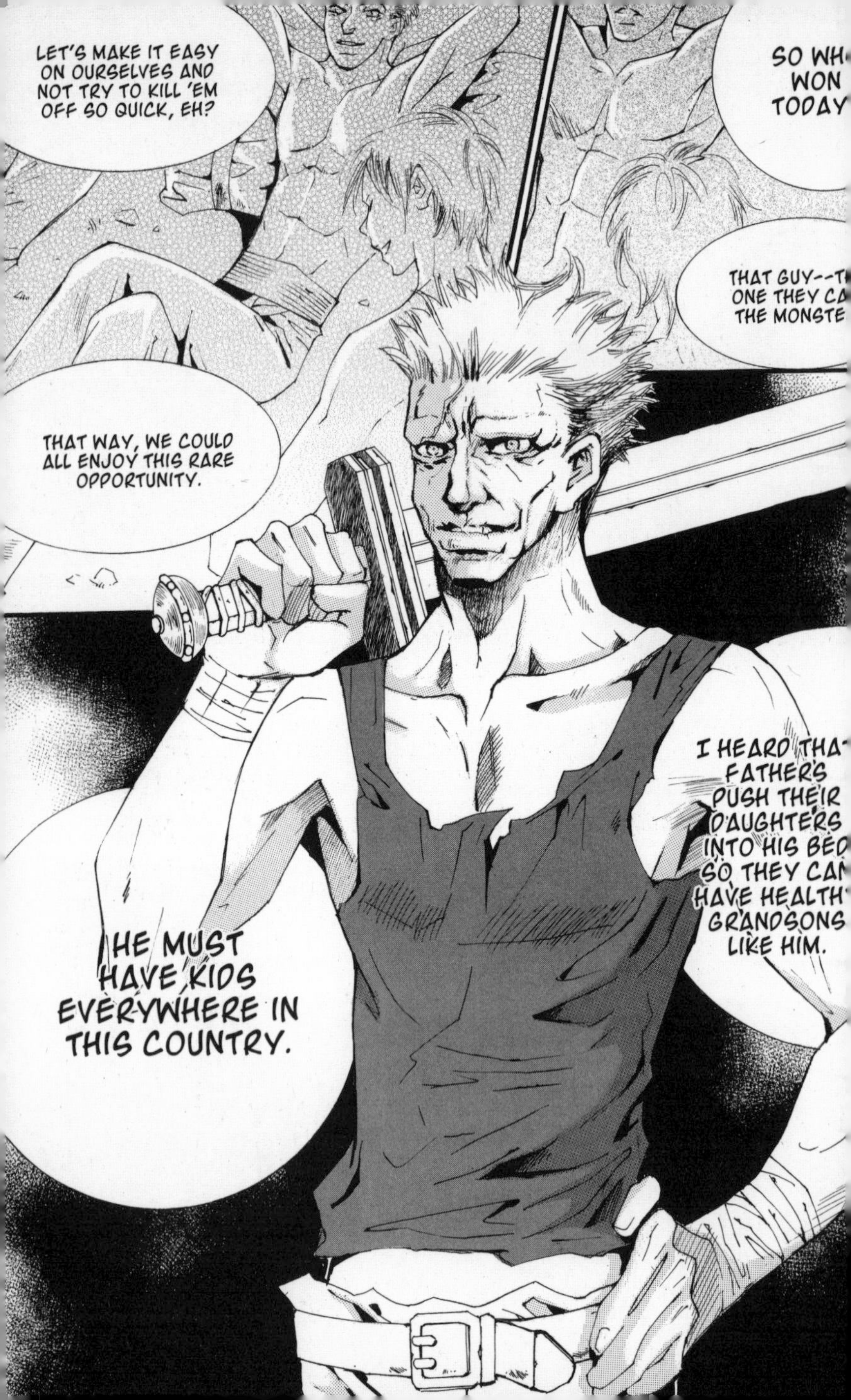

LET'S MAKE IT EASY ON OURSELVES AND NOT TRY TO KILL 'EM OFF SO QUICK, EH?
SO WH WON TODAY
THAT WAY, WE COULD ALL ENJOY THIS RARE OPPORTUNITY.
THAT GUY--T ONE THEY CA THE MONSTE
HE MUST HAVE KIDS EVERYWHERE IN THIS COUNTRY.
I HEARD THAT FATHER'S PUSH THEIR DAUGHTERS INTO HIS BED SO THEY CAN HAVE HEALTH GRANDSONS LIKE HIM.

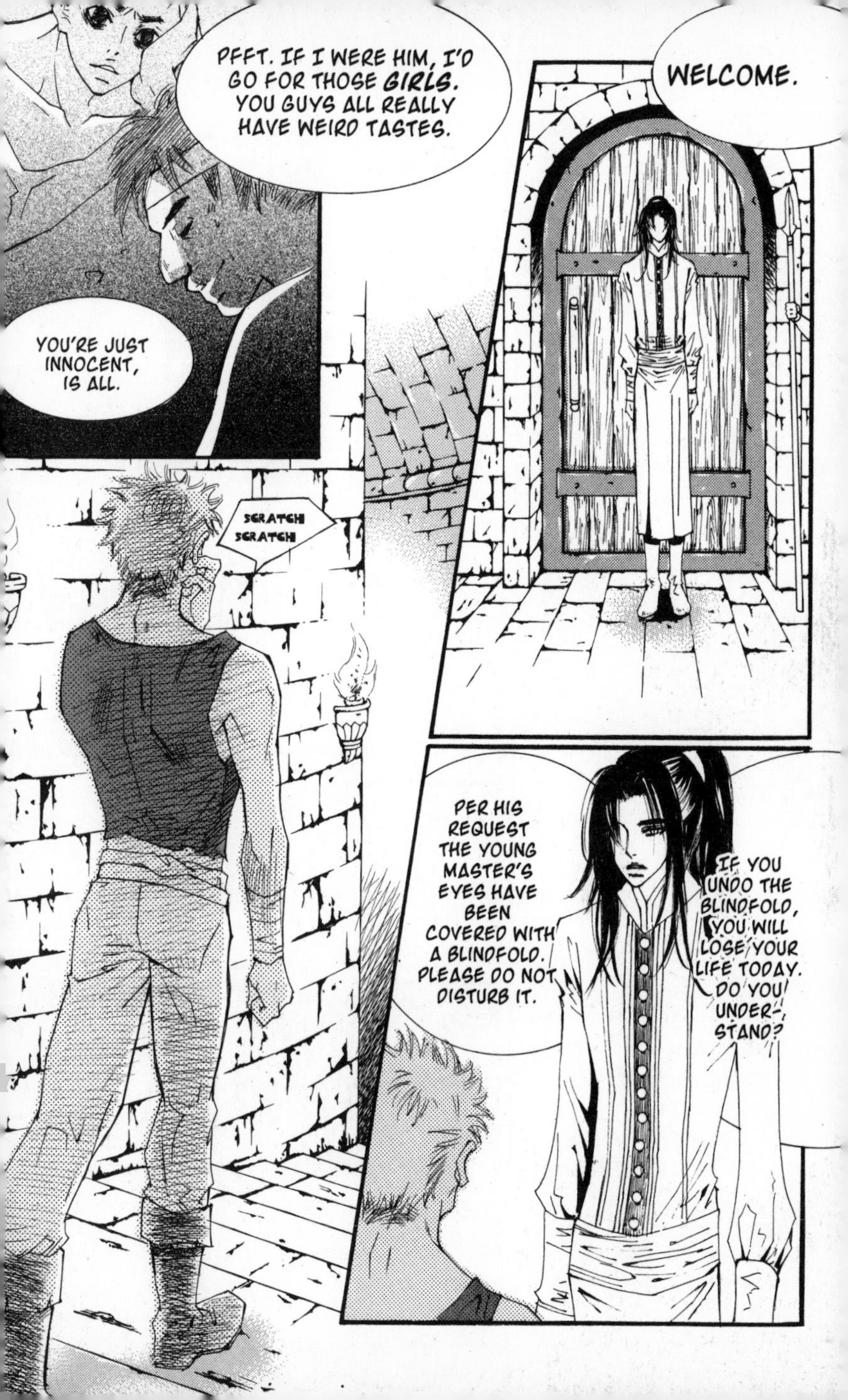
PFFT. IF I WERE HIM, I'D GO FOR THOSE GIRLS. YOU GUYS ALL REALLY HAVE WEIRD TASTES.
YOU'RE JUST INNOCENT, IS ALL.
WELCOME.
SCRATCH SCRATCH
PER HIS REQUEST THE YOUNG MASTER'S EYES HAVE BEEN COVERED WITH A BLINDFOLD. PLEASE DO NOT DISTURB IT.
IF YOU UNDO THE BLINDFOLD, YOU WILL LOSE YOUR LIFE TODAY. DO YOU UNDER-STAND?

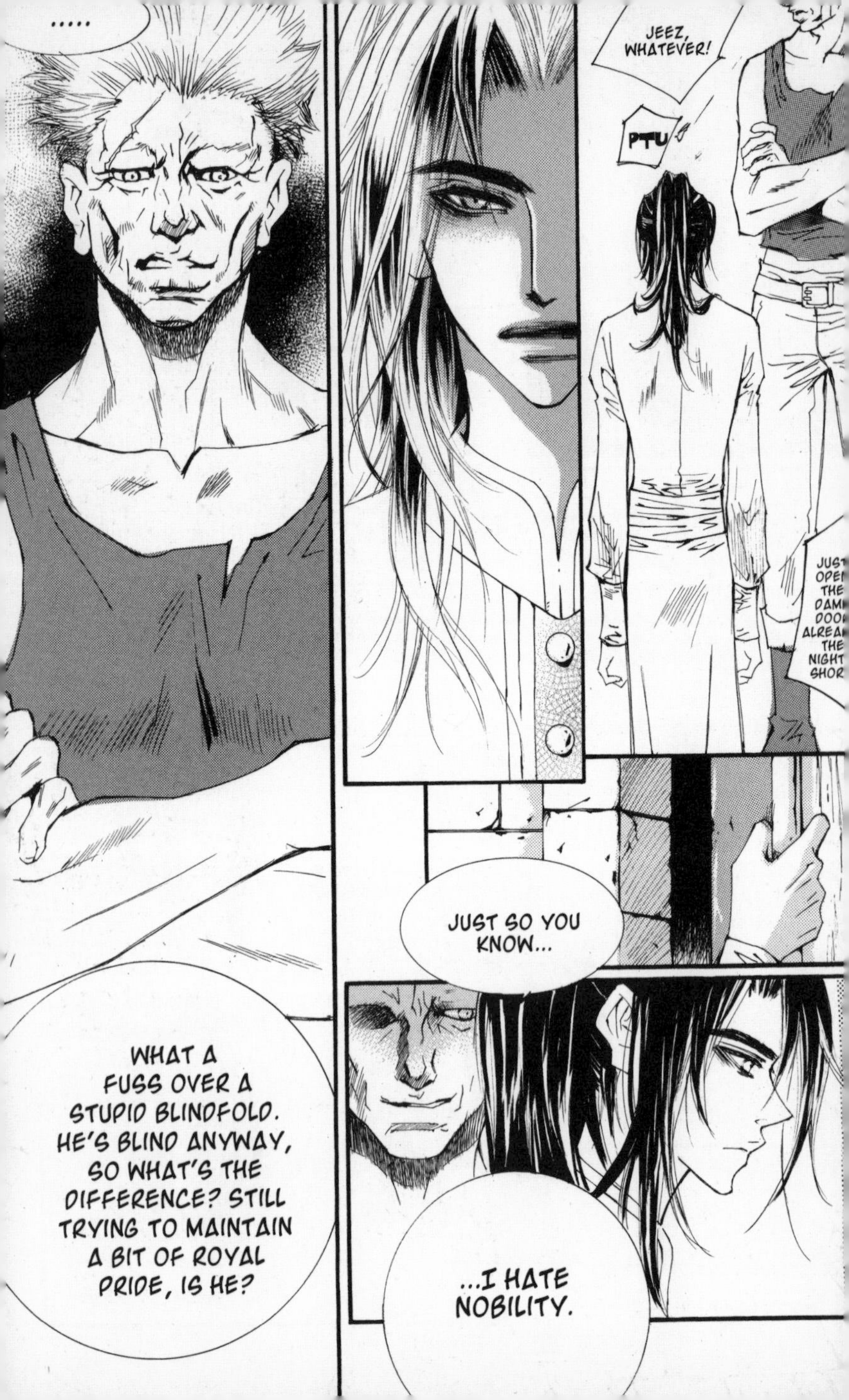
.....
WHAT A FUSS OVER A STUPID BLINDFOLD. HE'S BLIND ANYWAY, SO WHAT'S THE DIFFERENCE? STILL TRYING TO MAINTAIN A BIT OF ROYAL PRIDE, IS HE?
JEEZ, WHATEVER!
PTU
JUST SO YOU KNOW...
...I HATE NOBILITY.

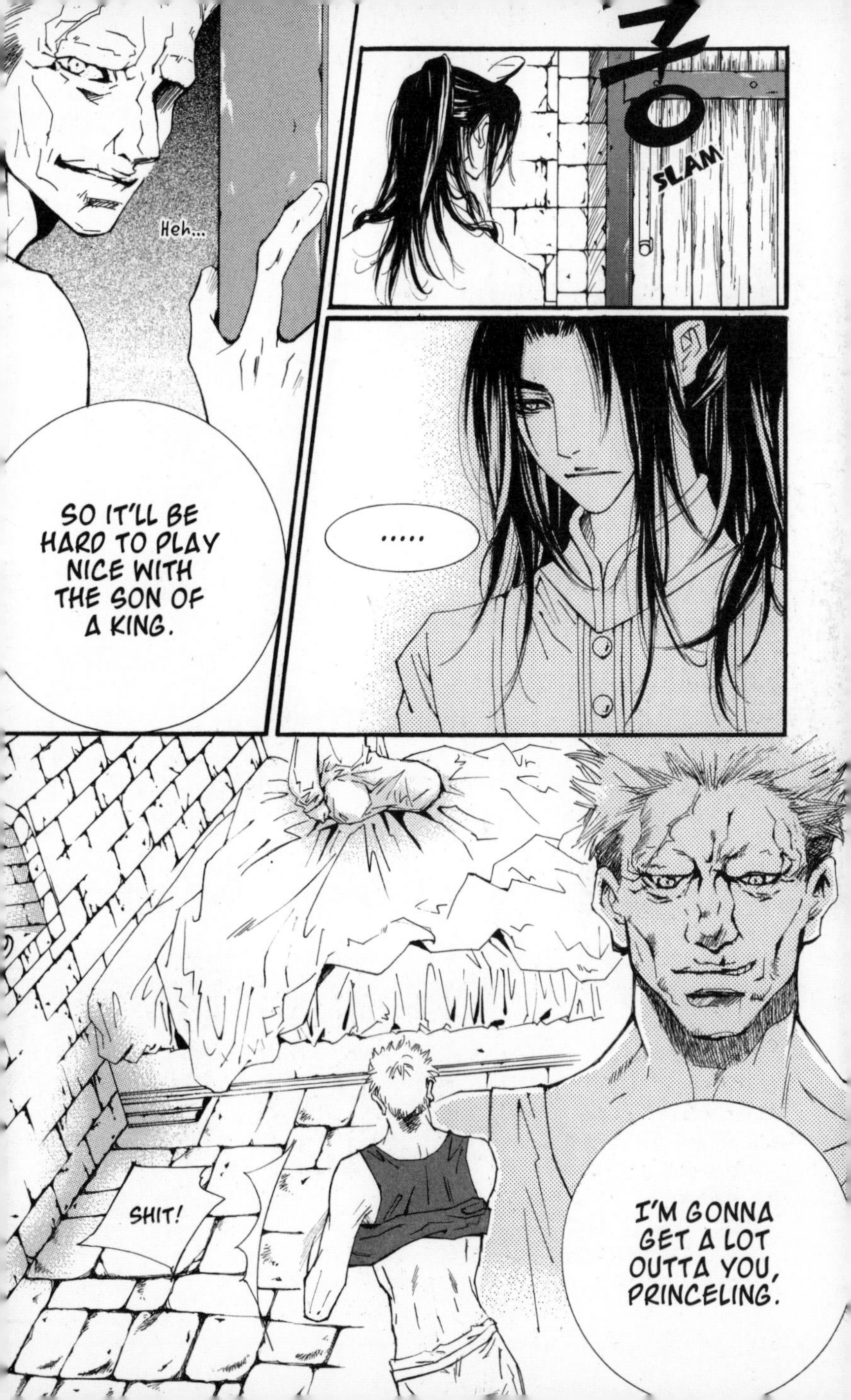

Heh...
SO IT'LL BE HARD TO PLAY NICE WITH THE SON OF A KING.
SLAM
.....
SHIT!
I'M GONNA GET A LOT OUTTA YOU, PRINCELING.

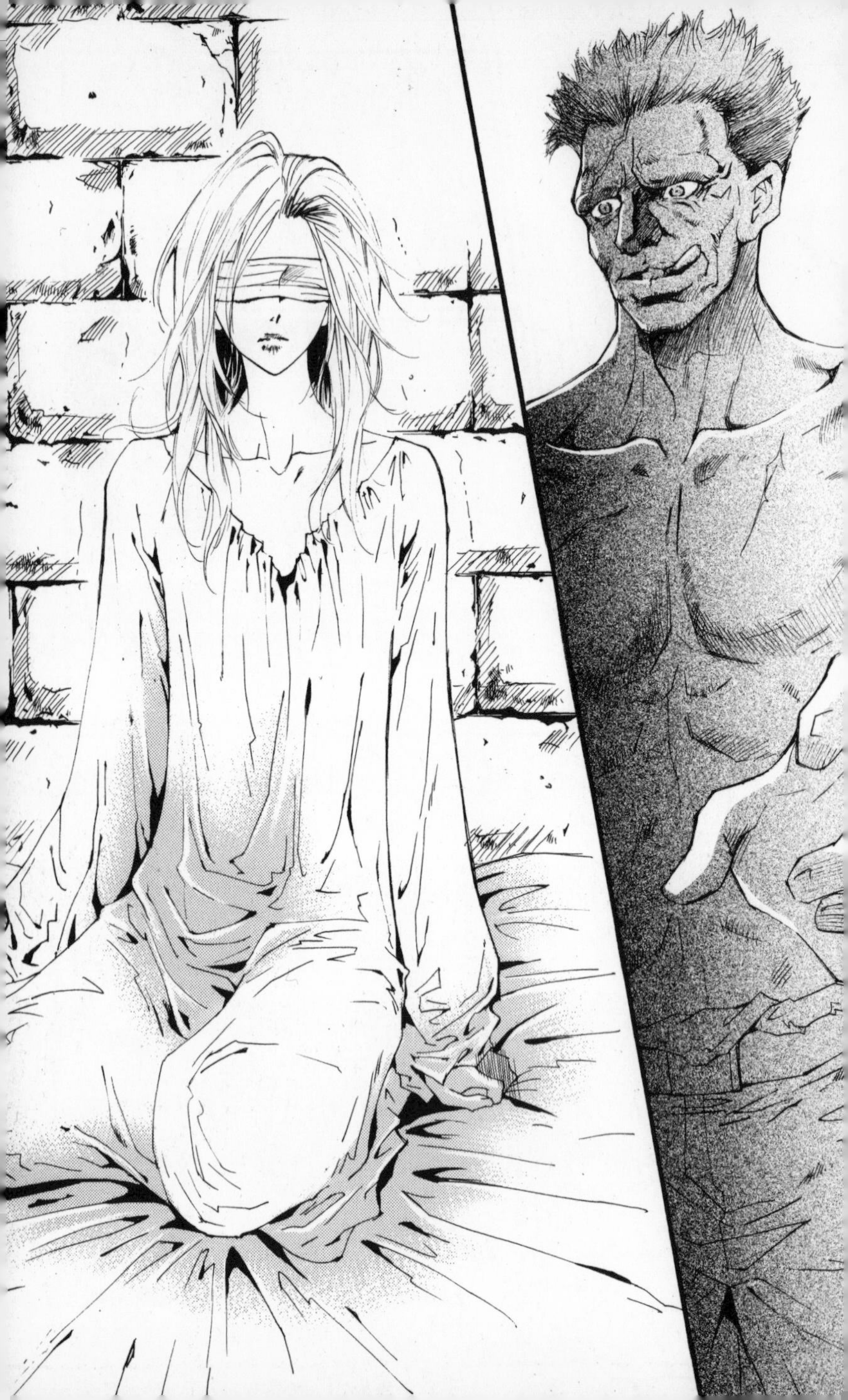

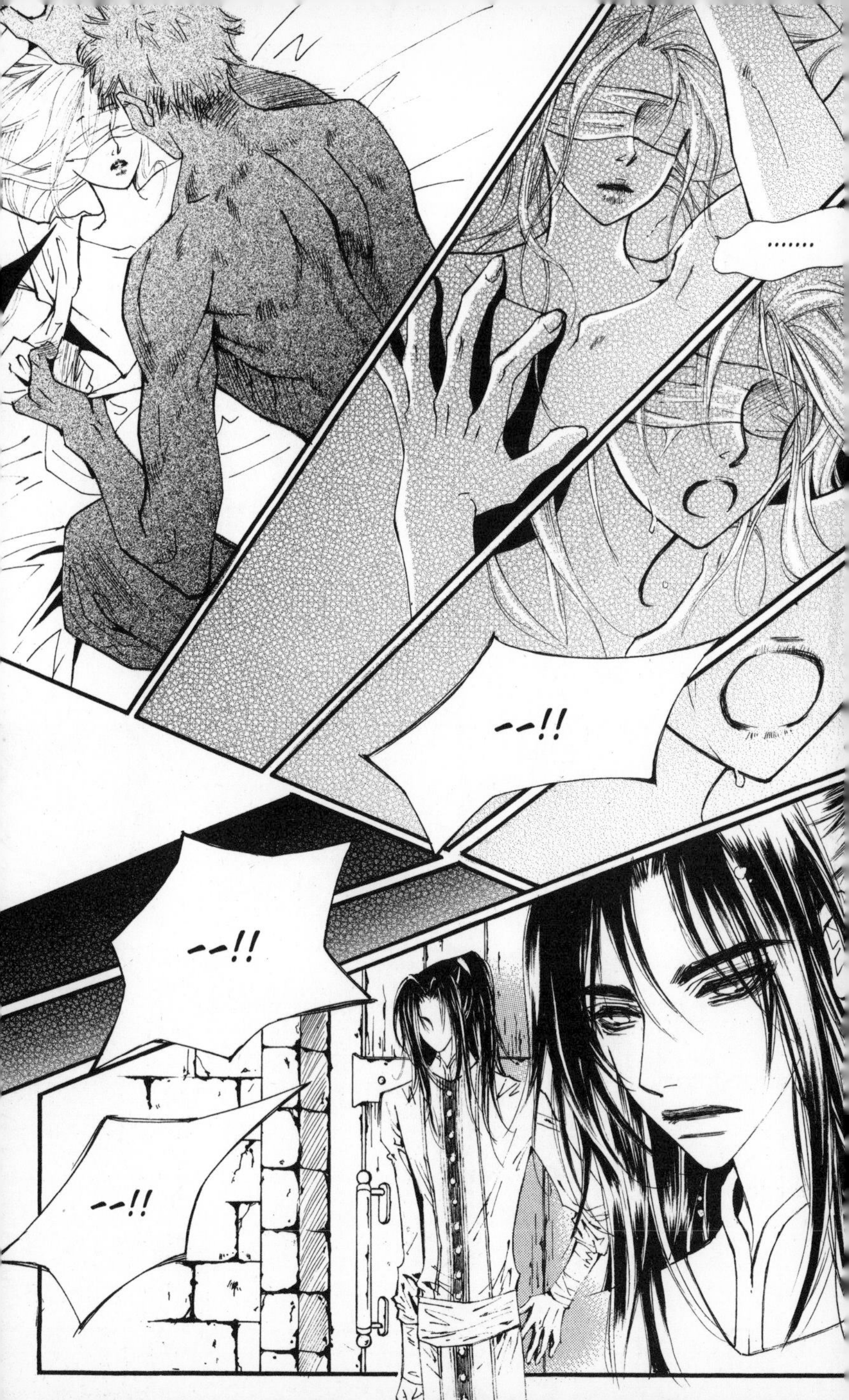

....
--!!
--!!
--!!

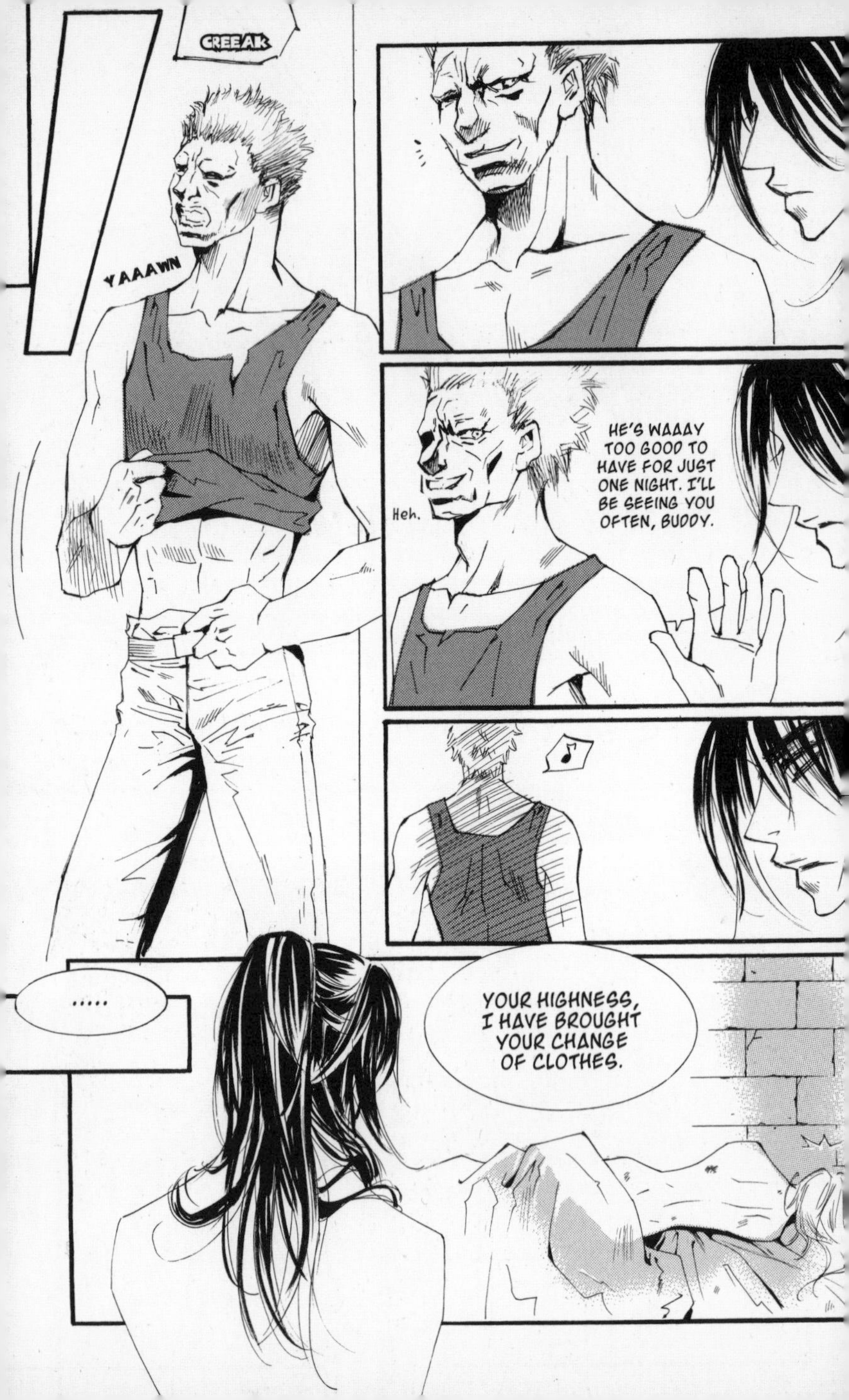
CREEAK
YAAAWN
Heh.
HE'S WAAAY TOO GOOD TO HAVE FOR JUST ONE NIGHT. I'LL BE SEEING YOU OFTEN, BUDDY.
......
YOUR HIGHNESS, I HAVE BROUGHT YOUR CHANGE OF CLOTHES.

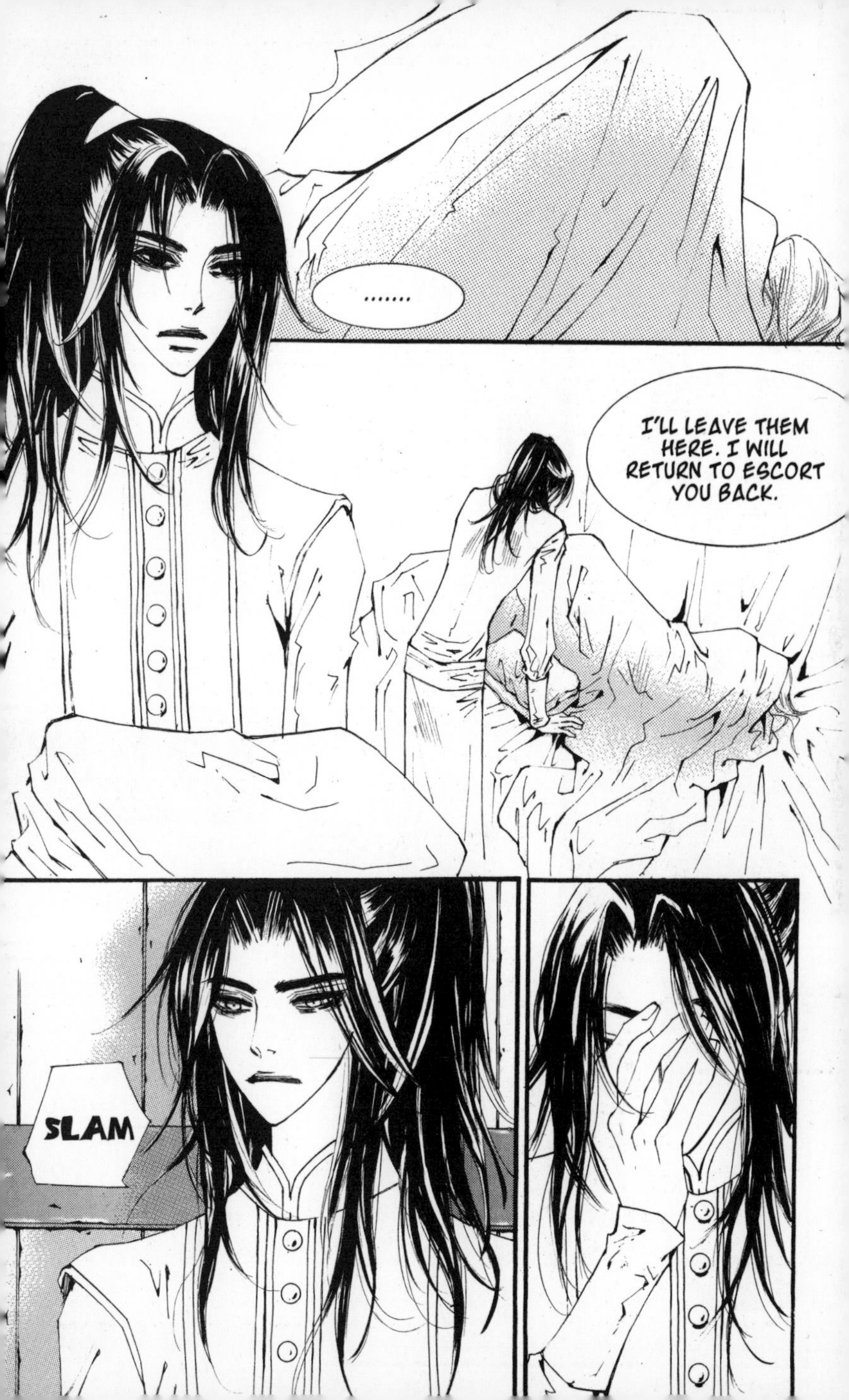
....
I'LL LEAVE THEM HERE. I WILL RETURN TO ESCORT YOU BACK.
SLAM

...FEELING UNCLEAN AND DESTROYED...

I CAN'T LET IT MATTER.

I'M JUST A BODY.

SO...

...AND THINKI THAT...

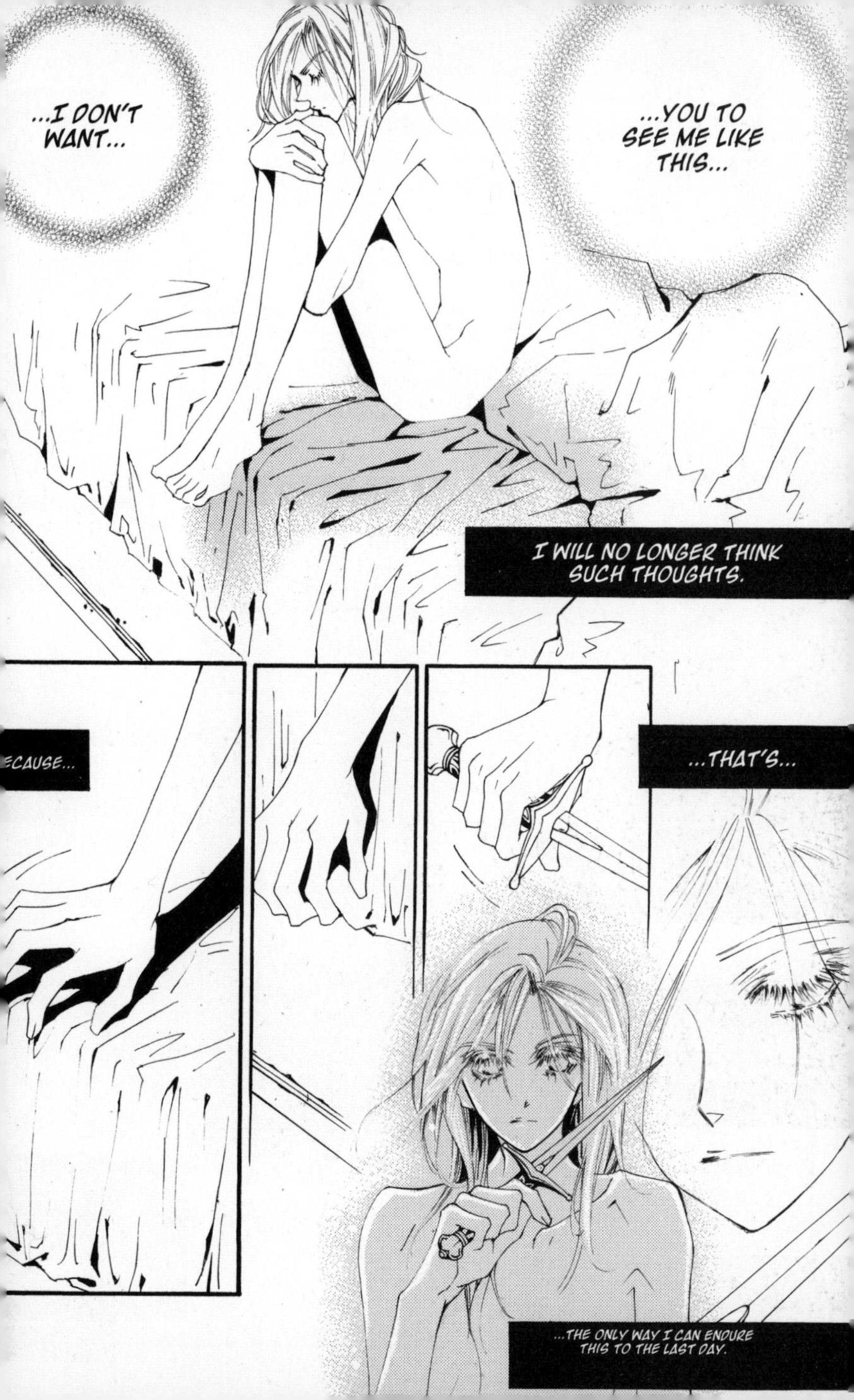
...I DON'T WANT...
...YOU TO SEE ME LIKE THIS...
I WILL NO LONGER THINK SUCH THOUGHTS.
ECAUSE...
...THAT'S...
...THE ONLY WAY I CAN ENDURE THIS TO THE LAST DAY.

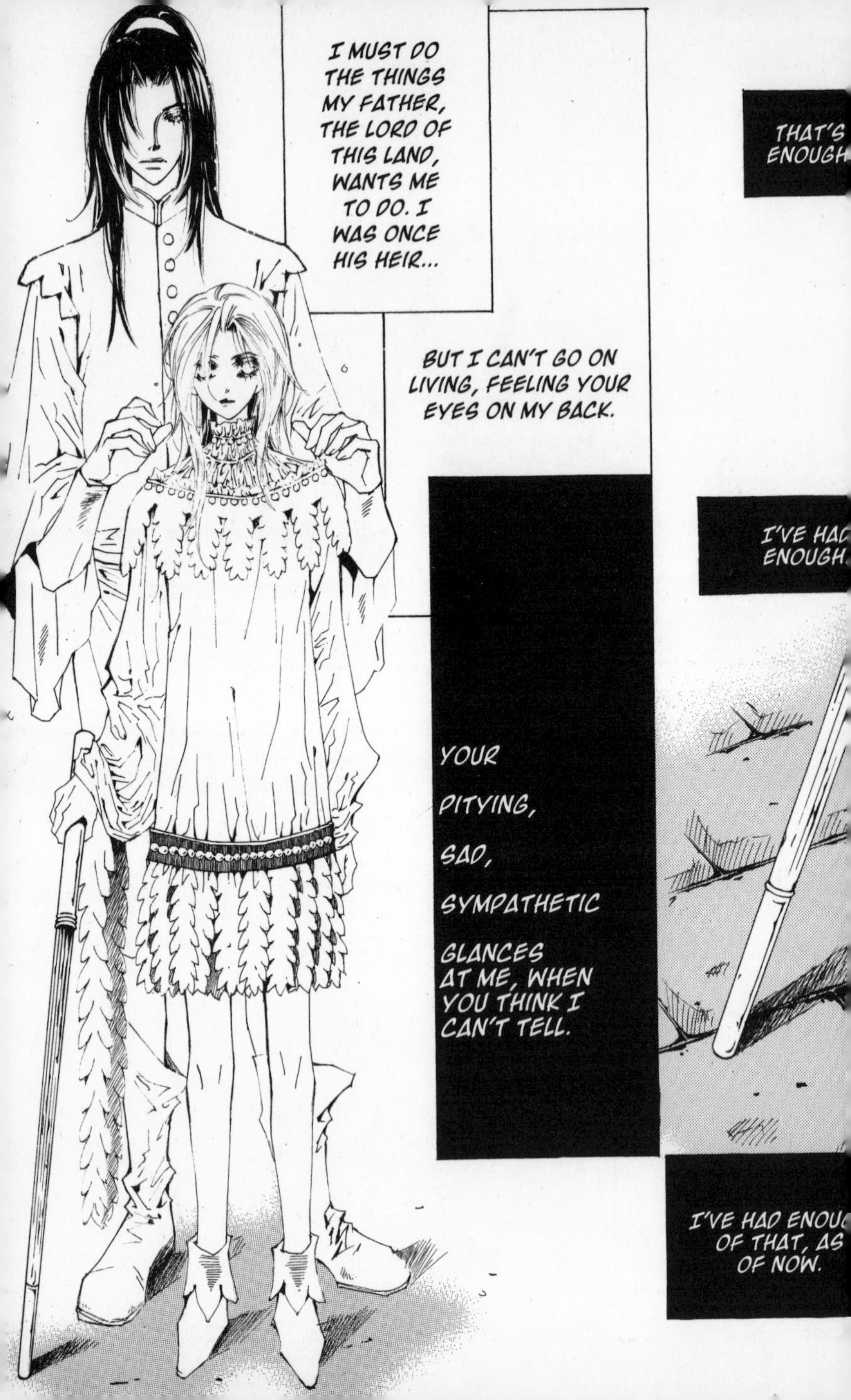
I MUST DO THE THINGS MY FATHER, THE LORD OF THIS LAND, WANTS ME TO DO. I WAS ONCE HIS HEIR...
BUT I CAN'T GO ON LIVING, FEELING YOUR EYES ON MY BACK.
YOUR PITYING, SAD, SYMPATHETIC GLANCES AT ME, WHEN YOU THINK I CAN'T TELL.
THAT'S ENOUGH
I'VE HAD ENOUGH
I'VE HAD ENOU OF THAT, AS OF NOW.

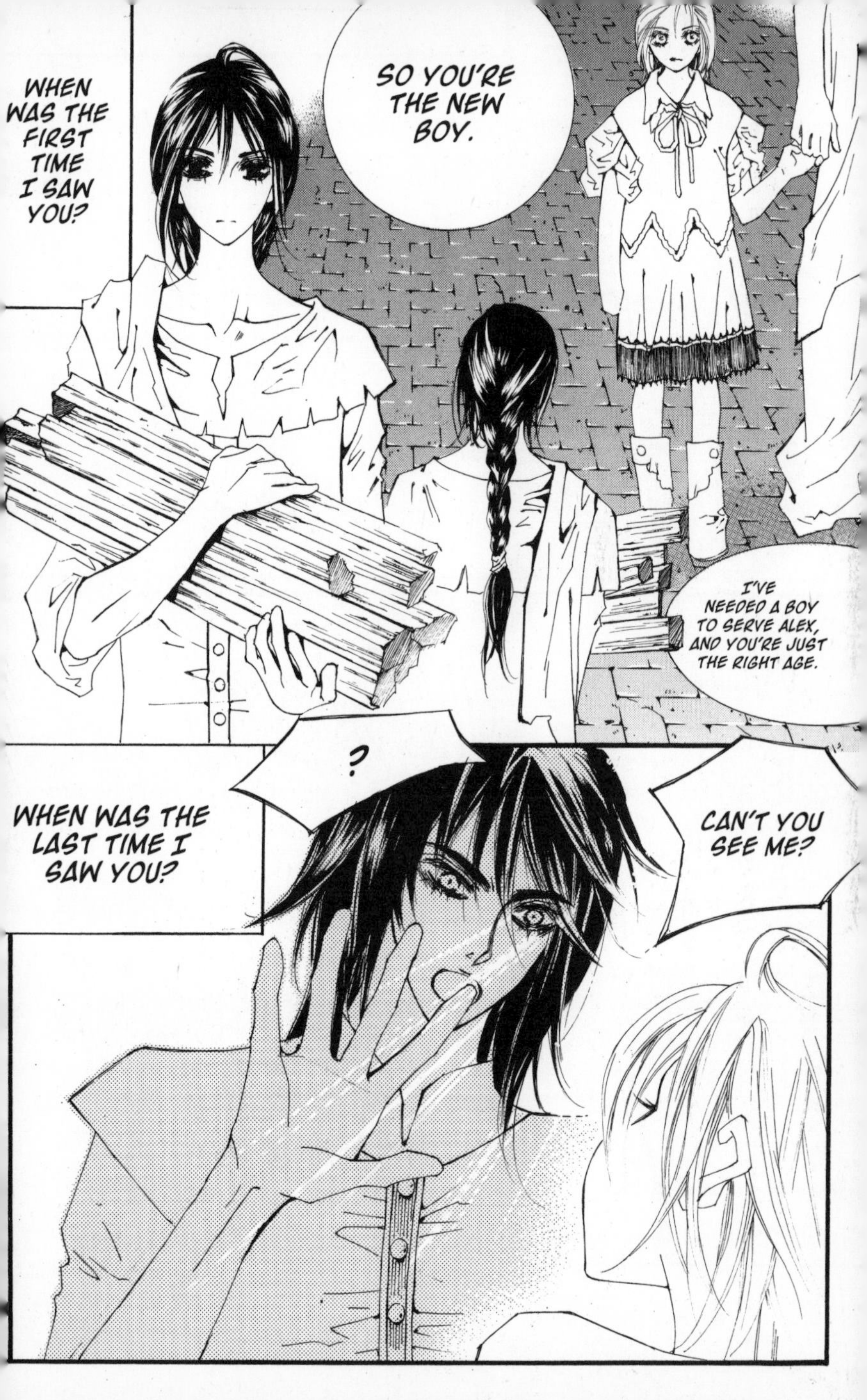
WHEN WAS THE FIRST TIME I SAW YOU?
SO YOU'RE THE NEW BOY.
I'VE NEEDED A BOY TO SERVE ALEX, AND YOU'RE JUST THE RIGHT AGE.
WHEN WAS THE LAST TIME I SAW YOU?
?
CAN'T YOU SEE ME?

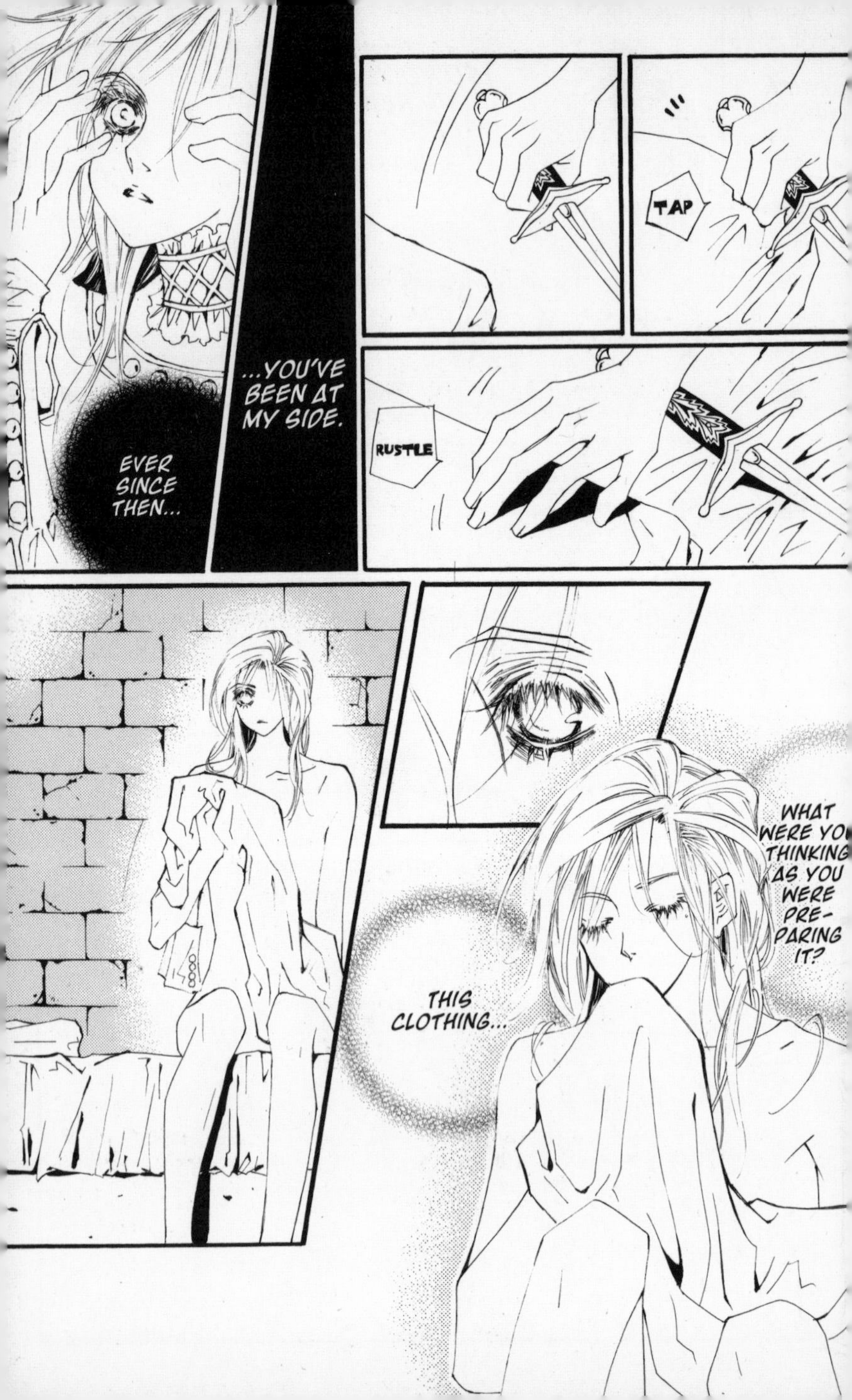
EVER SINCE THEN...
...YOU'VE BEEN AT MY SIDE.
TAP
RUSTLE
THIS CLOTHING...
WHAT WERE YO THINKING AS YOU WERE PRE-PARING IT?

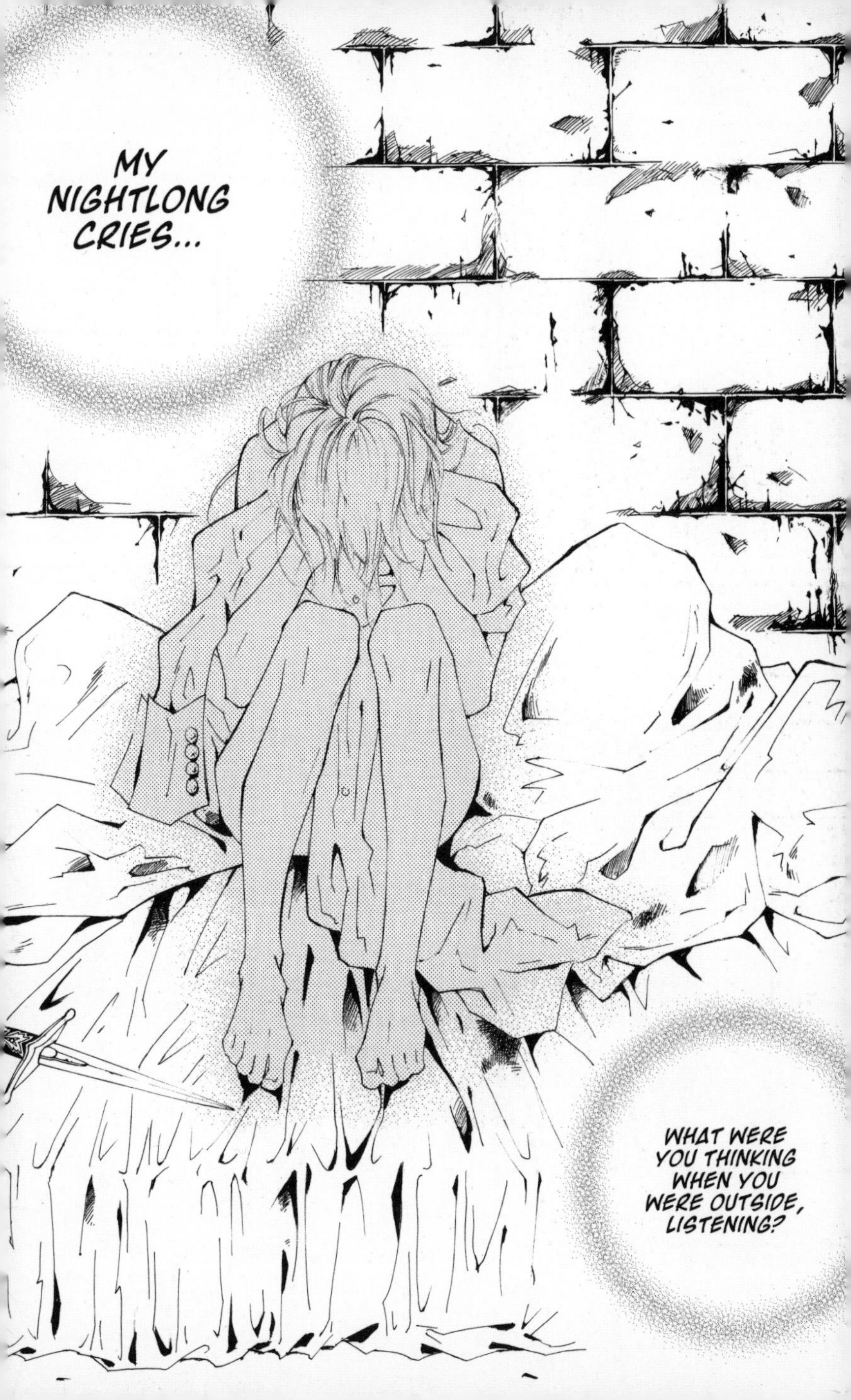
MY NIGHTLONG CRIES...
WHAT WERE YOU THINKING WHEN YOU WERE OUTSIDE, LISTENING?

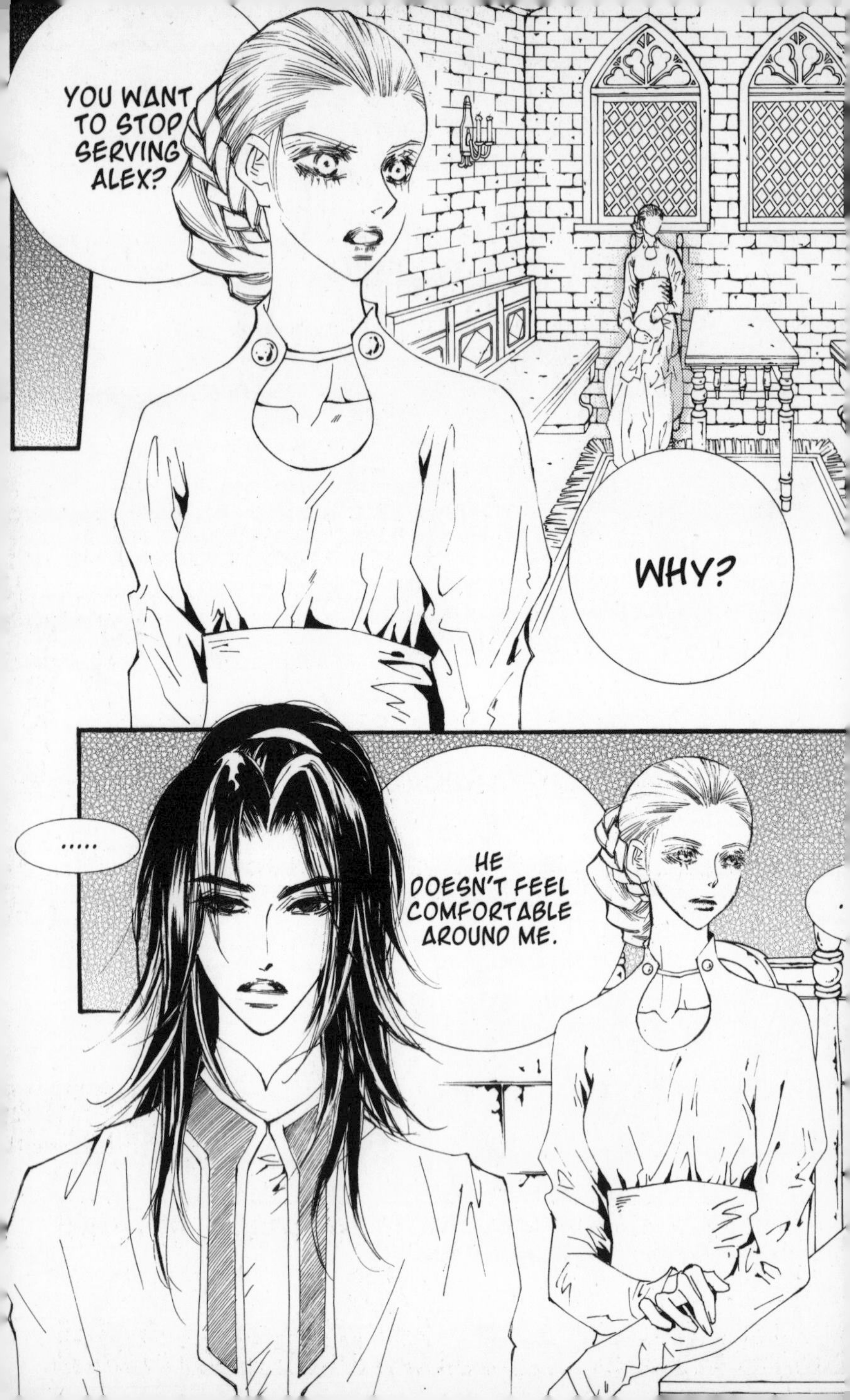
YOU WANT TO STOP SERVING ALEX?
WHY?
.....
HE DOESN'T FEEL COMFORTABLE AROUND ME.

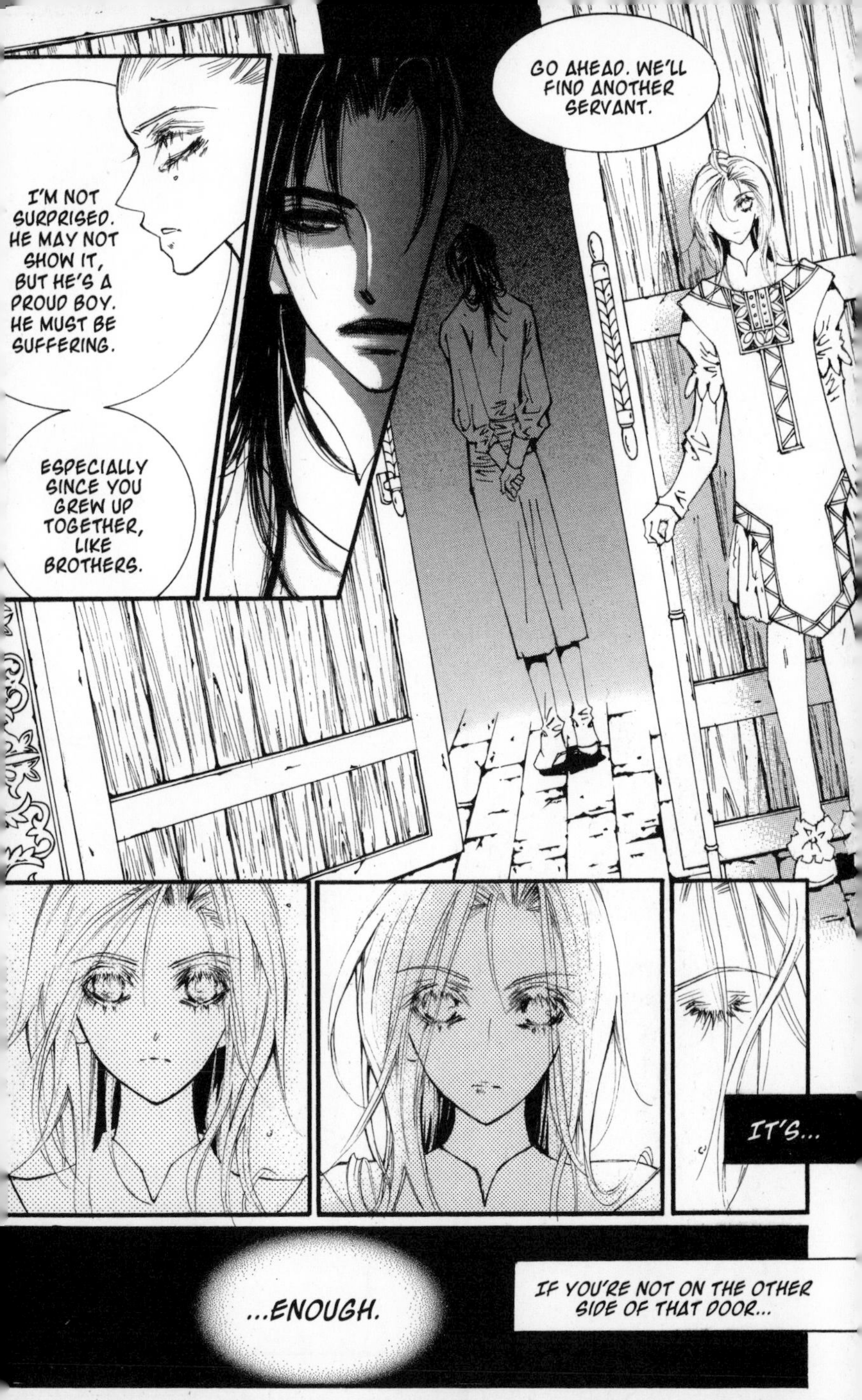
I'M NOT SURPRISED. HE MAY NOT SHOW IT, BUT HE'S A PROUD BOY. HE MUST BE SUFFERING.
ESPECIALLY SINCE YOU GREW UP TOGETHER, LIKE BROTHERS.
GO AHEAD. WE'LL FIND ANOTHER SERVANT.
IT'S...
...ENOUGH.
IF YOU'RE NOT ON THE OTHER SIDE OF THAT DOOR...

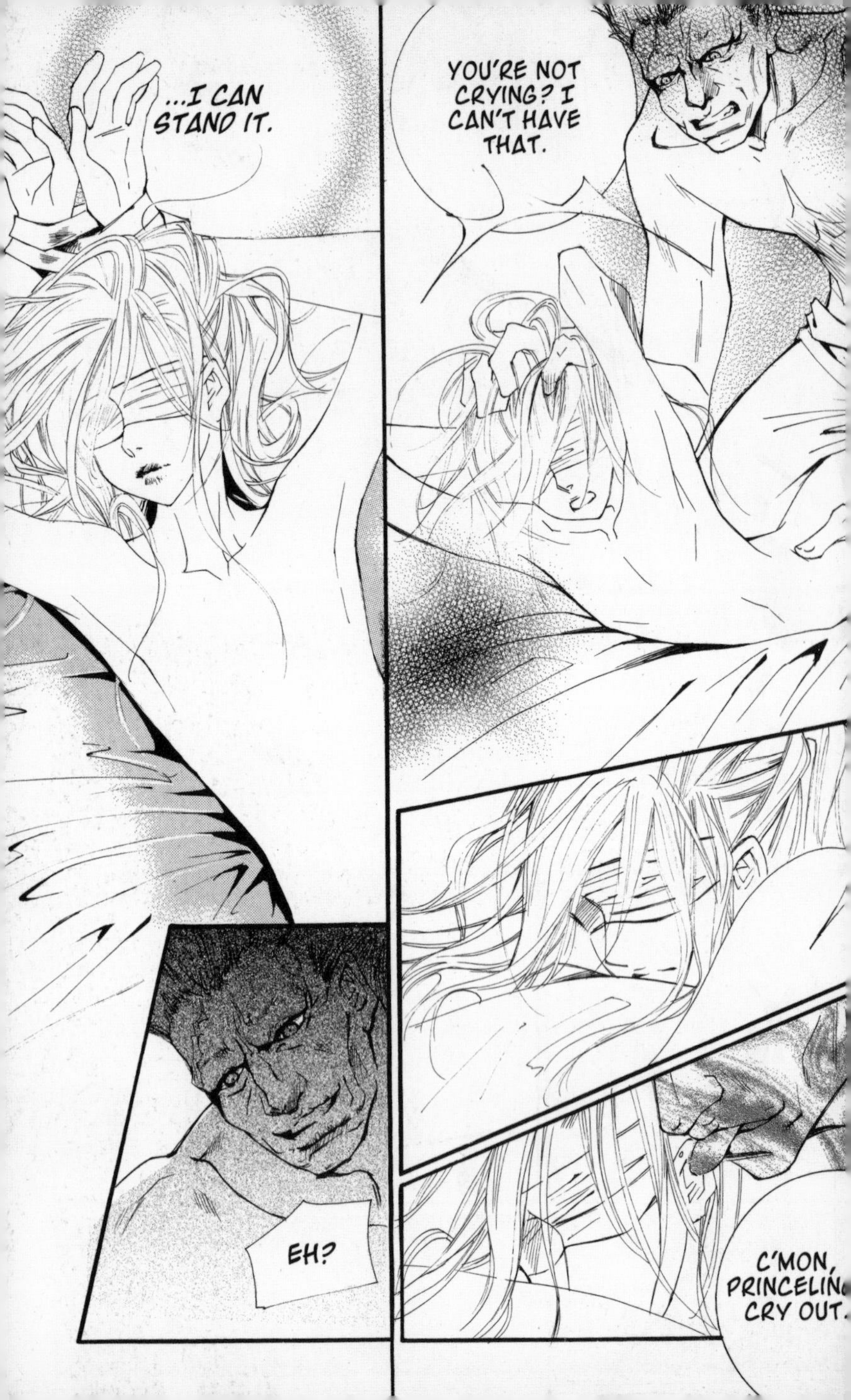
...I CAN STAND IT.
EH?
YOU'RE NOT CRYING? I CAN'T HAVE THAT.
C'MON, PRINCELING, CRY OUT.

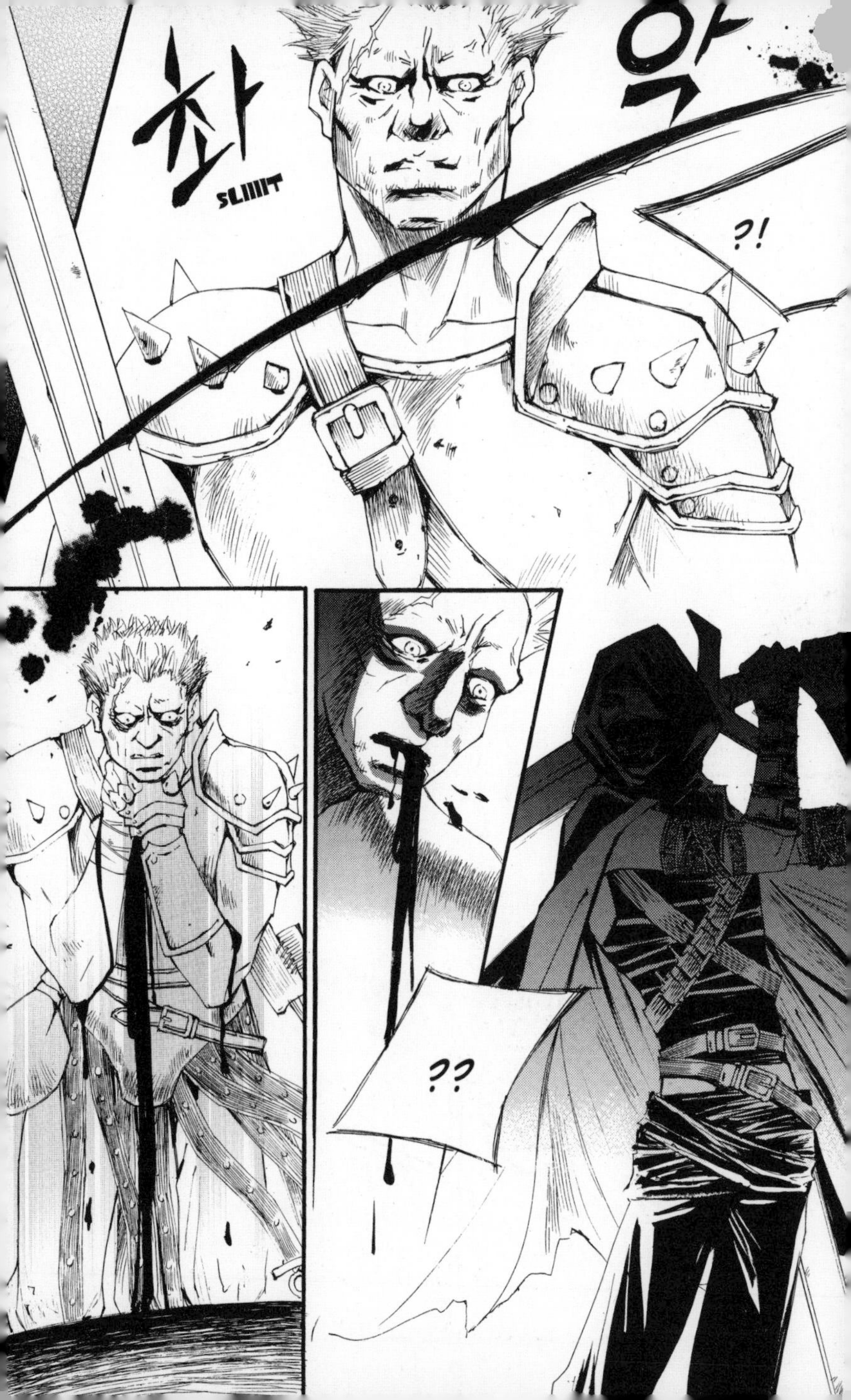
촤
SLIIIIT
악
?!
??

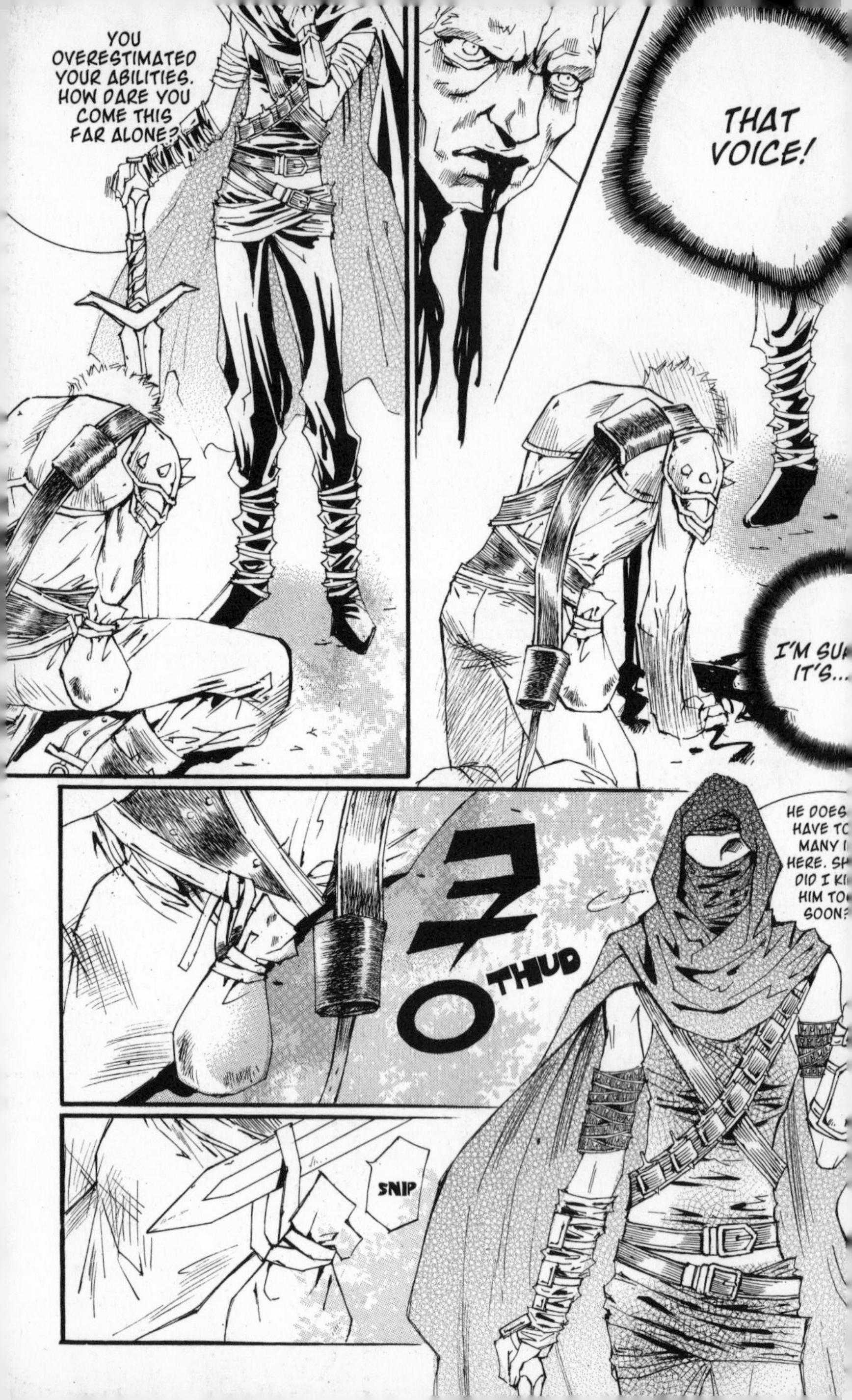
YOU OVERESTIMATED YOUR ABILITIES. HOW DARE YOU COME THIS FAR ALONE?
THAT VOICE!
I'M SU IT'S...
THUD
SNIP
HE DOES HAVE TO MANY HERE. SH DID I KI HIM TO SOON?

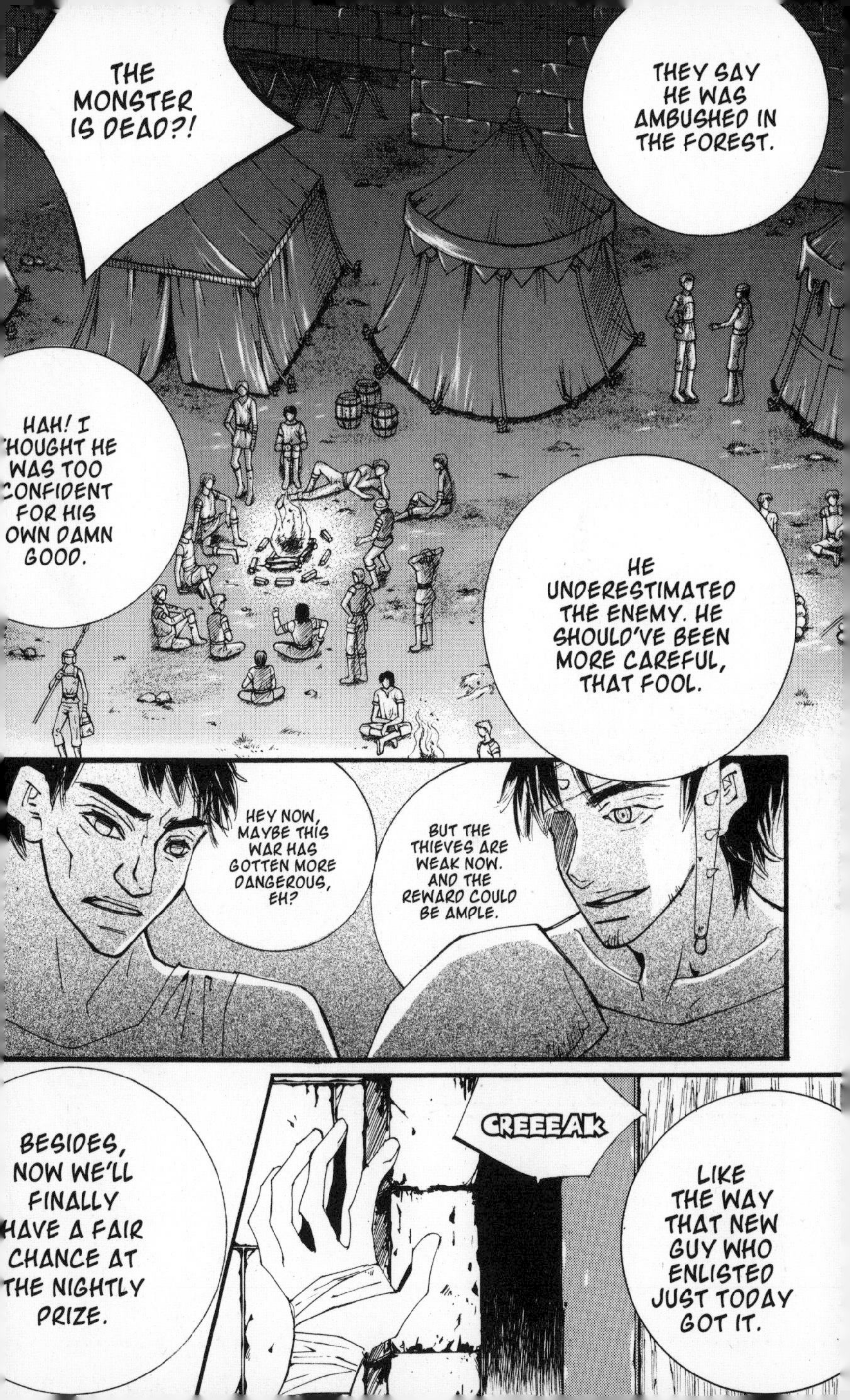
THE MONSTER IS DEAD?!
THEY SAY HE WAS AMBUSHED IN THE FOREST.
HAH! I THOUGHT HE WAS TOO CONFIDENT FOR HIS OWN DAMN GOOD.
HE UNDERESTIMATED THE ENEMY. HE SHOULD'VE BEEN MORE CAREFUL, THAT FOOL.
HEY NOW, MAYBE THIS WAR HAS GOTTEN MORE DANGEROUS, EH?
BUT THE THIEVES ARE WEAK NOW. AND THE REWARD COULD BE AMPLE.
BESIDES, NOW WE'LL FINALLY HAVE A FAIR CHANCE AT THE NIGHTLY PRIZE.
CREEEAK
LIKE THE WAY THAT NEW GUY WHO ENLISTED JUST TODAY GOT IT.

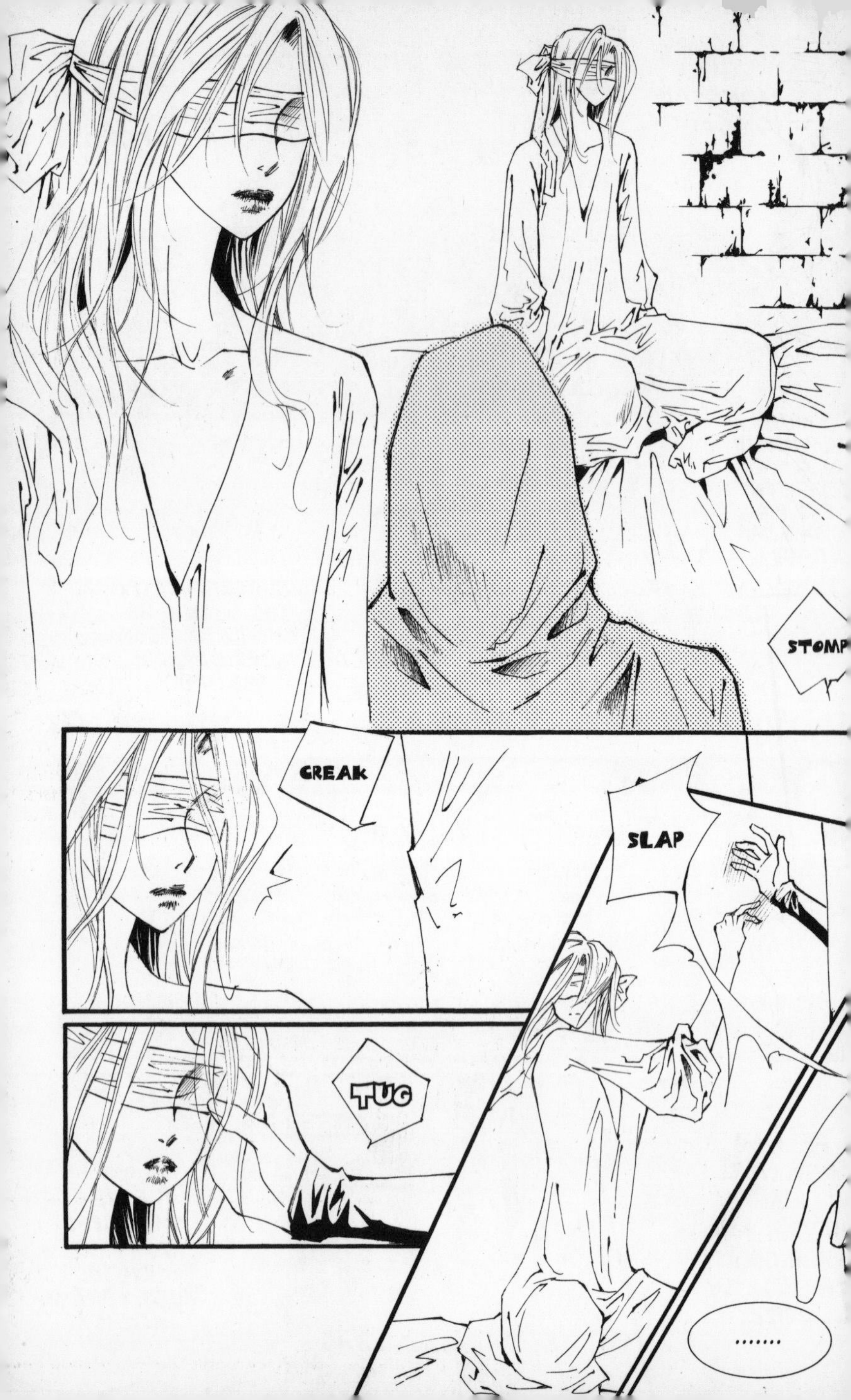
STOMP
CREAK
TUG
SLAP
....

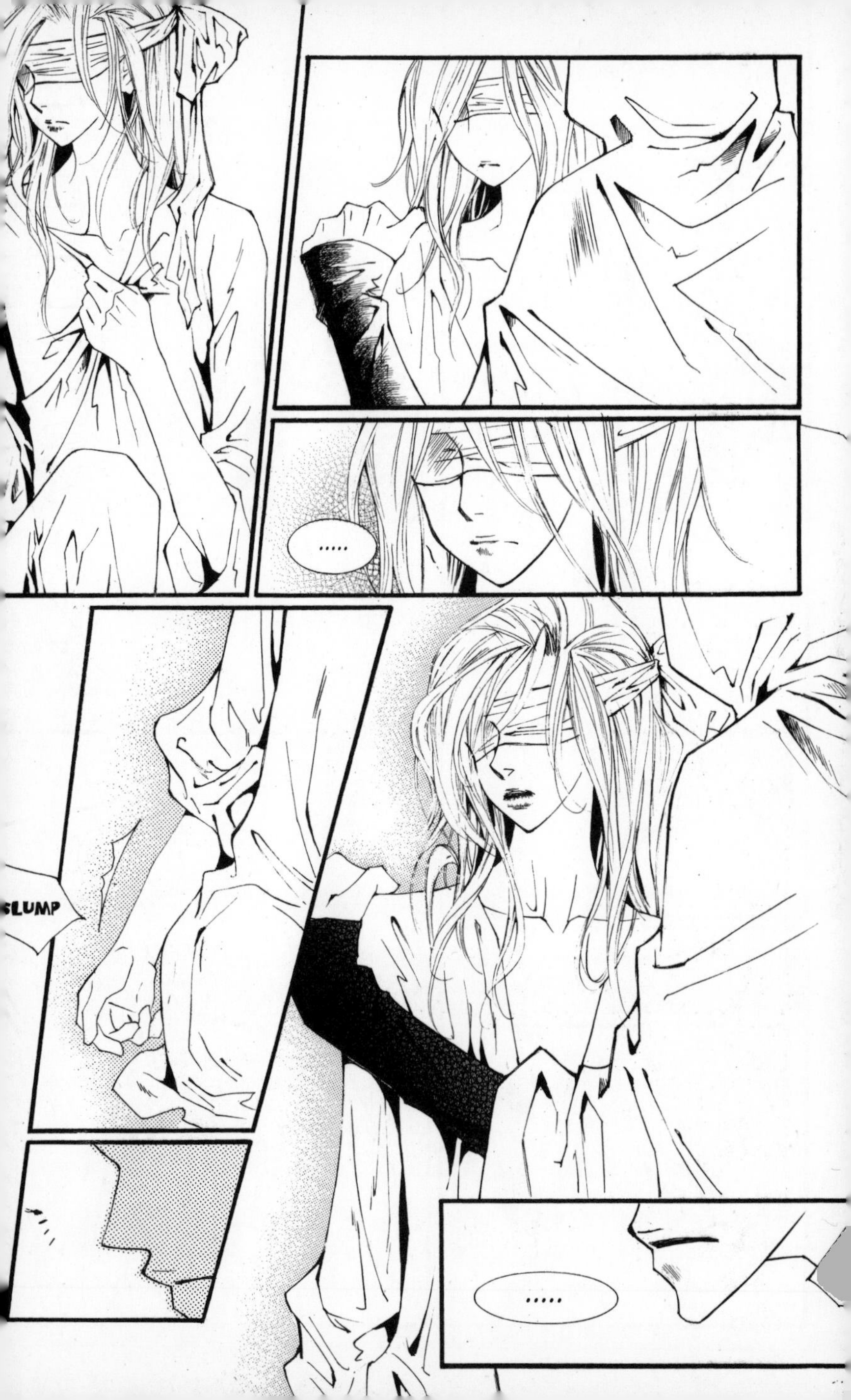
......
SLUMP
......

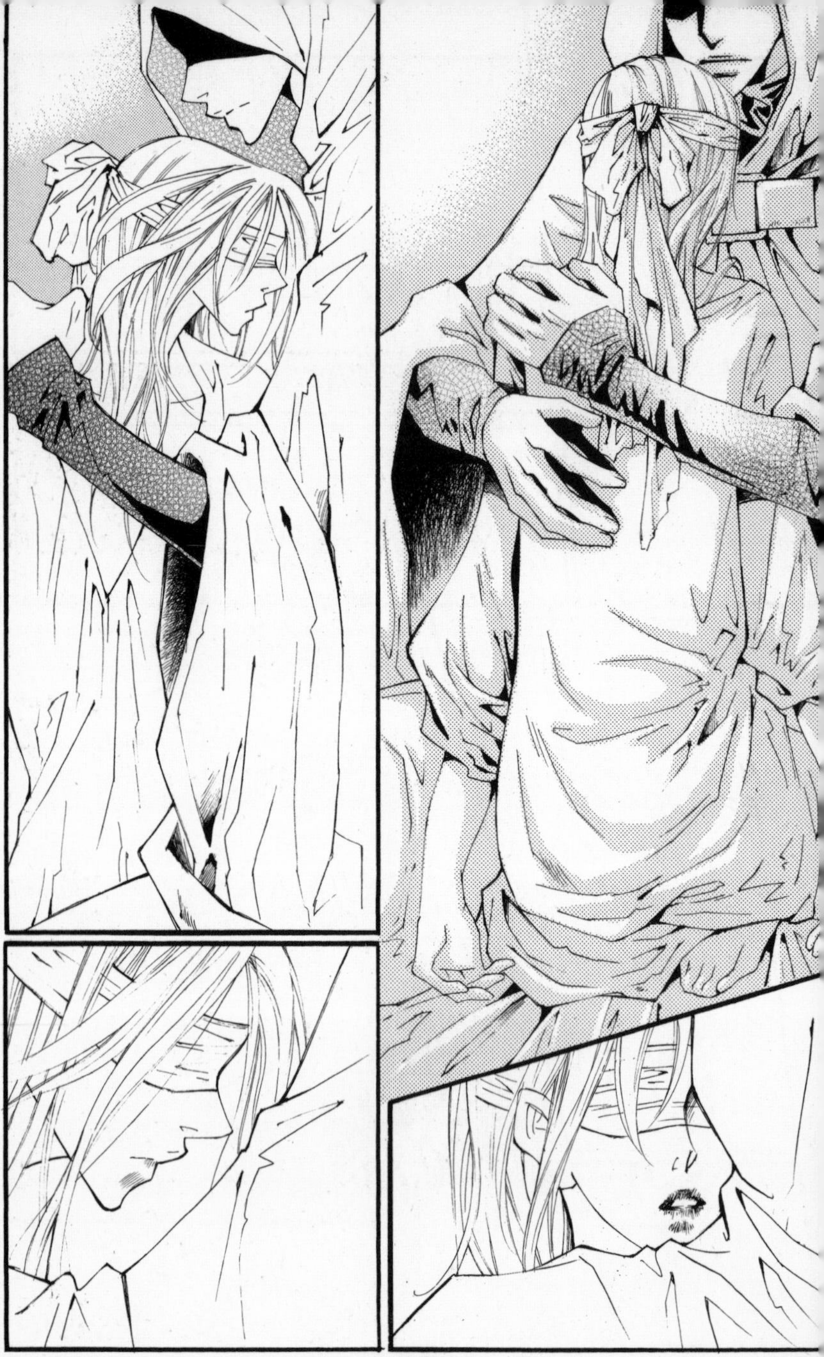

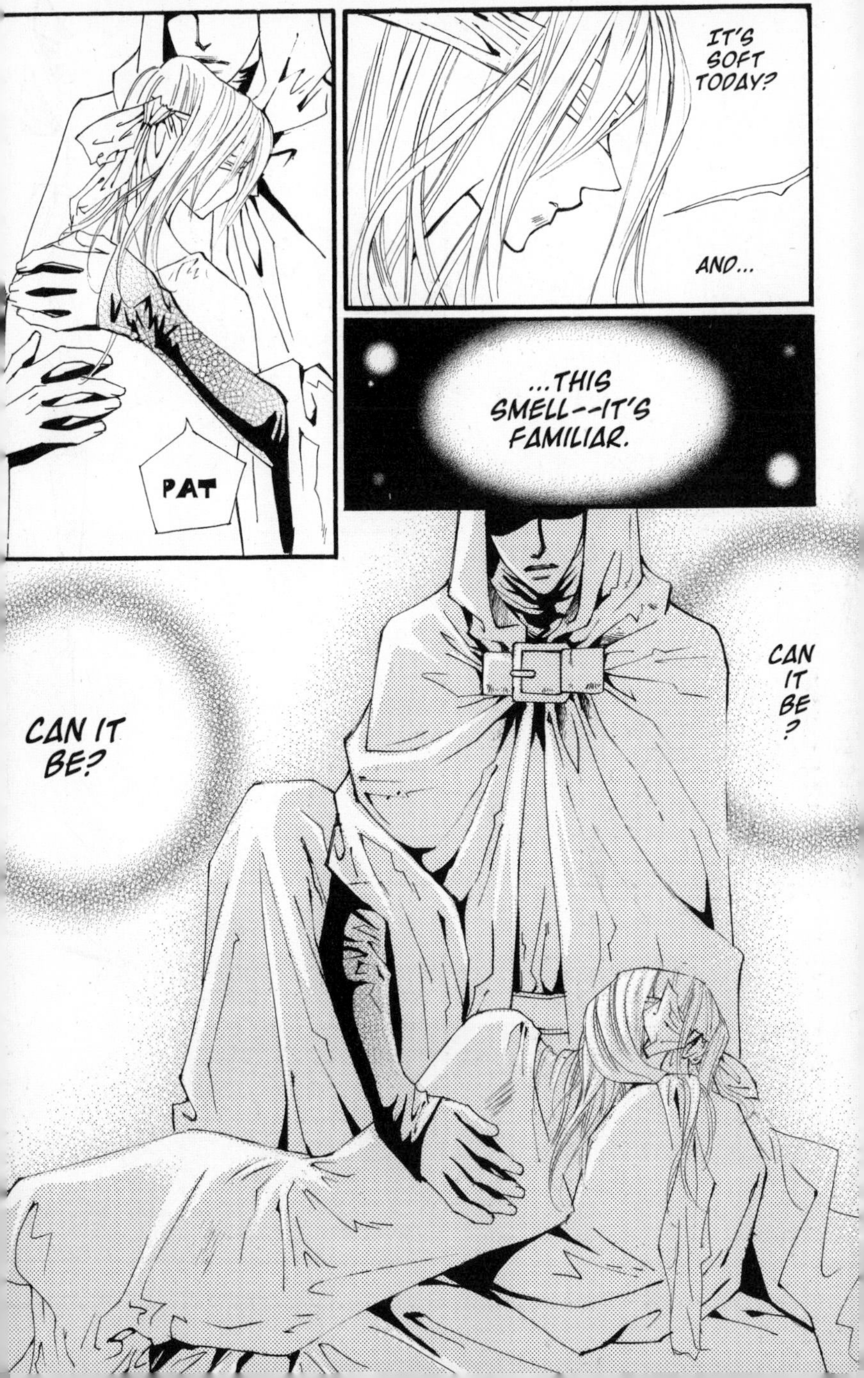
PAT
IT'S SOFT TODAY?
AND...
...THIS SMELL--IT'S FAMILIAR.
CAN IT BE?
CAN IT BE?

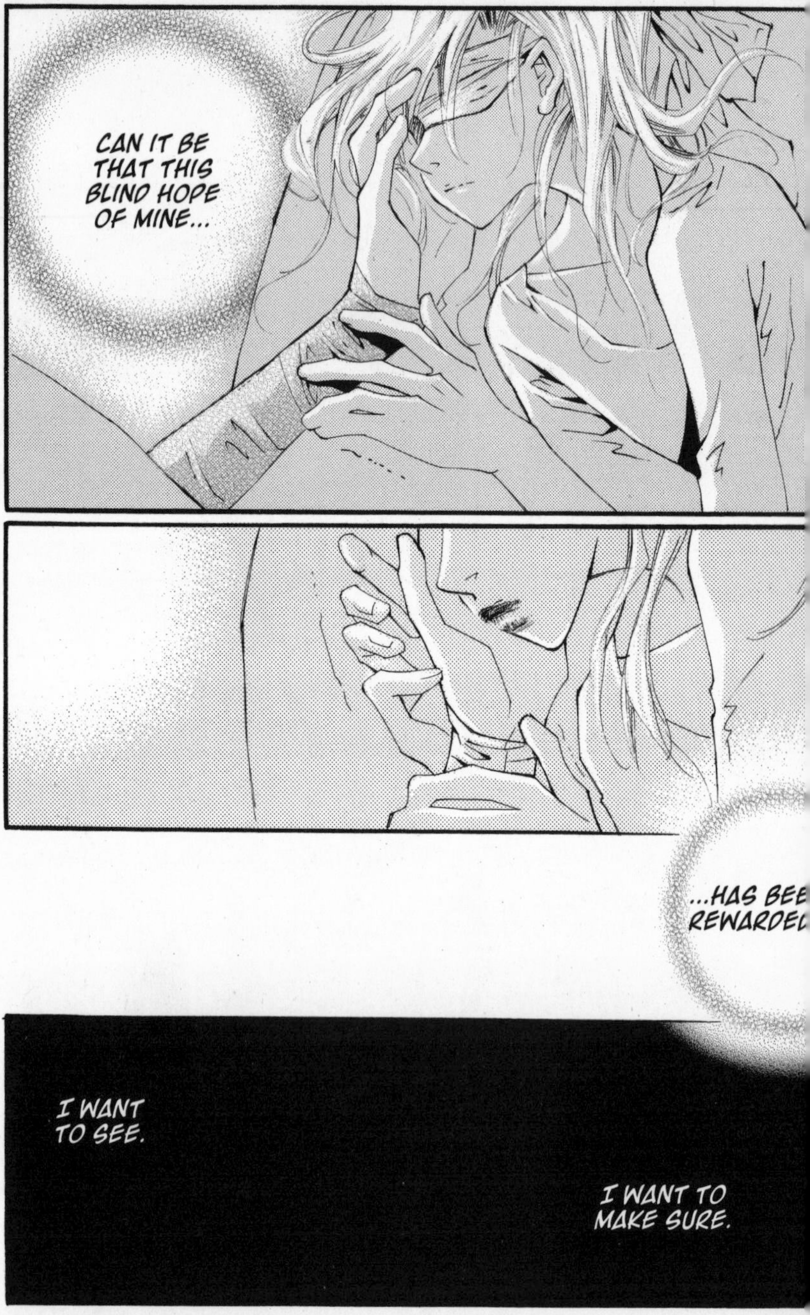
CAN IT BE THAT THIS BLIND HOPE OF MINE...
...HAS BEE REWARDE
I WANT TO SEE.
I WANT TO MAKE SURE.

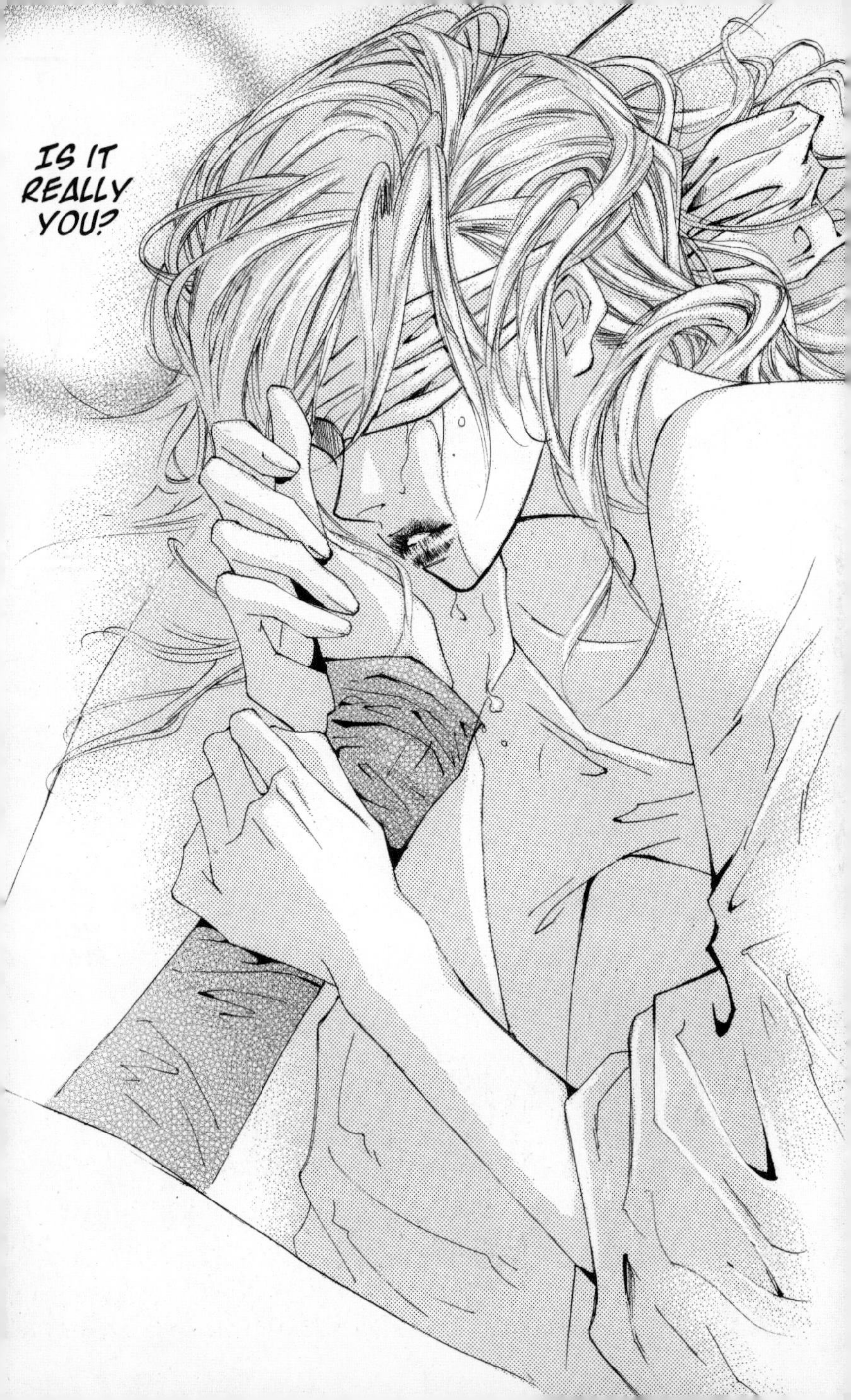
IS IT REALLY YOU?

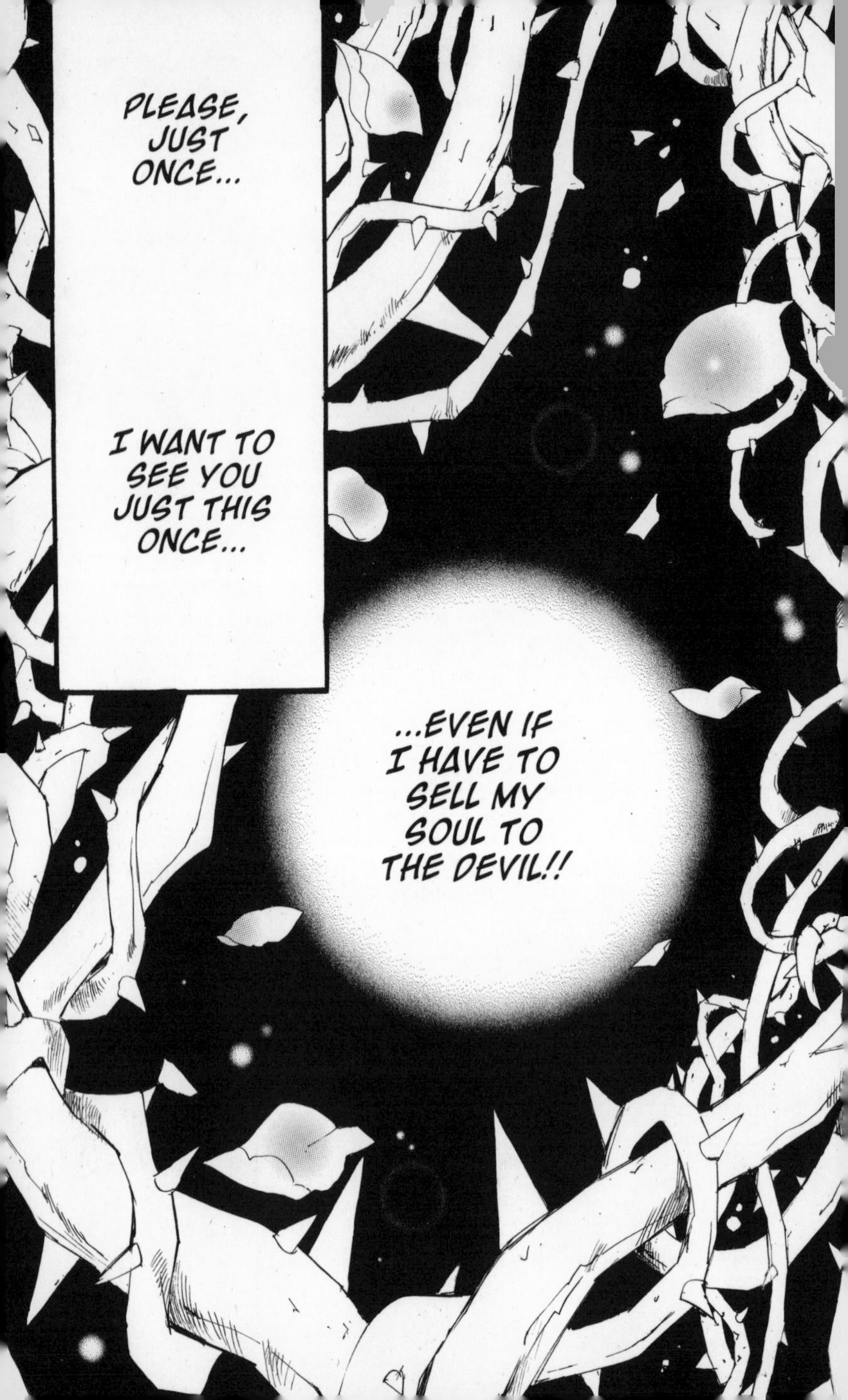
PLEASE, JUST ONCE...
I WANT TO SEE YOU JUST THIS ONCE...
...EVEN IF I HAVE TO SELL MY SOUL TO THE DEVIL!!

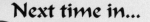
Next time in...

DEVIL'S BRIDE

WROUGHT WITH GUILT AND BLINDED BY HIS
DESIRE TO HAVE THE PERFECT BRIDE,
THE DEVIL CONTINUES HIS PURSUIT OF
HUMAN PARTS FOR THE CONSTRUCTION
OF LEY. WHILE HE LABORS TO PROCURE
THE NEXT ITEM ON HIS LIST--A BEATING
HEART--LEY MATURES INTO ADULTHOOD.
BUT AS LEY GROWS PHYSICALLY,
ALLOWING THE DEVIL TO INCH CLOSER
TO ACHIEVING HIS GOAL, THE DEVIL
BEGINS TO REALIZE A CRITICAL ERROR
IN HIS CALCULATIONS...THAT LEY WILL BE
GOVERNED BY HIS OWN PERSONALITY,
NOT BY HIS HUSBAND AND CREATOR.

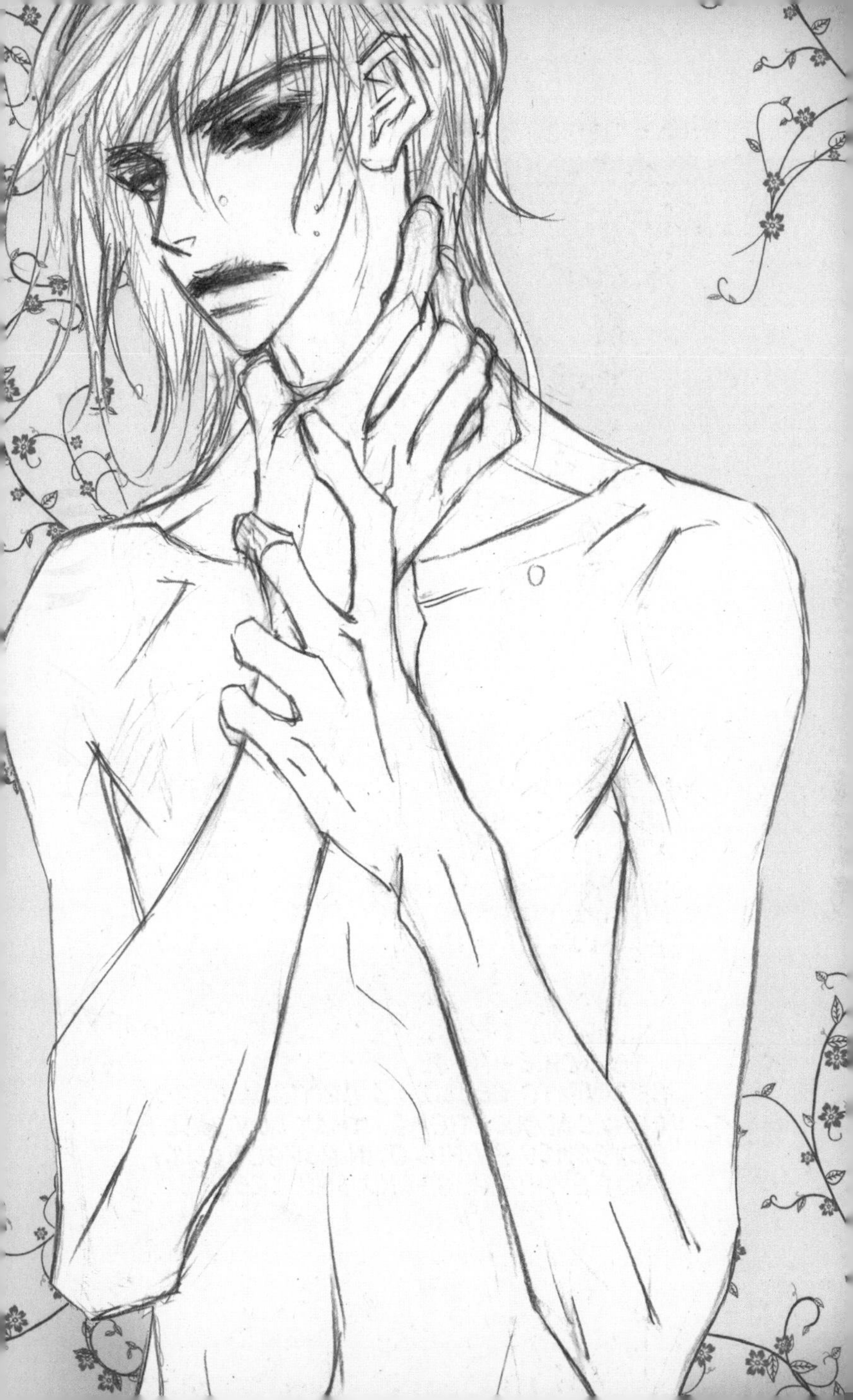

TOKYOPOP.com

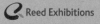

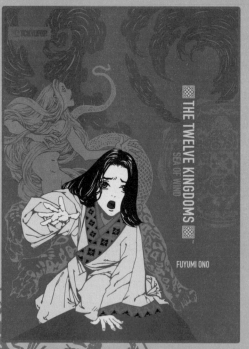

TOKYOPOP MANGA SUPPLEMENT

An anthology with new stories and art by
TOKYOPOP's top talent!

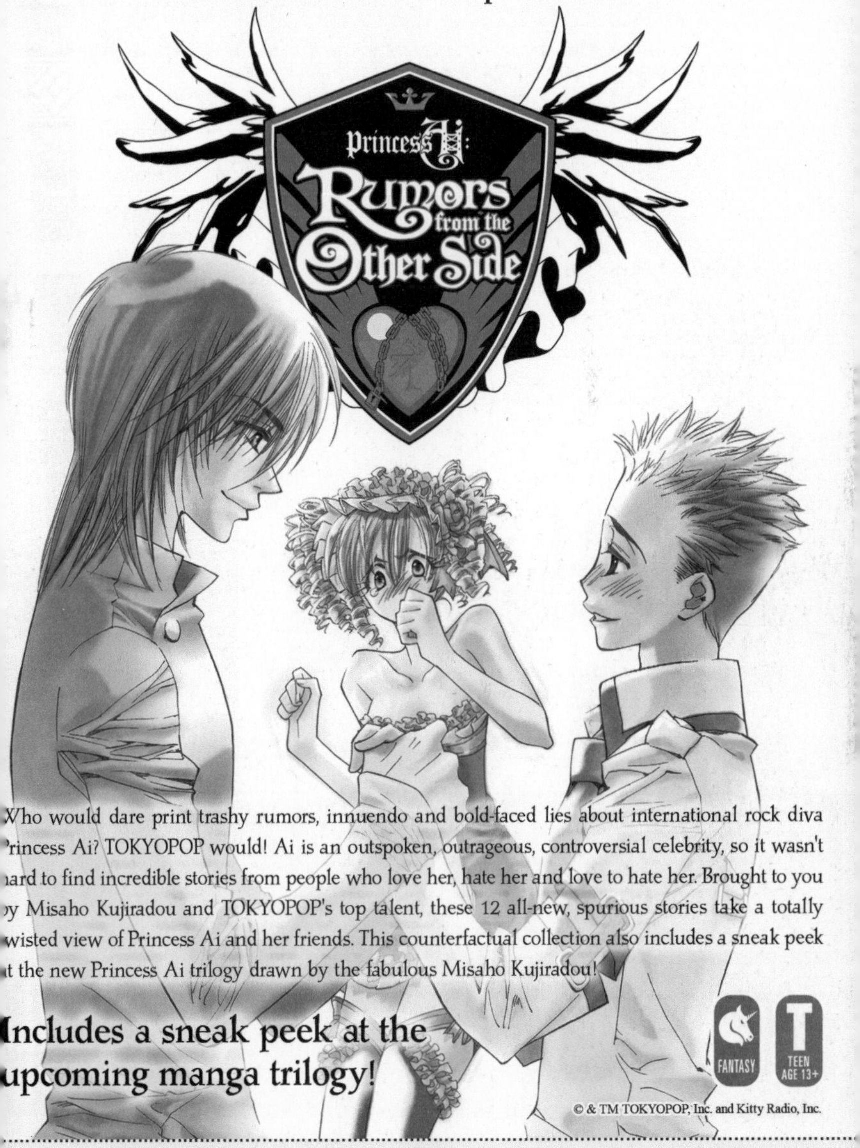
Princess Ai:
Rumors from the Other Side
FANTASY
T
TEEN
AGE 13+

Vho would dare print trashy rumors, innuendo and bold-faced lies about international rock diva 'rincess Ai? TOKYOPOP would! Ai is an outspoken, outrageous, controversial celebrity, so it wasn't ıard to find incredible stories from people who love her, hate her and love to hate her. Brought to you y Misaho Kujiradou and TOKYOPOP's top talent, these 12 all-new, spurious stories take a totally wisted view of Princess Ai and her friends. This counterfactual collection also includes a sneak peek t the new Princess Ai trilogy drawn by the fabulous Misaho Kujiradou!

Includes a sneak peek at the upcoming manga trilogy!

FOR MORE INFORMATION VISIT: WWW.TOKYOPOP.COM

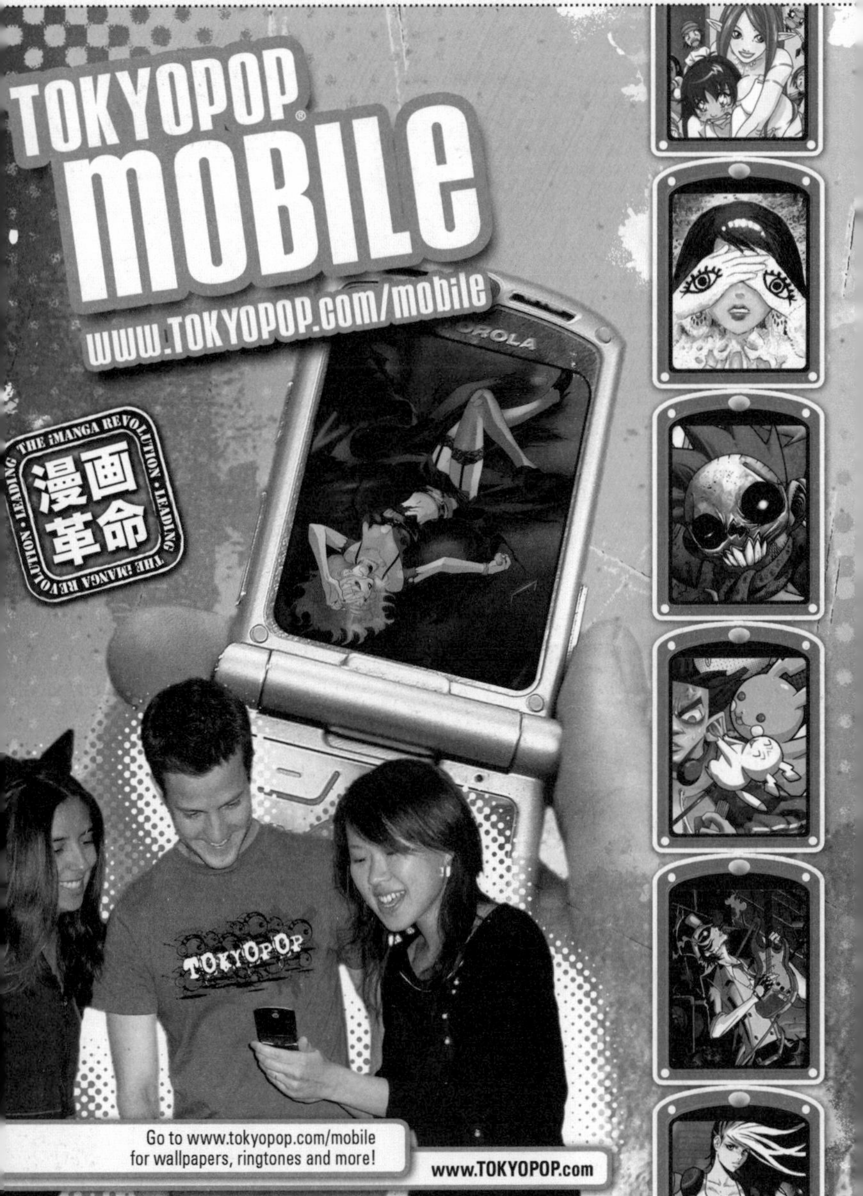
TOKYOPOP®
MOBILE
www.TOKYOPOP.com/mobile
THE iMANGA REVOLUTION · LEADING
漫画
革命
Go to www.tokyopop.com/mobile
for wallpapers, ringtones and more!
www.TOKYOPOP.com